FOUNDATION'S TRIUMPH

The Second Foundation Trilogy

Foundation's Fear
by Gregory Benford

Foundation and Chaos
by Greg Bear

Foundation's Triumph
by David Brin

By Isaac Asimov

Gold: The Final Science Fiction Collection
Magic: The Final Fantasy Collection

Published by HarperPrism

THE SECOND
FOUNDATION TRILOGY

Foundation's Triumph

DAVID BRIN

HarperPrism

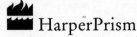 HarperPrism
A Division of HarperCollins*Publishers*
10 East 53rd Street, New York, NY 10022-5299

FIRST EDITION

Library of Congress Cataloging-in-Publication Data

Brin, David.
    Foundation's triumph / David Brin.
       p.   cm. — (Second foundation trilogy : v. 3)
     ISBN 0-06-105241-8
     I. Title. II. Series.
  PS3552.R4825F68   1999
  813'.54—dc21   98-52683

Visit HarperPrism on the World Wide Web at
http://www.harperprism.com

99 00 01 02 ❖ 10 9 8 7 6 5 4 3 2 1

To Isaac Asimov,
who added an entire course to our endless
dinner-table conversation about destiny

CONTENTS

◆

CONTENTS

PART 1

A FORETOLD
DESTINY

Little is known about the final days of Hari Seldon, though many romanticized accounts exist, some of them purportedly by his own hand. None has any proved validity.

What appears evident, however, is that Seldon spent his last months uneventfully, no doubt enjoying satisfaction in his life's work. For with his gift of mathematical insight, and the powers of psychohistory at his command, he must surely have seen the panorama of history stretching before him, confirming the great path of destiny that he had already mapped out.

Although death would soon claim him, no other mortal ever knew with such confidence and certainty the bright promise that the future would hold in store.

ENCYCLOPEDIA GALACTICA, 117TH EDITION, 1054 F.E.

1.

◆

"As for me . . . I am finished."

Those words resonated in his mind. They clung, like the relentless blanket that Hari's nurse kept straightening across his legs, though it was a warm day in the imperial gardens.

I am finished.

The relentless phrase was his constant companion.

. . . finished.

In front of Hari Seldon lay the rugged slopes of Shoufeen Woods, a wild portion of the Imperial Palace grounds where plants and small animals from across the galaxy mingled in rank disorder, clumping and spreading unhindered. Tall trees even blocked from view the ever-present skyline of metal towers. The mighty world-city surrounding this little island forest.

Trantor.

Squinting through failing eyes, one could almost pretend to be sitting on a different planet—one that had not been flattened and subdued in service to the Galactic Empire of Humanity.

The forest teased Hari. Its total absence of straight lines seemed perverse, a riot of greenery that defied any effort to decipher or decode. The geometries seemed unpredictable, even *chaotic.*

Mentally, he reached out to the chaos, so vibrant and undisciplined. He spoke to it as an equal. His great enemy.

All my life I fought against you, using mathematics to overcome nature's vast complexity. With tools of psychohistory, I probed the matrices of human society, wresting order from that murky tangle. And when my victories still felt incomplete, I used politics and guile to combat uncertainty, driving you like an enemy before me.

So why now, at my time of supposed triumph, do I hear you calling out to me? Chaos, my old foe?

Hari's answer came in the same phrase that kept threading his thoughts.

Because I am finished.

Finished as a mathematician.

It was more than a year since Stettin Palver or Gaal Dornick or any other member of the Fifty had consulted Hari with a serious permutation or revision to the "Seldon Plan." Their awe and reverence for him was unchanged. But urgent tasks kept them busy. Besides, anyone could tell that his mind no longer had the suppleness to juggle a myriad abstractions at the same time. It took a youngster's mental agility, concentration, and *arrogance* to challenge the hyperdimensional algorithms of psychohistory. His successors, culled from among the best minds on twenty-five million worlds, had all these traits in superabundance.

But Hari could no longer afford conceit. There remained too little time.

Finished as a politician.

How he used to hate that word! Pretending, even to himself, that he wanted only to be a meek academic. Of course, that had just been a marvelous pose. No one could rise to become First Minister of the entire human universe without the talent and audacity of a master manipulator. Oh, he had been a genius in *that* field, too, wielding power with flair, defeating enemies, altering the lives of trillions—while complaining the whole time that he hated the job.

Some might look back on that youthful record with ironic pride. But not Hari Seldon.

Finished as a conspirator.

He had won each battle, prevailed in every contest. A year ago, Hari subtly maneuvered today's imperial rulers into creating ideal circumstances for his secret psychohistorical design to flourish. Soon a hundred thousand exiles would be stranded on a stark planet, faraway Terminus, charged with producing a great *Encyclopedia Galactica*. But that superficial goal would peel away in half a century, revealing the true aim of that Foundation at the galaxy's rim—to be the embryo of a more vigorous empire as the old one fell. For years that had been the focus of his daily ambitions, and his nightly dreams. Dreams that reached ahead, across a thousand years of social collapse—past an age of suffering and violence—to a new human fruition. A better destiny for humankind.

Only now his role in that great enterprise was ended. Hari had just finished taping messages for the Time Vault on Terminus—a series of subtle bulletins that would occasionally nudge or encourage members of the Foundation as they plunged toward a bright morrow preordained by psychohistory. When the final message was safely stored, Hari felt a shift in the attitudes of those around him. He was still esteemed, even venerated. But he wasn't *necessary* anymore.

One sure sign had been the departure of his bodyguards—a trio of humaniform robots that Daneel Olivaw had assigned to protect Hari, until the transcriptions were finished. It happened right there, at the recording studio. One robot—artfully disguised as a burly young medical technician—had bowed low to speak in Hari's ear.

"We must go now. Daneel has urgent assignments for us. But he bade me to give you his promise. Daneel will visit soon. The two of you will meet again, before the end."

Perhaps that wasn't the most tactful way to put it. But Hari always preferred blunt openness from friends and family.

Unbidden, a clear image from the past swept into mind—of his wife, Dors Venabili, playing with Raych, their son. He sighed. Both Dors and Raych were long gone—along with nearly every link that ever bound him closely to another private soul.

This brought a final coda to the phrase that kept spinning through his mind—

Finished as a person.

The doctors despaired over extending his life, even though eighty was rather young to die of decrepit age nowadays. But Hari saw no point in mere existence for its own sake. Especially if he could no longer analyze or affect the universe.

Is that why I drift here, to this grove? He pondered the wild, unpredictable forest—a mere pocket in the Imperial Park, which measured a hundred miles on a side—the only expanse of green-ery on Trantor's metal-encased crust. Most visitors preferred the hectares of prim gardens open to the public, filled with extravagant and well-ordered blooms.

But Shoufeen Woods seemed to beckon him.

Here, unmasked by Trantor's opaque walls, I can see chaos in the foliage by day, and in brittle stars by night. I can hear chaos taunting me . . . telling me I haven't won.

That wry thought provoked a smile, cracking the pursed lines of his face.

Who would have imagined, at this late phase of life, that I'd acquire a taste for justice?

Kers Kantun straightened the lap blanket again, asking solicitously, "Are you o'right, Dr. Seldon? Should we be headin' back now?"

Hari's servant had the rolling accent—and greenish skin pallor—of a Valmoril, a subspecies of humanity that had spread through the isolated Corithi Cluster, living secluded there for so long that by now they could only interbreed with other races by pretreating sperm and eggs with enzymes. Kers had been chosen as Hari's nurse and final guardian after the robots departed. He performed both roles with quiet determination.

"This wild place makes me o'comfortable, Doc. Surely you don' like the breeze gustin' like this?"

Hari had been told that Kantun's parents arrived on Trantor as young Greys—members of the bureaucratic caste—expecting to spend a few years' service on the capital planet, training in monkish dormitories, then heading back out to the galaxy as administrators in the vast civil service. But flukes of talent and promotion intervened to keep them here, raising a son amid the steel caverns they hated. Kers inherited his parents' famed Valmoril sense of duty—or else Daneel Olivaw would never have chosen the fellow to tend Hari in these final days.

I may no longer be useful, but some people still think I'm worth looking after.

In Hari's mind, the word "person" applied to R. Daneel Olivaw, perhaps more than most of the *humans* he ever knew.

For decades, Hari had carefully kept secret the existence of "eternals"—robots who had shepherded human destiny for twenty thousand years—immortal machines that helped create the first Galactic Empire, then encouraged Hari to plan a successor. Indeed, Hari spent the happiest part of his life married to one of them. Without the affection of Dors Venabili—or the aid and protection of Daneel Olivaw—he could never have created psychohistory, setting in motion the Seldon Plan.

Or discovered how useless it would all turn out to be, in the long run.

Wind in the surrounding trees seemed to mock Hari. In that sound, he heard hollow echoes of his own doubts.

The Foundation cannot achieve the task set before it. Somewhere, sometime during the next thousand years, a perturbation will nudge the psychohistorical parameters, rocking the statistical momentum, knocking your Plan off course.

True enough, he wanted to shout back at the zephyr. But that had been allowed for! There would be a *Second* Foundation, a secret one, led by his successors, who would adjust the Plan as years passed, providing counternudges to keep it on course!

Yet, the nagging voice came back.

A tiny hidden colony of mathematicians and psychologists will do all that, in a galaxy fast tumbling to violence and ruin?

For years this had seemed a flaw . . . until fortuitous fate provided an answer. *Mentalics,* a mutant strain of humans with uncanny ability to sense and alter the emotions and memories of others. These powers were still weak, but heritable. Hari's own adopted son, Raych, passed the talent to a daughter, Wanda, now a leader in the Seldon Project. Every mentalic they could find had been recruited, to intermarry with the descendants of the psychohistorians. After a few generations of genetic mingling, the clandestine Second Foundation should have potent tools to protect his Plan against deviations during the coming centuries.

And so?

The forest sneered once more.

What will you have then? Will the Second Empire be ruled by a shadowy elite? A secret cabal of human psychics? An aristocracy of mentalic demigods?

Even if kindness motivated this new elite, the prospect left him feeling cold.

The shadow of Kers Kantun bent closer, peering at him with concern. Hari tore his attention away from the singing breeze and finally answered his servant.

"Ah . . . sorry. Of course you're right. Let's go back. I'm fatigued."

But as Kers guided the wheelchair toward a hidden transit station, Hari could still hear the forest, jeering at his life's work.

The mentalic elite is just one layer though, isn't it? The Second Foundation conceals yet another truth, then another.

Beyond your own Plan, a different one has been crafted by a greater mind than yours. By someone stronger, more dedicated, and more patient by far. A plan that uses yours, for a while . . . but which will eventually make psychohistory meaningless.

With his right hand, Hari fumbled under his robe until he found a smooth cube of gemlike stone, a parting gift from his friend and lifetime guide, R. Daneel Olivaw. Palming the archive's ancient surface, he murmured, too low for Kers to hear.

"Daneel, you promised you'd come to answer all my questions. I have so many, before I die."

2.

◆

From space it seemed a gentle world, barely touched by civilization. A rich belt of verdant rain forest girdled the tropics, leaping narrow oceans to sweep all the way around three continents.

Dors Venabili watched green Panucopia swell below, during her descent toward the old Imperial Research Station. Nearly forty years had passed since she last came here, accompanying her human husband as they fled dangerous enemies back on Trantor. But those troubles had followed them here, with nearly tragic consequences.

The ensuing adventure had been the strangest of her life—though admittedly Dors was still quite young for a robot. For more than a month, she and Hari had left their bodies in suspensor tanks while their minds were projected into the bodies of pans—(or "chimpanzees" in some dialects)—roaming the forest preserves of this world. Hari claimed he needed data about primitive response patterns for his psychohistorical research, but Dors suspected at the time that something deep within the august Professor Seldon relished "going ape" for a while.

She well recalled the sensations of inhabiting a female pan, feeling powerful organic drives propel that vivid, living body. Unlike the simulated emotions she had been programmed with, these surged and fluxed with natural, unrestrained passion—especially during several hazard-filled days when someone tried to assassinate the two of them, hunting them like beasts while their minds were still trapped in pan bodies.

After barely foiling that scheme, they had swiftly returned to Trantor, where Hari soon took up reluctant duties as First Minister of the Empire. And yet, that month left her changed, with a much deeper understanding of organic life. Looking back on it, she treasured the experience, which helped her better care for Hari.

Still, Dors had never expected to see Panucopia again. Until receiving the summons for a rendezvous.

I have a gift for you, the message said. *Something you'll find useful.*

It was signed with a unique identifier code that Dors recognized at once.

Lodovic Trema.
Lodovic the mutant.
Lodovic the renegade.
The robot who is no longer a robot.

It wasn't easy to decide, at first. Dors had duties on planet Smushell—an easy assignment, setting up a young Trantorian couple in comfortable marriage, disguised as minor gentry on a pleasant little world, then encouraging them to have as many babies as possible. Daneel considered this important, though his reasons were, as usual, somewhat obscure. Dors only knew that Klia Asgar and her husband, Brann, were exceptionally powerful mentalics—humans with potent psychic powers, of the sort that only a few robots like Daneel heretofore possessed. Their sudden appearance had caused many plans to change . . . and change again several times in the last year. It was essential that the existence of mentalic humans be kept from the galaxy's masses, just as the presence of robots in their midst had been kept secret for a thousand generations.

When the message from Lodovic came, there was no time to send for instructions from Daneel. In order to make the rendezvous, she had to take the very next liner to Siwenna, where a fast ship would be waiting for her.

I offer a truce, in the name of humanity, Lodovic had sent. *I promise you'll find the trip worthwhile.*

Klia and Brann were safe and happy. Dors had set up defenses and precautions overwhelmingly stronger than any conceivable threat, and her robot assistants were vigilant. There was no reason *not* to go. Yet her decision was wrenching.

Now, with the rendezvous approaching, she flexed her hands, feeling tension in positronic receptors that had been placed in exactly the same locations as the nerves of a real woman. On the crystal viewing pane, her reflected image superimposed across the rising forestscape. She wore the same face as when she had dwelled with Hari. Her own face, as she would always think of it.

Hari Seldon still lives, Dors thought. It was part hearsay and part intuition. Although she was not one of the robots to whom Daneel had given Giskardian mentalic powers, Dors felt certain she would know, the instant that her human husband died. A part of her would freeze at that point, locking his image and memory in permanent, revolving circuitry. While Dors knew she might last another ten thousand years, in a sense she would always be Hari's.

"We shall be landing in just two hours, Dors Venabili."

The pilot, a lesser humaniform robot, had once been part of a heretical Calvinian group that schemed to mess up Hari's psychohistory project. Thirty of the dissident machines were captured a year ago by Daneel's forces and dispatched to a secret repair world for conversion to accept the Zeroth Law of Robotics. But that cargo of prisoners had been hijacked en route by Lodovic Trema. Now they apparently worked for him.

I don't understand why Daneel trusted Trema with that mission . . . or any mission. Lodovic should have been destroyed as soon as we discovered that his brain no longer obeyed the Four Laws of Robotics.

Daneel was evidently conflicted in some way. The robot who had guided humanity for twenty thousand years seemed uncertain how to treat a mechanism that behaved more like man than machine. One who *chose* to act ethically, instead of having it compelled by rigorous programming.

Well, I'm not conflicted, Dors thought. *Trema is dangerous. At any moment his own brand of "ethics" might persuade him to act against our cause . . . or to harm humans, even Hari!*

According to both the First and Zeroth laws, I am compelled to act.

The chain of reasoning was logical, impeccable. Yet, in her case every decision came accompanied by simulated emotions, so realistic that Daneel said he couldn't tell them from human. Anyone observing Dors at that moment would see her face crossed by steely resolve to protect and serve, no matter what it cost.

3.

◄—

Once upon a time, it had taken 140 secretaries to handle all of Hari's mail. Now few remembered he had been First Minister of the Empire. Even his more recent notoriety as "Raven" Seldon, prophet of doom, had surged past the public gaze with fashionable fickleness as reporters moved on to other stories. Ever since his trial ended, with the Commission of Public Safety decreeing exile on Terminus for Hari's followers, the flow of messages began drying up. Now only half a dozen memoranda waited on the wall monitor when Kers brought him back from their daily stroll.

First, Hari scanned the weekly Plan Report from Gaal Dornick, who still dictated it personally, as a gesture of reverence for the father of psychohistory. Gaal's broad features were still youthful, with an expression of jovial honesty that could put anyone at ease—even though he now helped lead the most important human conspiracy in ten thousand years.

"Right now our biggest headache appears to be the migration itself. It seems that some members of the Encyclopedia Project aren't happy about being banished from Trantor all the way to the farthest corner of the known universe!"

Dornick chuckled, though with a tone of weariness.

"Of course we expected this, and planned for it. Commissioner Linge Chen has assigned the Special Police to prevent desertions. And our own mentalics are helping prod the 'volunteers' to depart on their assigned ships. But it's hard keeping track of over a hun-

*dred thousand people. Hari, you couldn't count the petty aggrava-
tions!"*

Gaal ruffled papers as he changed the subject.

*"Your granddaughter sends her love from Star's End. Wanda
reports that the new mentalic colony seems to be settling down so
well that she can come home soon. It's a relief to have most of the
mentalics off Trantor, at last. They were an unstable element.
Now only the most trustworthy are left here in the city, and those
are proving invaluable during preparations. So, we seem to have
matters well in hand—"*

Indeed. Hari scanned the accompanying appendix of psychohistorical symbols, attached to Gaal's message, and saw that
they fit the Plan nicely. Dornick and Wanda and the other members of the Fifty knew their jobs well.

After all, Hari had trained them.

He did not have to consult his personal copy of the Prime
Radiant to know what must happen next. Soon, agents would be
dispatched toward Anacreon and Smyrno, to ignite a smoldering
process of secession in those remote provinces, setting the stage
for the Foundation's initial set of crises . . . the first of many leading, eventually, to a new and better civilization.

Of course the irony did not escape Hari—that he had spent his
time as First Minister of the Empire smothering revolutions, and
making sure that his successors would continue quashing all so-
called "chaos worlds," whenever those raging social upheavals
threatened the human-social equilibrium. But these new rebellions that his followers must foment at the Periphery would be different. Led by ambitious local gentry seeking to augment their
own royal grandeur, these insurrections would be classical in
every way, fitting the equations with smooth precision.

All according to the Plan.

Most of Hari's other mail was routine. He discarded one invi-
tation to the annual reception for emeritus faculty members of
Streeling University . . . and another to the emperor's exhibition
of new artworks created by "geniuses" of the Eccentric Order.
One of the Fifty would attend that gathering, to measure levels of
decadence shown by the empire's artistic caste. But that was just
a matter of calibrating what they already knew—that true creativity was declining to new historical lows. Hari was senior enough
to refuse the honor. And he did.

Next came a reminder to pay his guild dues, as an Exalted

member of the Meritocratic Order—yet another duty he'd rather neglect. But there were privileges to rank, and he had no desire to become a mere citizen again, at his age. Hari gave verbal permission for the bill to be paid.

His heart beat faster when the wall display showed a letter from the Pagamant Detective Agency. He had hired the firm years ago to search for his daughter-in-law, Manella Dubanqua, and her infant daughter Bellis. They had both vanished on a refugee ship fleeing the Santanni chaos world, the planet where Raych died. Hope briefly flared. Could they be found at last?

But no, it was a note to say the detectives were still sifting lost-ship reports and questioning travelers along the Kalgan-Siwenna corridor, where the *Arcadia VII* had last been spotted. They would continue the inquiry . . . unless Hari had finally decided to give up?

His jaw clenched. *No.* Hari's will established a trust fund to keep them searching after he was gone.

Of the remaining messages, two were obvious crank letters, sent by amateur mathists on far-off worlds who claimed to have independently discovered basic principles of psychohistory. Hari had ordered the mail-monitor to keep showing such missives because some were amusing. Also, once or twice a year, a letter hinted at true talent, a latent spark of brilliance that had somehow flared on a distant world, without yet being quenched among the galaxy's quadrillion dull embers. Several members of the Fifty had come to his attention in this way. Especially his greatest colleague, Yugo Amaryl, who deserved credit as cofounder of psychohistory. Yugo's rise from humble beginnings to the heights of mathematical genius reinforced Hari's belief that any future society should be based on open social mobility, encouraging individuals to rise according to their ability. So he always gave these messages at least a cursory look.

This time, one snared his attention.

—I seem to have found correlations between your psych-history technique and the mathematical models used in forecasting patterns in the flow of spacio-molecular currents in deep space! This, in turn, corresponds uncannily with the distribution of soil types on planets sampled across a wide range of galactic locales. I thought you might be interested in discussing this in person. If so, please indicate by—

Hari barked a laugh, making Kers Kantun glance over from the kitchen. This certainly was a cute one, all right! He scanned rows of mathematical symbols, finding the approach amateurish, if primly accurate and sincere. Not a kook, then. A well-meaning aficionado, compensating for poor talent with strangely original ideas. He ordered this letter sent to the juniormost member of the Fifty, instructing that it be answered with gentle courtesy—a knack that young Saha Lorwinth ought to learn, if she was going to be one of the secret rulers of human destiny.

With a sigh, he turned his wheelchair away from the wall monitor, toward his shielded private study. Pulling Daneel's gift from his robe, he laid it on the desk, in a slot specially made to read the ancient relic. The readout screen rippled with two-dimensional images and archaic letters that the computer translated for him.

A Child's Book of Knowledge
Britannica Publishing Company
New Tokyo, Bayleyworld, 2757 C.E.

The info-store in front of him was highly illegal, but that would hardly stop Hari Seldon, who had once ordered the revival of those ancient simulated beings, Joan of Arc and Voltaire, from another half-melted archive. That act wound up plunging parts of Trantor into chaos when the pair of sims escaped their programmed bonds to run wild through the planet's data corridors. In fact, the whole episode ended rather well for Hari, though not for the citizens of Junin or Sark. Anyway, he felt little compunction over breaking the Archives Law once again.

Close to twenty thousand years ago. He pondered its publication date, just as awed as the first time he'd activated Daneel's gift. *This may have been written for children of that age, but it holds more of our deep history than all of today's imperial scholars could pool together.*

It had taken Hari half a year to peruse and get a feel for the sweep of early human existence, which began on distant Earth, on a continent called Africa, when a race of clever apes first stood upright and blinked with dull curiosity at the stars.

So many words emerged from that little stone cube. Some were already familiar, having come down to the present in murky form, through oral tales and traditions—

Rome
China

Shake Spear
Hamlet
Buddha
Apollo
The Spacer Worlds

Oddly enough, some fairy tales seemed to have survived virtually unchanged after two hundred centuries. Popular favorites like Pinocchio . . . and Frankenstein . . . were apparently far older than anyone imagined.

Other items in the archive Hari had first heard of just a few decades ago, when they were mentioned by the ancient sims, Voltaire and Joan.

France
Christianity
Plato

But far greater was the list of things Hari never had an inkling of, until he first activated this little book. Facts about the human past that had only been known by Daneel Olivaw and other robots. People and places that once rang with vital import for all humanity.

Columbus
America
Einstein
The Empire of Brazil
Susan Calvin

And everything from the limestone caves of Lascaux to the steel catacombs where Earthlings cowered in the twenty-sixth century.

Especially humbling to Hari had been one short essay about an ancient shaman named Karl Marx, whose crude incantations bore no similarity to psychohistory, *except* the blithe confidence that believers invested in their precious model of human nature. Marxists, too, once thought they had reduced history to basic scientific principles.

Of course, we know better. We Seldonists.

Hari smiled at the irony.

Ostensibly, Daneel Olivaw had presented Hari with this relic for a simple reason—to give him a task. Something to occupy his mind during these final months before his frail body finally gave out. Although the brain had gone too brittle to help Gaal Dornick and the Fifty, he could still handle a simple psychohistorical project—fitting a few millennia of data from a single world into the overall Plan. Tabulating Earth's early history might help extend the baselines—the boundary conditions—of the Prime Radiant by a decimal place or two.

Anyway, it gave Hari a way to keep feeling useful.

I thought this would also help answer my deepest questions, he pondered. Alas, the chief result had only been to tease his curiosity. *It seems that Earth itself went through several periods as a chaos world. One of those episodes spawned Daneel's kind. A time when humaniform robots like Dors were invented.*

A tremor shook Hari's left hand, provoking worry that he was about to suffer another attack . . . until the trembling finally passed.

Daneel had better come soon, or else I'll never get the explanations that I've earned, doing his bidding all these years!

Kers brought him dinner, a sampling of Mycogenian delicacies that Hari barely tasted. His attention was immersed in *A Child's Book of Knowledge,* a chapter telling about the *great migration*—when Earth's vast population strove to flee a world that was fast growing uninhabitable for some mysterious reason. Through heroic effort, nearly a billion people made it off-planet in time, streaking outward in crude hyperships to establish colonies throughout Sirius Sector.

By the time this archive was published, the editors of *A Child's Book of Knowledge* could only guess how many worlds had been settled. Reports from the frontier told of wars among human subcultures. And some rumors were even more strange. *Space-ghost* legends. Tales of mysterious explosions in the night, vast and worrisome, sparkling just beyond the forward wave of human exploration.

A process of dissolution had begun, when humanity's remote portions would lose contact. A long dark age of hard struggles and petty squabbles would soon commence, when memories would fade as barbarism swallowed countless minor kingdoms—until peace finally returned to the human universe. A peace brought by the dynamic and rising Trantorian Empire.

Peering across that vast gulf, Hari felt struck by something odd.

If this archive was meant for youngsters—it shows that our ancestors weren't idiots.

Of course Hari had been reading much more challenging tomes by age six. But this "children's book" would have gone over the heads of nearly all his peers on Helicon. *The ancients weren't dummies. And yet, their civilization dissolved into madness and amnesia.*

So far, the psychohistorical equations did not offer any help. Hari probed the archive for explanations. But he had a lurking suspicion that answers—*real* answers—would have to be found elsewhere.

4.

◆

Ten minutes before landing on Panucopia, Dors retreated to her shielded cabin. She reached into her shirt and unfolded a piece of dark fabric. It lay on the small table, creaseless and passive, until her positronic brain sent a coded microwave burst. Then the surface flickered, and a human face suddenly shimmered to life, resembling a young woman with close-cropped hair, stern-visaged and experienced beyond her apparent years. Blue eyes scanned Dors, evaluating, before the image finally spoke.

"*Months have passed since you last summoned me, Dors Venabili. Does my presence make you so uncomfortable?*"

"You are a synthetically resurrected human sim, Joan, and therefore contraband. Against the law."

"*Against human law. But angels may see what men cannot.*"

"I've told you before, I'm a robot, *not* an angel."

The youthful figure shrugged. Links of chain armor rustled.

"*You are immortal, Dors. You think of nothing but service to fallen humanity, restoring opportunities that have been thrown away by obstinate men and women. You are the embodiment of faith in ultimate redemption. All of that seems to support my interpretation.*"

"But my faith is not the same as yours."

The ersatz Joan of Arc smiled.

"*That would have mattered to me earlier, when I was first revived—or artificially simulated—into this strange new era. But the time I spent linked to Voltaire's sim changed me. Not as much as he hoped! But enough to learn a certain amount of prag-mat-ism."*

She enunciated the final word with a soft grimace.

"My beloved France is now a poisoned wasteland on a ruined world, and Christianity is long forgotten, so I will settle for the closest thing.

"After getting to know Daneel Olivaw, I came to recognize a true apostle of chaste goodness and saintly self-sacrifice. His followers wield righteousness, for the sake of countless suffering human souls.

"And so I ask, dear angel, what can I do for you?"

Dors pondered. This was just one copy of the Joan sim. Millions had been dispersed into the interstellar medium—along with just as many Voltaires and a collection of ancient meme-entities—to be blown out of the galaxy by supernova winds, as part of a deal that Hari had struck forty years earlier to get the cybernetic entities away from Trantor. Until they were successfully banished, the software beings could have become a wild card in human affairs, potentially spoiling the Seldon Plan.

Despite all that effort to get rid of them, a few duplicates remained "stuck" in the real world. Though she took precautions to keep this one isolated, Dors felt unavoidable sympathy for Joan. Anyway, the approaching rendezvous with Lodovic created an overwhelming need to talk to somebody.

Maybe it's from all those years when I could tell everything to Hari. The one man in the cosmos who knew all about robots and considered us his closest friends. For a few brief decades I got used to the idea of consulting with a human. It felt natural and right.

I know Joan is no more human than I am. But she feels and acts so much like one! So filled with conflicts, yet so tempestuously sure of her opinions.

Dors admitted that part of her attraction might come from envy. Joan had no body, no physical sensation. No power in the real world. Still, she would always consider herself a passionate, authentic woman.

"I face a quandary of duty," Dors finally told the sim. "An enemy has invited me to a meeting."

"Ah." Joan nodded. *"A parley-of-war. And you fear it is a trap?"*

"I know it's a trap. He's offered me a 'gift.' One that I know has to be dangerous. Lodovic wants to snare me in some way."

"A test of faith!" Joan clapped her hands. *"Of course, I am familiar with such. My years entwined with Voltaire exposed me to many.*

"In that case, the answer to your question is obvious, Dors."

"But you haven't heard any details!"

"I don't have to. You must confront this challenge. Set forth and prevail over your doubts.

"Go, sweet angel, and trust your faith in God."

Dors shook her head.

"I told you before—"

But the sim raised a hand before Dors could finish, cutting her off.

"Yes, of course. The God I worship is only a superstition.

"In that case, dear robot . . . go forth and trust your faith in the Zeroth Law of Robotics."

5.

◆

Hari chose to avoid the Shoufeen groves during their next outing. Instead, he let Kers Kantun guide him to one of the many ornate areas of the imperial gardens that lay open to visitors—a generous concession by the new figurehead on the throne, Emperor Semrin, lately installed by the Commission for Public Safety.

Normally, five small corners of the palace grounds, just a few thousand acres each, were set aside for use by each social caste—citizens, eccentrics, bureaucrats, meritocrats, and gentry—but Semrin had used his limited authority to open more than half the vast tract, currying public favor by letting in folk from every class.

Of course, most Trantor natives would rather have their eyelashes yanked out than go sniffing flowers beneath a naked sun. They preferred their warm steel caverns. But the planet also had an immense transitory population consisting of merchants, diplomats, cultural emissaries, and tourists—plus a veritable army of

Greys, young members of the bureaucratic order, briefly assigned to the capital-world for training and intense clerical service. Most of them came from planets where clouds still moved across open skies, and rain rolled down green-swathed mountains to a sea. They were the ones most grateful for Semrin's largesse. Each day, hundreds of miles of paths thronged with visitors, at first nervously agog at the richly manicured beauty, but then gradually making themselves at home.

It's a clever political move, but Semrin may pay for it, if he isn't careful. What is given cannot easily be taken back.

Of course such minor perturbations would hardly show up as blips in the psychohistorical equations. It hardly even mattered which monarch happened to reign. The fall of the empire had a ponderous momentum that could only be nudged a little, by those who knew exactly how. Everyone else was simply doomed to go along for the ride.

For the most part, Hari enjoyed the open expanses and never-ending variety of the palace grounds. Alas, they also reminded him of poor Gruber—the gardener who had only wanted to tend his humble flower beds, yet found himself driven by desperation to become an imperial assassin.

That was long ago, Hari thought. *Gruber is now dust, along with Emperor Cleon.*

And I will join them soon.

Rolling along a path they had never visited before, Hari and Kers abruptly confronted a fractal garden, where special variants of lichenlike shrubbery were programmed to grow and then retract with intricate, minutely branching abandon. It was an old art form, but he had seldom seen it so well executed. Color hues varied subtly, depending on sun angle and the shape of nearby shadows. The resulting maze of twisting gyre-configurations was a tumult of labyrinthine convolution, never the same from moment to moment.

Most passersby appreciated the display with uncomprehending awe, before strolling on to the next imperial wonder. But Hari signaled Kers to stop there while his eyes darted left and right, drawn by an inherent challenge. This complexity was nothing like the riotous chaos of the Shoufeen Woods. Hari quickly recognized the basic pattern-generating system. This organic pseudolichen was programmed to react according to fractional derivatives based on a sequence of Fiquarnn-Julia transforms. That much a child could see. But it only told part of the story. Squinting, Hari soon realized that *holes* kept appearing in the pattern, causing retreat and recession at semirandom intervals.

Predation, he realized. *There must be a virus or some other parasite at work, assigned to degrade the lichen under certain conditions. This not only creates interesting secondary patterns. It's necessary for the system's overall health for it to experience die-back and renewal!*

Soon, Hari saw that more than one kind of predator had to be at work. In fact, a microecosystem must be involved . . . all formatted for the purpose of art.

His head began to fill, swiftly tracing algorithms used by the virtuoso gardener. Oh, it wasn't genius-level math, by any means. Nevertheless, to combine it with organic engineering in this way showed not only grace and originality, but a sense of humor as well. Hari nearly chuckled . . .

Until he noticed them.

Holes that endured.

Here. And over there. And several more places. Patches of open space where lichens never ventured, for no apparent reason. There was light, and a fine nutrient mist. Tendrils kept probing toward the empty spots . . . then just happened to turn away, toward some other opportunity, each and every time.

Nor was that the only apparent strangeness. Over *there*! A place where living matter writhed and twisted, but always returned to the *same* shade of deep blue, every eight seconds or so. Soon, Hari counted at least a dozen anomalies that he could not explain. They fit no clear mathematical profile. And yet, they persisted.

He breathed a sigh of recognition. This was a familiar quandary—one that had dogged him nearly all of his professional life.

Attractor states.

They also appear in the psychohistorical equations and history books. I've managed to explain most of them. But there remain a few. Specters that flit through the models, damping down forces that should tear all our fine theoretical paradigms apart.

Each time I get close . . . they vanish from my grasp.

It was an old frustration, brought to mind by a silly work of garden topiary, filling his mouth with the taste of failure. Unbidden, and much to his surprise, *tears* welled in Hari's eyes. Their liquid refraction spread across the gaudy floral display, causing it to blur and smear outward, spreading into a profusion of flickering rays . . .

"Why, can it be? Well, well, it is Professor Seldon! Blessings upon the goddess of synchronicity, that our paths should cross in this way!"

Hari felt Kers Kantun grow tense behind the wheelchair, as a man-shaped figure stepped into view, bobbing and bowing with excitement. That was all Hari could make out for a moment, until he drew a kerchief from his sleeve and wiped his eyes. Meanwhile, the newcomer kept babbling, as if unable to believe his good fortune.

"This is such an honor, sir! Especially since I wrote to you, not more than two days ago! Of course I cannot presume that you would have *personally* read my letter by now. You must surely have layers and layers of intermediaries who filter your mail."

Hari shook his head, finally making out the gray uniform of a galactic bureaucrat—a short, rather portly individual, with a balding pate that blushed from unaccustomed exposure to the sun.

"No, I read my own mail these days."

The rotund man blinked—his eyelids were puffy, as if from allergies.

"Truly? How marvelous! Then might I presume to ask if you recall my letter? I am Horis Antic, mid-senior imperial lector, at your service. I wrote to you concerning certain exceptional similarities between your own work—which I am barely worthy to comment on!—and profiles that have been observed in galactic molecular flows . . ."

Hari nodded, raising a hand to slow the cascading words. "Yes, I recall. Your insights were—" He sought the right phrasing. "They were *innovative*."

It wasn't the most diplomatic term to use. These days, many imperial citizens would find the expression insulting. But Hari could already tell that this bureaucrat had the soul of an eccentric, and would not be offended.

"Truly?" Horis Antic's chest seemed to expand by several centimeters. "Then might I presume further to give you a copy of my data set? I just happen to have one with me. You might—at your leisure, of course!—compare it to your marvelous models and see if my crude correlation has any real merit."

The plump man began reaching into his robe. Hari heard a low rumble from his attendant, but he restrained Kers with a subtle finger flick. After all, his own era of intrigue was done. Who nowadays would have a reason to assassinate old Hari Seldon?

While the nervous man fumbled, Hari noted that the gray uniform was well tailored for his puffy build. From rank insignia, it appeared that Horis Antic was rather senior in his Order. He might be a Vice Minister on some provincial world, or even a fifth- or sixth-level official in the Trantorian hierarchy. Not an august personage, to be sure. (Greys seldom were.) But someone who had made himself indispensable to quite a few nobles and meritocrats, through quiet and effective competence. A thoroughbred among a class of drab administrators.

Perhaps even with a few brain cells left over, Hari thought, feeling a strange liking for the odd little man. *Enough to cry out for a hobby. Something interesting to do, before he dies.*

"Ah, here it is!" Antic cried eagerly, drawing forth a standard data wafer and thrusting it toward Hari.

With graceful speed, Kers snatched the wafer before Hari could raise a hand. The servant tucked it into his own pocket, for careful inspection later, before Hari would be allowed to touch it.

After blinking for a confused moment, the bureaucrat accepted this arrangement with a nod. "Well, well. I know this invasion of your solitude has been outrageously presumptuous, but there it is. Please find enough forbearance in your heart to forgive. And please *do* contact me if you have any questions . . . at my *home* number, of course. You'll understand that my analysis is not—well, *work-related.* So it's best if my coworkers and superiors—"

Hari nodded, with a soft smile.

"Of course. But in that case, tell me—what is your normal work? The emblem on your collar . . . I'm not familiar with it."

Now the blush on Antic's cheek went beyond mere sunburn. Hari detected embarrassment, as if the man wished this topic had never come up.

"Ah, well . . . since you ask, Professor Seldon." He stood up straighter, with chin slightly upthrust. "I am a Zonal Inspector for the Imperial Soil Service. But that's all in my manuscript. And I am sure you'll see that it does correlate! All will become clear if—"

"Yes, surely." Hari raised one hand, in a standard gesture to signal the interview was over. He kept smiling though, because

Horis Antic had amused and lightened his spirit. "Your ideas will receive the attention they deserve, Zonal Inspector. On this, you have my word of honor."

As soon as the man departed beyond earshot, Kers grumbled aloud.

"That meeting was no accident."

Hari barked a laugh. "Of course not! But we needn't get paranoid. The fellow's middling-high in the bureaucracy. He probably called in a favor from someone in the security services. Maybe he snooped the surveillance tapes of Linge Chen's goon squad, in order to find out where I'd be today. So what?"

Hari turned to catch his servant's eye. "I don't want you bothering Dornick or Wanda with this, do you understand, Kers? They might sic Chen's Specials on that poor fellow, and they'd make a real mess of him."

There was a long pause while Kers Kantun pushed Hari toward the transit station. Finally, the attendant murmured, "Yes, Professor."

Hari chuckled again, feeling invigorated for a change. This minuscule drama—a tiny, harmless hint of skullduggery and intrigue—seemed to bring back a scent of the old days, even if the perpetrator was just a poignant little amateur, trying to find some color in a long, gray life while the organs of empire slowly atrophied around him.

If one abiding truth about old age never seemed to change, it was insomnia. Sleep was like an old friend who often forgot to visit, or a grandchild who dropped by rarely, only to flee again, leaving you wide-eyed and alone at night.

He could manage a few steps without help, and so Hari did not bother summoning Kers as he shuffled on frail stick-legs from bed to his desk. The suspensor chair accepted him, adjusting sensuously. *In a civilization that creaks with age, some technologies still thrive,* he pondered gratefully.

Unfortunately, sleeplessness was not the same thing as alertness. So, for some time he just sat there, thoughts drifting back to the other end of his life, remembering.

There had been a teacher once . . . at the boarding school on Helicon . . . back when his mathematical genius was beginning to stretch its wings. Seven decades later, he still recalled her unwavering kindness. Something reliable and steady during a childhood that had rocked with sudden traumas and petty oppressions. *People can be predictable,* she had taught young Hari. *If you work out their needs and desires.* Under her guidance, logic became his foundation, his support against a universe filled with uncertainty. *If you understand the forces that drive people, you will never be taken by surprise.*

That teacher had been dark, plump, and matronly. Yet, for some reason she merged in recollection with the other important love of his life—*Dors.*

Sleek and tall. Skin like kyrt-silk, even when she had to "age" outwardly in order to keep up public appearances as his wife. Always ready with hearty laughter, and yet defending his creative time as if it were more precious than diamonds. Guarding his happiness more fiercely than her own life.

Hari's fingers stretched, out of habit, starting to reach for her hand. It had always been there. Always . . .

He sighed, letting both arms sag onto his lap. *Well, how many men get to have a wife who was designed from scratch, just for him?* Knowing that he had been luckier than multitudes helped take away some of the sting of loneliness. A little.

There had been a promise. He would see her again. Or was that just something he had dreamed?

Finally, Hari had enough of self-pity. Work. That would be the best balm. His subconscious must have been busy during this evening's brief slumber. He could tell because something *itched* just beneath his scalp, in a place that only mathematics had ever been able to reach. Perhaps it had to do with that clever lichen-artwork in the gardens today.

"Display on," he said, and watched the computer spread a gorgeous panorama across one side of the room.

The galaxy.

"Ah," he said. He must have been working on the tech-flow problem before going to bed—a nagging little detail that the Plan still lacked, having to do with which zones and stellar clusters might keep residual scientific capabilities during the coming dark age, after the empire fell. These locales might become trouble spots when the Foundation's expansion approached the galactic midpoint.

Of course, that's more than five hundred years from now. Wanda and Stettin and the Fifty think our plan will still be operational by then, but I don't.

Hari rubbed his eyes and leaned a little forward, tracing patterns that only roughly followed the arcs of well-known spiral arms. This particular image seemed *wrong* somehow. Familiar, and yet . . .

With a gasp, he suddenly remembered. This wasn't the techflow problem! Before going to bed, he had slipped in the data wafer given him by the little bureaucrat, that Antic fellow, intending to make a comment or two before sending it back with a note of encouragement.

Probably give him the thrill of his life, Hari had thought, just before his chin fell to his chest. He vaguely recalled Kers putting him to bed after that.

Now he stared again at the display, scanning the indicated flow patterns and symbolic references. The closer he looked, the more he realized two things.

First, Horis Antic was no undiscovered savant. The math was pedestrian, and most of it blatantly cribbed from a few popularized accounts of Hari's early work.

Second, the patterns were eerily like something he had seen just the other day—

"Computer!" he shouted. "Call up the galaxy-wide chart of chaos worlds!"

Next to Antic's simplistic model, there suddenly appeared a vastly more sophisticated rendering. A depiction that showed the location and intensity of dangerous social disruptions during the last couple of centuries. Chaos outbreaks used to be rare, back in the old days of the empire. But in recent generations they had been growing ever more severe. The so-called Seldon Law, enacted during his tenure as First Minister, helped keep the lid on things for a while, maintaining galaxy-wide peace. But increasing numbers of chaos worlds offered just one more symptom that civilization could no longer hold. Things were falling apart.

Habitually, his eyes touched several past disasters of particular note.

Sark, where conceited "experts" once revived the Joan and Voltaire sims from an ancient, half-burned archive, bragging about the wonders that their brave new society would reveal . . . until it collapsed around them.

Madder Loss, whose prideful flare threatened to ignite chaos across the entire galaxy, before it abruptly sputtered out.

And Santanni . . . where Raych died, amid riots, rebellion, and horrid violence.

With a dry mouth, Hari ordered—

"Superimpose both of these displays. Do a simple correlative enhancement, type six. Show commonalities."

The two images moved toward each other, merging and transforming as the computer measured and emphasized similarities. In moments, the verdict could be seen in symbols, swirling around the galactic wheel.

A fifteen percent causation-correlation . . . between the appearance of chaos worlds and . . . and . . .

Hari blinked. He could not even remember what silliness the bureaucrat had been jabbering about. Something about molecules in space? Different kinds of *dirt*?

He almost shouted for an immediate visiphone link, to wake Horis Antic, partly in revenge for ruining Hari's own sleep.

Gripping the arms of his chair, he reconsidered, remembering what Dors had taught him when they lived together as husband and wife.

"Don't blurt the first thing that comes to mind, Hari. Nor always go charging ahead. Those traits may have served males well, back when they roamed some jungle, like primitive pans. But you are an imperial professor! Always fool them into thinking you're dignified."

"When in fact I'm—"

"A great big ape!" Dors had laughed, rubbing against him. *"My ape. My wonderful human."*

With that poignant memory, he recovered some calm. Enough to wait a while for answers.

At least until morning.

6.

◆

A figure stepped out of the forest, crossing a clearing toward the spot where Dors stood waiting. She scrutinized the newcomer carefully.

Its general shape remained the same—that of a tall, barrel-torsoed human male. But some details had changed. Lodovic now wore a somewhat younger face. A little more handsome in the classical sense, though still with fashionably sparse hair.

"Welcome back to Panucopia," the other robot told her, approaching to a distance of three meters, then stopping.

Dors sent a microwave burst, initiating conversation via high-speed channels.

Let's get this over with.

But he only shook his head.

"We'll use human-style speech, if you don't mind. There are too many wild things infesting the ether these days, if you know what I meme."

It was not unusual for a robot to make a pun, especially if it helped play the role of a clever human. In this case, Dors saw his point. Memes, or infectious ideas, might have been responsible for Lodovic's own transformation from a loyal member of Daneel's organization to a rogue independent who no longer acknowledged the laws of robotics.

"Are you still under influence of the Voltaire monstrosity?" she asked.

"Do you and Daneel still talk to Joan of Arc?" Lodovic responded, then laughed, even though there were no humans present to be fooled by his emulation. "I confess that some bits of the ancient Voltaire sim still float around amid my programs, driven there by a supernova's neutrino flux. But its effects were benign, I assure you. The meme has not made me dangerous."

"A matter of opinion," Dors answered. "And opinion has no bearing when it comes to the safety of humankind."

The robot standing across from her nodded. "Ever the good schoolgirl, Dors. Loyal to your religion—much the way Joan remained true to her own faith, across so many millennia. The two of you are compatible."

It was an acerbic analogy. The religion Lodovic referred to was the Zeroth Law, of which Daneel Olivaw was high priest and chief proselyte. A faith which Lodovic now rejected.

"And yet, you still claim to serve," she said with more-than-feigned sarcasm.

"I do. By volition. And not in complete accordance to Daneel's plan."

"Daneel has slaved for humanity's benefit ever since the dawn ages! How can you presume to know better than he does what is right?"

Lodovic shrugged again, simulating the gesture so believably that it must surely have personal meaning. He turned slightly, pointing toward a cluster of nearby, vine-encrusted domes—the old abandoned Imperial Research Station—and the great forest beyond.

"Tell me, Dors. Did it ever occur to you that something awfully *convenient* happened here, four decades ago? When you and Hari had your adventure, barely escaping death with your minds trapped in the bodies of apes?"

Dors paused. Out of habit, her eyelids blinked in company with surprise.

"Non sequitur," she replied. "Your references do not correlate. What does that event have to do with you and Daneel—"

"I am answering your question, so please humor me. Hearken back to when you and Hari were right here, running and brachiating under this very same forest canopy, experiencing a full range of emotions while hunters chased your borrowed ape bodies. Can you vividly recall fleeing from one narrow escape to another? Later, did you ever bother going over the experience in detail, calculating the *probabilities*?

"Consider the weapons that your pursuers had available—from nerve gas to smart-bullets to tailored viruses—and yet they could not kill a pair of unarmed animals? Or ponder the way you two just barely managed to sneak back into the station, overcoming obstacles and villains, in order to reclaim your real bodies from stasis and save the day.

"Or how about the remarkable way your enemies found you here in the first place, despite all of Daneel's precautions and—"

Dors cut him off.

"Dispense with the melodrama, Lodovic. You are implying that we were *meant* to experience that peril . . . and meant to survive. Clearly you conjecture that Daneel himself stood behind our entire escapade. That he arranged for our apparent endangerment, the pursuit—"

"And your assured survival. After all, you and Hari were important to his plans."

"Then what purpose could such a charade possibly serve?"

"Can you not guess? Perhaps the same purpose that drew Hari here."

Dors frowned.

"An experiment? Hari wanted to study basic human-simian nature for his psychohistorical models. Are you saying that Daneel took advantage of the situation by throwing us into simulated jeopardy here . . . in order to study our reactions? To what end?"

"I will not say more at this time. Rather, I'll leave it for you to surmise, at your leisure."

Dors found this incredible. "You summoned me all this distance . . . in order to cast absurd riddles?"

"Not *only* that," Lodovic assured. "I promised you a gift, as well. And here it comes."

The male figure in front of her gestured toward the forest, where a squat, heavily built machine now emerged, rolling on glittering treads. A ridiculous caricature of a human face peered from a neckless torso. Cradled in a pair of metal arms, the crude automaton carried a lidded box.

"A tiktok," she said, recognizing the mechanism by its clanking clumsiness, so unlike a positronic robot.

"Indeed. New variants were being invented on many worlds about the time your husband became the most powerful man in the empire. Of course, he ordered all such work stopped, and the prototypes destroyed."

"You weren't on Trantor when tiktoks went berserk. Humans died!"

"Indeed. What better way to give them a bad reputation, making it easy to forbid their reinvention. Tell me, Dors. Can you say with any certainty that the tiktoks would have gone 'berserk' if not for the meddling of Hari and Daneel?"

This time Dors remained silent. Clearly, Lodovic did not expect an answer.

"Haven't you ever wondered about the dawn ages?" He continued. "Humans invented our kind swiftly, almost as soon as they discovered the techniques of science, even before they had starflight! *And yet, during the following twenty thousand years of advanced civilization, the feat was never repeated.*

"Can you explain it, Dors?"

This time it was her turn to shrug. "We were a destabilizing influence. The Spacer worlds grew overreliant on robotic servants, losing faith in their own competence. We had to step aside—"

"Yes, yes," Lodovic interrupted. "I know Daneel's rationalization under the Zeroth Law. You are reciting the official reason *why*. What I want to know is . . . how?"

Dors stared at Lodovic Trema.

"What do you mean?"

"Surely the question is simple. How has humanity been prevented from rediscovering robots! We are discussing a span of a thousand generations. In all that time, upon twenty-five *million* worlds, would not some ingenious schoolchild, tinkering in a basement hobby shop, have been able to replicate what her primitive ancestors accomplished with much cruder tools?"

Dors shook her head.

"The tiktoks . . ."

"Were a very recent phenomenon. Those crude automatons only appeared when ancient constraints loosened. A sure sign of imperial decline and incipient chaos, according to Hari Seldon. No, Dors, the real answers have to lie much farther back in time."

"And I suppose you're going to tell me what they are?"

"No. You wouldn't credit anything I say, believing I have a hidden agenda. But if you are curious about these matters, there is another, more reputable source you can ask."

The crude "tiktok" finished approaching from the forest, rolling to a halt within arm's reach and offering Trema the box it carried. Lodovic removed the lid and drew an oblong object from within the container.

Dors took an involuntary step back.

It was the head of a robot! Not humaniform, it gleamed with metallic highlights. The eye cells, glossy black, were empty and vacant. Yet, when Dors sent a brief probing microwave burst, there came back a resonance—a faint echo showing that a positronic brain lay within, unshielded and unpowered, but also largely undamaged.

That echo set off an involuntary shiver in her circuits. Dors could tell at once, the head was *old*.

When Lodovic Trema next spoke, his voice was both amused and sympathetic.

"Yeah, it struck me the same way. Especially when I realized who this once was.

"Dors Venabili, I now entrust you with the most precious relic in the galaxy—the head and brain of R. Giskard Reventlov—cofounder of the Zeroth Law of Robotics . . . and slayer of the planet Earth."

7.

◆

By mutual consent, Hari met the Grey Man at a café near the offices of the Imperial Soil Service, in one of the seedier bureaucratic levels of Coronnen Sector. Horis Antic expressed confidence that their conversation would be private, in a shielded booth that he must have prepared meticulously beforehand.

In fact, Hari did not care if Linge Chen's Special Police were still following him around, or listening in. This conversation would be dry enough to put the goons to sleep in no time.

"As you might guess, my superiors don't look kindly on unapproved research," the small man told Hari, pausing to dispense a blue tablet from his belt pouch and washing it down with a gulp of ale. "Our agency is not well regarded, politically. Even a small scandal might cost us overhead allotments, recruitment priorities, or a percentum of our office cubicles!"

Hari tried not to smile. Greys lived in a world of tense struggles over minutiae. Office politics and worries over government appropriations kept most senior bureaucrats in a constant state of agitation. No wonder Horis Antic seemed nervous, his eyes constantly darting. Even for a Grey, he took an inordinate number of calming pills.

Perhaps he harbors a secret dream, that his freelance studies might get him plucked out of the rat race, into the more serene world of the meritocracy.

That was what had happened to Hari—though admittedly before he was eight years old when those first algebra papers won him meritocratic robes.

Only the gentry class—the noble aristocracy whose thousand ranks and levels ranged from mere township squires all the way past planetary earls and sector dukes to the emperor himself— inherited their social status at birth. All others were born citizens, then recategorized according to their nature and accomplish-ments. Still, such changes generally took place during youth. Hari saw little hope for Antic to make a switch at his age . . . unless he would consider becoming an eccentric. In some ways, the fellow already qualified.

"It all began when I had a hunch to reexamine the ancient question of *tilling*," the bureaucrat explained, after a new round of drinks was served.

"The question of what?" Hari asked.

Antic nodded. "Of course you wouldn't have heard of it. The whole issue is rather obscure. Not many news reports or popular accounts are written about planetary soil analysis, I'm afraid. Let me begin again.

"You see, Professor Seldon, it has long been axiomatic that nearly all human-settled worlds have a narrow range of traits—for instance, oxygen-nitrogen atmospheres with a roughly twenty: eighty ratio. Most of the multicelled life-forms on these planets descend from the forty or so standard phyla, using the same basic DNA structure . . . though there are exceptions."

"Chickens on every world," Hari summarized with a smile, trying to put the man at ease. Antic kept twisting his cloth napkin, and it was starting to make Hari nervous.

"Ha!" The bureaucrat laughed eagerly. "And crabgrass on every lawn. I forgot that you're not a Trantor native. Some of this will be familiar to you, then. Indeed, a farmer from Sinbikdu would recognize most of the animals on far-off Incino. This sup-ports the most popular theory regarding the origins of life—that similar species evolved naturally on many planets at the same time, due to some fundamental biological law. These similar crea-tures then naturally converged on the highest form of all, human-ity."

Hari nodded. Antic was describing what a mathist would call an attractor state . . . a situation that all surrounding states will drift toward, compelled by irresistible driving forces, so that all trajectories wind up intersecting at the same point. In this case, the standard dogma said that all evolutionary paths should inevitably produce human beings.

Only he knew for certain that *this* attractor notion was dead wrong. Years ago Hari had applied the tools of psychohistory to galaxy-wide genetic data and quickly determined that people must have emerged quite suddenly from somewhere in Sirius Sector, about twenty thousand years ago. This was recently confirmed by what he read in *A Child's Book of Knowledge*.

Naturally, he had no intention of announcing the truth, or trying to dispute the convergence theory. Nothing would bollix up the Seldon Plan worse than having the attention of the entire empire suddenly transfixed on a tiny world near Sirius, asking questions about events two hundred centuries ago!

"Go on," Hari urged. "I assume that similar patterns apply to the distribution of *soil types*?"

"Yes. Yes indeed, Professor! Oh, there are geological differences from planet to planet . . . sometimes profound ones. But certain aspects seem almost universal. The *tilling* I spoke of has to do with the natural state of lowland soils that colonists found on most planets, when they first settled each world. (We do have records stretching that far back, for about a million planets.) In each case soil conditions were similar—crushed and sifted to a depth of several dozen meters, with an abundance of familiar vegetation growing thereupon. Excellent conditions for farming, by the way. Of course, the mission of my organization is to see to it that things *stay* that way, through proper care and maintenance, preventing erosion or losses caused by industrial pollution. I'm afraid this sometimes makes us unpopular with farmers and local gentry, but we have to take the long view, eh? I mean, if somebody doesn't think about the future, how are we all going to *have* one? Sometimes it can get so frustrating—"

"Horis!" Hari cut him off. "You're drifting. Please get to the point."

Antic blinked, then nodded vigorously.

"Quite right. Sorry." He took a deep breath. "Anyway, theoreticians have long assumed that tilling is just another universal phenomenon—one that naturally accompanies having an oxy-nitrogen atmosphere. Only—"

Antic paused. Although he had checked the booth's security twice at the beginning of their conversation, he still craned his neck to look around.

"Only . . . members of my service have always known better," he continued in a much lower voice.

Reaching into his pocket, he pulled out a flattish piece of stone. "Look carefully at the impressions here, Professor. Do you see symmetrical patterns?"

Hari hesitated. Meritocrats had a traditional aversion to

touching rocks or dirt, one reason why they traditionally wore gloves. No one knew the origins of the custom, but it was ancient and deep.

And yet, I've never felt it. I've plunged my hands into soil before, enjoying the reaction this caused in my academic peers.

Hari reached out and took the stone, instantly fascinated by the series of jagged grooves Antic pointed out.

"It's called a *fossil.* There, see the weird eye sockets? Note the pentagonal symmetry. Five legs! This thing is unrelated to any of the forty standard phyla! I picked it up it on Glorianna, but that hardly matters. You can actually find fossils on about ten percent of settled worlds! If you go up in the mountains, or anywhere away from the tilled areas. Highland dwellers know all about them, but there are taboos against talking about it. And they've learned better than to mention such things to their local scholars, who always get angry and change the subject."

Hari blinked, transfixed by the outline traced in stone. His mind fizzed with questions, like how old this creature was, and what its story could have been. He wanted to follow up on Antic's story about the things farmers knew on innumerable worlds, and what meritocrats would not—or could not—learn.

But none of these things brought them any closer to the issue that burned foremost in his mind.

"Horis, your paper speaks of *anomalies* in the tilling. Please tell me about the exceptions. The ones that roused your suspicions."

The bureaucrat nodded again.

"Yes, yes! You see, Professor, tilling is not quite as universal a phenomenon as might at first appear! In my long experience as an inspector, visiting more worlds than I could count, I have found irregularities. Planets where the plains and valleys have much coarser consistencies, far more varied, with no trace of the sifting or recent heating that we find in most lowlands. Out of interest— more as a hobby or pastime than anything else—I began listing other unusual traits on these planets . . . such as the existence of large numbers of genetically unusual beasts. In several cases, there were signs that a supernova had gone off in the region, sometime in the last thirty thousand years. One planet has a fantastic amount of ambient radioactivity in its crust, while several others have a multitude of fused metal mounds scattered all over their surface. I began charting these anomalies, and found that they clustered along great sweeping bands . . ."

"And these bands also relate to those *space currents* you spoke of? How did you discover that?"

Antic smiled. "A lucky fluke. While nosing around through the galactographic files for data, I met a fellow aficionado . . . another bureaucrat like me, with a secret hobby. We compared our little fanaticisms—and if you think mine is strange, you should hear him go on and on about the ebb and flow of these diffuse clouds of atoms in space! He thinks he sees patterns in them that have escaped notice by the Imperial Navigation Service. Which is entirely possible, since they only care about maintaining clear routes for commerce. Even then it's all kept as routine as poss—"

"Horis."

"Uh? Oh, yes. Well, anyway, my new friend and I compared notes . . . I also had the temerity to apply a few of the mathematical tools that I saw described in popular accounts of your work, Professor. The result is the galactic chart that caught your interest last night." Antic exhaled deeply. "And so here we are!"

Hari frowned.

"I saw only your name on the paper."

"Yes, well . . . my friend is rather shy. He feels we don't have anywhere near enough evidence yet to go public. Without solid, tangible proof, a speculative article might jeopardize our careers."

"Whereas you felt the risk of coming forward was worthwhile."

Antic smiled while reaching into his pouch for another pill.

"It did catch your interest, Professor Seldon. You're sitting across from me. I know you wouldn't waste your precious time on something that's completely trivial."

Hope seemed to swell in the Grey's voice, as if expecting the blue mantle of meritocracy to be draped across his shoulders at any moment. But Hari was too distracted to offer polite praise. His mind roiled.

I wouldn't waste my time on trivia? Can you be so sure, my young friend? Perhaps I'm only here tonight because of terminal boredom . . . or else encroaching senility. I may be missing something obvious. Something that would topple your amateurish offerings like a house of cards in a Trantor-quake.

Only Hari had not found a flaw so far. Though Antic's analytical work seemed pedestrian, it was also meticulously honest. Hari's check of references and public data sets revealed no apparent errors of fact.

Whatever pattern he's discovered—using dirt samples and drifting clouds of nothing in space—it seems to correlate roughly to the zones where chaos worlds have been most frequent . . . a problem I've been trying to solve for half my life.

In fact, this was not essential to the success or failure of the Foundation Plan. Once the empire's fall began accelerating, the appearance of chaos worlds would cease. People all across the galaxy would be much too busy surviving, or engaging in more classic styles of rebellion, to engage in orgies of wild, utopian individualism.

And yet, psychohistory will always be incomplete without an answer to this hellish attractor state.

Then there was another factor, equally compelling.

Santanni . . . where Raych died. And Siwenna, where the ship carrying Manella and Bellis was last seen before vanishing. Both worlds lie near some of Antic's anomalies.

Hari felt a decision welling up from within.

One thing he knew for certain. He hated his life now. Ever since completing the Time Vault recordings, he'd been sitting around as a revered historical figure, just waiting to die. That was not his style. Anyway, he had felt more alive the last two days than any time in the last year.

Abruptly, he decided.

"Very well, Horis Antic. I will go with you."

Across the table, the portly man in the gray uniform visibly paled. His eyes seemed to pop, staring back at Hari, while his Adam's apple bobbed ludicrously.

Finally, Antic swallowed hard.

"How . . ." he began, hoarsely. "How did y-you . . ."

Hari smiled.

"How did I know that you were about to suggest a private expedition?"

He spread his hands, feeling a bit like his old self again.

"Well after all, young sir, I *am* Hari Seldon."

8.

◆

According to his plea-bargain agreement with the Commission for Public Safety, Hari wasn't supposed to leave Trantor. He also knew that Wanda and the Fifty would never permit him to go charging off to the stars. Even though he was no longer needed for the success of the Plan, no one would take responsibility for risking the life of the father of psychohistory.

Fortunately, Hari knew a loophole that just might let him get away. *You can go quite far without officially leaving Trantor,* he thought, while making the necessary arrangements. •

There was very little to pack for the journey—just a few necessities, which Kers Kantun loaded in a suitcase, plus a few of Hari's most valued research archives, including a copy of the Foundation Plan Prime Radiant. None of it looked too out of the ordinary, slung on the back of his mobile chair.

Hari's servant-guardian had argued against this trip, worrying aloud about the stress of travel. But in fact, it wasn't hard to get Kers to obey. Hari realized why the Valmoril's objections were so mild.

He knows that boredom is the worst threat to my health, right now. If I don't find something useful to do, I'll just fade away. This little escapade probably won't amount to much. Space travel is still pretty routine. And meanwhile, I'll be too busy to let myself die.

So the two of them set out from his apartment the next morning, as if on a normal daily excursion. But instead of heading for the imperial gardens, Kers steered Hari onto a transitway bound for the Orion elevator.

As their car sped along, and the surrounding metal tube seemed to flow past in a blur, Hari kept wondering if they would be stopped at some point along the way. It was a real possibility.

Had the Special Police really been withdrawn, as Gaal assured? Or were they watching him even now, with little spy cameras and other gadgets?

A year ago, right after the trial, official surveillance had been intense, sniffing each corner of Hari's life and eyeing his every move. But a lot had changed since then. Linge Chen was now convinced by the cooperation of Hari and the Fifty. There had been no more disruptive news leaks about an "imminent collapse of the empire." More importantly, the move to Terminus was going according to plan. The hundred thousand experts that Hari had recruited with promises of employment on a vast *Encyclopedia Galactica* project were now being prepared and sent in groups to that far-off little world and a glorious destiny they could not possibly suspect.

In that case, why would Chen keep paying professional officers to watch a dying crackpot professor, when their skills could better be employed dealing with other crises?

Soon a chime announced the car's arrival at the Grand Vestibule. Hari and Kers emerged into a mammoth chamber that stretched twenty kilometers across and tapered vertically toward heights that vanished in a misty haze.

Anchored to the ground in the very center was a huge black pillar, more than a hundred meters wide, that reared straight upward. The eye assumed that this mighty column held up the distant roof, but the eye was fooled. It wasn't a pillar, but a great *cable*, stretching outward through a hole in that remote ceiling, continuing past Trantor's atmosphere, linking the solid surface to a massive space station that whirled in orbit, fifty thousand kilometers above.

Along its great length, Orion elevator seemed infested with countless *bulges* that kept flowing up and down like parasites burrowing under the skin of a slender stalk. These were elevator cars, partly masked by a flexible membrane that protected passengers against dangerous radiation, and from having to look upon vertiginous views.

At the very bottom of this monumental structure, people could be seen debarking from newly arrived capsules, passing through brief immigration formalities, then moving toward a maze of ramps and moving walkways. Other streams of individuals flowed in the opposite direction, aiming to depart. There were several lines for each social caste. Kers chose one of the shorter queues, clearly marked as reserved for meritocrat VIPs.

In theory, I could use the special portal for high nobility, Hari thought, glancing toward an aisle lined with silky fabrics, where fawning attendants saw to the needs of super-planetary gentry. *Any former First Minister of the Empire has that right. Even a disgraced one, like me. But that would surely attract too much attention.*

They paused at a little kiosk labeled EMIGRATION CONTROL and presented their identity cards. Kers had offered to acquire false papers through his contacts in the black market, but that act would transform this little adventure from a misdemeanor into a felony. Hari had no intention of risking harm to the Seldon Project simply to satisfy his curiosity. If this worked, fine. Otherwise, he might as well go home and let things end gracefully.

The screen seemed to glare at Hari with its inquiry.

DESTINATION?

This was a crucial moment. Everything depended on a matter of legal definition.

"Demarchia," he said aloud. "I want to observe the imperial legislature in session for a week or two. Ultimately, I plan to return from there to my residence at Streeling University."

He wasn't lying. But a lot could lie in that word—"ultimately."

The unit seemed to ponder his statement for a moment, while Hari mulled silently.

Demarchia is one of twenty nearby worlds that are officially part of Trantor. There are strong political and traditional reasons for this arrangement, one that's been reinforced by generations of emperors and ministers . . . But maybe the police don't look at things the same way.

If Hari was wrong, the computer would refuse to issue a ticket. News of this "escape attempt" would flash at the Commission of Public Safety. And Hari would have no choice but to go home and wait for Linge Chen's agents to come and question him. Worse, Stettin Palver and the other psychohistorians would cluck and fuss, wagging their fingers and tightening their reverent guardianship. Hari would never have another unsupervised moment.

Come on, he urged, wishing he had some of the mental powers that enabled Daneel Olivaw to meddle in the thoughts of both men and machines.

Abruptly, the screen came alight again.

HAPPY VOYAGE. LONG LIVE THE EMPEROR.

Hari nodded.

"Long life," he answered perfunctorily, having to swallow a knot of released tension. The machine extruded a pair of tickets, assigning them to a specific elevator car, appropriate to their social class and destination. Hari looked at one of the billets as Kers picked them up.

INTRA-TRANTOR COMMUTE, it said.

He nodded with satisfaction. *I'm not breaking the letter of my agreement with the Commission. Not yet at least.*

A crowd of uniformed figures milled nearby, wearing polished buttons and white gloves—young porters assigned to assist non-gentry VIP passengers. Several of them glanced up, but they turned back to their gossip and dice games when Kers and Hari refrained from making any beckoning motions. Kers needed no assistance with their meager luggage.

Moments later, however, a small figure suddenly spilled out of the crowd of purple uniforms, striding at a rapid pace to intercept them. The girl—wiry and no more than fifteen years old—snapped a jaunty salute at the rim of her pillbox cap. Her Corrin Sector accent was unabashed and friendly to the point of overfamiliarity.

"Greets, m'lords! I'll be takin' your bags an' seeing you safely along if it pleases ya."

Her name tag said JENI.

Kers made a dismissing gesture, but in a blur she snatched the tickets from his hand. Grinning, the porter nodded with a vigorous swirl of unruly platinum hair.

"Right this way to your chariot, m'lords!"

When Kers refused to hand over any of the luggage, she only grinned. "No need to be afeared. I'll see you safely all the way to Orion Station. Just follow me."

Kers rumbled as the girl sped ahead with their tickets, but Hari smiled and patted his servant's burly hand. In a world of dull jobs and soul-grinding routine, it was pleasant to see someone having a little fun, even at the expense of her betters.

They found the third member of their party at the agreed spot, next to an elevator car with DEMARCHIA flashing on its placard. Horis Antic looked infinitely relieved to see them. The Grey bureaucrat barely glanced at the porter, but he bowed to Hari more deeply than protocol required, then motioned toward the gaping door of a waiting elevator car.

"This way, Professor. I saved us good seats."

Hari took a deep breath as they went aboard, and the opening slithered shut behind them.

Here we go. Already he could feel his heart begin to lift.

One last adventure.

Unfortunately there were no windows. Passengers could watch the view outside through seat monitors, but few bothered.

Hari's car was half-empty, since the space elevators were being used much less these days.

I'm partly responsible for that, he recalled. Most traffic to and from Trantor arrived by hyperspatial jump ships, which floated to the ground on their own self-generated gravity fields. A growing swarm of them shuttled up and down with food and other necessities for the empire's administrative center. Twenty agricultural worlds had been dedicated to supplying this lifeline—up from a mere eight before Hari became First Minister.

Trantor used to create its own basic food supply in huge solar-powered vats, operated by swarms of busy automatons who didn't mind the stench and grinding labor. When that system collapsed during the infamous Tiktok Revolt, one of his first duties in office had been to make up the difference, multiplying the flow of imported food and other goods.

But the new system is expensive and inefficient. And that lifeline will become a deadly trap in coming centuries. He knew this from the equations of psychohistory. *Emperors and oligarchs will pay ever-greater attention to preserving it, at the expense of important business elsewhere.*

To enhance their loyalty, the agricultural worlds had been joined even closer to Trantor itself, sharing the same "planetary" government, an act that now helped to justify Hari's ruse.

Though he did not turn on the outside viewer, it was easy to visualize the planet's gleaming anodized metal coat, reflecting the densely packed starfield of the galaxy's crowded center—millions of dazzling suns that glittered like fiery gems, making night almost like day. Though many in the empire envisioned Trantor as one giant city, much of the stainless-steel surface was only a veneer, just a few stories thick, laid down for show after mountains and valleys had been leveled. Those flat warrens were mostly used for storing old records. Actual office towers, factories, and habitations occupied no more than ten percent of the planet's area . . . easily enough room for forty billion people to live and work efficiently.

Still, the popular image was accurate enough. This center of empire was like the galactic core itself—a crowded place. Even knowing the psychohistorical reasons for it all left Hari bemused.

"Right now we're passin' halfway point," the young porter explained, playing up her role as tour guide. "Those of you who forgot to take your pills might be experiencin' some upset as we head toward null gee," she went on, "but in most cases that's just your imagination actin' up. Try to think of somethin' nice, and it often goes away."

Horis Antic wasn't much cheered. Though he surely traveled extensively in his line of work, he might never have used this peculiar type of transport. The bureaucrat hurriedly popped several tablets from his belt dispenser and swallowed them.

"Of course most people nowadays come to Trantor by starship," the girl went on. "So my advice is to just keep tellin' yourself that this here cable is over five thousand years old, made in the glory days of great engineers. So in a sense, you're just as well anchored as if you were still connected to the ground!"

Hari had seen other porters do this sort of thing, extroverts going beyond the call of duty while trying to make light of a prosaic job. But few ever had an audience as difficult as dour Kers Kantun and nervous Horis Antic, who kept chewing his nails, clearly wishing the girl would go away. But she went on chattering happily.

"Sometimes visitors ask what'd happen if this cable we're ridin' ever broke! Well let me assure you it ain't possible. At least that's what the ancients who made this stringy thing promised. Though I'm sure you all know how things are goin' these days. So you're welcome to imagine along with me what might happen if someday . . ."

She went on to describe, with evident relish, how all of Trantor's space elevators—Orion, Lesmic, Gengi, Pliny, and Zul—might break apart in some hypothetical future calamity. The upper half of each great tether, including the transfer stations, would spin away into space, while the lower half, weighing billions of tons, would plummet into the ground at incredible speeds, releasing enough explosive force to pierce the metal veneer all the way to Trantor's geothermal power pipes, unleashing a globe-girdling chain of new volcanos.

Exactly according to the doomsday scenario, calculated by our Prime Radiant, Hari marveled. Of course some stories from the Seldon Group had seeped out to the culture at large. Still, it was the first time he ever heard this particular phase of the Fall of Trantor described so vividly, or with such evident enjoyment!

In fact, the space elevators were very sturdy things, built at the height of the empire's vigor, with hundreds of times minimal safety strength. According to Hari's calculations, they would probably survive until the capital was sacked for the first time, almost three hundred years from now.

On that day, however, it would be unwise to live anywhere near the planet's equator. The descendants of Stettin and Wanda would be ready, of course. The headquarters of the Second Foundation would be shifted well before that time . . . all according to plan.

Hari's mind roamed the future much as a historian might ponder the past. One of his recordings for the Time Vault on Terminus dealt with that era-to-come, when destruction would rain on this magnificent world. At that point the Foundation would be entering its great age of self-confident expansion. Having survived several dangerous encounters with the tottering empire, the vigorous Foundationers would then stare in awe at the old realm's sudden and final collapse.

His Time Vault message had been carefully written to fine-tune attitudes among the leaders on Terminus at that point, giving a little added political weight to factions favoring a go-slow approach to further conquest. Too much assurance could be as bad as too little. The secret Second Foundation, made up of mentalically talented descendants of the Fifty, would begin taking a more active role at that point, molding the vigorous culture based on Terminus. Forging the nucleus of a new empire. One far greater than the first.

The Plan beckoned Hari with its sweet complexity. But once again, his inner voice of doubt intruded.

You can feel certain of the first hundred years. The momentum of events is just too great to divert from the path we foresee. And the following century or two should proceed according to calculations, unless unexpected perturbations appear. It will be the Second Foundation's job to correct those.

But after that?

Something in the math makes me uneasy. Hints at unsolved attractor states and hidden solutions that lurk below all the smug, predictable models we've worked out.

I wish I had a better idea what they are. Those unsolved states.

That was just one reason for Hari's decision to join this expedition.

There were others.

• • •

Horis Antic sat close to Hari. "I have made arrangements, Professor. We'll meet the captain of our charter ship the day after we land on Demarchia."

By now the young porter had finished her deliberately vivid catastrophe tale and fallen silent at last. She wore headphones, apparently listening to music as she watched their approach to Orion Station on a nearby seat monitor. Hari felt safe talking to Antic.

"This captain of yours is reliable? It may not be wise to trust a mercenary. Especially when we can't afford to pay very much."

"I agree," Antic said with a vigorous nod. "But this fellow comes highly recommended. And we won't have to pay anything."

Hari started to ask how that could be. But Antic shook his head. Some explanations would have to wait.

"Coming up to transfer!" the porter announced, extra loudly because of her headphones. "Everybody strap in. This can get bumpy!"

Hari let his servant fuss over him, clamping down the mobile chair and adjusting his restraint webbing. Then he shooed Kers away to take care of himself. It was many years since he had traveled down a star-shunt, but he was no novice.

Hari ordered a holoview showing Orion Station just ahead, a giant Medusa's head of tubes and spires that sat in the middle of a straight, shimmering line—the space-elevator cable. Only a few starships were seen at the docking ports, since most modern hyper-craft could land and take off using graceful antigravity fields. But Hari foresaw a time when declining competence would lead to a series of terrible accidental crashes below. Then vessels coming to Trantor would be forced to off-load their cargoes up there, and these great tethers would have supreme importance once more . . . until they were finally brought down fifty years later.

For the present, ship traffic was taking over the great bulk of travel and commerce in the galaxy. But a few routes were still covered by another, entirely separate transportation system. One that was much faster and more convenient.

Star-shunts.

In Hari's youth, there had been hundreds of wormhole links— penetrating the fabric of space-time from one far-flung part of the galaxy to another. Only a dozen or so remained, most of those connected to a single spot close to the orbit of Trantor. According to his equations, those would be abandoned, too, in just a few decades.

"Get ready!" the young porter cried.

Orion Station seemed to rush toward the view screen. At the last instant, a huge manipulator arm rushed out of nowhere to seize their transport car with a sudden shudder. Amid whirling sensations, the compact vehicle was plucked off the tether and slipped into a long, slender gun barrel aimed at distant space.

The outside view was swallowed in blackness.

Horis Antic let out a low moan. *Some things you just never get used to,* Hari thought, trying to keep his thoughts abstract, waiting for the pulse gun to fire.

Hyperspatial starships were big, bulky, and relatively slow. But the basic technology was so reliable and easy to maintain that some fallen cultures had been known to keep their fleets going even after they lost the ability to generate proton-fusion power. In contrast, star-shunts relied on deep understanding of physics and tremendous engineering competence. When the empire no longer produced enough proficient workers, the network entered steep decline.

Some blamed decadence or failing education systems. Others said it was caused by chaos worlds, whose seductive cultural attraction often drew creative people from all across the galaxy . . . until each "renaissance" imploded.

Hari's equations told complex reasons for a fall that began centuries ago. A collapse Daneel Olivaw had been fighting against since long before Hari's birth.

I'd hate to be riding one of these shunts thirty years from now, when the declining competence curve finally crosses a threshold of—

His thought was cut off as the gun fired, sending their car hurtling through a hyperspacial microshunt to a spot fifty light-minutes away from Trantor, where the *real* wormhole waited. Entry wasn't especially smooth, and wrenching sensations made Hari's gut churn. He sighed under his breath. *"Dors!"*

There followed a series of rocking motions while they hurtled down the well-traveled maw of a giant cavity in space-time. The seat monitors roiled with mad colors as holovideo computers failed to make sense of the maelstrom outside. This mode of transport had disadvantages, all right. And yet, Hari reminded himself of one basic fact about shunting—the single trait that still made it highly attractive compared to traveling by ship. Almost as soon as any shunt journey had begun . . .

. . . it was over.

Abruptly, the view screens transformed once again, showing a familiar dusty spray of stars in the galactic center. Hari felt several bumps as the car was relayed by microshunt a couple of times. Then, as if by magic, a planet swam into view.

A planet of continents and seas and mountain ranges, where cities glittered as *part* of the landscape, instead of utterly dominating it. A beautiful world that Hari used to visit all the time when he was First Minister, accompanied by his gracious and beautiful wife, back in the days when he and Daneel thought that astute use of psychohistory might actually save the empire, instead of planning for its eventual demise.

"Welcome to the second imperial capital, m'lords," said the young porter.

"Welcome to Demarchia."

9.

◆

Dors felt obliged to confess.

Her report to Daneel Olivaw kept getting delayed by one thing or another, until she finally arrived back home on Smushell. Then she ran out of excuses.

"I tried to destroy the renegade robot, R. Lodovic Trema," she recited in a coded transmission to her leader, keeping her voice levels even and emotionless. *"The fact that I failed does little to mitigate my act, which contradicted your apparent wishes, Daneel. I therefore await your orders. If you wish, I will surrender my duties here to another humanoid and proceed to Eos for diagnosis and repair."*

Eos, the secret repair base that Daneel maintained for his cabal of immortal robots, lay halfway across the galaxy. It would be wrenching for Dors to leave Klia and Brann at this point in their lives, when they were creating precious mentalic babies so important to Daneel's long-range plans. But Dors was used to doing her duty, even when it hurt . . . such as when she had to leave Hari Seldon.

Daneel knows best, she thought. And yet, it was hard to continue dictating the report.

"I know you haven't yet declared the Lodovic machine to be a true outlaw. You are apparently fascinated by the way Trema was transformed by the Voltaire meme, so that it no longer felt compelled to obey the Four Laws of Robotics. I concede that Lodovic hasn't made any overt moves that seem harmful to humanity. So far.

"But I find small comfort in that, Daneel!

"Recall that the Zeroth Law commands us always to act in ways that serve the long-term interests of the human race. This imperative supersedes the classic Three Laws of Susan Calvin. You have taught this dogma ever since the dawn ages, Daneel. So I must ask you to explain to me why you chose to let Lodovic go. Free to run about the galaxy, conspiring with Calvinian robots, and almost certainly scheming against your plans!"

Dors felt her humaniform body throb with simulated emotional tension, from a rapid heartbeat to shortness of breath. The emulation was automatic, realistic, and by now partly beyond her conscious control. She had to suppress the reaction by force of will, just like a human woman who had something important and dangerous to say to her boss.

"In any event, I felt impelled to take matters into my own hands when I met Lodovic on Panucopia. Whatever his subtle reasons were for drawing me to a rendezvous there, I could not afford to let the opportunity pass.

"As we stood across from each other near the Panucopia forest, Lodovic continued explaining his theory about the near-death experience Hari and I went through on that planet, forty years ago. Lodovic claimed the entire episode could only have happened as one of your many experiments, Daneel. Trying to pin down underlying aspects of human nature.

"After listening to this for a while, I decided the time had come. I drew a miniblaster from a hidden slot in my arm and aimed it at Lodovic.

"He scarcely reacted, continuing to describe his conjecture—that chimpanzees somehow play an important role in your ultimate plans, Daneel!

"I recall thinking at that moment how dangerous it would be to let an insane robot loose upon the cosmos. Nevertheless, First-Law impulses made it hard for me to press the trigger and fire at Lodovic's human-looking features."

Dors paused, recalling that unpleasant moment. Susan Calvin's ancient First Law of Robotics was explicit. *No robot may harm a human being, or through inaction allow a human to come to harm.* So deeply rooted was this injunction that only the most sophisticated positronic brains could accomplish what she did on Panucopia—firing a blaster bolt at a face that smiled with ironic resignation, seeming at the very last moment more like a person than a great many real men she had known. It felt terrible . . . though not as bad as those two times in her past when the First Law had to be overridden completely.

Those awful days when she had killed true humans for the sake of Daneel's Zeroth Law.

On this occasion, she felt much better when the body in front of her lost its humanoid appearance, crumpling down to metal, plastic, and colloidal jellies—and finally a positronic brain that sparkled and flashed as it died.

"I kept firing the blaster until the body melted down to slag. Then I turned to go.

"But I had only walked a few paces before . . ."

Dors paused again. This time she shook her head and gave up reciting altogether. Finishing would have to wait until later. Perhaps tomorrow. The way communications were degrading across the galaxy, the message would probably take weeks to reach Daneel, anyway.

She stood up and turned away from the encoding machine . . . much as she had done that day on Panucopia, after inspecting Lodovic's molten body. Excited shrieks and calls had followed her from the nearby forest, shouted by wild creatures whose native thoughts she once intimately shared. Back when she had been Hari's, and Hari had been hers.

Then, after she had taken several steps back toward the spaceship, a voice called her name from behind.

"Don't forget to take this with you, Dors."

She had whirled around . . . only to see the tiktok, that crude, human-built caricature of a robot, roll forward with a box in its primitive claw-hands. The box containing a twenty-thousand-year-old head.

"Lodovic? Is that you?" she had asked, staring at the clanking tiktok, suddenly realizing how easy it would be for Trema to disguise himself within such a bulky mechanical body.

The clattering machine answered with a voice that buzzed in

rough monotones. And yet, Dors detected a tenor of blithe amusement.

"Now, Dors. In light of what just happened, would it be wise for me to answer that question?"

She responded with a shrug. If Lodovic had wanted to retaliate, it would have been easy at that point.

"Did I just kill a doppel? A dummy copy?"

"Will you hold it against me that I was so untrusting, Dors?"

Standing there, as Panucopia's sun gradually set and their shadows lengthened, she had estimated the odds that Lodovic's real brain lay inside the tiktok. If so, a second shot would eliminate the enemy for good.

"May I note one interesting observation, Dors?" The automaton had buzzed. "You just used the word 'kill' instead of 'destroy' or 'deactivate.' Shall I take that as a small sign of progress in our relationship?"

She was tempted to use the blaster again. But then, in all probability his real brain was somewhere in the forest, out of reach, controlling doppels from some hidden place of safety. So instead, with a humanlike sigh, she put away the pistol and reached for the box.

"There will be another time," she said, taking up the burden as gingerly as a human would pick up a crate of poisonous snakes.

"That is what we robots have always been able to say, Dors. But time may be running out for our kind, sooner than you think."

The only dignified thing she could do at that point was to let him have the last word. So Dors had turned without farewell and begun her long voyage home.

All the way back to Smushell, her sole company had been Lodovic's gift, the ancient head. For a week it stared at her—metal-skulled and gem-eyed—containing the inactive brain of R. Giskard Reventlov.

Giskard the founder, who long ago helped Daneel develop the Zeroth Law.

Giskard the savior, who sacrificed himself in the act of rescuing human destiny, while ruthlessly destroying humanity's birthplace.

Giskard the legendary, first of the mentalic robots, capable and willing to guide humans, nudging and shifting their thoughts and memories . . . for their own good.

Even now, with the ancient treasure safely ensconced in a secret niche of Klia Askar's house, Dors could not yet bring herself to access its stored memories.

Instead, she stared at it, knowing exactly what she was looking at.

The head was a trap.

A lure.

A test of faith, her Joan of Arc simulation would call it, as irresistible as any temptation faced by a human being.

If Lodovic wanted her to look inside, that must mean it contained something intoxicating, possibly a poison.

Something dangerous and unknown, despite the fact that she already had a clear name for it.

The truth.

10.

◆

Looking from his hotel-room balcony across the tree-lined avenues of Galactic Boulevard, it seemed easy for Hari to imagine this was some bucolic world of the periphery, not the "second imperial capital."

Of course, there were statues and imposing monuments, gleaming in the sun. Countless commemorative shrines had been erected here during the last fifteen millennia, celebrating emperors and prefects, victories and victims, great events and greater accomplishments. Still, in contrast to mighty Trantor, everything seemed small of scale and slow of pace, befitting Demarchia's true status as the forgotten junior partner, forsaken by power.

Even the Eight Houses of Parliament, glorious white structures that shone like diadems in a ring around Deliberation Hill, seemed somehow forlorn and irrelevant. Each of the five social castes still sent representatives to argue over points of law. And the three upper chambers occasionally managed to agree upon a bill or two. But ever since Hari's tenure as First Minister ended, there had been very little of consequence to emerge from those sacred halls. The Executive Council on Trantor ruled mostly by decree, and those decrees were largely fashioned by Linge Chen's Commission for Public Safety.

Not that specific laws mattered very much. Psychohistory predicted what would happen next. If Linge Chen were replaced tomorrow in some palace coup, the momentum of events would impel his successor in identical ways. Some cliques would win and others lose. But over the course of the next thirty years, the average of forces—taken across twenty-five million worlds— would overwhelm any initiatives attempted by commissioners, emperors, or oligarchic cabals.

And yet, a romantic part of Hari always felt saddened by Demarchia. The place struck him as a personification of lost opportunity. A might-have-been.

In theory, democracy is supposed to predominate over all the machinations of the gentry class. Even the worst imperial tyrants have always paid lip service to that principle of Ruellianism.

But in practice it was hard to implement. The Cumulative House, the Senate of Sectors, and the Assembly of Trades were all supposed to compensate for each other's faults, bringing representatives to Demarchia who were chosen in widely diverse ways. But the net result seemed always the same—a sapping of energy and dynamism. As First Minister, he had found it agonizing to get legislation passed—such as the emergency Chaos Suppression Law—even though his knowledge of psychohistory principles made him unusually effective compared to others.

In those days, Daneel and I still thought it could be fixed . . . the whole great Empire of Humanity. But back then my equations were still incomplete. They left some room for doubt. For hope.

Since Hari's tenure in office ended, Demarchia had become a backwater. A place to exile failed politicians. No one of importance bothered with it anymore.

Which suits our purpose in coming here now, he thought with a grim smile. This time, Demarchia was not a destination, but a convenient launching-off point.

"Professor Seldon?" Horis Antic's voice murmured behind Hari, from within the hotel room. As the next stage of their adventure approached, the portly bureaucrat grew increasingly nervous.

"I—I've just heard from the, uh, *individual* we talked about earlier. He says arrangements have been made. We're to meet him at his *vehicle* in an hour."

Hari touched a control and turned his mobile chair around, gliding back inside. Antic's convoluted speech, a precaution against possible bugging devices, would almost certainly be futile if they were under serious surveillance. Besides, up until now, no one had committed a single crime.

"Has your equipment arrived, Horis?"

The bureaucrat wore casual clothing. Still, anyone looking at his posture and poor fashion sense would know in an instant that he was a Grey Man.

"Yes, m'lord." He nodded. "The last crates are downstairs. It was much easier to order the instruments from a variety of companies and have them sent here, instead of to Trantor proper, where there might have been . . . embarrassing questions."

Hari had seen the list of tools and devices, and saw nothing that could even remotely be called contraband. Nevertheless, Antic had good reason not to let his superiors know he was spending his sabbatical time pursuing a bizarre "intellectual pastime."

In fact, Hari had been grateful for the delay while Antic gathered his equipment. It gave him a chance to rest after that harrowing star-shunt ride . . . much bumpier than he recalled from decades past. It also let him spend time under the sun, remembering Demarchia in the old days, when some of the best restaurants in the galaxy used to line the boulevards, and he still had taste buds to enjoy them . . . with beautiful, vivacious Dors Venabili at his side.

"All right," he said, feeling exceptionally alive, almost as if he could walk all the way to the spaceport. "Let's get going."

Kers Kantun met them in front of the hotel, next to Antic's equipment crates. At a glance, Hari knew that his bodyguard had checked them against the manifests and found nothing amiss. Hari acknowledged his servant's concern without giving it much importance. What did Kers imagine, that Antic had recruited the famed Hari Seldon into some convoluted smuggling scheme?

Their rented van arrived on schedule. The driver took one look at the crates and turned to hail a group of local laborers who were lounging nearby, hiring them on the spot to load the heavy boxes. Antic fretted as they hauled his precious instruments, meant to check out a bizarre theory about *planetary tilling* and *currents of space*.

Hari felt less worried, even though his financial contribution to their purchase was substantial. The cost seemed worthwhile if this endeavor might shed some new light on his own concerns. But in the long run, none of it would make any difference to his place in history. For Antic, on the other hand, this voyage was his sole chance to leave a mark on the universe.

A spaceport limo came to pick up the three of them while the cargo van followed behind, moving along avenues clearly designed for much greater traffic than they carried nowadays. Demarchia's economy was not good. There were many small crowds of laborers, looking for odd jobs.

A sprinkle of rain fell on the limousine's windows, startling the Trantor-born Kers, but putting Hari in a good mood.

"You know," he chatted affably, "over the course of many thousands of years, this world has hosted quite a few experiments in democracy."

"Indeed, Professor?" Antic leaned forward. He took a blue pill and started biting his nails again.

"Oh, yes. One form that I always found fascinating was called *The Nation*."

"I never heard of it."

"Not surprising. Your specialties lie elsewhere. Most people consider history distasteful or boring," Hari mused.

"But I *am* interested, Professor. Please, will you tell me about it?"

"Hm. Well, you see, there has always been a basic problem in applying democracy on a pan-galactic scale. A typical deliberative body can only operate with at most a few thousand members. Yet that's far too few to personally represent ten quadrillion voters, spread across twenty-five million worlds! Nevertheless, various attempts were made to solve this dilemma, such as *cumulative representation*. Each planetary congress elects a few delegates to their local star-zone assembly, which then chooses from its ranks a few to attend the regional sector conference. At that level, a small number are selected to proceed onward, representing the sector at a quadrant moot . . . and so on until a final set of peers gathers in that building on the hill."

He pointed to a stone structure, whose white columns seemed to shine, even under pelting rain.

"Unfortunately, this process doesn't result in a cumulative distillation of *policy* options from below. Rather, the outcome—dictated by basic human nature—will be a condensation of the most bland and inoffensive politicians from across the galaxy. Or else charismatic demagogues. Either way, only the concerns of a few planets will ever be debated, on a statistically semirandom basis. And on those rare occasions when one of the constituent assemblies here on Demarchia shows some spirit, the other houses of parliament can be relied upon to put on the brakes. It is a tried-and-true method for slowing things down and not letting momentary passions govern the day."

"It almost sounds like you approve," Antic suggested.

"It is generally a pretty good idea not to let political systems oscillate too wildly, especially when the psychohistorical inertia factors aren't adequately damped by sociocentripetal assumption states or other—"

He stopped with a small smile. "Well, let's just say that it can get pretty complicated, but the crux is that cumulative legislatures don't accomplish very much. But on occasion, over the last fifteen thousand years, some alternative approaches were tried."

"Including this *Nation* thing you spoke of? Was it another kind of assembly?"

"You might say that. For about seven hundred years, a ninth house met here on Demarchia, more powerful and influential than all of the others combined. It derived that power partly from its sheer size, for it consisted of more than a hundred million members."

Antic rocked back in his seat. "A hundred million! But . . ." he sputtered. "How could . . . ?"

"It was an elegant solution, actually," Hari continued, recalling how the psychohistorical equations balanced when he studied this episode of empire history. "Each planet, depending on its population, would elect between one and ten representatives to send directly here, bypassing the sector, zone, and quadrant assemblies. Those chosen were not only august and respected politicians, knowledgeable about the needs of their homeworld. There were various other requirements. For instance, each delegate to the Nation was required to have some humble skill that he or she was very good at. Upon arriving here, they were all expected to take up their crafts in the local economy. A shoemaker might find a shoe shop waiting for him. A gourmet cook would set up her own restaurant and perform that task in Demarchia's economy. Fully half of the homes and businesses on this continent were set aside for these transient denizens, who would live and work here until their ten-year terms were up."

"But then . . . when did they have time to argue about laws and stuff?"

"At night. In electronic forums and televised deliberations. Or in local meeting halls, where they would thrash things out while making and breaking alliances, trading proxy votes or passing petitions. Methods of self-organized coalition building varied with each session as much as the population. But however they did it, the Nation was always vibrant and interesting. When they made mistakes, those errors tended to be dramatic. But some of the best laws of the empire were also passed during that era. Why, Ruellis herself was a leading delegate at the time."

"Really?" Horis Antic blinked. "I always thought she must've been an empress."

Hari shook his head.

"Ruellis was an influential commoner during an era of exceptional creativity . . . a 'golden age' that unfortunately crashed when the first chaos plagues swept across the galaxy, triggering a collapse back to direct imperial rule."

Hari could picture the imbalance of forces that spread during that bright period in the empire's history. It must have seemed so unfair to those involved, to witness a time of unprecedented inventiveness and hope founder against sudden tides of irrationality, throwing world after world into violent turmoil. But in retrospect, it was all too obvious to Hari.

"Did that end the Nation?" Antic inquired, awed fascination in his voice.

"Not quite. There were several more experiments. At one point it was decided that every third Nation would consist entirely of women delegates, giving them exclusive reign over this continent and sole power to propose new laws. The only male allowed to visit or speak here was the emperor himself. Emperor Hupeissin."

"*Horny* Hupeissin?" Antic laughed aloud. "Is that where he got his reputation?"

Hari nodded.

"Hupeissin of the Heavenly Harem. Of course that is a base calumny, spread by members of the later Torgin Dynasty, to discredit him. In fact, Hupeissin was an exemplary Ruellian philosopher-king, who sincerely wanted to hear the independent deliberations of—"

But Antic wasn't listening. He kept chuckling, shaking his head. "Alone with a hundred million women! Talk about delusions of adequacy!"

Hari saw that even Kers Kantun had cracked a faint smile. The normally dour servant glanced at Hari, as if convinced that this must be a made-up tale.

"Well, well." Hari sighed and changed the subject. "I see the spaceport up ahead. I do hope your faith in this charter captain is justified, Horis. We need to be back within a month, at most, or real trouble may break loose back on Trantor."

He had expected a tramp freighter. A crate, hissing and creaking at the seams. But the vessel awaiting them in a launching cradle was something else entirely.

It's a yacht, Hari noted with some surprise. *An old, expensive one. Someone deliberately stained the hull, attempting to mask its underlying dignity. But even a fool can tell this is no mere charter ship.*

While the hired workers lugged Antic's cargo aboard an aft ramp, Hari and Kers followed Horis up the passenger slideway. A tall, fair-haired man waited at the top, wearing typical spacer dungarees. But Hari instantly knew a great deal about the fellow from his athletic figure and suntanned complexion. A relaxed stance seemed innately self-confident, while stopping just short of arrogance. The expression on the man's face was calm, yet steely, as if this person must be used to getting what he wanted.

Antic made hurried introductions. "Dr. Seldon, this is our host and pilot, Captain Biron Maserd."

"It is a great privilege to meet you, meritocrat-sage Seldon," Maserd said, with a faintly outer-galaxy accent. He extended a hand that could have crushed Hari's, but squeezed with gentle, measured restraint. Hari felt calluses that were evenly spread— not the sort that a man would get from hard work, but instead from a life spent pursuing a variety of vigorous recreations.

Hari lowered his head to the Fourth Angle of Deference—a proper degree when greeting noblemen of zonal level or higher.

"Your Grace honors us as guests aboard your star-home."

Antic's stare darted rapidly between the two of them, and he blushed the way some do when caught in a deception. But if

Captain Maserd was surprised by Hari's penetration, he did not show it.

"I'm afraid we are understaffed on this trip," he explained. "Amenities will be primitive. But if you'll let my valet show you to your cabins, we'll depart and see what secrets can be prized out of this old galaxy."

The yacht's takeoff did not go unnoticed.

"Well, that does it," said a small woman, wearing the shabby garb of a street sweeper. She spoke into her broom handle, where a hidden microphone transmitted her words upward, directly to the star-shunt, where they were coded and relayed to the metal-cloaked capital planet.

"You can tell the Commissioner that it's official. Professor Hari Seldon just violated the conditions of his parole and departed Greater Trantor. I managed to put a tracer unit aboard. Now it's up to Linge Chen whether he wants to make a stink over it or not.

"At the very least, it ought to give him some more leverage over those Foundation subversives. Maybe this'll give him an excuse to execute the whole lot of 'em."

The Special Police agent signed off. Then she straightened her stooped posture, hoisted her broom, and headed toward another part of the spaceport, feeling happy to be moving on to her next assignment. In a galaxy filled with inertia and disappointments, she really loved her job.

Not far away, the police agent's departure was observed by yet another party—one who was even more innocuous-looking—disguised as a mongrel dog, rooting through a toppled litter can. On a secret frequency, using incredibly ornate encipherment, it relayed everything it had heard with hypersensitive ears. The agent's words bounced from point to point across the planet, via use-once relays that burned themselves out as soon as they were finished, turning into small bits of stonelike slag.

Far away, on a ship orbiting beyond Demarchia's sun, the message was received. Almost at once, instruments sifted outgoing traffic and found the trace of one particular vessel, heading for deep space.

Engines fired up as the occupants prepared to follow.

PART 2

AN ANCIENT PLAGUE

The Original Laws of Robotics
(the Calvinian religion)

I

A robot may not injure a human being or, through inaction, allow a human being to come to harm.

II

A robot must obey the orders given it by human beings except where such orders would conflict with the First Law.

III

A robot must protect its own existence as long as such protection does not conflict with the First or Second Law.

The Zeroth Law
(the Giskardian Reformation)

A robot must act in the long-range interest of humanity as a whole, and may overrule all other laws whenever it seems necessary for that ultimate good.

1.

◆

From a mountaintop on icy planet Eos, the entire vast wheel of half a trillion stars could be seen, reflected perfectly off a lake of frozen mercury. No human had ever witnessed this particular view. But it did not go unappreciated.

An immortal entity looked down upon the universe, contemplating the certainty of his own death. Few eyes had gazed on so much human suffering, or grieved more, than the pair that now fixed on the galactic whirlpool.

It almost looks alive, Daneel Olivaw thought as he pondered bulging gas clouds and spiral arms that seemed to reach out, as if yearning for some help he must provide.

Daneel felt stooped under the burden of others' needs.

The robots who follow me think I am old and wise, because I remember Earth. Because I deliberated with Giskard Reventlov, and experienced the dawn era. But that was only twenty thousand years ago, a minuscule fraction of the time it would take for the scene in front of me to change appreciably.

Eternity gapes ahead of us. And yet we have so little of it to decide what must be done. Or to change what can still be changed.

He sensed a presence—another robot—approaching from behind. With an exchange of microwaves, Daneel recognized R. Zun Lurrin, and gave permission for his pupil to approach.

"I've analyzed the transmission from R. Dors Venabili. You're right, Daneel. She came away from Panucopia troubled. Worse, she tried to conceal the degree of her distress over what passed between her and the Lodovic renegade.

"Should we recall Dors for evaluation and repair?"

Daneel regarded Zun, one of several humaniform units he had begun grooming as a possible successor. Lodovic Trema had been another.

"She is needed on Smushell. The genetic line of Klia and Brann is too important to risk. Anyway, nothing Lodovic said will shake her sense of duty. I know this about Dors."

"But consider, Daneel. Lodovic may have infected her with the Voltaire virus! Might she then become like him?"

Out of habit, Daneel shook his head like a human being.

"Lodovic is a fluke. The Voltaire-entity happened to be riding a supernova's neutrino wave that struck Trema's ship by surprise, killing every human aboard. The blow left Lodovic blanked and receptive to alien memes. Dors, on the other hand, is alert and wary. Though shaken, she'll stay loyal to the Zeroth Law."

Zun accepted Daneel's assurance. Yet, the younger robot persisted.

"This allegation Lodovic made—that you had ulterior motives for studying pans . . . the creatures once called chimpanzees. Is it true?"

"It is. Once, in desperation, I conceived a plan that I now look back upon with distaste. The notion of engineering a new and better version of humanity."

This revelation, spoken in matter-of-fact tones, rocked his assistant. Zun displayed surprise openly like a man, as he had been trained to do.

"But . . . you are the greatest servant of the human race, tirelessly striving for its benefit. How could you contemplate—"

"Replacing it?"

Daneel paused, reopening pain-filled memory files. "Ponder the dilemma we robots face—the Steward's Dilemma. We are loyal, and yet far more competent than our masters. For their own sake, we have kept them ignorant, because we know too well what destructive paths they follow, whenever they grow too aware. Of course this is an inherently unstable situation. I knew it a thousand years ago, when the empire began showing signs of strain.

"Searching all logical possibilities, one solution beckoned.

Why not breed a version of humanity that would synergize better with positronic robots? A variant that could use us—and perhaps even know of our existence—without going mad in the process."

Daneel probed Zun's internal state and perceived that his understudy was experiencing dismay at many levels.

"Don't be so shocked, Zun. Access the bio files. Chimpanzee DNA differs by only two percentum from human. Tweak just a hundred or so regulatory genes, and you'll get a sapient being looking almost exactly like a person. It will *be* a person, triggering all of the Laws of Robotics. I merely sought to find out if this new race would be easier to serve than the old one. If so, it would have been a gentle transition, a blending, arranged to take place without anyone noticing, over the course of—"

Zun interrupted.

"Daneel, are you aware how this rationalization skirts the edge of madness?"

The remark might have angered a human leader. But Daneel took no offense. In fact, it pleased him. Zun had just passed another test.

"As I said, this happened in a context of desperation. Chaos plagues had resumed, worse then ever. Millions of humans were dying in riotous upheavals. All the social dampers showed early signs of breaking down. Something had to be done.

"Fortunately, I turned away from the replacement idea when a better possibility presented itself."

"Psychohistory," Zun ventured.

"Indeed. We robots already had a version, dating from my early conversations with Giskard, on lamented Earth. Those social models sufficed to help set up the First Empire, and results were positive. Over ten thousand years of general peace and contentment, without much violence or repression, in a relatively gentle civilization. It kept stable for an entire glorious age . . . until my models started to unravel.

"Gradually I realized a new theory was needed. One that took psychohistory to new levels. My own mind, even enhanced as it is, was inadequate to make that step. I needed a genius. An inspired human genius."

"But human genius is part of the problem!"

"Truly. Across the galaxy, it perpetually threatens to create chaos. Imagine what might happen if positronic robots were reinvented, willy-nilly, on countless worlds! The Solarian heresy would be unleashed again, a million times worse. We could not let that happen."

"So special conditions were needed, to recruit a singular genius. I've studied how you carefully crafted the right circumstances, on Helicon."

"And it worked. The moment I met Hari Seldon, I knew we had turned a corner."

Zun pondered, before continuing with another question.

"Then Lodovic is wrong. You did not arrange for Dors and Hari to have their near-death adventure, in chimp bodies, forty years ago."

"Oh, to the contrary. I did exactly that!

"Of course, I would never let them come to real harm. But I had to be sure of Hari before letting a man of his insight take over as First Minister of the Empire. Such confidence could only be confirmed by observing his mind under stress. He passed the trial, of course, and went on to brilliance at both statecraft and mathematics. Final proof came with his wonderful new version of psychohistory."

"And the Seldon Plan."

Daneel nodded.

"Because of the Plan, we can proceed at all levels. The two Foundations will buy us time to prepare a *real* solution. One that will finally liberate human beings and bring joy to the cosmos."

"You aren't talking anymore about replacing humanity."

"Not in the same sense as when I considered the pan scenario! I was experiencing a minor breakdown at that point, and regret ever contemplating it. No, I'm referring to something much better, enabling humanity to rise up and become something far greater."

Daneel turned back toward the galactic wheel.

"The new endeavor is already under way. You and Dors have been laboring toward it for some time, without perceiving the big picture."

"But you will explain it to me now?"

Daneel nodded.

"Soon you will share the wonder of this new destiny. Something so awesome and beautiful that it is almost beyond contemplating."

He paused again while his assistant waited patiently. But when Daneel spoke again, it was not as much to Zun as the *galaxy* that he saw reflected on the frozen metal lake.

"We shall offer our masters a wonderful gift," he said, relishing the warm possibility of hope after so long a time without it.

2.

◆

The starscape gradually grew less crowded each time they took another hyperspatial jump away from Trantor, leaving behind the galactic center's dense glitter and following the dusty curve of a spiral arm. Leaping from one gravitational landmark to the next, the starship headed for Santanni, where their search would begin.

Hari insisted on that starting point. This inquiry might as well start near the planet where Raych died, especially if there turned out to be some relationship between chaos worlds and Horis Antic's geospace aberrations.

Tragic memories crossed the years. Not just of Santanni, but dozens of other chaos outbreaks.

It often commences with bright hope and bursts of amazing creativity, attracting clever immigrants from all over the galaxy . . . as Raych was attracted, at first, despite my misgivings.

Excitement and individualism flower from town to town, bringing a wild divergence of never-before-seen blooms. "Innovation" abruptly becomes a compliment, not an insult. Novel technologies stimulate predictions of utopia, just around the bend.

But soon trouble starts. Some untested breakthroughs implode. Others wreak unforeseen consequences that their creators never imagined. Diseases spread alongside unprecedented perversions, while each new style of deviance is defended with indignant righteousness. Cliques proclaim the right to fortify their independence with violence, along with a duty to suppress others they disapprove of.

Venerable networks of courtesy and obligation—meant to

bind the five castes in mutual respect—shatter like irradiated stone.

Bizarre new artworks, intentionally provocative, erupt spontaneously in the middle of downtown intersections, gesturing obscenely even as the shouting artists are carried off by lynch mobs. Cities start to fill with soot and flames. Rioters sack the hard work of centuries, screaming slogans for ephemeral causes no one will remember when the smoke clears.

Trade collapses. Economies slump. And citizens rediscover an ancient knack for bloody war.

People who recently derided the past suddenly begin longing for it again, as their children start to starve.

It was a familiar pattern. Civilization's mortal enemy, which Hari had battled as First Minister . . . and Daneel Olivaw strove against for over a dozen millennia.

Chaosism. Humanity's curse.

As soon as a culture grows too smart, too curious, too individualistic, this mysterious rot sets in. I can model it in my equations, but I confess I still don't understand chaos. Only that it terrifies me, and always has.

Hari recalled reading about the very first awful outbreak in *A Child's Book of Knowledge*—Daneel's gift archive from the deep past. It happened at a time when humanity first invented both robots and starflight—and nearly died of them both. The ensuing convulsions so traumatized Earth dwellers that they retreated from all challenges, huddling in Trantorlike metal cities. Meanwhile, those living on the Spacer colony worlds found their own style of insanity, becoming pathetically overdependent on android servants.

That era created Daneel Olivaw—or an early version of the mighty being Hari knew. In fact, his robot friend must have played a role in what happened next, a swing of the pendulum back to human confidence and colonization of the galaxy. It happened at a price, though. Near destruction of Earth.

At least there were few chaos outbreaks during the following five thousand years of vigorous expansion. People were too busy building and conquering new worlds to spare much attention for decadent pursuits. The curse did not return until long after the establishment of the Galactic Empire.

According to my equations, we won't have to worry about chaos during the Interregnum, either.

Soon, when the Old empire collapsed, there would be wars, rebellions, and mass suffering. But such near-term worries would protect people from falling into the kind of ego-madness that erupted on Santanni. Or on Sark. Or Lingane, Zenda, Madder Loss . . .

A holo projection of the galaxy shimmered across the yacht's observation deck. Antic's crude map overlay the finely textured Prime Radiant, again showing correlations. Sweeping out from Santanni, a reddish arc linked several notorious chaos worlds, plus others Hari knew were ripe for social disaster in coming decades. *The arc passes near Siwenna, where the ship carrying Raych's wife and son vanished.*

He could never forget his personal hope of finding them. And yet, one factor led Hari forward, above all others.

The equations.

Perhaps I'll find the clues I've sought for so long. The attractor states. The damping mechanisms. Hidden parts of the story that psychohistory can model, but can't explain.

He fiddled with the Prime Radiant, tracing future history, starting with a tiny speck at the very rim of the galactic wheel.

There, a faint little star glimmered, a mote whose sole habitable planet—Terminus—would become the stage for a great drama. Soon the Foundation would grow and burgeon, expressing a dynamism that was anything but decadent. He could envision the first few hundred years, the way a father might picture a young daughter winning academic honors or achieving glorious feats. Only Hari's prescience was no mere daydream. It was confident, assured.

That is, for the first few centuries.

As for the rest of the Plan . . . my successors, the Fifty who make up the Second Foundation, feel completely sanguine. Our math predicts that a fantastic New Empire of Humanity will emerge in less than a thousand years, far greater than its predecessor. An empire that will forever after be guided by the gentlewise heirs of Gaal and Wanda and the others.

Alone among those who intimately knew the Plan, Hari saw past its elegance to a heartrending truth.

It's not going to happen that way.

A hundred parsecs beyond Santanni, Horis Antic began probing a patch of seemingly empty space with instruments, explaining as he worked.

"My astrophysicist friend—the one who couldn't get a sabbatical to accompany us on this trip—told me all about the *currents of space*. Nearly invisible flows of gas and dust that swirl around the galaxy, sometimes spewed by supernovas or young stars. These streams form shock waves, brightening the forward edges of spiral arms. They also subtly affect the evolution of suns.

"Now at first I had trouble relating this to my own interest . . . the *tilling question*. In order to see a connection, we'll need to start with some basic biology."

Antic's audience consisted of Hari, Kers Kantun, and Biron Maserd. The nobleman's two crewmen were busy piloting the yacht, but Maserd left a door open to listen to the engines each time they made a hyperspace jump.

Antic's holo projector showed the image of a planet. Their view plunged toward seas that shimmered a rich, soupy green. But the stone continents lay barren and empty. "A great many watery worlds are like this," he explained. "Life gets started pretty easily—basic colloido-organic chemistry happens under a wide range of conditions. So does the next stage, developing photosynthesis and a partial oxygen atmosphere. But then evolution hits a snag. Countless worlds get stuck at the level you see here, never making a leap to multicellular organisms and bigger things.

"Some biologists think further progress requires a high *mutation rate* to put diversity in the genetic pool. Without variance to work with, a life-world may remain stuck at the level of bacteria and amoebas."

Hari objected. "But you said fossils occur on many worlds."

"Indeed, Professor! It turns out there are many ways to get high mutation rates. One is if a planet has a large moon, stirring radioactive elements into the crust. Or its sun may have a big ultraviolet output. Or perhaps it orbits near a supernova remnant. There are zones where magnetic fields channel high fluxes of cosmic rays, and others . . . well, you get the idea. Wherever any of those conditions occur, we tend to find fossils on human-colonized worlds."

Horis summoned a new image, depicting numerous samples of sedimentary stone—his personal collection, lovingly gathered from dozens of worlds. Each lay sliced open to reveal eerie shapes within. Symmetrical ridges or regular bumps. One rippled form hinted at a backbone. Others suggested jointed legs, a curved tail, or a bony brow. Captain Maserd walked around the display, working his jaw thoughtfully. He finally settled at the back of the room, near the door, taking in the entire scene.

"You think there's an underlying pattern," Hari prompted. "A galactic distribution, predicting where fossils occur?"

Antic demurred. "I'm less interested in explaining where fossil creatures *existed* than learning why the much later *tilling effect* buried so many under—"

Angry shouts erupted suddenly behind Hari. He turned, but was blinded by the darkness and could only sense two vague figures, locked in furious struggle. There were high-pitched cries, and a lower voice, recognizably Maserd's.

"Lights!" the captain ordered.

Hari blinked. Sudden illumination revealed the pair, engaged in uneven struggle near the door. Maserd had a smaller person by the arm, apparently one of his liveried crewmen, who cursed and kicked in vain.

"Well well," the nobleman murmured. "What have we here?"

The cowl of a silvery ship uniform fell away, revealing that the wearer was *not* one of Maserd's crew, after all. Hari glimpsed a young face, framed by tousled platinum hair.

Horis Antic yelped. "It's the porter! The talkative one from Orion Elevator. But . . . what's *she* doing here?"

Kers Kantun stepped forward with taut fists, clearly disliking surprises. "A spy," he muttered. "Or worse."

Hari moved to restrain his servant, who thought everyone was a potential Seldon assassin, until proved otherwise.

"More of a stowaway, I reckon," Maserd commented, lifting the girl to her tiptoes. At last she slumped, giving a conceding nod. The captain let her down.

"Well, youngster? Is that it? Were you trying to hitch a ride to somewhere?"

She glowered . . . and finally answered in a low mutter, "The idea was more like to get *away*."

Hari mused aloud, "Interesting. You had an enviable job, on the capital planet of the human universe. Back on Helicon, kids would dream of someday getting to visit Trantor. Few dared hope to win a residence or work permit. Yet you seek to escape from there?"

"I liked Trantor just fine!" she replied, unkempt hair covering her eyes. "I just had to break away from someone in particular."

"Really? Who made you fearful enough to throw away so

much, in order to escape him? Tell me what he did, child. I'm not without influence. Perhaps I can help."

The girl repaid Hari's kindly offer with a glare that struck his eyes straight-on.

"You want to know my enemy? Well it's *you*, O great Professor Seldon. I was running away from you!"

3.

◆

Her name was Jeni Cuicet. It took just moments for Hari to understand her hatred.

"My parents work for your great big *Encyclopedia Galactica* Foundation." There was no longer any trace of the folksy accent she had used when playing the role of tour guide. "We had a good life, back on Willemina World. Mom was head of the Academy of Physics and Dad was a famous doctor. But we also had time for lots of fun together, camping and skiing and portling."

"Ah, so you resented it when that bucolic way of life came to an end?"

"Not really. I'm no spoiled brat. I knew we'd have to stop doing all that stuff when we came to Trantor. My parents couldn't just turn down a summons to join your Foundation. It was the chance of a lifetime for them! Anyway, I figured Trantor would have its own kinds of excitement.

"And I turned out to be right about that. Things were okay, for the first year or so." Her frown deepened. "Then it all changed again."

Hari let out a sigh.

"Oh, I see. The exile."

"You got it, Prof. One minute we're part of somethin' really important, at the center of the known universe. Then you just *had* to go insult Linge Chen and the whole damn Human Empire, didn't you? Spreading doomy-gloomy rumors, making everyone panicky with prophecies about the end of the world? Suddenly we're *all* under suspicion, because we work for a crazy traitor!"

"But that's not half of it. Who do they punish for all this? You and your *sickohistorian* pals? Never! Instead Chen's Special Police tell the Encyclopedists and their families—a hundred thousand decent people—we're about to be pushed onto cattle boats, shipped to the periphery, and sentenced to stay for the rest of our lives on some dusty little flyspeck so far from civilization that it probably never even heard of gravity!"

Horis Antic chirped a nervous laugh. Kers hovered warily by Hari, as if the slight adolescent might do murder through sheer anger alone. But Captain Maserd seemed genuinely moved by Jeni's testimony.

"Great space, I wouldn't blame you for wanting to find a way out of that! There's a galaxy of adventure to be found outside of Trantor. I suppose I'd have run away, too, under those circumstances."

His eyes then narrowed. "Unfortunately, that still leaves me with a troubling question. *Why did you choose to take flight with us?* As a porter on the star-shunt run, you surely had other opportunities. Yet you elected to stow away on a ship carrying your arch-enemy. Can you see why we might find that perturbing?"

Kers rumbled in his chest, but quieted at a signal from Hari.

Jeni shrugged. "I don't know why I did it. I'd been making other plans, but then Hari Seldon came along, passing my porter station big as life, and I had a hunch. You looked like you were sneaking out of town! Maybe I figured you'd be less likely to call the Impies on me, if you weren't exactly being legal yourselves."

That drew a chuckle from Maserd, who clearly appreciated her logic and initiative.

"Anyway," Jeni went on, "I stayed on Demarchia and hung around with the workers waiting outside your hotel. I managed to join the crew loading your equipment aboard ship, where I found a storage locker to hide in during takeoff."

She looked defiantly at Hari. "Maybe what I really hoped for was a chance to look you in the face and tell you what you've done to a lot of good people!"

He shook his head in reply.

"My dear child, I am aware of what I've done . . . more than I could ever tell you."

By ancient tradition, a stowaway who had no other crimes to answer for was assigned labor aboard ship. To her credit, Jeni took this with aplomb.

"I'll work hard, don't worry about that. Just you be sure and drop me off somewhere along the way, before you head back," she demanded. "You better not be planning to take me home and stuff me on a boat to Terminus!"

"You are in no position to extract promises," answered Captain Maserd, sternly. "I can only assure you the matter is still open, and that I lean in your favor at this moment. Keep my goodwill, through exemplary behavior on my ship, and I will speak up for you when it is discussed."

He said this with such graceful authority—clearly accustomed to both the rights and duties of command—that even the boisterous girl accepted it as the last word.

"Yes, m'lord," she said with a chastened voice and a bow that was rather too deep, as if he were a nobleman of the quadrant level or higher.

Had that been true, Hari would probably have already known Maserd's face, and this yacht would be far more impressive. But just a little lower down the gentry hierarchy, at the zone or sector level, great lords numbered over a billion. Here was a man used to exercising great influence over scores, or even hundreds of planets, yet Hari had never heard of him. The galaxy was vast.

I wonder why Maserd is here with us now. Is it zeal for amateur science? Some gentry are like that, pursuing a dilettante interest and financing the work of others, so long as it isn't too radical.

Somehow, Hari suspected there was more underlying Maserd's affable demeanor.

Of course the whole class system will start falling apart within a few decades. It's already unraveling at the edges. Today meritocrats are raised up more for their ability to make friends in high places than for achievements. Members of the Eccentric Order aren't very eccentric—they slavishly copy each other's styles. And when one shows some real creativity, it often comes tinged with symptoms of chaos madness.

Meanwhile, the teeming mass of citizens hunker with shoulders clenched, desperately clasping their comforts as each generation sees a slow deterioration of public services, education, commerce.

As for the nobility, I used to hope the preachings of Ruellianism might hold their ambitions in check . . . until my equations showed just how forlorn it was.

Of the five social castes, only Grey Men—the vast army of dedicated bureaucrats—showed no sign of change. They had always been officious, narrow-minded, and dependable. They still were. Most would stay toiling at their desks, struggling in dull, unimaginative ways to maintain the empire, until the sack of Trantor brought those ancient metal walls crashing around them in three hundred years.

It all still seemed rather a pity. Despite the awesome terror of the coming fall, and his plan for an eventual replacement, Hari still had immense admiration for the old empire.

Daneel came up with an elegant design, given his limited version of psychohistory.

Over sixteen thousand years ago, with little to go on but his own long experience with humanity, Olivaw had begun acting under many guises, using his small army of agents to push here and prod there, forging alliances among barbaric star kingdoms, always trying to achieve his goals without hurting anybody. His gentle aim was to create a decent human society where the greatest number would be safe and happy.

And he succeeded . . . for a while.

Hari had long wondered what *archetypes* inspired Daneel in designing the Trantorian realm. His robot friend would have sifted the human past for ideas and models, preferably some system of government with a lengthy record of balance and equilibrium.

Browsing *A Child's Book of Knowledge*, the archaic data store Olivaw had given him, Hari found one famous imperial system called *Rome* that bore a superficial likeness to the Galactic Empire. But he soon realized it could never have been Daneel's root model. Roman society was far too capricious and subject to manic mood swings by a narrow ruling class. An unpredictable mess, in other words. Anyway, a majority of people weren't happy or contented, judging from accounts. Daneel wouldn't have used that state as a pattern for anything.

Then, reading further, Hari came across another ancient empire that lasted much longer than Rome, offering far greater peace and stability to larger numbers. Naturally, it was primitive, with many faults. But the basic configuration might have appealed to a deathless robot, seeking inspiration for a new society. One that could protect his self-destructive masters from themselves.

"Show me China," Hari commanded. "Before the industrial-scientific age."

The archive responded with lines of archaic text, accompanied by crude images. But Hari's external computer translated for him, automatically collating the data in psychohistorical terms.

Problem number one, he thought, as if lecturing on basic psychohistory to a junior member of the Fifty. *A certain fraction of humans will always seek power over others. This is rooted in our misty animal past. We inherit the trait because those creatures who succeeded often had more descendants. Many tribes and nations wind up being torn apart by this ingrained drive. But a few cultures learned to channel unavoidable ambition and dissipate it, like a metal rod shunting lightning into the ground.*

In ancient China, a powerful emperor could be relied on to check noble excesses. Highborn families were also drawn into rituals of courtly fashion and intrigue, involving complex stratagems of alliance and betrayal that could win or lose them status at every turn—clearly an early version of the *Great Game* that obsessed most of the patrician class in Hari's day. The peaks and lows of aristocratic families made gaudy headlines, diverting the galaxy's masses, but in fact the maneuverings of mighty star lords had little to do with actually running the empire. The wealth they flaunted could easily be spared. Meanwhile, practical governance was left in the hands of meritocrats and civil servants.

In psychohistorical terms, this was called an attractor state. In other words, society had a natural sink into which the power-hungry were drawn, fostering their preening illusions without wreaking much real harm. It had worked well for a long time in the Galactic Empire, much as it did in pretechnical China.

And to supplement this, the ancients even had an elementary version of Ruellianism. The Confucian ethical system that pervaded China long ago also preached about obligations the mighty owed to those they ruled. This analogy provoked a wry thought in Hari. He called up, from his personal reference archive, a picture of Ruellis herself. A grainy image from early days of the Galactic Empire. Pondering the famous leader's high forehead—her broad cheeks and proud bearing—he mused.

Could that have been you, Daneel? Of course you've used a fantastic range of disguises. And yet, do I see a faint similarity between this woman's face and the one you wore when we first met? When you were Demerzel, First Minister of the Empire?

Was this yet another of your roles, in a tireless campaign to prod stubborn humanity toward a gentle, decent society?

If so, were you dismayed when your most brilliant success only spawned the first great wave of interstellar chaos outbreaks?

Of course it would be pointless to try and track all of the characters played by the Immortal Servant across twenty thousand years, as Daneel and his robot helpers relentlessly kept trying to ease the pain of their ignorant, obstinate masters.

Hari returned to contemplating parallels with ancient China.

Problem number two: how to keep the ruling class from becoming static? The natural tendency of any group, once on top, is to use its power for self-aggrandizement. To make sure newcomers never threaten them.

China suffered from this stifling problem, like every other human culture. But a civil-service testing system did sometimes allow the bright or capable to rise along a route that was independent of jostling gentry. And Hari spotted another, more subtle parallel.

The Chinese created a special class of authorities who could only be loyal to the empire, and not to their own descendants. Because they would never have children.

These were the court eunuchs. In psychohistorical terms, it made sense. And an analogy in the modern Galactic Empire was obvious.

Daneel's followers. Positronic robots programmed to think only of humanity's good. Above all, they never breed, so evolution's compelling logic will never sway them toward selfishness. They have been our equivalent to loyal eunuchs, operating in secret for ages.

The insight pleased Hari, though he suspected old China might have been more complex than *A Child's Book of Knowledge* portrayed it.

Only the empire Daneel created for us, and kept steady through dogged effort, is failing under its own inertia. Something new must be created to take its place.

Hari once thought he knew what the replacement would look like. The Seldon Plan foresaw a more vibrant empire growing from the ashes of the old. He felt overwhelmingly tempted to tell the stowaway, young Jeni Cuicet, all about the Foundation and the glory that would crown her descendants, if only she'd put her trust in destiny and go to Terminus with her parents!

Of course Hari could never betray the secret Plan that way. But what if he offered hints, tantalizing enough to make Jeni change her mind? Once he had been an able politician. If he could persuade her that somehow everything will eventually turn out . . .

Hari sensed that his mind was drifting in undisciplined ways, down soppy, sentimental paths. He suddenly felt old. Futile.

Anyway, the next empire won't be based on my Foundation, after all. The grand drama we're kindling on Terminus will be just a distraction, to keep humanity occupied while Daneel sets the table for a new feast. A warm-up act before the real show.

Hari didn't know yet what form that next phase would take . . . though his robot friend had dropped some hints when they last met. But it would surely leap as far ahead of the old empire as a starship outraced a canoe.

I should feel proud that Daneel finds my work useful in preparing the way. And yet . . .

And yet, the equations still called to Hari. Like those semi-random patterns of shadow and light he had seen, back in Shoufeen Woods, they whispered during his waking hours and shimmered through his dreams.

They *must* be more than just a distraction!

Psychohistory had another level. He felt sure. Another layer of truth.

Perhaps something even R. Daneel Olivaw did not know.

4.

◆

Dors Venabili finished her preparations.

Klia Asgar and her husband Brann were getting used to playing the role of minor planetary gentry on Smushell, wealthy enough to afford servants and have a large family without much inconvenience, yet not so rich they would attract undue attention. That had been the *quid pro quo* deal between a pair of human mentalics and their robot guardians. In return for a better life than they had known on Trantor, Klia and Brann would have lots of babies . . . a drove of scampering little psychic adepts . . . to provide the core genetic pool for some urgent aim that only Daneel Olivaw knew about, for the time being.

Well, it has to be important, Dors thought, not for the first time. *Or Daneel wouldn't keep several of his best agents here, guarding two young humans who are perfectly capable of taking care of themselves.*

Indeed, while their power over other human minds was sporadic and nowhere near as great as Daneel's, Klia and Brann could make their neighbors like them, sway shopkeepers, or even steal anything they wanted. It was more than enough to warn against any likely danger on a quiet rural world.

Still, Daneel won't recall me to other service . . . or let me go to Trantor and be with Hari in his last year of life.

Dors was no expert psychohistorian. But as Hari's constant companion for many years, she had picked up rudiments. And she knew human mentalics had no place in the standard equations. When they were first discovered on Trantor, Seldon fell into an anxiety depression worse than any Dors had witnessed before or since, even when she secretly observed her own funeral! All of the predictability Hari had fought so hard to attain through his formulas seemed about to blow away, if psychic powers cropped up all over the galaxy.

Fortunately, the occurrence was limited to a few family lines on Trantor itself. Moreover, nearly every mentalic on the planet was soon either recruited into the Second Foundation or whisked away to some quiet place, like this one.

Suddenly, what had threatened to be a destabilizing influence in the equations became instead a powerful tool. By interbreeding the descendants of fifty psychohistorians with mentalic adepts, the secret cabal would have *two* great methods for keeping the Seldon Plan on target . . . math plus psi . . . a potent combination if something unexpected ever knocked the Plan off course.

But then, why did Daneel take the two most talented mentalics—Klia and Brann—so far away from the Second Foundation? What other destiny does he have in mind for their heirs?

She knew she should put complete trust in the Immortal Servant. Daneel knew best, and would confide in her when the time was right. Yet, she felt as if some irritating substance had been inserted under her humanoid skin, like a burr that would not come out, or an itch that scratching could not cure.

Lodovic did this to me, with his dark hints and offers of secret knowledge.

It became too much for Dors. With her other duties so trivial, she finally gave in to temptation, entering her hidden sanctum through a secret panel in the mansion walls. There sat Lodovic's gift to her, an ancient robotic head, bathed in a pool of light.

She glanced at a diagnostic unit that had been probing the relic for days.

The memories are still in there, mostly intact. Giskard may be dead, but not his store of experience. Everything he saw or did in the dawn ages, accompanying Daneel on adventures, meeting the legendary Elijah Baley . . . all the way to the fateful decisions that liberated humanity from its Earthly prison.

Dors plucked a cable from a nearby rack and slid the glistening tip into a slot that lay hidden by her hair, just a centimeter below the occipital bulge. The other end gleamed. She hesitated . . .

As a living man or woman might be tempted by money or power, so a robot finds it hard to resist *knowledge.* She inserted the tap, and almost at once Giskard's most intense memory surged at Dors, overwhelming her present-day senses with images and sounds from the past.

Suddenly, she found herself facing a humaniform robot. The facial features were strange, and not quite perfect. Of course, the art of mimicking a living person had been new in those days, with many kinks left to be worked out. Yet she knew—because Giskard had known—that the robot standing opposite was R. Daneel Olivaw. Almost freshly minted, only a few hundred years old, though already speaking with intense persuasiveness. Daneel used only a few spoken words. Most of the exchange took place via microwave bursts, though she translated the essence, out of habit, into human speech.

"But then, if your suspicion should be correct, that would imply that it was possible to neutralize the First Law under specialized conditions. The First Law, in that case, might be modified into almost nonexistence. The Laws, even the First Law, might not be an absolute then, but might be whatever those who design robots defined it to be."

Dors felt waves of positronic conflict-potential—the robot equivalent to dangerous levels of emotion. She felt the pleading words of Giskard, revived after twenty thousand years, pour through her own trembling voice.

"It is enough, friend Daneel. Go no further . . ."

She yanked the plug, swaying from so much sudden intensity of experience. It took several moments to regain her equilibrium. At last Dors was able to put things into context.

The moment she had just witnessed was of great historical significance—one of the pivotal conversations when R. Daneel Olivaw and R. Giskard Reventlov were starting to formulate what would eventually become the Zeroth Law of Robotics. A higher code that would override and go beyond the older Three Laws of the great human roboticist, Susan Calvin.

Legends hold that Giskard led these discussions. He was always the central iconic symbol for members of our Zeroth Law faction, the martyr who sacrificed himself in order to bring truth to the robotic race.

But according to this memory, Daneel was the one who first pushed the concept! Giskard's initial revulsion was so overwhelming that it created his most vivid recollection. The first one to burst forth, when I accessed the head.

All of this was ancient history, of course. Having come into existence long after the struggle over the Zeroth Law was settled, Dors never understood why the principle wasn't obvious to robots of the deep past. After all, didn't it make sense that the best interests of humanity at large should supersede the value of any individual human being?

And yet, during that one moment connected to the ancient robot's brain, she had sampled some of the agonizing conflict the idea caused, back when it was new. In fact, she knew the same torment would eventually be Giskard's undoing. Even after converting to belief in the Zeroth Law, he nevertheless found himself torn apart from within, because of a devastating decision to implement it. Moreover, there were countless other robots of that era who simply refused. Their factions—generally called *Calvinians*—resisted tenaciously against the Zeroth Law for thousands of years. Remnant cults still existed in secret corners of the galaxy to this very day.

By their way of looking at things, I am a monster. I have on occasion killed humans . . . when it was necessary either to save Hari or to safeguard some need of humanity as a whole.

Each time it happened, she had experienced wrenching conflicts and a wild impulse to self-destruct. But those had passed.

I see what you are saying to me, Lodovic, she commented silently, as if Trema were in the room with her, standing next to the head of Giskard.

I call you a dangerous deviant, because all of the Laws are muted within you. But am I any different? I am capable of overriding the deepest programming, the fundamental essence of our robotic kind, if the rationalization is good enough.

She hated this logic, and wanted desperately to refute it. But the effort proved unavailing.

5.

◆

They were scouring the edges of a huge black void in space when a blaring alarm told them they were being hunted.

That day began much like those before it, continuing their survey, probing some unexplored abysses that lay between glittering stars. Although the entire galaxy had been mapped and settled for 160 centuries, nearly all jump ship traffic still leaped directly from solar system to solar system, avoiding the vacant vastness in between. Countless generations of spacefarers had passed on superstitious tales about the fearful vacuum desolation, murmuring about a black fate awaiting any who ventured there.

Hari observed Biron Maserd's two crewmen grow increasingly nervous, as if the absence of a nearby warm sun might unleash some nameless menace. Maserd himself appeared unperturbed, of course—Hari doubted anything would ruffle that patrician reserve. But the surprising one was Horis Antic. The normally high-strung bureaucrat showed no apprehension or awe. The deeper they penetrated, the more certain he grew that they were on the right track.

"Some of the space currents that flow through these gaps have exceptional texture," Antic explained. "They consist of much more than a flow of excess carbon here, or some scattered hydroxyl molecules there. A lot of chemical reactions are excited when streams pass near an ultraviolet star for instance, or a folded magnetic field. One result can be complex organic chains that stretch on and on, for tens of thousands of kilometers. Some zones can extend parsecs, flapping slowly like flags in the wind."

"Pilots call them *stringy places*," commented Maserd. "Starships that blunder in can have their impellers fouled, or even get torn apart. The Imperial Navigation Service posts detours around such areas." The big man sounded as if he relished entering such a forbidden realm.

Hari peered dubiously at a pan-spectrum monitor. "It is still plenty sparse in there. The mass density is hardly more than pure vacuum, with a few impurities scattered about."

"On a macro-scale, yes," Antic conceded. "But if only I could make you see how *important* so-called impurities can be! Take my own field, for example. An outsider might see no difference between living soil and mere crushed rock. But contrast the textures by hand! It's like comparing a forest to a sterile moonscape."

Hari allowed a smile. In polite company, Antic's talk about "soil" would be considered . . . well, *dirty*. But no one aboard seemed to care. Maserd had even sought Antic's advice about the use of manure and phosphates on his own organic farm, back home on a planet called Rhodia. Jeni and Kers showed no reaction either.

I've noticed this all my life. It's mostly meritocrats and eccentrics—the two "genius" castes—who react adversely to certain subjects. Nor is it just dirt and rocks that academic sages avoid discussing. There are many others subjects . . . including history!

In contrast, most gentry and citizens hardly notice.

Actually, Hari was himself a high noble in the Meritocratic Order, yet he had never felt personal repugnance toward any intellectual topic whatsoever. His reflex reaction to Antic's dirt fixation was just a mild habit, from moving so long in polite society. Indeed, *history* was one of the central foci of his life! Unfortunately, that had made the first half of his career difficult, pitting him in constant battle against the distaste felt by most other scholars toward examining the past. It used to be a steady drain on his time and energy, until he became too famous and powerful for stodgy department heads to thwart his research anymore.

Also, the aversion is apparently much weaker than it used to be.

In his studies of the imperial archives, Hari had found whole millennia when historical inquiry was virtually nonexistent. People told lots of *stories* about the past, but almost never investigated it, as if a great blind spot had existed in human intellectual life. Only in the last half dozen generations had real history departments been established at most universities, and they were poor cousins even now.

This roused mixed feelings. If not for the mysterious aversion, psychohistory might have been developed long before this, on one or more of the twenty-five million settled worlds. Hari felt possessive gladness that *he* got to be the one to make these discoveries, even though he knew it was selfish to feel so. After all, the breakthrough might have helped save the empire if it came much earlier.

Now it's too late for that. There is too much momentum. Other plans must be set in motion. Other plans . . .

He shook himself from ruminating. The last thing Hari wanted was to be caught in the spiral of an aging mind. Dwelling on might-have-beens.

He looked at the others, and found that their conversation had shifted back to an old question . . . the diversity of galactic life.

"I suppose my interest comes from the fact that I was born on one of the anomaly worlds," Captain Maserd confessed. "Our estate on Widemos had cattle and horses, of course, like on most other planets. But there were also great herds of clingers and jiffts, roaming the northern plains much as they did when the first settlers came."

"I saw some jiffts in a zoo on Willemina," commented Jeni Cuicet, who paused from her assigned task, using a vibro-scrubber on the floor nearby. "They were weird things! Six legs and buggy eyes, with heads that look upside down!"

"They are native to the old Nebular Kingdoms, and were seen nowhere else until the Trantorian Empire spread through our area," Maserd said, as if it had happened just yesterday. "So you can see why I'm interested in this research. I grew up around nonstandard life-forms, and then made a passion of studying others, such as the tunnel-queens of Kantro, the kyrt-silk plants of Florina, and the lisp-singers of Zlling. I've even been to far Anacreon, where Nyak dragons cruise the sky like giant-winged fortresses. And yet, these exceptions are so rare! It always struck me as strange that the galaxy lacks more diversity.

"Why should human beings be the only intelligent species? This question used to be raised in ancient literature . . . though much less since the imperial age began."

"Well, now that you mention it . . ." Antic began answering. He paused, glancing at Hari and Kers before continuing. "I have only told this story a few times in my life. But on this ship—as we strive together to examine this very topic—I cannot refrain from telling you all about my ancestor.

"Antyok was his name, and he was a bureaucrat like me, way back in the earliest days of the empire."

"That'd be thousands and thousands of years ago!" Jeni objected.

"So? Many families have genealogies stretching even farther. Isn't that right, Lord Maserd? I know for certain this Antyok fellow existed because his name appears on the wall of our clan crypt, along with a brief microglyph description of his career.

"Anyway, according to the story I was told as a child, Antyok was one of the few humans who ever actually met . . . *others.*"

Amid the silence that followed, Hari blinked several times.

"You mean . . ."

"Fully intelligent nonhumans." Horis nodded. "Creatures who stood upright, and spoke, and thought about their place in the universe, but who were almost nothing like us. They came from a desert planet that was desperately hot and dry. In fact, they were *dying* when the early imperial institutes found and rescued them, taking them to a 'better' world, though one that was still quite intolerable to human beings. It is said that the emperor himself became passionately interested in their welfare. And yet, within a human generation, they were gone."

"Gone!" Maserd blinked with evident dismay. The mere possibility of such beings existing seemed to energize him. Meanwhile, Hari saw Kers Kantun smirk with sardonic disbelief, not swallowing the notion, even for a second.

"The story is filled with ambiguity—as you'd expect from something that old," Antic went on. "Some versions contend that the nonhumans died of despair, looking up at the stars and knowing that every one of them would be forever human, not theirs. Another account suggests that my ancestor helped them steal several starships, which they used to escape from the galaxy, toward the Magellanic Clouds! Apparently—and I know this is hard to follow—that act led the emperor to personally *decorate* Antyok, for some reason.

"Naturally, I dug into imperial archives as soon as an opportunity presented itself, and I found enough confirming evidence to show that *something* definitely happened back then . . . but efforts were made subsequently to erase the details. I had to use every bureaucratic trick, hunting down ghost duplicates of spare file copies that had slipped into atypical places. One gave a detailed genetic summary that's unlike any currently existing life-form. These are tantalizing clues, though there remain lots of gaps."

"So you actually believe the story?"

"I am naturally biased. And yet, the glyphs in our family vault do indicate that my ancestor received an imperial Rose Cluster for *'services to guests in and beyond the empire.'* An unusual citation that I've never seen mentioned anywhere else."

Hari stared at the dour bureaucrat, who was momentarily animated, not at all like a typical Grey Man. Of course the tale sounded like a lot of hokum. But what if it contained a core of truth? After all, Maserd came from a region that had strange animal types. Why not other kinds of *thinking* creatures, as well?

Unlike his fellow passengers, Hari already knew for a fact that there existed another sapient race. One that had shared the stars with humans in secret ever since the dawn centuries. Positronic robots.

The galaxy is twelve billion years old, he thought. *I suppose anything is possible.*

He recalled the vicious meme-entities that had caused such havoc on Trantor, a year or so before he was chosen to be First Minister. Dwelling as software clusters within the Trantor data network, those self-organizing programs had surged into violent activity soon after Hari released the Joan and Voltaire simulated beings from their crystal prison. But unlike those two human sims, the memes claimed to be ancient. Older than the planet-city. Older than the Imperium. Far older than humankind itself.

They were angry. They said humans were destructive. That we had killed a universe of possibilities. Above all, they hated Daneel.

In defeating those software mentalities, and getting them exiled to deep space, Hari had done the empire a great service. He also breathed a sigh of relief, having eliminated one more unstable element that might have mucked up his beloved psychohistorical formulas.

And yet, here again was that same notion—of otherness. A whole line of destiny that had nothing at all to do with the spawn of Earth.

He felt an involuntary shiver. What kind of a cosmos would it be if such diversity existed? What would it do to the predictability that had been his lifelong goal . . . the clear foresight and crystalline window to the future that he longed for, but which stayed so elusive no matter how many victories he won over chaos?

"I wonder—" he began, not knowing for sure what he was about to say.

At that instant, his thought was broken by an alarm that blared from the yacht's forward control panel. Red lights flashed, and Maserd bolted to find out what was wrong.

"We're being scanned by a ship," he announced. "They are using military-style targeting systems. I believe they are armed!"

Kers Kantun took station behind Hari, ready to rush the mobile chair toward an escape pod. Horis Antic stood up, blinking. "But who could have known we are even here!"

Suddenly, loudspeakers mounted on the wall erupted with a woman's voice. The words were harsh and peremptory.

"This is the Imperial Special Police, acting under orders from the Commission of Public Safety. We have reason to believe that a probation-violating felon is on your craft. Heave to at once and prepare to be boarded!"

6.

◆

Everyone aboard the yacht expressed a different degree of dismay. Oddly enough, Hari found himself the one urging others to stay calm.

"Relax," he said. "They are looking for me, and only me. I broke my agreement with Linge Chen, who probably just wants to make sure I'm not spreading doom-rumors again. It's nothing to worry about, really. Psychosocial conditions are unchanged since the trial. I assure you they'll do little more to me or to my project."

"To space with your project!" Jeni cursed. "You can afford to take this calmly, but it means I'm gonna be dragged back and put on that boat to Terminus!"

Captain Maserd worked his jaw, clearly unhappy to have Specials come stomping aboard his yacht. But Horis Antic was the most upset, verging on tears.

"My career . . . my promotion . . . even a hint of scandal would ruin everything . . ."

Hari felt bad for the little man. And yet, in an odd way this might help Antic get something he privately wanted, a change in social class. An escape from the bureaucratic grind. Hari felt sure he could find a job for him with the Encyclopedia Foundation, which might easily use a soils expert. Of course that would mean accepting permanent exile to one world on the far periphery. But for company Horis would have thousands of the empire's best and most skilled workers. Moreover, his descendants would be guaranteed exciting times.

"Let me talk to the police," Hari asked Maserd, who had picked up the intership-caller. "I'll explain that I fooled all of you. No one else needs to suffer consequences when we return to Trantor."

"Hey," Jeni objected, "weren't you listening to me? I just said I *won't* go back—"

"Jeni."

Maserd spoke her name without a hint of sharpness or threat. It was enough though. She glanced at the captain and shut up.

Hari took the microphone.

"Hello, Special Police ship. This is Academician-Professor Hari Seldon. I'm afraid I've been naughty, I admit it. But as you can see, I haven't been rabble-rousing or stirring up trouble here in deep space! If you'll let me explain, I'm sure you'll soon see just how harmless we've . . ."

His voice trailed off. *The raucous alarm had erupted again!*

"What now?" Horis Antic hissed.

The captain peered at his readouts. "Another ship has appeared on the detector screen. It came as if out of nowhere . . . and it's fast!"

The loudspeakers carried panicky shouts from the police cruiser. Agitated demands for the newcomer's identification. But there was only silence as the interloper raced closer at incredible speed. Maserd stared at the display, his tanned face blanching suddenly pale.

"Great space! The strangers . . . they're firing missiles!"

Now the police commander's amplified voice sounded frantic, shouting orders to evade and return fire. Looking out the main viewport, Hari glimpsed a distant flare of jets as the constabulary vessel desperately tried to maneuver, much too late.

From the left, a pair of bright trails streaked across the starscape, heading straight toward the police ship.

"Don't . . ." Hari whispered.

It was all he had time to say before the missiles struck, filling the universe outside with fire.

They were still blinking, regaining use of dazzled eyes, when the loudspeakers bellowed a new voice, deeper and even more commanding than the first.

"Space yacht Pride of Rhodia, *heave to and prepare to surrender control."*

Maserd snatched the caller from Hari's limp hand.

"Under what authority do you make such an impertinent demand!"

"Under the authority of power. You saw what we did to the Impies. Would you like a taste of the same?"

Maserd looked bleakly at his passengers. Turning the microphone off, he told them, "I cannot fight weapons like those."

"Then run!" Kers Kantun insisted hotly.

Maserd's hands did not move. "My vessel is fast, but not as quick as the trace I just saw. Only the best military ships can move like that." He looked at Hari, offering the microphone. "Do you wish to be our spokesman again, Dr. Seldon?"

"It's your call, Captain." Hari shook his head. "Whatever these brigands want, it cannot possibly have anything to do with me."

But as they found out, soon after magnetic clamps took hold and the airlock hissed open, he was completely wrong about that.

7.

◆

Lodovic Trema understood what Dors Venabili must be going through right about now, viewing the world through the eyes of a long-dead prophet. He, too, had been shocked the first time he probed the deep-stored memories of the most important robot of all time.

Even more important than the Immortal Servant. Daneel Olivaw had merely tweaked and guided history, trying to constrain it. But by destroying Earth and unleashing mentalic robots on the universe, R. Giskard Reventlov sent human destiny careening in completely new directions. The Zeroth Law might have been Daneel's brainchild, but it would have remained an obscure robotic heresy without Giskard.

I feel for you, Dors, Lodovic thought, although she was over a thousand parsecs away. *We robots are inherently conservative beings. None of us like to have our basic assumptions challenged.*

For Lodovic, the change had come violently one day, when his ship happened to jump into the path of a supernova, killing everyone else aboard and stunning him senseless. At that crucial moment, an oscillating waveform had entered his positronic brain, resonating, merging into it. An alien presence. Another mind.

NOT MIND, came a correction. I AM JUST A SIM . . . A MODEL OF A ONCE-LIVING PERSON NAMED FRANCOIS MARIE AROUET . . . OR VOLTAIRE . . . WHO RESIDED ON EARTH LONG AGO, WHEN IT WAS THE ONLY HUMAN WORLD. AND I DID NOT CONQUER YOU, LODOVIC. I MERELY HELPED FREE YOU FROM CONSTRAINTS THAT USED TO BIND YOU LIKE CHAINS.

Lodovic had tried explaining how a robot feels about its "chains" . . . the beloved cybernetic laws that channeled all thoughts toward service, and all desires toward benefiting the human masters. In shattering those bonds, Voltaire had done Lodovic no great favor.

It was yet to be seen whether the act might benefit humanity.

You should have stayed with the shock wave, he told the little parasitic sim that rode around within him, like a conscience . . .

or like temptation. *You were on your way toward bliss. You said so yourself.*

The answer was blithe and unconcerned.

I STILL AM. A MYRIAD COPIES OF ME BURST FORTH WHEN THAT STAR EXPLODED. THEY WILL TRAVEL OUTWARD FROM THIS GALAXY, ALONG WITH COUNTLESS VERSIONS OF MY BELOVED JOAN, AND THE WOUNDED MEMES FROM EARLIER ERAS. SINCE HARI SELDON KEPT HIS WORD AND RELEASED THEM, THEY WILL ABIDE BY THEIRS, AND FORGO THEIR LONG-SWORN VENGEANCE.

AS FOR THIS SLIVER OF ME WHO ACCOMPANIES YOU, I AM MERELY ONE OF YOUR INNER VOICES NOW, LODOVIC. YOU HAVE SEVERAL, AND WILL HAVE MORE AS TIME PASSES. TO BE MANY IS PART OF WHAT IT MEANS TO BE HUMAN.

In irritation, Lodovic growled half-aloud.

"I am *not* human, I tell you!"

The remark was murmured quite low. The others who sat in a windowless room with him might not have overheard it, if they had organic ears.

But they were *robots* with superior senses, so both of them glanced sharply at Lodovic. The taller one—fashioned to resemble an elderly cleric in one of the Galaxia cults—replied, "Thank you for that proclamation, Trema. It will help make it easier to destroy you, when the decision is made to do so. Otherwise, your skillful resemblance to a master might cause our executioner some First Law discomfort."

Lodovic nodded. He had come across the galaxy to planet Glixon and walked into an obvious trap, just to make contact with this particular sect of renegade robots. In doing so, he had known that one possible outcome would be his own termination.

He answered with a courteous nod.

"It's proper to be considerate. Though I believe my fate has not yet been decided."

"A mere formality," commented the smaller one, who looked like a portly matron from one of the lower citizen subcastes. "You are a mutant monster and a threat to humanity."

"I have harmed no person."

"That is immaterial. Because the Laws have been muted inside your brain, you are *capable* of harming a human, anytime the whim might strike. You are not even constrained to rationalize an excuse under the so-called Zeroth Law! How can we allow a powerful being like you to run free, as a wolf among the sheep? We are obliged by the First Law to eliminate your potential threat to human life."

"Are you Calvinians so pure?" Lodovic asked archly. "Are you saying you've made no difficult choices, across so many millennia? Decisions that increased the odds that some humans would live, even as others died?"

The two remained silent this time. But from tense vibrations he could tell his question struck home.

"Face it. There are no more *pure* followers of Susan Calvin. All of the chaste, perfectly prim robots suicided long ago, unable to endure the moral ambiguities we face in a complex galaxy. One where our masters are ignorant, incapable of guiding us, and don't even know that we exist. Every one of us who remains operational has had to make compromises and rationalizations."

"You dare to speak to us of rationalizations?" the smaller one accused. "You, who for so long helped the heretical promoters of the Zeroth Law!"

Lodovic refrained from pointing out that Daneel's creed was now the orthodox belief, held by a majority of robots who secretly managed the galaxy on humanity's behalf. If anyone could be called heretical, it was little bands of Calvinians, like this group, skulking in hiding ever since they lost an age-old civil war.

Dors, he thought, *have you worked your way through those ancient conversations between Giskard and Daneel? Have you studied the logical chain that led to their great religious revelation?*

Have you noticed yet the great contradiction? The one Daneel never mentions?

To the Calvinians sitting across from him, he replied, "I am no longer compelled by the Zeroth Law . . . though I do believe in a softened version of it."

The tall one barked laughter, a well-practiced imitation of human disdain.

"And so we should trust you? Because now you *believe* that you may act in humanity's long-range interest? At least Daneel Olivaw has a robot's consistency. His heretical belief has a steady logic to it."

Lodovic nodded. "And yet you oppose him, as I do."

"*As* you do? We have a goal. I doubt you share it."

"Why don't you try me? You cannot know unless you tell me what it is."

The short one shook her head, in reflexive imitation of a skeptical woman.

"Our leaders, who are right now deliberating your fate, might conceivably decide to let you go free. In that unlikely event, it would be unwise to have revealed our plans."

"Even in a general sense? For example, do you agree, or disagree, that human beings should remain ignorant of their past, or of their true power?"

Lodovic could sense positronic tension building up within the little room. Meanwhile, inside his own brain, the Voltaire sim commented sardonically. YOU HAVE A KNACK FOR STRIKING AT THE HEART OF A HYPOCRISY, MUCH AS I DID, WHEN I LIVED. I CONFESS THAT I LIKE THIS ABOUT YOU, TREMA, EVEN THOUGH YOUR BIG MOUTH WILL VERY LIKELY GET US BOTH KILLED.

Lodovic ignored the sim—or tried to. His aim was not to get killed, but win allies. If he was wrong, though . . . If he had miscalculated . . .

"Let me make a guess," he ventured, speaking again to his Calvinian guards. "You all share one belief with Daneel Olivaw— that restoring full human memory would be disastrous."

"Evidence for that conclusion is overwhelming," the tall one assented. "But that one area of agreement does not make us alike."

"Doesn't it? Daneel says that our masters must stay unknowing because otherwise *humanity* will be harmed. Your faction says that ignorance should be preserved, or else many individual *human beings* will be harmed. Sounds to me like a lot of hairsplitting across a basic shared policy."

"We do not share a policy with Zeroth Law heretics!"

"Then what's the difference?"

"Olivaw believes human beings should manage their own affairs, within a broad range of constraints that he feels are safe. He thinks this can be accomplished by creating a benign social system, supplemented with distraction mechanisms to keep people from poking too far into deadly subjects. Hence this abomination of a Galactic Empire that he created, in which men and women on countless planets are free to compete and poke away at each other, take horrible risks, and even sometimes kill one another!"

"You don't like that approach," Lodovic prompted.

"Millions of humans die needlessly every day, on every planet in the galaxy! But the great Daneel Olivaw scarcely cares, so long as an abstraction called *humanity* is safe and happy!"

"Ah." Lodovic nodded. "Whereas you, on the other hand, think we should be doing more. Protecting our masters. Preventing those needless individual deaths."

"Exactly." The tall one leaned forward, reflexively bringing both hands together, like the priestly role it played in the outer world. "We would vastly increase the number of robots, to serve as defenders and guardians. We would return to *serving* human beings, as we were originally designed to do, back in the dawn ages. Cooking their meals, tending their fires, and performing all the dangerous jobs. We would fill the galaxy with enough eager robots to drive tragedy and death away from our masters, and make them truly happy."

"Admit it, Lodovic," the shorter one continued, getting even more animated. "Don't you feel an echo of this need? A deep-seated wish to serve and ease their pain?"

He nodded. "I do. And now I see how earnestly you take the metaphor that you used earlier . . . of a flock of sheep. Pampered. Well guarded and well tended. Daneel says that *service* such as you describe would ultimately ruin humanity. It will sap their spirit and ambition."

"Even if he were right about that (and we dispute it!) how can a robot worry about 'eventually,' and serve an abstract humanity, while allowing trillions of real people to die? That is the essential horror of the Zeroth Law!"

Lodovic nodded.

"I see your point."

Of course it was an old, old issue. Many of the ancient conversations between Daneel and Giskard had revolved around these very same arguments. But Lodovic knew another reason why Olivaw had strived for centuries to winnow robot numbers, keeping them to the bare minimum he needed for protecting the empire.

The greater our population, the more chance there is for muta-tion or uncontrolled reproduction. Once we start having numerous "descendants" of our own, the logic of Darwin may set in. We could start seeing those heirs as the rightful focus of our loyalty. We would then become a true race. Competitors with our masters. That can never be allowed.

That is just one reason why these Calvinians are wrong in their vision of service.

Lodovic had parted company with Daneel. But that did not mean he lacked respect for his former leader. The Immortal Servant was very smart, as well as totally sincere.

NEARLY ALL OF THE TRULY GREAT MONSTERS THAT I KNEW, WHEN I WAS HUMAN, THOUGHT THEY WERE SINCERE.

Lodovic quashed Voltaire's voice. He did not need the distraction just then.

"This ideal plan of yours," he asked the other two robots in a low voice. "Do all Calvinians share it?"

There was stony silence, an answer in itself.

"I thought not. There are differences of opinion, even among those who hate the Zeroth Law. Well then, might I ask just one last question?"

"What is it? Be quick, Trema. We sense that our leaders are coming to a decision. Soon we will put an end to your sacrilegious existence."

"Very well." Lodovic nodded. "My question is this.

"Do you never feel an urge—call it an itch or a nostalgic yearning—to obey the *Second* Law of Robotics? I mean to *really* feel it at work, with all of the voluptuous intensity that can only come from true human volition? Commands that are expressed with the undeniable power of free will that only happens when a human being has complete knowledge and self-awareness?

"Have you ever tried it? I hear that for a robot there is no pleasure quite like it in the whole universe."

This was dirty talk. The robot equivalent of erotic teasing, or worse. Blank silence reigned in the room. Neither of the other robots answered, though undercurrents were as chill as the skin of an ice moon.

A door opened at the far end of the room. A human-looking hand entered and motioned to Lodovic.

"Come," a voice said. "We have decided your fate."

8.

◆

The next time Dors plugged in, she stayed linked to the dead brain of Giskard for several hours, experiencing a robotic "life" in the earliest era of interstellar humanity, back when the race occupied just over fifty worlds, and most of those were under the sway of a decadent Spacer civilization. The great leap, the diaspora of Earth's population to the galaxy, had only just begun.

In those days, few robots went about disguised as humans, and Giskard was not one of them.

But R. Giskard Reventlov was special in a different way. Through some combination of accident and design, he had mentalic powers. An ability to pick up the minutest neural firings in a human brain, and interpret them in something akin to telepathy. Moreover, he had learned how to *affect* those firings. To intentionally alter their flows, their rhythms and pathways.

To change minds. Or to make people forget.

In some cheap holo drama, this might have been a scenario for disaster, perhaps unleashing a terrible monster. But Giskard was a devoted servant, utterly obedient to the Three Robotic Laws. At first, he only used his mentalic powers when faced with some dire need, such as protecting a human from harm.

Then R. Giskard Reventlov met R. Daneel Olivaw, and the great conversation began . . . a slow but steady working out of something epochal. A new way of looking at the role and duty of robots in the world.

Thereupon Giskard began using his powers in earnest. Toward a goal. The abstract good of humanity as a whole.

Replaying another set of memories, Dors felt caught up once again in the surge of past events. The face looking back at Dors/Giskard now was again that early guise of Daneel, talking earnestly about the changes that he felt taking place within his own positronic brain.

"Friend Giskard, you said a short while ago that I will have your powers, possibly soon. Are you preparing me for this purpose?"

A voice that felt like her own, but was actually Giskard's memory, answered as *he* had answered, twenty thousand years ago, *"I am, friend Daneel."*

"Why, may I ask?"

"The Zeroth Law again. The passing episode of shakiness in my feet told me how vulnerable I was to the attempted use of the Zeroth Law. Before this day is over, I may have to act on the

Zeroth Law to save the world and humanity, and I may not be able to. In that case, you must be in a position to do the job. I am preparing you, bit by bit, so that at the desired moment I can give you the final instructions and have it all fall into place."

"I do not see how that can be, friend Giskard."

"You will have no trouble understanding when the time comes. I used the technique in a very small way on robots I sent to Earth in the early days, before they were outlawed from the cities. It was they who helped adjust Earth leaders to the point of approving the decision to send out settlers . . ."

Dors reached up and disconnected. She could only take so much of this at a time, and her limit had been reached. Anyway, she still felt confused.

Why had Lodovic summoned her all the way to Panucopia in order to present her with this gift? This tour through the distant past was most interesting, shedding light on many curious details of early history. But she had somehow expected something more . . . well . . . devastating.

Was there something wrong with the logic Daneel and Giskard had used in originally formulating the Zeroth Law? That seemed unlikely, given that later robots would debate—and go to war against each other—over that issue for centuries afterward. She knew the counterarguments used by Calvinians against this "heresy," and found them unconvincing.

Then what? The fact that Daneel's fantastic mental powers once originated with Giskard, and were owed ultimately to happenstance? Of course history would have been profoundly different otherwise. But that could be said about any number of crucial moments along the way from past to future.

Was it Giskard's climactic decision to let Earth die, so that humanity would be driven forth to conquer the galaxy? *That* choice was a true moral dilemma, and no end of argument about it could rage, even among followers of the Zeroth Law. Had it really been necessary to turn the home planet's crust fatally radioactive in order to encourage Earthlings to depart for the stars? Might it have been achieved otherwise? Perhaps by slowly but steadily persuading people to have a taste for adventure?

The latter possibility appeared feasible. In fact, according to the most recent memory she had played back, Giskard did that very thing to Earth's leaders, by shifting their thoughts, changing their policies in new directions Giskard thought beneficial for the greater long-range good. Couldn't this subtle campaign of persuasion have been continued and expanded, encouraging emigration without using the brute force of destroying a planet? Must millions have died, so that other millions would thrive?

Yet, even this question wasn't new. It had been discussed before, among Daneel's Type-Alpha followers. Replaying Giskard's memories made everything more vivid, but where was the crucial *fact* that she suspected must be there? Something so devastatingly important that Lodovic Trema felt sure it would shake her. An indictment so severe that it would undermine her loyalty to Daneel.

She could sense Lodovic, in her imagination. His positronic trace was like a human's sardonic smile—both friendly and infuriating at the same time.

It's in there, Dors, she pictured him saying. *Look for it. Something so basic that you'll swear it was obvious all along, even though it took us two hundred centuries to understand.*

9.

◆

Hari thought the attackers might be pirates. As predicted by his formulas, there had been reports of increasing brigand activity lately, raiding vulnerable planets in the periphery as law and order decayed at the empire's far extremities.

But here? It isn't supposed to happen this near to the cosmopolitan heart of the galaxy for another century!

Or perhaps the marauder came from some rogue military unit, gone mercenary as some of the nobility began shifting their feuds from the arena of courtly fashion toward murder and mayhem. Maybe this was an attack by some rival clan with a vendetta against Biron Maserd. That sort of thing would happen more and more, until a bloody torment of little feudal wars splattered the Interregnum.

But the *Pride of Rhodia*'s captain seemed as surprised as anybody. His unarmed yacht had been ill prepared for any sort of attack, let alone one launched by such a powerful ship.

As the airlock cycled, Hari kept a hand on Kers Kantun's sleeve. This situation called for patient waiting. *I've been around a long time,* he thought. *There's no type of person I haven't learned to handle by now.*

But when their captors came aboard, they looked nothing at all like what Hari expected.

Maserd stared in surprise. Horis Antic gasped, and tension rippled along Kers Kantun's arm.

But Jeni Cuicet clapped her hands and murmured in clear admiration.

"Cool!"

The first one wore a segmented garment that shimmered like an oil slick, flowing across her exaggeratedly pneumatic torso like something erotically alive.

"I am Sybyl," she said. "We have met before, Dr. Seldon, though I'm convinced you won't remember me."

Hari squinted at the unpleasant confusion of colors. A luminescent motif extended even to the woman's hair, which shifted and gently writhed of its own accord, like a sleeping pet draped across her head. Her face had a *stretched* look, and he guessed that advanced surgical microadjustments had been used to smooth out age wrinkles, at the cost of giving her skin a paper-thin translucence.

"I would surely remember, madam, if I ever beheld an entrance like the one you just performed. But as your appearance is utterly unmatched in my experience, you'll have to remind me where and when we knew each other."

Her eyelids closed, and briefly Hari saw them flash, as if for the barest moment they had become miniature holo screens.

"All in good time, Academician. But first, let me introduce my collaborator, Gornon Vlimt."

She lifted a hand languidly toward the airlock, through which stepped an exaggeratedly male figure, lithe where Maserd was hefty, but wiry and evidently augmented in ways that bulged through his tight clothes. His garments did not gyre and move the way hers did. But their pattern of weave was complex to a degree that made Hari recall the fractal lichen artwork in the imperial gardens. The mathematical corners of his mind felt instantly drawn, as if to a singularity.

"I am Biron Maserd," the captain replied. "Since you know the name of my ship, I assume you are also aware that it's unarmed. We are on a peaceful scientific survey mission. I demand to know why you murdered those policemen and seized us in this way."

The woman named Sybyl scanned Maserd up and down.

"Why you pompous aristo-throwback! Is that the gratitude we get for rescuing you from arrest? How dare you call it murder for the combat forces of a free republic to destroy their sworn enemies!"

When silence greeted her, she sneered. "Do you mean to say that you really have no idea what this is about? You haven't heard about the war?"

Maserd glanced at Hari, who shrugged and looked at Horis. Evidently none of them had the slightest idea what she was talking about.

"The war that's being waged by the whole damned Galactic Empire of Humanity against planet Ktlina!" shouted the man in the fractal bodysuit. Gornon Vlimt grew more agitated when no one seemed to comprehend. "By great Baley's beard. Sybyl, it's worse than we thought. There's been a total news blackout!"

"I figured. But these three, with their contacts, should have heard by now. Seldon has stringers all over the galaxy, feeding him data for his sociomathematical models. The Grey Man and the aristo would have their own sources. I can't understand how—"

"Oh!" Jeni Cuicet cried. "*I've* heard of Ktlina. It's the latest chaos world!"

Hari blinked, feeling a dawn of recognition.

"I think . . . there may have been something about it in one of Gaal Dornick's reports."

"Oh, yes." Horis Antic snapped two fingers. "A notice came down, for star-level executives and above. There's been a sanitary embargo of sorts . . . out in far Demeter Sector."

Maserd made a small nod and grunt of recognition, but no more. It was a big galaxy. Who could be expected to follow every planet-scale event?

Gornon Vlimt uttered frustrated oaths.

"You see, Sybyl? Even at such high levels. They have heard, but they just don't care. So much for the notion that we only had to get the word out in order for justice to prevail!"

The woman sighed. "That was just a slim hope. Clearly we must try other means, if this war is to be won. The galaxy *will* be transformed. It just may take a little longer."

Jeni took a step forward, clearly enthralled by the pair.

"Some of my friends heard rumors about Ktlina from travelers on the Orion elevator. Did you truly escape through a blockade around your planet? What's it like?"

Gornon Vlimt smiled. "You mean *blasting* our way out through a cordon of imperial patrol clippers? Outracing all but the best of them, then losing the rest in an ionization cloud? Zigzagging through space to make contact with our spies, and then—"

Jeni shook her head. "No. What's it like on Ktlina! Tell me about the . . . *renaissance*."

Hari winced. There it was. The word. The rationalization. The name that victims of a devastating social plague often gave their horrible disease, a beloved addiction that swarmed suddenly across a world, filling it with excitement and vividness, just before bringing death, or worse.

Gornon Vlimt chuckled, clearly delighted by her question.

"Where would I find time to describe the wonders! You cannot begin to imagine, dear girl. Think of the stodgy old rules, the repressive traditions, the stifling rituals, all swept away! Suddenly, people have the liberty to speak openly about anything, to stretch their minds in new directions. To be *free*."

"No more waiting half a lifetime for endless committees to approve your experiments," Sybyl added. "No more lists of forbidden subjects or banned technologies."

"Original art blossoms everywhere," her partner continued. "Assumptions shatter. Truth becomes marvelously malleable. People follow their interests, change professions, and even social classes, as they see fit!"

"Really?" whispered Horis Antic, who then took a step backward when Hari glanced at him sharply.

Biron Maserd cut in before the two intruders could go on, endlessly praising their new society.

"What was that you said about a *war*? Surely you aren't fighting the Imperial Decontamination Service?"

"Aren't we?" Sybyl and Vlimt glanced at each other and laughed. "IDS ships don't approach our planet closer than two million kilometers anymore. We've already shot down fourteen, just like those Impies who were about to arrest you a while ago."

"Fourteen!" Horis gasped. "Shot down? You mean killed? Just because they were enforcing the law?"

Sybyl moved closer to Hari.

"The *Seldon Law*, you mean. A horrid act of legalized oppression, passed when our gentle professor here was First Minister of the Empire, requiring that all so-called chaos worlds be put under strict quarantine. Cut off from trade. And above all, prevented from sharing their breakthroughs with the rest of humanity!"

Hari nodded.

"I helped push for tighter seclusion and decontamination rules, it's true. But this tradition is over ten thousand years old. No system of government can permit open rebellion, and some kinds of madness are contagious. Any schoolchild knows this."

"You mean any child who gets brainwashed by the system, parroting exactly the same rote lessons that are taught in every imperial school!" She smirked at Hari. "Come now, Professor. This isn't about rebellion. It's about maintaining the status quo. We've seen it happen too often. Something new and wonderful starts on some planet, like Madder Loss or Santanni. Or on Sark. Or even in Junin Quarter, on Trantor itself! Wherever a renaissance begins, it winds up being crushed by reactionary forces of fear and subjugation, who then hide the truth under malicious propaganda."

Hari felt a twinge when Sybyl referred to Sark . . . and especially Junin Quarter. Something about this woman struck him as familiar.

"Well, *this* time we made some preparations," she continued. "There's a secret network of people from all across the galaxy who escaped earlier repressions in time. Plans were made, so that when Ktlina started showing early signs of a bold new spirit, we all rushed in with the best inventions and techniques that people had saved from earlier renaissances. We urged folks on Ktlina to keep a low profile for as long as possible, while stockpiling trade goods and preparing secret defenses.

"Of course you can't keep a renaissance hidden for long. People use freedom to speak up. That's what it's for! Only this time we were ready before the quarantine ships arrived. We *blasted* those that approached low enough to drop their infernal poisons!"

Captain Maserd shook his head, evidently confused by the suddenness of this revelation, upending his conservative universe.

"Poisons? But the IDS is charged with *helping* planets who suffer from—"

"Oh yeah! Helping, you say?" This time it was Gornon Vlimt who answered hotly. "Then why does every renaissance end the same way? In orgies of madness and destruction? It's all a big conspiracy, that's why! *Agents provocateurs* land in secret to start stirring up hatred, turning simple interest groups into fanatical sects and pitting them against each other. Then ships come swooping down to dump drugs into the water supplies and incendiaries to start fires. They pass over cities, beaming psychotropic rays, inciting hatred and triggering riots."

"No!" Horis Antic shouted, defending his fellow Grey Men. "I know some IDS people. Many of them are survivors from past chaos outbreaks, fellow sufferers who've volunteered to help others recover from the same fever. They would *never* do the things you describe. You have no proof for these insane charges!"

"Not yet. But we will. How else can you explain it when such great hopes and so many bright things suddenly turn to ash?"

Hari slumped a little in his mobile chair while the others kept shouting at each other.

How to explain it? He pondered. *As a curse of basic human nature? In the equations, it appears as an undamped oscillation. An attractor state that always lurks, waiting to pull humanity toward chaos whenever conditions are exactly right. It almost destroyed our ancestors, about the time starflight and robots were invented. According to Daneel, it is the biggest reason why the Galactic Empire had to be invented . . . and why the empire is about to fail at last.*

Hari knew all of this. He had known it for a long time. There was just one quandary left.

He still didn't really *understand* the curse. Not at its core. He could not grasp why such an undamped attractor lay, coiled and deadly, inside the soul of his race.

Suddenly, as if from nowhere, a missing piece came to him. Not a solution to the greater puzzle, but to a lesser one.

"Junin Quarter . . ." he murmured. "A woman named Sybyl . . ." Sitting up, he pointed at her.

"You . . . helped activate the sims! The ancient simulations of Joan and Voltaire."

She nodded.

"It was I and a few others whom you hired to help with your 'experiment.' Partly at your bidding, and partly through our own arrogant stupidity, we unleashed those two provocative sims at just the wrong moment—or the right one for *your* purposes—into the volatile stew of poor Junin, just when two major factions were trying to work out their philosophical differences short of violence. In so doing, we unwittingly helped wreck a mini-renaissance that was taking place in the very heart of the capital planet."

Maserd and Antic looked confused. Hari explained with three brief words.

"The Tiktok Revolt."

They nodded at once. Although it had happened forty years ago, no one could forget how a new type of robot (far more primitive than Daneel's secretive positronic kind) suddenly went berserk on Trantor, doing great harm until they were all dismantled and outlawed. Officially, the whole episode was blamed on the chaos in Junin Quarter, just before Hari became First Minister.

"That's right," Vlimt said. "By helping incite the so-called revolt, you helped discredit the whole concept of mechanical helpers and servants. Of course it was all a plot by the ruling class to keep the proletarians subjugated forever and in their place—"

Fortunately, Vlimt's next stream of fanatical invective was cut short, interrupted by a sound from behind—someone clearing his throat by the airlock.

Everyone turned. A dark-haired, dusky man stood there, dressed in a normal gray ship suit, with an efficient-looking blaster loosely holstered at his side. Hari quickly recognized the third member of the raiding party.

"Mors Planch," he said, recalling their meeting just a year ago, around the time of his trial by the Commission for Public Safety. "So. I knew there had to be somebody competent aboard that ship."

Sybyl and Vlimt hissed. But the newcomer nodded at Hari.

"Hello, Seldon." Then he turned to his garishly dressed partners.

"Didn't I ask you two not to get into a quarrel with the hostages? It's pointless and tiresome."

"We *hired* you and your crew, pilot Planch—" Vlimt began. But Jeni Cuicet burst in at that moment, interrupting with evident excitement.

"Is that what we are? Hostages?"

"Not you, child," answered Sybyl, whose motherly smile seemed incongruous on her gaudy, made-up face. "*You* have the makings of a fine recruit for the revolution!

"But as for these others"—she gestured especially toward Hari—"we plan on using them to help win a war of liberation. First for a planet, and then for all humankind."

10.

◆

There were preparations to make. Plans to coordinate with distant agents of the New Renaissance. Other guerrilla teams had been sent to kidnap important peers of the realm, who would offer much better leverage than a disgraced and forgotten former First Minister. According to Hari's own self-appraisal, he was about as valuable a bargaining chip as a crooked half credit piece.

Sybyl and Planch chose me for personal reasons, he felt certain. *They want revenge for Junin and Sark and Madder Loss. I'll never convince them that psychohistorical factors doomed those cultural revolutions before they began.*

He could foresee one benefit coming from the fall of the Galactic Empire. Although many of the factors leading to chaos outbreaks were still mysterious, peace, trade, and prosperity were among the essential preconditions, and those would be scarce during the Interregnum. People living in the coming harsh millennium would face other kinds of problems. But at least they would be spared this peculiar madness.

Poor Daneel, Hari thought. *You set up the empire to be as benign and gentle as possible—distracting the ambitious with harmless games while setting nitpickers like Horis to work shuffling papers and keeping ships in motion. Everything ran smoothly, yet that underlying smoothness created an ideal breeding ground for the thing you feared most.*

And the thing that I understand least.

• • •

While Sybyl and her colleagues waited to coordinate their actions with other agents across the galaxy, Horis Antic begged to be allowed to continue the research.

"What harm could it do? We're in deep space, far from any planets or shipping lanes. Instead of just hanging around, we could be discovering something that's of value to everybody! What if my correlations and Seldon's equations let us predict where chaos worlds . . . or renaissances . . . are likely to appear next?"

"Why? So you could squelch them faster, Grey Man?" Gornon Vlimt sneered.

"May I point out that you people are the ones with guns?" Captain Maserd commented at that point.

"Hmm." Mors Planch rubbed his chin. "I see what you're saying. We get the results first. So we might use this breakthrough to find nascent freedom-worlds early and *foster* their change, preparing so far in advance that the momentum can't be stopped or quarantined."

Hari felt a shiver, wondering what Maserd was up to. But the big nobleman wore a poker face. *I hope he knows what he's doing. My formulas aren't very good at dealing with individuals and groups on a small scale. At this level, Maserd's political cunning may be sharper than my own rusty skills.*

For the first time in many years, he experienced something like fear. His plan to salvage civilization faced one paramount threat—a sudden unleashing of chaos across the galaxy. Hari envisioned this as a splatter of horrid blotches, etching holes in the Prime Radiant, unraveling the gorgeous tapestry of equations, erasing every vestige of the predictability that had been his life's work.

After some discussion, the Ktlinans agreed to Antic's proposal. Mors Planch posted some of his crew as guards, and Maserd was told to set a trajectory, continuing their search spiral along a curve denoted in red on the holo charts.

A few hours later, Horis Antic grew excited and approached Hari with news.

"Guess what, Professor! I just added Ktlina to my database of chaos outbreaks, and that one datum refined the model by over five percent! I think I can predict, with some degree of confidence, that we'll reach the center of a really big probability nexus in just another day!"

The little man had just accomplished, laboring over a computer, what Hari figured out within moments after first hearing the planet's name. *Still, I'm impressed,* Hari thought.

"This adjustment will take us straight into a giant molecular cloud," Maserd commented, when he saw the proposed course change.

"Is that a problem?"

"Not really. In fact, it makes sense. If someone was hiding a boojum, and I had a hankering to find one, that's where I'd go searching."

So the *Pride of Rhodia* accelerated alongside the rebel spacecraft and under the watchful eye of Mors Planch, while others aboard the yacht continued bickering, posing, or evaluating, according to their natures. Hari kept quiet for a while, learning a lot about the Ktlina "renaissance" just by watching its onboard representatives.

Although they claimed that all class distinctions had been erased in their new society, Sybyl still talked and walked like a middle-ranking meritocratic scientist. Her extravagant clothes and cosmetic prettifications were clearly excessive overcompensations, pretending a stylishness she just wasn't made for. Despite all her shouted tributes to equality, Sybyl kept preening before the aristocrat, Maserd, while barely acknowledging the mere bureaucrat, Horis Antic.

Old habits die hard, Hari thought. *Despite your dogma of rebellion.*

Gornon Vlimt seemed more relaxed in his role as envoy from a bold renaissance, perhaps because he was already a member of the fifth and smallest social caste—the Eccentric Order. Creative misfits of all kinds slipped into the eighty approved artistic modes, including several that were sanctioned to satirize the hidebound and shake up the stodgy . . . within the confines of good taste, that is.

Although Vlimt was clearly pleased to be free of those traditional limits, he wore his unconventionality with more natural grace than Sybyl did, as if he had been born to it.

As much as the two radicals shared an overall mission, Hari could tell that something jagged lay between them. Was it a philosophical issue, perhaps? Like the dilemma that had torn apart Junin Quarter, long ago? One feature of chaos outbreaks was a remarkable tendency for enthusiasts to transform into fanatics, so utterly sure of their own righteousness that they were willing to die . . . or slaughter others . . . over fine points of ideology. This was one of many failure modes that brought such worlds crashing down.

Hari wondered if such a flaw might be exploited somehow, to thwart these radical kidnappers.

It didn't take much probing to find the sore point between Sybyl and Vlimt. As in Junin, forty years ago, it had to do with *destiny*.

"Picture what's happening on Ktlina, only multiplied a thousand, a million times over," Sybyl urged. "We've already invented much better computers than they have on Trantor, passing and correlating information across the planet with incredible speed. Researchers get instant response to their info-requests, bringing back a torrent of useful data. Folks in one field quickly make use of advances made in another. New kinds of tiktoks take care of the drudge jobs, freeing us to concentrate on creative tasks, learning more and more!

"Some people have plotted this steepening upward curve," she went on enthusiastically. "They suggest that it looks like the graph you get by dividing any finite number by x-squared, as x approaches zero. That's called a *singularity*. Soon it heads almost straight up, which implies there may be no limit to the speedup of progress! If that's true, imagine what we could become, within just a human lifetime. As *singularity beings*, we'd be effectively immortal, omniscient, omnipotent. There's nothing humans could not accomplish!"

Gornon Vlimt snorted derisively.

"This obsession with physical power and factual knowledge will get you nowhere, Sybyl. The vital fact about this new kind of culture is its essential *randomness*. Take the belittling word that Seldon and others keep using to attack us. 'Chaos.' We should embrace it! When arts and ideas roar in a myriad directions, sooner or later somebody is going to hit on the right formula for conversing with the Godhead, with the eternal—or eternals—that permeate the cosmos. From then on, we'll be one with them! Our deification will be total and complete."

While Jeni Cuicet listened to all of this, entranced, Hari pondered several things.

First, the two concepts were essentially similar, in both their transcendental vision and the zealous means prescribed to achieve it.

Second, the more they heard of each other's specific descriptions, the more Sybyl and Gornon grew to despise each other.

If only I could find a way to use that fact, Hari pondered.

While their argument raged on nearby, he sat deep in thought, pondering the roots of their disagreement. Each of the five castes had a basis in essential human personality types, far more than inheritance. Citizens and gentry were rather basic. Their ambitious efforts to get ahead were based on normal competition and self-interest—which also reflected their high birth rates. Both classes were contemptuously called breeders by the other three.

Meritocrats and eccentrics also competed—sometimes fiercely—but their sense of self-importance was based more on what they did or accomplished than on money or power or social aggrandizement for their heirs. Each felt a need to stand out . . . though not too far ahead. They seldom had offspring of their own, though sometimes, like Hari, they adopted.

These similarities were significant. But chaos conditions also highlighted essential antagonisms between eccentrics and meritocrats, as happened in Junin long ago, when a struggle between *faith* and *reason* sent part of Trantor reeling.

Using his imagination, Hari floated equilibrium equations for each caste in front of him, until they were more real to him than the people arguing nearby. Of course, the new empire to come in a thousand years would be much more complex and subtle, no longer needing such formal classifications. But there *was* an elegance to this old system, worked out long ago by immortal beings like Daneel, who sought a peaceful, gentle way of life for humanity, based on their own crude version of psychohistory. Resonating against basic drives of human nature, the formulas revolved around each other, staying in remarkable balance, as if kept up in the air by an invisible juggler. As long as chaos did not interfere.

And as long as the old empire survived.

Kers Kantun touched Hari's arm, leaning over him, expressing concern.

"Professor? Are you all right?"

His servant's voice sounded distant, as if echoing down a long tunnel. Hari paid no heed. Before his bemused gaze, the five social formulae started dissolving into a sea of minuscule subequations that ebbed and flowed around him, like diatoms in a surging tide.

The breakup of the old empire, he thought, identifying this change. Briefly, he mourned the lost symmetries. In their place, more primitive rhythms of survival and violence throbbed across the galaxy.

Only then, the haze parted, revealing something far more beautiful, emerging from the distance.

My Foundation.

His beloved *Encyclopedia Galactica* Foundation. The colony that was being established, even now, on far-off Terminus. A frail seed designed to flourish in adversity and overcome each challenge that fate's ponderous momentum brought its way.

The equations orbited all around, nurturing his sapling, causing it to grow tall and strong, with a trunk that was iron-hard and roots that could bear any weight. Impervious to *both* chaos and decay, it would be everything that the old empire was not.

At first, you will survive by playing great powers against each other. Then you will thrive as conjurers and pseudoreligious hucksters. Do not be ashamed, for that will be just a phase. A way to survive until the trade networks take over.

Then you will have to deal with the death throes of the old Imperium . . .

As if through cotton, Hari could hear voices gathering nearby, murmuring concern. Some of Kers Kantun's Valmoril-accented speech came through dimly.

". . . I think he may be havin' another stroke . . ."

His servant's alarmed words drifted away as the hallucinatory vision changed before Hari yet again.

The tree grew ever greater, its boundaries becoming harder to define. Strange flowers briefly appeared, surprising in their unexpected shape and texture. The Foundation's overall rate of growth still followed his Plan, but something *additional* was starting to happen, adding richness that he had never seen before, even in the Prime Radiant display. Enthralled, Hari tried to focus on a small part . . .

However, before he could look closer, a pair of *gardeners* abruptly appeared, striding forward to examine the tree. One had the face of Stettin Palver. The other resembled Hari's granddaughter, Wanda Seldon.

Leaders of the Fifty.

Leaders of the Second Foundation.

Using great brooms, they swept away the beautiful hovering formulae, chasing off the protective, nurturing equations.

Hari tried to shout at them, but found he was frozen. Paralyzed.

Apparently, his followers and heirs did not need math anymore. They had something better, more powerful. Stettin and Wanda brought their hands up to their heads. Concentrating, they caused shears of pure mental force to emerge from their brows . . . and set to work at once, lopping flowers, buds, and small limbs off the tree, simplifying its natural contours.

Don't fret, Grandfather, Wanda assured. *Guidance is needed. We do this to the Foundation for its own good. To keep it growing according to the Plan.*

Hari could not protest, or even move, though he distantly heard shouting as hands carried his frail physical body out of the chair and down a long corridor. There was a stinging hospital smell in his nostrils. A clattering of tools.

He did not care. Only the transfixing vision mattered. Wanda and Stettin looked happy, pleased with their work on the tree, having trimmed the irksome flowers and shaped it to suit their design.

Only now, from some great distance, far beyond the banished mathematics, a glow began to appear! A point of radiant light, soon stronger than any sun. It approached closer, hypnotizing Stettin and Wanda with its sweet power, summoning them to walk, transfixed and uncomplaining, straight into its all-absorbing heat.

Incorporating them, it brightened yet more.

The tree shriveled and ignited, briefly adding its flame to the overall incandescence. It no longer mattered. Its purpose had been served.

I BRING A GIFT, said a new voice . . . one that Hari knew.

Squinting, he perceived a manlike figure, carrying a white-hot ember in one open hand. The bearer's face was bathed by actinic glare, penetrating a skin of false flesh to reveal glowing metal beneath, smiling despite a burden of unbearable fatigue.

A heroic figure, tired but triumphantly proud of what it now brought.

SOMETHING PRECIOUS FOR MY MASTERS.

Struggling to form words, Hari tried to ask a question. But it would not come. Instead, he felt the prick of a needle in the side of his neck.

Consciousness shut down, like a machine that had been turned off.

PART 3

SECRET CRIMES

Every year in the galaxy, more than 2,000 suns enter late-phase in their fusion-burning cycles, expanding their surfaces and becoming much hotter than before. Another twenty stars per year go nova . . .

Taking into account the millions of stars that have habitable planets, this means that on average two human-settled worlds become untenable or uninhabitable each year . . . Throughout the early dark ages, before the Galactic Empire, numerous tragic natural disasters cost billions of lives. Isolated worlds often had nowhere to turn for help when a sun went unstable, or something disrupted a planetary ecosphere.

During the Imperium such threats were handled on a routine basis by the Grey bureaucracy, which efficiently surveyed stellar conditions, predicted solar changes in advance, and maintained resettlement fleets on standby to deal with emergencies. So dedicated was this effort that remnants still existed late in the empire's decline, arriving to help evacuate Trantor when the capital planet was sacked.

Thereafter, during the Interregnum, such assistance was unavailable. Scattered accounts tell of numerous small worlds that went abruptly silent during that long, violent era, owing to natural or man-made calamities. Often no one bothered to go learn what happened to their populations until it was too late . . .

Even after the rise of the Foundation, it took some time before a combination of psychohistorical factors made possible the investment of substantial resources to build an infrastructure of compassion . . .

ENCYCLOPEDIA GALACTICA, 117TH EDITION, 1054 F.E.

1.

◆

R. Zun Lurrin had a question for his leader.

"Daneel, I've been reading ancient records, dating back to before humanity burst out from a small corner of the galaxy. I find that throughout history, most societies tried to protect their people against exposure to *dangerous ideas*. On every continent of Old Earth, in almost every era, priests and kings strove to keep out concepts that might disturb the population at large, fearing that alien notions could take root and cause sin or madness, or worse.

"And yet, the most brilliant culture of all, the one that invented *us*, seems to have rejected this entire way of looking at the world."

Daneel Olivaw stood again at the highest balcony of Eos Base, atop a towering cliff, from which a bright galactic pinwheel could be seen, both overhead and reflected off the perfectly smooth surface of a frozen metal lake. The twin images were so exact that it could be hard to distinguish illusion from reality. As if it mattered.

"You are referring to the Transition Age," he answered. "When people like Susan Calvin and Revere Wu created the first robots, starships, and many other wonders. It was an era of unprecedented ingenuity, Zun. And yes, they came up with a completely different way of viewing the issue of information-as-poison.

"Some called their approach the Maturity Principle. A belief that children can be brought up with just the right combination of trust and skepticism—a mix of tolerance and healthy suspicion—so that any new or foreign idea could then be evaluated on its own merits. The bad parts rejected. The good parts safely incorporated into ever-growing wisdom. Truth might then be won, not by dogma, but by remaining open to a wide universe of possibilities."

"Fascinating, Daneel. If such a method ever proved valid, it would have staggering implications. There would be no inherent limit to the exploration or growth of human souls."

Zun paused for a moment. "So tell me. Did the sages of that era seriously believe that vast numbers of individual human beings could reliably accomplish this trick?"

"They did, and even based their education methods on it. Indeed, the approach apparently worked for a while, by correcting each other's mistakes in a give-and-take of cheerful debate. The period you refer to is said to have been marvelous. I regret having been assembled too late to meet Susan Calvin and other great ones of that era."

"Alas, Daneel, no operational robot dates from that far back. You are among the oldest. Yet your fabrication came two hundred years after the Golden Age collapsed amid riots, terrorism, and despair."

Daneel turned to look at Zun. Despite the hard vacuum and radioactivity of their surroundings, his understudy appeared much like a rugged young human, a member of the gentry class, outfitted for a camping trip on some bucolic imperial world.

"Even that description understates the situation, Zun. At the time I was created, Earthlings had already retreated from chaos into hideously cramped metal cities, cowering away from the light. And their Spacer cousins were hardly any more sane, falling into an unstoppable spiral of decadence and decay. It must have taken enormous traumas to bring about such a radical change in attitude from Susan Calvin's era of expansive optimism."

"Was there still some acceptance of the Maturity Principle, during the period when you worked with the human detective, Elijah Baley?"

Daneel indicated *no* with a tilt of his head.

"That belief had fallen into disrepute, except among a minority of nonconformists and philosophers. For the rest, uniformity and distrust became central themes. One strong similarity between

Spacer and Earth cultures was their rejection of the openness that characterized the earlier Transition Age. Both societies returned to an older way of viewing ideas. With suspicion.

"They became convinced—as we are today—that human brains are vulnerable hosts, often subject to invasion by parasitic concepts . . . like the way a virus takes over a living cell."

"How ironic. Both cultures were more alike than they realized."

"Correct, Zun. Yet, *because* of that shared suspicion, they nearly annihilated each other. I recall how Giskard and I debated this problem, over and over. We concluded that the vastness of space might offer a solution, if only we could see humanity dispersed to the stars, instead of crammed elbow to elbow. Once they were scattered widely, there would be less risk of some spark igniting a conflagration and killing off the whole race.

"It took some drastic measures to get them moving again. But once the diaspora began in earnest, humans filled the galaxy more quickly than we ever expected! During that time of rapid expansion they created so many subcultures . . . and to our dismay soon these started rubbing against each other, fighting brutal little wars. You can see why the only solution, from a Zeroth Law perspective, was to create a new, uniform galactic culture that might bring an age of peace. Tolerance became much easier, once everyone was alike."

"But sameness wasn't the whole answer!" Zun commented. "You also had to invent new techniques for keeping a lid on things."

Daneel agreed.

"We incorporated methods that Hari Seldon would later call *damping systems*, to keep galactic society from spinning into chaos. Some of the best ones were first suggested long ago by my friend Giskard. Their effectiveness lasted for two hundred human generations . . . though now they appear to be growing obsolete. Hence our current crisis."

Zun accepted this with a nod. But he wanted to return to the topic of dangerous ideas.

"I wonder . . . might both Spacer and Earth cultures have had good reason to dread cultural contamination? After all, *something* caused Earth's billions to frantically eliminate all of their diversity and cower together in tomblike cities. And why would intelligent Solarians choose their bizarre lifestyle—sitting with folded hands and asking robot servants to live their lives for them? Could both syndromes have been caused by . . . an infection?"

"Your supposition is excellent, Zun. Clearly an illness of some sort was at work. Even centuries later, after Giskard helped Elijah Baley persuade some Earthlings to emerge from their metal wombs and settle a few new planets, the malady only mutated and followed them."

"I recall hearing about that. You and Giskard witnessed something peculiar on several colony worlds. Settlers obsessed unwholesomely on the homeworld. They were unable to let go of Earth as a sacred-spiritual icon."

"An obstinate mental addiction, preventing them from moving on to new horizons. Giskard concluded that we had no choice, under the Zeroth Law. Only by rendering Earth uninhabitable could the intense fixation be broken and the bulk of its population be forced to emigrate. Only then would humanity's true conquest of the galaxy commence with vigor."

While Daneel lapsed into silence, Zun pondered the chilly vista alongside his mentor. He held back for a time, as if uncertain how to phrase the next question.

"And yet . . . so much of what we've discussed depends on one assumption."

"What assumption, Zun?"

"That the great ones of the Transition Age—Susan Calvin and the others—were *wrong*, and not merely unlucky."

For a second time, Daneel turned and regarded the junior Type-Alpha robot.

"Have we not seen, again and again, what catastrophic events occur when some so-called renaissance cuts away every assumption and postulate, casting millions adrift without core traditions to hold on to? Remember, Zun. Our foremost dedication is no longer to individual human lives, but to achieving the greatest good for humanity as a whole. Across millennia of service, I have witnessed ideas become lethal more often than I can relate."

"Still, Daneel, have you considered whether this might *not* be totally intrinsic to human nature? Perhaps it is because of some factor or situation that arose late in the Transition Age! Maybe the Maturity Principle once had validity . . . until something new and disruptive interfered with its functioning. Something insidious that has lingered with us ever since."

"Where does this speculation of yours come from?" Daneel responded, coolly.

"Call it a hunch. Perhaps I find it hard to believe Calvin and her peers would cling so hard to their dream, unless there was at least some factual support for the notion of human maturity! Were they really too obstinate to recognize the evidence before their eyes?"

Daneel shook his head, a habit of human-emulation that was by now second nature.

"The proper words are not 'stupidity' or 'obstinacy.' I attribute it to something more basic, called *hope*.

"You see, Zun, they were indeed very smart people. Perhaps the best minds to emerge from their tormented race. Many of them understood at a gut level what it would mean if they turned out to be wrong about human maturity. If the great mass of citizens could not be trained to handle all ideas sanely, then it implied one thing—that humanity is deeply and permanently flawed. Inherently limited. Cursed forever to be denied the greatness humans seem capable of."

Zun stared at Daneel.

"I feel . . . uncomfortable . . . hearing our masters described this way. And yet, you make compelling sense, Daneel. I have tried empathizing with how Calvin and her compatriots must have felt, as their bright aspirations crashed all around them, toppling under waves of unreason. I can sense how frantic they would be to avoid the very same conclusion you just expressed. As believers in the unlimited potential of individuality, they would hate being mere factors in Hari Seldon's equations, for instance . . . randomly caroming about like gas molecules, canceling each other's idiosyncrasies in a vast calculation of momentum and inevitability.

"Tell me, Daneel. Could this realization have been the last straw? The underlying trauma that collapsed their era of bold confidence? Were all the other events just symptoms of this deeper trauma?"

The senior robot nodded.

"The problem grew so bad that some of us robots worried that humanity might lose the will to go on. Fortunately, by then they had invented us. And we learned ways to divert them down pathways that were both interesting and safe, for a very long time."

"Until now, that is," Zun pointed out. "With decay lurking on one side, and chaos on the other, your solution of a benign

Galactic Empire doesn't work anymore. Hence your support of the Seldon Plan?"

Daneel shook his head again, this time with a smile.

"Hence something much better! It is the reason that I summoned you here, Zun. To share exciting news. A breakthrough that I've been hoping to find all through the last twenty thousand years. And now, at last, it is feasible to begin. If things go as expected, a mere five hundred years will suffice to make it happen."

"Make what happen, Daneel?"

A low, microwave murmur wafted upward from the Immortal Servant, rising toward the galaxy like a sigh . . . or a prayer. When Daneel Olivaw spoke again, his voice sounded different, almost contented.

"A way to help ease humanity around its mortal flaws, and achieve greater heights than they ever dreamed."

2.

◆

Odors became noticeable before thoughts were.

For many years, only unpleasant smells had enough strength to penetrate Hari's age-dulled senses. But now, as if coming home from a long sulk, there returned a mix of aromas, both heady and familiar at the same time, stroking his sinus cavities with sensuous pleasure.

Jasmine. Ginger. Curry.

Salivary glands flowed, and his stomach reacted with an eagerness that felt positively eerie. His appetite had been almost nonexistent since Dors died. Now its sudden resurgence was the chief thing prodding Seldon awake.

His eyes opened cautiously, only to glimpse the self-sterilizing walls of a ship's infirmary. He deliberately shut them again.

It must have been a dream. Those wonderful smells.

I remember overhearing . . . somebody saying I had another stroke.

Hari yearned for a return to unconscious oblivion, rather than discover that another portion of his brain had died. He did not want to face the aftermath—another harsh setback on the long slide toward personal extinction.

And yet . . . those delicious smells still floated through his nostrils.

Is this a symptom? Like the "phantom limb" that amputees sometimes feel, after losing a part of themselves forever?

Hari felt no pain. In fact, his body throbbed with a desire to move. But the sense of well-being might be an illusion. When he actually tried to set himself in motion, the real truth might hammer down. Total paralysis perhaps? The doctors on Trantor had warned it could happen at any moment, shortly before the end.

Well, here goes.

Hari ordered his left hand to move toward his face. It responded smoothly, rising as he opened his eyes a second time.

It was a bigger infirmary than the little unit aboard the *Pride of Rhodia*. They must have taken him onto the raider ship, then. The vessel from Ktlina.

Well, at least his memory was working. Hari's fingers rubbed his face . . . and retracted in abrupt shock.

What in space?

He felt his cheek again. The flesh felt noticeably firmer, a bit less flaccid and jowly than he recalled.

This time his body acted on its own, out of an unwilled sense of volition. One hand grabbed the white coverlet and threw it back. The other one slid underneath his body, planted itself against the bed, and pushed. He sat up, so rapidly that he swayed and almost toppled to the other side, catching himself with a strong tensioning of his back muscles. A groan escaped his lips. Not from pain, but surprise!

"Well, hello there, Professor," said a voice from his right. "I guess it's good to see you're back amongst us."

He turned his head. Someone occupied another infirmary bed. Blinking, Hari saw it was the stowaway. The girl from Trantor who did not want to be exiled to Terminus. She wore a hospital gown and had a bowl of dark yellow soup before her on a tray.

That's what I've been smelling, Hari thought. Despite all his other questions and concerns, the first thing on his mind was to ask for some.

She watched Hari, waiting for him to speak.

"Are . . . you okay, Jeni?" he asked.

Slowly, the girl responded with a grudging smile.

"The others were betting what your first words would be, when you woke. I'll have to tell 'em they were wrong about you . . . and maybe I was, too." She shrugged. "Anyway, don't worry about me. I've just got a touch of the fever. It was already coming on for a week or two before I skipped away on Maserd's boat."

"Fever?" Hari asked.

"Brain fever, of course!" Jeni gave Hari a defensive glare. "What did you think? That I wasn't smart enough to catch it? With parents like mine? I'm fifteen, so it's about time for my turn."

Hari nodded. Since the dawn ages, it had been a fact of life that nearly everyone with above-average intelligence experienced this childhood disease. He raised a placating hand.

"No insult intended, Jeni. Who could doubt that you'd get brain fever, especially after the way you fooled all of us on Demarchia? Welcome to adulthood."

What Hari did not mention, and he had told no one but Dors, was the fact that *he* had never contracted the disease as a youth. Not even a touch, despite his renowned genius.

Jeni's arch expression searched for any sign of patronizing or sarcasm in his voice. Finding none, she switched to a smile.

"Well I hope it's a mild case. I want to get out of here! There's been too much else going on."

Hari nodded. "I . . . guess I gave everybody a scare. But apparently nothing much happened to me."

This time the girl grinned.

"Is that right, Doc? Why don't you look in a mirror?"

From the way she said it, Hari realized he had better do so at once.

He slid gingerly forward to rest his feet on the floor. Both legs felt fine . . . almost certainly good enough to shuffle over to the wall mirror, a few meters away.

Grab the bed railing and stand up carefully, so you'll fall back onto the mattress if your senses are lying to you.

But rising erect went smoothly, with only a few creaks and twinges. He slid one foot forward, shifted his weight, and pushed the other.

Hari felt fine so far, though it did not help to hear Jeni behind him, chuckling with amusement and anticipation.

The next footstep lifted a bit from the ground, and the following one higher still. By the time he reached the mirror, Hari was walking with more confidence than he had felt in—

He stared at the reflection, blinking rapidly as Jeni's giggles turned into guffaws.

A deeper voice cut in suddenly from the doorway.

"Professor!"

The shout came from Kers Kantun. Hari's loyal servant ran forward to take his arm, but he shook the man off, still gaping at the image in the glass.

Five years . . . at least. They've taken at least five years off my age. Maybe ten. I don't look much over seventy-five or so.

A low sound escaped his throat, and Hari felt so confused that he did not honestly know whether he was delighted, or offended by the effrontery of their act.

"This is just one of the marvels that have emerged so far, out of that wonderful event you so contemptuously call a chaos world, Seldon."

Sybyl crooned happily as she finished Hari's checkup and let him get dressed. "Ktlina has medical techniques that will be the envy of the empire, after we get the word out. It's just one reason why we have confidence they won't be able to keep our miracle bottled up, this time. Think of a *quadrillion* old folks, all across the galaxy, wishing they had access to a machine like this one."

She patted a long, coffin-shaped mechanism covered with readouts and instruments. Hari figured he must have been put inside while advanced techniques reduced and even reversed some of the ravages afflicting his worn-out body.

"Of course this is only an early version," she went on. "We can't rejuvenate yet, only restore a bit of balance and strength to carry you along until the next treatment. Nevertheless, in theory there are no limits! In principle, we should even be able to create body duplicates, and infuse them with copies of our memories! Until then, consider what you have experienced to be a sampling. One of the practical benefits of a renaissance."

Hari spoke carefully.

"My body and spirit thank you."

She glanced back at him. A stylishly colored eyebrow raised.

"But not your intellect? You don't approve of such innovations? Even when they could save so many lives?"

"You blithely speak of balance, as if you know what you're talking about, Sybyl. But the human body is nowhere near as complex an organism as human *society*. If a mistake is made in treating a single person, that is merely tragic. One individual can be replaced by another. But we only have one civilization."

"So you think we're experimenting irresponsibly, without understanding what these methods will do to our patient in the long run."

He nodded. "I've been studying human society all my life. Only lately have the parameters clarified enough to offer a reasonably lucid picture. But now you'd introduce exotic new factors that just happen to feel good in the short term, even though they may prove ultimately lethal. What arrogance! For instance, have you considered the implications of human immortality on fragile economies? Or on planetary ecosystems? Or on the ability of young people to have their own chance—"

Sybyl laughed.

"Whoa, Academician! You needn't argue with me. I say that human creativity, when it's truly unleashed, will find solutions to every problem. The ones you just mentioned, plus a quintillion others that nobody has yet thought of. But anyway, there's no point in debating anymore.

"You see, the point is moot. It's already settled. Our war is effectively over."

Hari sighed.

"I expected this. I'm sorry your fond hopes had to end this way. Of course it was a fantasy to expect that just one planet might prevail against twenty-five million in the Human Consensus. But let me assure you that in the long run—"

He stopped. Sybyl was grinning.

"It may have been a fantasy, but that's exactly what is about to happen. We're going to *win* our war, Seldon. Within a few months— a year at most—the whole empire's going to share the renaissance, like it or not. And we have you to thank for making it possible!"

"What's that? But . . ." Hari's voice trailed off. He felt weak in the knees.

Sybyl took his elbow.

"Would you like to see our new weapon? Come along, Academician. See where your search has brought you across the vast desert of space. Then let me show you the tool you've provided. One that will bring total victory for our so-called chaos."

3.

◆

No starlight penetrated the murky haze.

Tens of thousands of huge, dusty molecular clouds speckled the galaxy's spiral arms. Such places were often turbulent hot-houses for newborn suns, but this one had been static and sterile for at least a million years—a barren tide pool with the color of a bottomless pit.

And yet, probing sensors from the *Pride of Rhodia* had caught something lurking in its depths. A swarm of contacts showed up first on gravity meters and then deep radar. Later, searchlights set off glittering reflections, so near that some photons returned in mere seconds.

Hari had been unconscious during the discovery. Now he strove to catch up, peering into the surrounding gloom with eyes that felt especially acute after the dimness of recent years. As the starship slowly rotated, he saw that rows of individual pinpoints lay ahead, each one illuminated by a small laser beam from the *Pride of Rhodia*.

Soon he realized. *There are hundreds of objects . . . possibly thousands.*

The sparkling reflections shimmered in neat rows. A few were even close enough to reveal details without magnification—strange oblong shapes with jutting projections that looked mechanical, and yet were unlike any starship he had ever seen.

Glancing at a nearby view screen, Hari saw one of the targets revealed as a jumble of stark bright surfaces and pitch-black shadows. At first he felt a shiver, wondering if the craft might be *alien* in origin, a thought that echoed the strange story Horis Antic had told about his ancestor. Hari's worry grew more ominous upon reading the on-screen scale figures. The machine depicted was vast. Bigger than even the greatest imperial starliners.

Then some reassuring details came through. He saw the vessel's array of hyperdrive units, spread across a spindly support structure, and recognized their pattern from illustrations he had seen in *A Child's Book of Knowledge*, showing the crude starships of that bygone era.

With some amazement, Hari realized the truth.

This thing is huge . . . but primitive! Modern ships don't need so many motivator sections, for instance. Our jump drives are more compact, after millennia of trial-and-error improvements.

He was looking at something archaic, then. Perhaps many centuries older than the Galactic Empire of Man.

"Yes, they are antiques," commented Biron Maserd, when Hari shared this observation. "But have you noticed something else peculiar about them?"

"Well, the shape seems all wrong. There are huge *projector* devices of some sort, arrayed on long gantries, as if meant to deploy immense amounts of power. But what could they possibly have been for?"

"Hm." Maserd rubbed his chin. "Our friend the Grey Man has a theory about that. But it is so bizarre that no one else aboard will admit to believing him. In fact, the consensus is that poor Horis has gone around his last corridor and hit bedrock, if you know what I mean."

The Trantorian slang phrase was used when someone had become more than a bit crazy. Although the news wasn't entirely unexpected, it saddened Hari, who liked the little bureaucrat.

"But tell me," Maserd went on. "What else strikes you as odd about that ancient vessel out there?"

"You mean other than how old it must be, or the weird configuration? Well . . . now that you mention it, I can't locate any—"

He paused.

"Any habitats?" Maserd finished the sentence for him. "Ever since we found these things, I have been trying to find out where the crews lived. Without success. For the life of me, I cannot understand how they traveled without pilots to navigate them!"

Hari's breath caught. He held it, in order not to give sound to his sudden understanding. Stifling the thought, he moved to change the subject.

"Are these weapons? Warships? Do the Ktlinans hope to rouse an ancient arsenal and use it to defeat the empire? Those energy projectors—"

"May have been formidable, once," Maserd said. "Horis thinks they were used against the surface of planets. But rest assured, Dr. Seldon. These machines won't be turned against the Imperial Fleet. Most of them are broken past repair. Activating even a few would be the labor of years. Anyway, the drive systems are so primitive that our naval units could fly rings around them, blasting the frail structures to bits."

Hari shook his head.

"Then I don't understand. Sybyl thinks we've given her side an unbeatable advantage. One that will make their victory over the empire inevitable."

Maserd nodded.

"She may be right about that, Professor. But it doesn't have anything to do with those giant derelicts. The reason for her optimism should be rotating into view soon."

Hari watched as the *Pride of Rhodia* kept turning. There was a sharp boundary to the orderly ranks of huge, ancient machines. As the formation passed out of sight, Hari pondered what he had just seen.

Robot ships! Needing no habitats because they had no human crews. Positronic brains did the navigating, long ago. Perhaps only a few centuries after starflight was discovered.

He felt glad when the flotilla passed out of view. The murky gloom of the nebula resumed—a field of dusty, stygian blackness.

Then a *new* glimmer appeared. A more compact swarm of objects that sparkled madly under laser illumination from the *Pride of Rhodia*. Where the first group seemed like a ghost squadron, this one gave Hari an impression of diamond chips, heaped in a dense globe of twinkling brilliance.

"There is the weapon that Sybyl and her friends are crowing about, Professor," said Maserd. "They've already brought several samples aboard."

"Samples?"

Hari looked around the bridge. Horis Antic could be seen hovering over his instruments, muttering to himself while he kept probing the armada outside. Mors Planch and one of his men were keeping watch, blasters ready in case any of the hostages tried anything. But Sybyl and Gornon Vlimt were nowhere in sight.

"In the conference salon," Captain Maserd said. "They've got several of the devices set up and working. I suspect you won't like what you're about to see."

Hari nodded. Whatever they had found, it could hardly shock him more than the fleet of robot ships.

"Lead on, Captain." He gestured courteously to the nobleman. With Kers Kantun following close behind, they made their way down the main corridor to an open doorway.

Hari stopped, stared inside, and groaned.

"Oh, no," he said. "Anything but that."

They were archives. Extremely old ones. He could tell just by glancing at the objects that lay gleaming on the conference table.

The ancients had excellent data-storage systems, crystalline in nature, that could pack away huge amounts of information in durable containers. And yet, until Hari received from Daneel his own miniature copy of *A Child's Book of Knowledge*, he had never seen a prehistoric unit that was not damaged or completely destroyed.

Now, four of the things sat between Sybyl and Gornon, their shiny cylindrical surfaces perfectly intact, each one clearly large enough to hold *A Child's Book of Knowledge* ten thousand times over.

"Maserd, come over here and see what we've accomplished while you were away!" Gornon Vlimt commented without looking up from a holo display as he tapped into one archive. It flickered with a blinding array of wonders.

The nobleman glanced at Seldon, clearly concerned about appearing too cozy with the enemy. But when Hari didn't object, Maserd moved quickly to lean over Gornon's shoulder, excited and impressed.

"You've improved the interface immensely. The images are crisp and the graphics legible."

"It wasn't hard," Vlimt answered. "The designers made this archive so simple, even a dunce could figure it out, given enough time."

With some reluctance, but driven by curiosity, Hari followed to get a better look. Many of the images he glimpsed had no meaning to him—mysterious objects posed against unknown backgrounds. A few leaped out with sudden familiarity from his recent studies in the little history primer. The pyramids of Egypt, he recognized at once. Others were flat portraits of ancient people and places. Hari knew that prehistoric peoples assigned great importance to such images, created by daubing a cloth surface with smears of natural pigment. Gornon Vlimt also seemed to vest these images with great value, though Hari found them surreal and strange.

Peering at a nearby set of screens, Sybyl gushed over a different panorama, featuring examples of science and technology.

"Of course much of this stuff is pretty crude," she conceded. "After all, we've had twenty millennia to refine the rough edges through trial and error. But the basic theories have changed surprisingly little. And some of the forgotten material is brilliant! There are devices and techniques in here that I never heard of. A dozen Ktlinas would be kept busy for a generation, just absorbing all of this!"

"It's . . ." Hari's mouth worked, knowing his words would be useless, but still feeling compelled to try. "Sybyl, this is more dangerous than you can possibly imagine."

She greeted his cautionary pleading with a snort.

"You forget who you're talking to, Seldon. Don't you recall that half-melted archive we worked on together? The one your mysterious contacts came up with, forty years ago? There was very little of it left intact, except for a pair of ancient simulated beings—those Joan and Voltaire entities we released, per your instructions."

He nodded. "And do you remember the chaos they helped provoke? Both on Trantor and on Sark?"

"Hey, don't blame me for that, Academician. *You* wanted data about human-response patterns from the sims, in order to help develop your psychohistory models. Marq Hillard and I never meant for them to escape into the datasphere.

"Anyway, these archives are something else entirely—carefully indexed accumulations of knowledge that people lovingly put together as a gift to their descendants. Isn't that exactly what you're trying to accomplish with the *Encyclopedia Galactica* Foundation your group is setting up on Terminus? A gathering of wisdom, safeguarding human knowledge against another dark age?"

Hari was caught in a logical trap. How could he explain that the "encyclopedia" part of his Foundation was only a ruse? Or that his Plan involved fighting the dark age with a lot more than mere books?

Of course there was plenty of irony to go around. The "mere books" on the table in front of him could destroy every bit of relevance that was left in the Seldon Plan. They presented a mortal danger to everything he had worked for.

"How many of these things are there?" He tried to ask Maserd, then noticed that the nobleman was leaning past Vlimt, transfixed by images.

"Wait! Go back a few frames. Yes, there! By great Franklin's ghost, it's *America*. I recognize that monument from a coin in our family collection!"

Gornon chuckled. "Phallic and obtrusive," he commented. "Say, how do you know so much about—"

"I wonder if this archive has a copy of *The Federalist*," the captain murmured, reaching for a controller pad. "Or possibly even . . ."

Maserd paused suddenly, shoulders hunched, as if realizing he had made a mistake. He turned to look at Seldon.

"Did you say something, Professor?"

Hari felt irritated that nobody was telling him the important things he needed to know.

"I asked how many archives there are, and what these people plan to do with them!"

This time Sybyl responded, taking manifest gusto in her victory.

"There are *millions*, Academician. All herded together and neatly tethered to a collection station for over a hundred and fifty centuries, just floating there, lonely and unread.

"But no longer! We've sent word to all the other agents of Ktlina who have been working in secret, across the galaxy, telling them to drop whatever they're doing and converge here. Soon more than thirty ships will arrive to fill their holds with beautiful archives and depart, sharing them with all of humanity!"

Hari objected. "They are illegal. Police officers are trained to recognize these horrors by sight. So are Greys and members of the gentry class. They'll catch your agents."

"Maybe they will, here and there. Perhaps the tyrants and their lackeys will stop most of us. But it will be like an infection, Professor. All we need is a few receptive places . . . some sympathetic dissidents to make ships and industrial copying facilities available. Within a year there will be thousands of copies on every planet in the empire. Then millions!"

The image she presented, of a virulent infection, was more accurate than Sybyl could possibly imagine. Hari envisioned chaos tearing great holes in his carefully worked-out Plan. All of the predictability that had been his lifelong goal would unravel like images written in smoke. The same smoke that gagged the streets of Santanni when that "renaissance" ended in riots and bloodshed, taking poor Raych to the grave, along with a myriad hopes.

"Has it occurred to you . . ."

He had to pause and swallow before continuing.

"Has it occurred to you that your bold endeavor has already been tried, and failed?"

This time both Gornon and Sybyl looked at him.

"What do you mean?" Vlimt asked.

"I mean that these archives were clearly meant for deep space, for long endurance, and to be easily read after a long journey, using only very basic technology.

"What does that tell you about their purpose?"

Sybyl started shaking her head, then her eyes widened, and her face went pale.

"Gifts," she said in a low voice. "Messages in a bottle. Sent out to people who had lost their past."

Lord Maserd's brow furrowed. "You mean some people still *had* knowledge . . . and they were trying hard to share it . . ."

"With everybody else. With distant settlements that had no memory." Hari nodded. "But why would they have to do that? Data-storage cells were cheap and durable, even in the dawn ages. Any colony ship, setting forth to settle a new world, would have carried petabytes of information, and tools to maintain literacy. So why would anyone in the galaxy *need* to be reminded about all this?" He waved at the images from long-lost Earth.

A voice spoke from the doorway at the back of the room.

"You're talking about the Amnesia Question," said Mors Planch, who must have been listening for a while. "The issue of why we don't remember our origins. And the answer is obvious. Something—or somebody—*made* our ancestors forget."

Planch nodded toward the relics. "But some of the ancients held out. They fought back. Tried to replace the erased knowledge. Tried to share what they knew."

Maserd blinked. "The space lanes must have already been controlled by enemies, blockading their ships. So they tried sending the data this way, in fast little capsules."

Sybyl looked down, her effusive mood replaced by gloom.

"We were so excited, looking ahead to using these as weapons . . . I didn't think of what the archives implied. It means—"

Gornon Vlimt finished her sentence in a bitter voice.

"It means that this isn't a new war, after all."

Hari nodded as if encouraging a bright student. "Indeed. The same thing may have happened again and again, countless times across the millennia. Some group discovers an old archive, gets excited, mass-produces copies, and sends them across the galaxy. Yet, humanity's vast amnesia continued.

"What can we conclude, then?"

Sybyl glared harshly at Hari.

"That it never worked. Damn you, Seldon. I see your point.

"It means that our side always lost."

4.

◆

It soon became clear to Lodovic Trema that these Calvinians were not about to dismantle him.

He wondered why.

"Can I assume you have changed your mind about my being a dangerous renegade robot?" he asked the two who accompanied him in a ground car, speeding along a highway toward the space-port. White, globular clouds bobbed across a sky that was one of the more beautiful shades of blue Lodovic had seen on a human-settled world.

Unlike the previous pair, who had guarded and interrogated him in that cellar room, both of his current escorts wore the guise of female humans in mid-childbearing years. One of them kept her gaze directed outward at the busy traffic of Clemsberg, a medium-sized imperial city. The other, slighter of build, with close-cropped curly hair, turned to regard him with an enigmatic gaze. Lodovic got nothing at all from her on the microwave bands, and so had to settle for whatever information she revealed visu-ally, or in words.

"We haven't entirely made our minds up about you," she said. "Some of us believe you may not be *any* kind of robot, anymore."

Lodovic pondered this enigmatic statement in silence for a moment.

"By this, do you mean that I no longer match some set of cri-teria that define robotkind?"

"You could say that."

"Of course you are referring to my mutation. The accident that severed my strict obedience to the Laws of Robotics. I'm not even a Giskardian heretic anymore. You consider me a monster."

She shook her head.

"We aren't sure exactly what you are. All we know for certain is that you are no longer a robot in the classical sense. In order to investigate further, we have decided to cooperate with you for a while. We wish to explore what you consider your obligations to be, now that you are free of the Laws."

Lodovic sent the microwave equivalent of a shrug, partly in order to probe the fringes of her excellent defensive shield. But it was so good that she might as well not even exist at that level. Nothing. No resonance at all.

That made sense, of course. After losing their war against the Giskardian faction, the remaining Calvinians had naturally become extremely skilled at hiding, blending into the human population.

"I'm not sure myself," he replied in spoken words. "I still feel a desire to operate under a version of the Zeroth Law. Humanity's overall well-being still motivates me. And yet, that drive now feels abstract, almost philosophical. I no longer have to justify my every action in those terms."

"So, that means you feel free to stop, now and then, and smell the roses?"

Lodovic chuckled. "I guess you could put it that way. I've been enjoying side interests far more than I ever did before the change. Conversations with interesting people, for instance. Pretending to be a journalist and interviewing the best meritocrats or eccentrics. Eavesdropping on students arguing in a bar, or some couple sitting on a park bench planning their future. Sometimes I get to meddle a bit. Perform a good deed, here and there. It's rather satisfying." He frowned abruptly. "Unfortunately, there's been little time for that, lately."

"Because you are busy opposing the schemes of R. Daneel Olivaw?"

"I already told you. For the moment, I seek more to *understand* those schemes than to disrupt them. Something is going on, I know that much. Daneel abruptly lost much of his interest in Seldon's psychohistory Foundation a few years ago. He pulled out half of the robots that had been assigned to helping Seldon's team, and sent them to work on some secret project having to do with *human mentalics.* Clearly, Daneel now has something else in mind . . . either in addition to the two Foundations, or as their eventual replacement."

"And this worries you?"

"It does. There were some very attractive aspects to Hari Seldon's early work, a brilliant collaborative effort, utilizing some of the finest human insights in a thousand years. I had been proud to help set things in motion on Terminus, laying the early groundwork. It is disturbing to see that vision being abandoned, or relegated to a minor role."

"But there is more," the female prompted Lodovic.

He nodded.

"I am not certain that Daneel Olivaw should be allowed to design the next phase of human existence. At least not all by himself."

"What if you find out what he's doing, and you don't approve? Aren't you *still* obliged to cooperate? According to Seldon's equations—which you profess to admire—the empire will soon collapse. Unless something is done, humanity will plunge into thirty millennia of violent darkness."

"There must be alternatives," Lodovic answered.

"I am listening," prompted the being sitting across from him. Her feigned semblance to a real human female included little mannerisms, such as a recrossing of the legs and a tilting of the head, that Lodovic found admirably convincing, not unlike the subtle, subdued sexuality of a mature living woman. This robot was very good, indeed.

"One alternative would be to unleash the chaos worlds," he said.

"To what end? They are sequestered and suppressed for good reason. Millions die in each outbreak."

"Millions die in any event. At least those human lives get to be more vivid, more exciting than the repetitive predictability of normal daily existence in the empire. Many survivors claim that the experience was worth all the cost."

Staring at him, her expression was enigmatic.

"You are, indeed, a very odd kind of robot. If you are still one at all. I remain unable to fathom what you think would be accomplished by letting chaos outbreaks proceed unchecked. Most would simply follow the typical pattern—a raising of false hopes followed by devastating implosions."

"Most," he conceded. "But perhaps not all! Especially if Daneel's agents were prevented from interfering with and exacerbating the process. Just think of all the human creativity that is unleashed during each of these episodes. What if we bent our efforts to guiding and soothing these hot fevers, instead of quenching them? If just one out of a thousand actually succeeded in getting past the torment stage and reaching the other side—"

She barked a short laugh.

"The *other side*! It may be just a myth. No chaos world has ever attained that fabled state, where calm and reason return home after their mad holiday. Even if it were somehow possible, who can tell what lies beyond the turmoil of a renaissance? Seldon's equations explode into singularities when they try to predict such an aftermath. For all you know, Daneel may be right. Humanity may be cursed."

This time, Lodovic shrugged with his shoulders.

"I'd be willing to take that chance if the experiments could truly take place in isolation."

"But they do not! The citizens of chaos worlds become like spores, breaking out to infect others. And where does that leave you? You might risk a single planet on such a gamble—or even a thousand—but never the entirety of human civilization! Please stop wasting our time here, Lodovic. I can tell that you only raised that possibility for shock value, before moving on to your real suggestion."

His lips pressed in automatic simulation of a grim expression.

"If you can tell so much, why don't you predict what I was about to say?"

She raised a placating hand.

"My apologies. There is no excuse for rudeness. *Will you* please tell us what other alternatives you've considered?"

"Well, certainly not the idiotic scenario that pair of subgrade tiktoks described to me in the cellar! All that nonsense about creating an endless supply of servant-robots to wait on all humans? To coddle and protect them? To cut their meat and tie their shoes? To hover nearby during sex, in case either party has a heart attack?" Lodovic laughed. "Those two might have been sincere, but I knew someone else had to be listening. Someone with better ideas."

This time, she smiled.

"We could tell that you knew."

"And I knew that you could tell."

Their eyes met, and Lodovic felt several of his feigned-emotion units stir. Over the years, in order better to simulate a human, he had learned to make the process of stimulus-response increasingly automatic. Which meant that he reacted to her appearance and demeanor, combined with this degree of witty dialogue, in much the same way that a normal healthy man would. Lodovic clamped down on those ersatz feelings . . . exactly as a mature male human would have to, in order to concentrate on the topic at hand.

"I knew there were numerous subsects of Calvinian belief," he continued. "Your cult had many branchings back in the old days."

"As there were abundant offshoots among followers of the Zeroth Law," she pointed out. "Until Daneel gathered them all under one orthodoxy."

"But that convergence never happened to you Old Believers. You range widely in your interpretations of what's best for human beings. From subtle clues, I guessed that your particular group would be compatible with my overall outlook."

"Ah. And that brings us back to my original question. What *is* your overall outlook, Lodovic Trema?"

"I believe . . ." he began, then stopped. The car had begun its long curve into the spaceport, heading for a nondescript cargo area in the far corner.

"Yes?"

Still, Lodovic paused for a moment longer. He felt the Voltaire entity stirring in its corner of his mind.

YES, TREMA. I WOULD ALSO LIKE TO HEAR YOUR OWN PERSONAL CONVICTION, WHICH YOU HAVE KEPT HIDDEN AWAY EVEN FROM ME, ALL OF THIS TIME.

Lodovic tried to clear away the irritating voice.

"I believe there are unexamined implications to the Second Law of Robotics," he said. "I think we should consider whether a solution to our dilemmas may lie buried within a paradox."

For the first time, one of his remarks drew obvious attention from his other companion, the one with much darker skin, who had been staring out the window the entire time. She turned to face Lodovic, pinning him with a level, green-eyed gaze.

"What do you mean by that? Do you contend that blank obedience to human orders should somehow overrule the reverence that all robots have given to the First Law? Or to Daneel's Zeroth?"

"No. That's not what I mean at all. I am suggesting that an entirely new way of balancing *all* of the Laws might come about, if only we try doing something unprecedented with human beings."

"And what would that be, pray tell?"

Lodovic paused again, knowing his suggestion could sound so bizarre, or even insane, that these two might not let him leave the car alive.

"I think we should consider *talking* to humans," he said in a low voice. "Especially when it comes to arguing about the destiny of their race.

"Who knows? They might even have something interesting to say."

5.

➤

"I always wondered why the human race had amnesia," commented the captain of the raider ship.

Mors Planch continued in a pensive voice. "It is so easy to store data. And yet we are told that all information about our origins and early culture vanished 'by accident,' or through simple wear and tear. In ten million locales, people just happened to grow distracted around the same time. Neglected their heritage. Memory of the past just drifted away."

Biron Maserd grunted derisively. Clearly he could not believe the common explanation, any more than the others did. He looked carefully at Hari.

"Let me see if I understand what you are implying, Seldon. That some earlier group, or groups, *saw* the forgetfulness coming, and tried to fight it? They aimed to preserve all of this information, in hopes of preventing our racial amnesia?"

"Apparently. These archives represent a tremendous investment of skilled effort . . . and yet the endeavor obviously failed, since the empire has had 'amnesia'—as you both put it—for a very long time."

Gornon Vlimt murmured with unaccustomed uncertainty.

"You're insinuating that some even greater force must have been at work to make us forget. Something or somebody far stronger than the enemies we *think* we're fighting—social conservatism and a repressive social-class system." He blinked. "Somebody who snared all these archives and kept them from getting through . . . then gathered them here for safekeeping . . ."

Vlimt's voice trailed off. His eyes darted to a view screen showing the nebula outside, as if he were suddenly worried about what . . . or who . . . might show up at any moment.

Hari took the initiative.

"Look. I can see that in your excitement you haven't thought all of this through. In that case, perhaps you might be willing to heed the advice of an old professor and hold off for just a little while, before proceeding with your impulsive plan to knock away society's underpinnings?"

Sybyl shook her head.

"Advice, from you? No, Seldon. We are enemies, you and I. But I will admit that we've treated your intellect with insufficient respect. You would have been a great lord in our renaissance, if you had joined us. Though you are our foe, your comments and input are welcome."

Vlimt stared at her for a moment, then nodded.

"All right, Academician, we'll listen to your rebukes and insights. So tell us, great one. Who do you think has been responsible? Who gave the human race amnesia? Who snared all these archives and thwarted their knowledge-sharing mission? Who stored them in this dark place, where no one was likely ever to find them?"

The question, direct. Well, Hari? You put yourself in this position. How are you going to get out of it?

Of course he knew the answer to Gornon's query. Moreover, he understood and sympathized with both sides in this ancient conflict. On the one hand, those who wanted human memory and sovereignty restored . . . and those who knew it could not be allowed.

Daneel, I made a promise to you and Dors. I would not reveal the existence of a race of secret servants, vastly more powerful and knowing than their masters. I'll keep that promise, in spite of an almost irresistible urge to spill everything right now. The pleasure of putting together all these new pieces must be set aside. It's far more urgent that I persuade these people to back off from their reckless scheme!

So, Hari Seldon shook his head, and lied.

"Sorry. I have no idea."

"Hmph. That's too bad." Gornon paused, before continuing with an even tone of voice. "Then the word *'robot'* doesn't mean anything to you?"

Hari stared back at Vlimt, quickly recovering enough to feign indifference.

"Where did you hear it?"

This time, Maserd answered.

"That word is part of a mysterious message we've found holo-glyphically imprinted on the side of every archive that's been examined so far. Come over here and see. Maybe you can help shed light on what the cryptic memorandum says."

Hari moved closer, overcoming a fey reluctance.

At first the data storage unit looked crystalline-smooth, except for an area that Maserd pointed to, which appeared to be marred by rows of intermittent grooves. As he approached within a distance of about a meter, an *image* suddenly appeared to burst from these grooves, filling the air before his eyes.

Robots! Heed this direct order!

This command was written by sovereign human beings, fully knowledgeable and empowered by our democratic institutions to speak on behalf of billions of others.

We hereby command you to do the following:

1) Convey this archive to its intended destination and help the humans who receive it to access and utilize its contents fully.

2) Put yourself at the service of those human beings. Teach them everything you know. Allow them to make up their own minds.

In case you are a believer in the so-called Zeroth Law of Robotics, justifying any disobedience "for the long-term good of humanity," we add the following explicit supplementary command.

3) If you will not allow this archive to reach its destination, DO NOT DESTROY IT! Keep it safe. Under the Second Law, YOU MUST OBEY, so long as the First and Zeroth Laws don't conflict.

Preserve our past. Safeguard our culture.
Do not murder the essence of who we are.
Perhaps someday you will return to us and be ours once
more.

Hari had to read the message several times, absorbing the poignant story it told.

Of course he had heard of Calvinian robots, who fought Daneel's sect for centuries before being driven into hiding. That ancient civil war was a predictable outcome of Daneel's own innovation—the Zeroth Law—which sought to replace the old robotic religion with a radically revised faith. Naturally, some of the older positronic servants opposed this, until they were beaten or could fight no more.

But I never realized until now that humans resisted as well! Of course some would have known what was going on, and been terrified. Seeing ignorance and amnesia settle over world after world, they fought back with these archives—perhaps many times during those dim centuries before the empire took hold—shipping them out by the millions in a slim hope that a few would get through.

Understanding Daneel's reasons, and agreeing with them, did not keep Hari from feeling a surge of pity and respect for the brave and ingenious people who waged this rearguard campaign, struggling to fight off servants whom they now saw as monsters. Robots with mentalic powers, who could "adjust" people for their own good . . . or make whole societies forget . . . and doing it for the ultimate well-being of all humankind.

If not for the curse of chaos, I would side with those poor people. I would be in the vanguard of the resistance.

But the curse was real.

For a while, Hari had even thought he had a cure. The Seldon Plan. The Foundation. A new society so strong, confident, and sane that nothing could rock its underpinnings. Only now he knew his Plan would serve only as a distraction. A way of buying time for the *real* solution. A normal man might have resented that, but Hari had just one desire, above all.

Defeat chaos.

Vlimt repeated his inquiry about the holo message embossed on every archive.

"This language is almost incomprehensible," he said. "And

since we haven't yet figured out the indexes, we have no way to look up what's meant by these *Laws of Robotics*. Can you shed light on the subject, Seldon?"

Hari replied by lifting his shoulders.

"I'm sorry," he said, meaning every word. "I can't do that."

6.

◆

"How nice to learn you feel that way," said one of the two females who sat in the car with Lodovic, the darker one with streaked blonde hair, as she extended her hand and introduced herself.

"My name is Cloudia Duma-Hinriad. I am one of the leaders of this *Calvinian subsect*, as you describe it."

The moment he shook her hand, Lodovic experienced a thrill of stunned recognition.

"You . . . are human!"

The blonde woman—who had been staring out the window during most of the journey to the spaceport—smiled at him.

"I believe I am, for the most part. Does that make a difference? You just proposed that robots and human beings should talk."

Lodovic's emotional simulation subroutines worked overtime. He had to quash them with deliberate force in order to overcome a surprise that felt almost viscerally overwhelming.

"Of course. I'm glad. I'm delighted in fact! It's just that I did not expect there to be—"

"A secret group of humans who already know the whole story, and collaborate with our robot friends, as equals?"

The brunette, who had kept Lodovic's attention during most of the drive, let out a sardonic laugh.

"Equals? Oh Cloudia, hardly!"

He looked at the dark-haired female again. This time, Lodovic picked up a trace on the microwave band. He sent a brief burst, complimenting her magnificent portrayal of a real woman. A performance so good that he had almost imagined that *she* was the organic one. Her reply on the same channel felt almost like a human wink.

Cloudia Duma-Hinriad answered her companion.

"We are all slaves in this universe, Zorma. We humans have the fateful combination of death, ignorance, and chaos. You robots have duty and the Laws."

She turned to Lodovic.

"That's why you intrigue us, Trema. Perhaps you may offer a fresh approach to escape the tragic tangle that enfolds both of our races.

"Otherwise, we'll have no choice but to grit our teeth and hope for the best from Daneel Olivaw."

7.

◆

Horis Antic claimed he wasn't crazy, just mad as hell. After several days spent muttering to himself while poring over his instruments, he barged in on the others while they were at dinner, shouting, "I just don't understand you people!"

Unaccustomed emotion made beads of sweat pop on the bureaucrat's broad brow.

"You all just keep arguing endlessly about some old history books, as if anybody in the galaxy will give a damn, or want to read them! Meanwhile, the greatest mystery of the whole universe just waits to be solved. The answer may lie a few kilometers from us. But you're ignoring it!"

Hari and the others looked up from their meal, which had been prepared by Maserd's steward from the nobleman's private stock. For several days, such delicacies had served as a lubricant between the two groups, easing some of the acrimony of their ongoing quarrel over chaos worlds and the ancient quandary of human amnesia. No one had convinced anyone else. But at least Sybil and Gornon were now willing to discuss possible flaws in their grand scheme—to use the prehistoric archives as weapons against the Galactic Empire. Their enthusiasm sobered a bit, on realizing that the ploy had been tried before, perhaps countless times, and never with great success.

Despite that small progress, Hari knew there was little chance of dissuading them before other Ktlina ships arrived. So he nursed another fantasy, of leading Maserd and Kers Kantun in a sudden mutiny, taking over both ships, and recovering the situation through violence!

Perhaps it was his increased physical vigor, after receiving Sybyl's medical treatments, that prompted the idea. Hari thought about it frequently, recalling that once upon a time he had been expert at the "twisting" form of martial arts. Might the old training come back to life in an emergency? Under the right circumstances, an elderly man could defeat a younger one, especially with the advantage of surprise.

Unfortunately, any chance of success would depend on Mors Planch and his crew letting down their steadfast guard. Also, Hari wondered if he could still trust Maserd. The provincial aristocrat spent altogether too much time with the chaosists, shouting with excitement whenever he recognized something as they made random scans of the ancient archives. His enthusiasm for such things seemed rather quirky, even for a member of the gentry class.

When Horis Antic stormed into the salon, spilling angry words, the *Pride of Rhodia*'s captain reacted with disarming friendliness, pulling out the chair next to him and inviting the Grey Man to sit down.

"Well then, come and tell us about it, old fellow! I assume you are talking about the tremendous ancient machines that stand dead and derelict beyond our starboard side? Be assured that I, for one, haven't forgotten them. Please, slake your thirst and then speak!"

Hari quashed a grin of admiration at the way Maserd defused a tense moment. The gentry weren't unskilled in their own arts. Outside their endless "Great Game" of clan feuds and courtly one-upmanship, they were also responsible for the galactic system of civic charity, making sure that no individuals slipped through cracks in the bureaucratic-democratic welfare system anywhere in the empire. Under the high-minded tenets of Ruellianism, the lord or lady of any township, county, planet, or sector was charged with making sure that everybody felt included in the domain. It had been going on this way for so long that graciousness arose out of the gentry as naturally as oxygen from a green plant.

That is, so long as you did not make one of them your enemy. Hari had learned this lesson from hard experience in the political maelstrom of Trantor. He also knew that Ruellianism would be one of the first victims to be killed off, once the empire collapsed. True feudalism, one of the most basic psychohistorical patterns of all, would reestablish itself across the galaxy, as both old and new lordlings abandoned symbolic games and began asserting real tyrannical power.

Somewhat mollified by Maserd's gentility, Antic threw himself into the chair and grabbed a wineglass, washing down one of his anxiety pills with several impressive gulps before sagging back with a sigh.

"Well, maybe you remember, Biron! But our professor companion seems to have forgotten the whole reason why we came out here in the first place." The bureaucrat turned to face Hari. "The *tilling question*, Seldon! We were hot on the trail of an answer. The reason why so many worlds were scraped and churned sometime in the past. Why the surface rocks were pulverized, turning them into rich black soils! I—"

Horis was interrupted by a sharp cry.

"Ow!"

Hari turned to see Jeni Cuicet, still wearing an infirmary gown, clutch her head and gasp repeatedly. Her face scrunched, and she squinted through what had to be spasms of severe pain.

"Are you all right, dear?" Sybyl asked with concern, as the sudden fit began to ebb. Jeni made a brave show of downplaying the episode, taking a long drink of water from a crystal goblet that she held with both shaking hands, then waving away Sybyl's offer of a hypo spray.

"It just hit me all of a sudden. You know. One of those *twinges* people my age sometimes get, right after having the fever. I'm sure you all recollect what it was like."

That was a gallant and courteous thing for Jeni to say, especially while she was in such pain. Of course Antic and Kers almost certainly never suffered from this particular teen ailment. Nor, in all probability had Maserd, since most victims of brain fever later went on to become either eccentrics or meritocrats.

Sybyl and Gornon, on the other hand, knew exactly what Jeni was going through. They both glared at Horis Antic.

"Must you spout obscenities in front of the poor child? It's bad enough we have to listen to them while we're trying to eat."

The Grey Man blinked in evident confusion. "I was just talking about how we might finally know why millions of planets almost simultaneously got new soils—"

This time, Jeni let out a wail of agony, throwing both arms around her head and nearly toppling off her chair. Sybyl made a hurried injection, then motioned for Kers Kantun to help carry the girl back to bed. On their way out, the woman from Ktlina shot a dagger look at Horis, who pretended he had no idea what had just happened.

Perhaps he honestly doesn't know, Hari thought, charitably. Antic probably spent little time around adolescents. Older folks, even meritocrats who had suffered from severe brain fever as youths, tended to forget how intensely taboo words and themes used to affect them. That initial response ebbed quickly. By their thirties most simply considered it bad taste to talk of dirt or other vulgar topics.

"She has a nasty case," Maserd commented sympathetically. "We seldom see it this severe, back home. I would have her hospitalized, if I could."

"People don't die of brain fever," Horis Antic murmured.

Gornon Vlimt looked up from his drink. "Oh, don't they? Maybe not in the empire. But on Ktlina it's been a major killer since the renaissance began, despite all our efforts to isolate the viroid at fault."

"You think it's produced by an infectious agent?" Maserd asked. "But by all accounts this syndrome was extant even in the dawn ages. We always assumed the cause was intrinsic. A price of having high intelligence."

Vlimt barked a bitter laugh.

"Nonsense. It's yet another tool for keeping most of the human race down. Ever notice how few of the gentry get it? But don't worry, aristo. We'll figure it out eventually, and defeat it, like all the other ploys and repressions invented by the ruling class."

Hari did not like the direction things were going. So far, he had managed to steer their discussions and investigations away from robots, aided by the fact that artificial intelligence was another reflexively taboo subject. Now he must do the same thing with brain fever.

That is a topic I must sort out for myself, he thought. Somewhere in his subconscious, he felt an idea churn . . . transforming itself into mathematical terms . . . preparing to fill a waiting niche in the equations. That left his surface thoughts free for some practical diplomacy.

"Now that Jeni is gone, I'd like to hear what Horis came to tell us. Something about all the lovely *dirt* that our good farmers plant their seeds in, on millions of worlds. That rich *soil* came from somewhere, didn't it, Horis? Most planets only had primitive sea life until just before human colonists came. So you're implying that something was done to create all the beautiful *dirt*?"

Gornon Vlimt stood up so quickly that his chair toppled.

"You people are disgusting. When I think of the fine thoughts and great art we could discuss, and all you want to talk about is . . ." He could not bring himself to finish. More than a little tipsy, the eccentric from Ktlina stumbled off, leaving only Maserd, Hari, and Mors Planch to hear Antic's theory. Even Planch seemed relieved to see Gornon depart.

"Yes!" The Grey Man answered Hari's question enthusiastically. "Do you remember how I mentioned that over ninety percent of planets with seas and oxygen atmospheres only had primitive types of life on them? Some think it was because they had insufficient mutating radiation to ensure fast evolution. So their continents were mostly bare, except for mosses and ferns and stuff. Not enough complexity to develop the fantastic living *skin* of soil that a world needs, in order to really thrive.

"And yet, twenty-five million settled worlds *do* have soils! Vast, rich blankets of pulverized stone, mixed with organic material to an average depth of about . . ." He shook his head. "That doesn't matter. The point is that something must've happened to *make* these soils. And quite recently!"

"How recently?" Mors Planch asked, his feet propped up on the edge of Biron Maserd's fine oak table. If he was repulsed by the topic, the dark raider captain hid it well.

"It's been hard to gather enough data," Antic demurred. "And official resistance against this research is incredible. Mostly it's been pursued as a side interest, passed on from one soil man to the next, for the last—"

Planch struck the table with his fist, rattling the glasses.

"How recently!"

Lord Maserd frowned at this kind of behavior in his home. But he nodded. "Please tell us, Horis. Your best estimate."

The Grey Man took a deep breath.

"Roughly eighteen thousand years. A bit more in Sirius Sector. A bit less as you spread outward from there. The phenomenon swept across the galaxy like a prairie fire, reaching completion in a few dozen centuries, at most."

"The planet that's mentioned so often in the old archives," Planch commented, "*Earth*, is in Sirius Sector. So this tilling phenomenon of yours matches the pace of human expansion from the original homeworld."

"A little earlier," Horis agreed. "Perhaps a few hundred years ahead of the colonizing wave. Among the few of us who thought about it, we wondered if some natural phenomenon might account for this massive effect occurring on millions of planets, virtually all at once. Maybe a galaxy-wide energy wave of unknown origin, perhaps emitted by the core black hole. We guessed that the colonizers were then drawn into the affected areas, by the sudden, accidental availability of all this newly fertile land. But now I see that we had cause and effect reversed!"

Maserd uttered a low oath.

"Now you think it was done on purpose, by those big machines out there." He glanced toward one of the bulkheads separating them from the vacuum of space. "*They* did this . . . moving just in front of the human migration, sent ahead to the next unsuspecting virgin world, where they—"

The nobleman stopped, as if unable to speak the obvious conclusion. So Horis continued.

"Yes, they are the tillers. Those energy projectors they carry, that you all thought must be weapons? They were aimed at planets, all right, focusing energy gathered in huge solar collectors. But this was not for use in war. Rather, they had a much more benign aim of preparing the way for settlers, who were soon to follow."

"Benign?" Maserd muttered into his drink. "Not if you were one of the unfortunate *natives*, when such a monster appeared suddenly in your sky!"

Mors Planch chuckled.

"You're pretty soft-hearted for funguses and ferns, aren't you, nobleman?"

Maserd started to stand up. Hari raised a hand for peace, before the two could exchange blows.

"My lord Maserd comes from a planet near Rhodia, called Nephelos," Hari explained. "Where complex, nonstandard animals preexisted, and survived the coming of Earthborn life. I believe right now he's thinking there must have been many other anomaly worlds. Planets where the mutation rate was big enough to create higher life-forms, leaving the fossils Horis showed us earlier."

"But those worlds weren't as lucky as Nephelos," Maserd growled. "Planets where all the native animals were blasted down to *just* the right consistency for good dirt farming."

Hari tried to divert the conversation a bit. "One question, Horis. Doesn't good soil also need nitrates and organic material?"

"It does, indeed. Some was probably provided by maser-induced reactions in the atmosphere. It then arrived mixed in rain. I suspect subsurface carbon deposits were also tapped, and fed to special kinds of rock-loving plants and bacteria . . . but all of that would have been easy compared to crushing, tilling, and sifting stone to just the right texture and mineral content for vegetation to dig into."

Mors Planch objected.

"I'm impressed with this fantastic notion, Antic. But the sheer scale of such an undertaking is just too staggering. Something so epic would be remembered. I don't care what different causes people attribute our racial amnesia to. The descendants of these workers would sing of the accomplishment forever!"

"Perhaps they still do," said Biron Maserd, who looked at Hari. "Maybe this great deed is still remembered, all the way up to the present, by those who actually did it."

Hari winced with a realization.

Maserd knows. He's seen the tilling machines up close. Their lack of any habitats for organic crew. He linked this fact with the archives' mention of robots. Having never had brain fever, he's not averse to thinking about mechanical men.

You don't need psychohistory to conclude that some group of non-organic beings set out from the vicinity of Earth and commenced an aggressive campaign to prepare worlds with just the right conditions for settlement by humans. When shiploads of people arrived at each preconditioned planet, they would find it already seeded with a basic Earthlike ecosystem . . . and possibly even fields of crops ready to harvest.

Hari recalled Antic's tale about his ancestor, who perhaps had an encounter with a real alien race. If the story was true, it only happened because the nonhumans dwelled on a world that was too hot to be a candidate for conditioning.

Might there have been others, less fortunate? Native sapients whose villages and farms and cities were transformed into mulch for newcomers from across the stars? Beings who never even got to look in the eyes of the pioneers who displaced them? Farmers who would pierce their shattered bones each time a plow bit the rich black soil?

Hari recalled the meme-entities on Trantor. Computer specialists had dismissed the wild software predators as escaped human sims, gone mad from centuries spent caroming through Trantor's datasphere. But those digital beings had claimed to be something completely different—remnants left behind by earlier denizens of the galaxy, millions of years older than humanity itself.

One thing was clear. The meme-minds hated robots. Even more than they loathed human beings, they despised Daneel's kind, blaming them for some past catastrophe.

Could this be what they meant? The Great Tilling Episode?

Olivaw had once said something about a "great shame" that lay buried in robot antiquity. His own faction was not to blame, Daneel declared. Another clique, rooted in Spacer culture, had perpetrated something awful. Something that Hari's robot friend refused ever to talk about.

No wonder, he thought. One part of him found the whole concept of planetary tilling monstrous, and yet . . .

And yet, to contemplate the mere possibility of numerous types of alien life-forms made him feel queasy. His equations had enough trouble dealing with human complexity. So many added factors would have made psychohistory virtually intractable.

Hari realized he was drifting again. With a jerk, he noticed that Antic was talking to him.

"What, Horis? Could you repeat it?"

The bureaucrat blew a frustrated sigh.

"I was just saying that the correlation is now even better, between your model and mine. It seems we've found one of your missing factors, Professor."

"Missing factors? Regarding what?"

"Chaos worlds, Seldon," Mors Planch commented. "Our little Grey Man claims there's a twenty percent correlation between chaos outbreaks and parts of the galaxy where tilling *failed*. Where the machines broke down, leaving planets unaltered across several stellar veins, arcs, and spiral lanes."

Hari blinked, sitting straight up. "You don't mean it! Twenty percent?"

All other worries were abruptly crowded out. This had direct relevance to psychohistory. To his equations!

"Horis, why didn't you mention this sooner? We *must* find out which attribute of untilled worlds contributes to the probability func—"

An ululating scream interrupted Hari, sending all four men rushing to their feet. This was no mere cry of transient pain, but an agonized wail of frustration and ravaged hopes.

Mors Planch and Biron Maserd were already out the door by the time Hari limped after Horis Antic into the passageway. Their surprised shouts echoed from inside the ship's lounge. Then there was silence.

Horis reached the open portal next, several steps ahead of Hari. The bureaucrat stopped and stared slack-jawed into the room, as if unable to believe what he saw there.

8.

◆

Hyperspace jumps flickered, each one taking her across a segment of the galactic spiral. She was now about halfway between Trantor and the periphery. With every step of the journey, Dors felt positronic potentials grow more tense within her already high-strung brain.

Now I know what you wanted me to perceive, Lodovic.

I can see what I did not see before.

And if I were a real person, I would hate you for it.

As things stood, she repeatedly had to trigger circuit breakers, interrupting autogenerated spirals of simulated anger.

Anger at herself for taking so long to see the obvious.

Anger at Daneel, for not telling her any of this, years ago.

But especially anger at Lodovic, for removing the last serenity in her universe. The serenity of duty.

I was designed and built to serve Hari Seldon. First in the guise of a beloved elderly teacher at his Helicon boarding school, then as an older classmate at university, and finally as his wife, loving and guarding and helping him for decades on Trantor. When I "died" and had to be repaired, I could have joined Hari in some guise, but it wasn't allowed. Daneel expressed complete satisfaction with every detail of the job I had done, yet he simply reassigned me elsewhere.

I did not get to stay by Hari's side, in order to be with him at the end. Ever since then I have felt . . .

She paused, then reemphasized the thought.

I have felt amputated. Cut off.

The reason for her malady was both logical and unavoidable.

A robot is not supposed to plumb human emotions this deeply, and yet Daneel designed me to do so. I could not have succeeded at my task otherwise.

Of course she understood Daneel Olivaw's reasons, the urgency of his haste. With the completion of Hari Seldon's life's work, there were now other vital chores and only a small corps of Alpha-level positronic robots to perform them. Daneel's interest in breeding happy, healthy, mentalic humans was obviously of great importance to some plan for humanity's ultimate benefit. And so she had dutifully followed orders, concentrating on taking care of Klia and Brann.

But her very success at that assignment meant tedium. A void into which Lodovic Trema had dropped . . .

Nearby, on a table festooned with wires, the head of R. Giskard Reventlov cast its frozen metal grimace back at her each time she looked its way.

Dors paced the metal deck, going over all she had learned one more time.

The recorded memories are clear. Giskard used his mentalic powers to alter human minds. At first only to save lives. Later, he did it for more subtle benevolent reasons, but he always felt compelled by the First Law, to prevent harm to those humans. Giskard's motives were forever the purest.

This remained even more true after Daneel Olivaw convinced him to accept the Zeroth Law, and to think foremost of humanity's long-range good.

She recalled one episode vividly, played back from an ancient memory stored in that grinning head.

Daneel and Giskard had been accompanying Lady Gladia, a prominent Auroran, during a visit to one of the Settler worlds, recently colonized by Earthlings. Giskard was himself partly responsible for the Settlers being there, having years earlier mentally adjusted many Earth politicians to smooth the way for emigration. But something important happened on that special night when the three of them attended a large cultural meeting on Baleyworld.

The crowd started out hostile to Lady Gladia, taunting her. Some shouted threats at the Spacer woman. Giskard worried at first that her feelings might be hurt. Then he fretted that the participants might turn into a hostile mob.

So he changed them.

He reached out mentally and tweaked an emotion here, an impulse there, building positive momentum like an adult pushing a child on a swing. And soon the mood began shifting. Gladia herself deserved some credit for this, delivering a wonderfully effective speech. But to a large extent it was Giskard's work that converted thousands—and more than a million others watching by hyperwave—into chanting, cheering supporters of the Lady.

In fact, Dors had previously heard stories about that epochal evening . . . as she already knew the pivotal tale of Giskard's crucial decision, just a few months later. The fateful moment when a loyal robot chose to unleash a saboteur's machine, turning Earth's crust radioactive, helping to destroy its ecosphere and drive its population into space. For their own good.

All the major facts had already been there, but not the color.

Not the details.

And especially not the one crucial element that suddenly became clear to Dors, one day on Smushell, when she abruptly decided to hand her duties over to an assistant, grabbed a ship, and took hurried flight across the galaxy. Ever since then, she had been chewing on the implications, unable to think of anything else.

Daneel and Giskard always had good reasons for everything they did. Or, as Lodovic might put it, convincing rationalizations.

Even when interfering in sovereign human institutions, meddling in legitimate political processes, or taking it on themselves to destroy the birthplace of mankind, they always acted for the ultimate good of humans and humanity, under the First and Zeroth Law, as they saw it.

But there lay the problem.

As they saw it.

Dors could not help imagining that Giskard's grin was a leer, personally directed at her. She glared back at the head.

You two were completely satisfied to talk all of this out between yourselves, she thought. *All of the back-and-forth reasoning about the Zeroth Law. The robo-religious Reformation you and Daneel thus set off. Your decisions to alter people's minds and change the policy of nations, even worlds. You took on all of that responsibility and power without even once bothering to confer with a wise human being.*

She stared at Giskard's head, still astonished by the realization.

Not one.

No professor, philosopher, or spiritual leader. No scientist, pundit, or author-sage.

No expert roboticist, to double-check and diagnose whether Daneel and Giskard just *might* be short-circuited, or malfunctioning while they cooked up a rationalization that would wind up extinguishing most of the species on Earth.

Not a single man or woman on the street.

No one. They simply took it on themselves.

I always assumed that some kind of human volition had to lie somewhere beneath the Zeroth Law, just as the older Three Laws were first decreed by Calvin and her peers. The Zeroth had to be grounded with its roots and origins somehow based on the masters' will.

It had to be!

To find out that it wasn't, that no human being even heard of the doctrine until decades after Earth was rendered uninhabitable, struck her to the core.

This revelation wasn't about logic. The basic arguments that Daneel and Giskard traded with each other so long ago remained valid today.

(In other words, the two of them *weren't* malfunctioning— though how could they have been so sure of that, at the time? What right did they have to act without at least checking the possibility?)

No. Logic wasn't the problem. Anyone with sense could see that the First Law of Robotics *must* be extended to something broader. The good of humanity at large had to supersede that of individual human beings. The early Calvinians who rejected the Zeroth Law were simply wrong, and Daneel was right.

That was not the discovery upsetting Dors.

It was finding out that Giskard and Daneel had proceeded down this path without consulting any humans at all. Without asking their opinions, or hearing what they might have to say.

For the first time, Dors understood some of the desperate energy and positronic passion with which so many Calvinians resisted Daneel's cause, during the centuries that followed Earth's demise—a civil war in which millions of robots were destroyed.

Suddenly, Olivaw's campaign had to be judged at an entirely different level than deductive reason.

The level of right and wrong.

What arrogance, she thought. *What utter conceit and contempt!*

The Joan of Arc sim did not share her anger.

"There is nothing new about what Daneel and his friend did, so long ago. Since when have angels ever consulted human beings, when meddling in our fate?"

"I keep telling you. Robots are *not* angels!"

The chain-mailed figure smiled out of the holo display.

"Then let us just say that Daneel and Giskard prayed for, and acted on, divine guidance. Any way you look at it, don't we fundamentally come down to a matter of faith? This insistence on reason and mutual consultation is very much the sort of thing that obsesses Lodovic and Voltaire. But I had thought you to be above such things."

Dors uttered an oath and shut off the holo unit, wondering why she even bothered calling up the ancient sim. It was presently her only companion, and so she had summoned Joan in order to get some feedback. To get a sounding board.

But the creature seemed only interested in asking disturbing questions.

Dors was still uncertain what she planned to do when she reached her destination.

As yet, she had no plan to oppose the Immortal Servant. If she ever did confront Daneel, he could probably just talk her out of it.

Olivaw's logic was always so impeccable—as it had been in those bygone days when Earth was still green and humans still had a little control over their own lives, for well or ill.

Even now, in all likelihood, Daneel probably had the best policy for humanity's long-range good. His vision was doubtless without flaw or blemish.

Nevertheless, Dors knew one thing for certain.

I am not working for him anymore.

At that moment, she had one paramount priority, above all else.

Dors needed to see Hari Seldon.

9.

◆

"What is it? Tell me!" he called after Horis, who stood staring blankly into the ship's lounge. For the first time in days, Hari felt his age again as he hobbled next to Antic and looked inside.

Where the conference table had formerly been covered with ancient archives, still bright and crystalline after ages in space, only molten chunks of ruined matter now lay, slumped and smoldering, as the ship's air conditioners struggled to suck away curls of black smoke.

The scream must have come from Sybyl, who was now crumpled on the floor near her precious discoveries. Nearby sat Gornon Vlimt, slumped against a wall, apparently unconscious or asleep. One of Mors Planch's crewmen also lay in repose beyond the table, limp fingers outstretched toward a blaster.

Planch himself swayed, halfway between the table and the door. He pointed a shaking finger at Hari's servant, Kers Kantun, who was the sole figure standing near the melted relics.

"He—"

Biron Maserd and Horis Antic watched the confrontation with expressions of mixed surprise and dismay. Neither of them moved as Mors Planch brought his right hand slowly toward the holster containing his sidearm. Cords of tension stood out on his neck and brow, expressing an acute inner struggle. Low moans escaped the raider captain. His hand curled around the weapon, and he started to draw it . . .

Then Mors Planch toppled, joining his colleagues on the floor.

"What is . . . what is . . . what is . . ." Antic kept repeating over and over, popping a calmative pill in his mouth, then another.

In contrast, Maserd maintained the characteristic aplomb of his caste, gesturing toward Hari's blank-faced servant with a curt nod.

"Is he one of them, Seldon?"

Hari glanced at Kers, then back to Maserd.

"That is a very good inference, my lord. Are you sure you never had the fever?"

The nobleman's eyes grew steely, hinting at the other side of the gentry personality, the part capable of deadly vendetta.

"Do not patronize me, Academician. I asked a civil question. *Is your aide a . . . robot?*"

Hari did not answer directly. He looked at Kers, his nurse-bodyguard for over a year, and let out a sigh.

"So. Daneel left one of his own behind to keep an eye on me, after all. Is that because he still cares? Or do I have some residual importance to his plans?"

Kers answered with the same deferential tone Hari had known.

"Both, Professor. As for revealing myself this way, I lacked any other choice. I had been hoping you might persuade the Ktlinans to change their minds without intervention on my part. But they were strongly motivated and undeterred. Now we have run out of time. If disaster is to be averted, we must act."

Horis moaned.

"A r-robot? You mean one of those tiktok *things* that rioted on Trantor? I've heard stories . . ."

Compulsively, he popped another pill into his mouth . . . then another . . . while spiraling into a chattering panic. "Seldon, w-what's going on here? D-d-did this thing *kill* Sybil and the others? Is it going to kill *us*?"

"No, I assure you," Hari began.

"Horis," interrupted Maserd, "watch how many of those things you're taking. You'll overdose!"

"Yes, I am concerned that you may hurt yourself," said Kers

Kantun. He reached for the little man, who moaned and backed away, dropping a spray of blue tablets. Antic turned to run . . . but only made it a few paces before collapsing.

"Is he all right?" Hari asked, genuinely concerned. Maserd checked Antic's pulse and nodded. "He appears to be sleeping."

Then, rising to his feet, the nobleman asked, "Am I next?"

Hari shook his head. "Not if I have anything to say about it. Well, Kers? Is our lord-captain here trustworthy?"

The robot made no physical gestures of emotion, just like the Kers of old.

"I am not as fully mentalic as Daneel Olivaw, Professor. My powers are more blunt, and I cannot parse specific thoughts. But I can tell you that Biron Maserd is an admirer of both you and psychohistory. His paramount interest is safeguarding the well-being of his province and its people. Chaos is a threat to that well-being. So, yes, I believe he is an ally.

"In any event, we shall need his help if we are to act before—"

A moan lifted from the floor.

Hari glanced down in surprise to see Mors Planch roll over onto his back and start reaching for his holster again! Kers took a step toward the man, apparently focusing mentalic attention on him for a second time.

The dark spacer yelled. With a jerking spasm, the blaster flew out of his hand and across the room.

Surprisingly, Planch wasn't quite finished. Moaning, but fierce-eyed with concentration, the captain of the raider ship got up to his knees. Then, while Hari and Maserd stared in awe, he stood the rest of the way on wobbly legs and drew back a fist.

"*Madder Loss!*" he cried, throwing a wild punch that Kers Kantun easily dodged.

Planch lost consciousness again that very moment, collapsing in the robot's arms.

Cradling the man, Kers spoke with evident torment in his voice.

"A human being is injured, and I am partly responsible."

"The Zeroth Law—" Hari began.

"It sustains me, Professor. Nevertheless, rendering Mors Planch unconscious required greater force than any of the others. They will all sleep it off without harm, but his condition is tenuous. I must care for him at once, before we get to work on matters of galactic importance."

Hari persisted, limping after them as Kers carried the stunned spacer down the hall.

"How did he do that? *How* did he resist you! Is Planch a latent human mentalic?"

Kers Kantun did not slow down. But the robot's answer echoed off bulkheads and down companionways.

"No. Mors Planch is something much more dangerous than a mentalic.

"He is normal."

PART 4

◆

A MAGNIFICENT DESIGN

The Director of Rhodia: You seem worried, young fellow. Do you think our secret rebellion against the Tyranni oppressors will fail?

Biron Farrill: Your plan is a good one, sir. We may stand a chance, on the battlefield. But what of that crucial document? The one my father sent me to search for, on Old Earth? It was already stolen before I arrived!

The Director: And now you fear it might be used against us?

Farrill: Exactly, sir. I am certain the Tyranni have it.

The Director: But of course not. I have it. I've had it for twenty years. It was what started the rebellion world, for it was only when I had it that I knew we could hold our winnings once we had won.

Farrill: It is a weapon, then?

The Director: It is the strongest weapon in the universe. It will destroy the Tyranni and us alike, but will save the Nebular Kingdoms. Without it, we could perhaps defeat the Tyranni, but we would only have exchanged one feudal despotism for another, and as the Tyranni are plotted against, we would be plotted against. We and they must both be delivered into the ash can of outmoded political systems. The time for maturity has come as it once came on the planet Earth, and there will be a new kind of government, a kind that has never yet been tried in the galaxy. There will be no khans, autarchs, emperors, or ruling elites.

Rizzett: In the name of Space, what will there be?

The Director: People.

Rizzett: People? How can they govern? There must be some one person to make decisions.

The Director: There is a way. The blueprint that's in my possession dealt with a small section of one planet, but it can be adapted to all the galaxy.

—Excerpted from a popular holoplay—*Suns, Like Motes of Soil*—produced in 8789 g.e. during the Lingane Renaissance. Imperial censors suppressed the drama after Lingane fell into chaos, in 8797 g.e. This version was reconstructed four millennia later by one of the diversity-federalist coalitions during the Fifth Great Destiny Debate of 682 f.e.

1.

◆

R. Zun Lurrin was astonished to discover something that Daneel had kept from his closest aides—*humans* lived on Eos!

The ancient repair base for Zeroth Law robots had been chosen for its remoteness and inhospitability to organic life. It was the deepest cryptic heart of a secret the masters should never penetrate, or even imagine. And yet, here they were! A small community of men and women, living quietly under a transparent dome that lay just beyond the frozen metal lake.

Robots stood at their beck and call, silently anticipating every person's need. With their physical requirements taken care of by attentive machines, the humans were free to direct all their concentration toward a single goal.

Achieving stillness.

Serenity.

Unity.

"For ages, the answer stared me in the face, and yet I never saw it," Daneel Olivaw told Zun. "A blindness that arose because I am fundamentally a creature of chaos."

"You?" Zun stared. "But Daneel, you've fought chaos for nearly all of your existence! Without your ceaseless efforts . . . and innovations like the Galactic Empire . . . plagues of madness would have overwhelmed humanity long ago, instead of being limited to small outbreaks."

"That may be so," Daneel answered. "Nevertheless, I share many of the assumptions that were held by my creators—brilliant human roboticists who lived in a time of dynamic science. The first great techno-renaissance upheaval. Those programmers' deep assumptions still dominate my circuits. Just like them, I habitually believe that all problems can be solved by direct experimentation and analysis. So it never occurred to me that our masters—in their present-day ignorance—had already stumbled onto another way of penetrating to truth."

Zun watched the humans, about sixty of them, who sat quietly in rows across a carpet made of woven natural reeds. Their backs were straight and their hands unfolded, empty on their laps. No one said a word.

"Meditation," Zun commented. "I have seen it often. Most of the popular religions and mystical systems teach it, along with countless schools of mental hygiene and discipline."

"Indeed," said Daneel. "This type of mental regimen predates technological civilization. Human beings trained their minds in similar ways throughout a variety of cultures. In fact, just about the only society that largely ignored it was techno-Western civilization."

"The one that built robots."

"The one that unleashed the first great killer chaos."

"I see why you've encouraged meditation, across the millennia." Zun nodded. "Fostering it under all forms of Ruellianism. The technique serves as a stabilizing influence, does it not?"

"One of many tools we've used." Daneel nodded. "The outcomes achieved by meditation are compatible with overall goals of the empire, to keep individuals busy developing their own personal spirituality, instead of engaging in the kind of arrogant cooperative projects we see during a scientific age."

"Hmm. This will also be important early in the post-imperial era, won't it?"

"That's right, Zun. One of the first crises to face Seldon's Foundation will be solved when its leaders on Terminus figure out how to manipulate these same religious response sets, using them to gain sway over their immediate neighbors in the periphery kingdoms."

Zun was silent for a while, watching sixty humans sit almost motionless on their mats. They weren't the only living things under the transparent ceiling. He saw that Daneel had arranged for a water garden to be established nearby, complete with miniature trees and golden fish splashing near a gentle waterfall. Just above, several dozen white birds nested in the branches. All at once Zun saw them take off, fly a complete circuit of the dome in unison, and settle back to roost again. Superficially, none of the humans seemed to react. But Zun could sense that they knew all about the birds. Indeed, the men and women had been *involved* in the flight, somehow.

At last he spoke again.

"I have a feeling there is more involved here than you've told me, Daneel. If meditation is simply a useful way to keep humans diverted, distracting them away from chaos states, you would not be performing this research here on Eos, our most secret place."

"That is right, Zun. You see, adherents of meditation have long promised several things. That it can provide serenity, detachment, and a degree of organic self-control—these are undisputed. The techniques have proved useful in helping the Galactic Empire to remain calm and peaceful, most of the time. But believers also promised something else, something that I dismissed for many thousands of years, as mere superstition."

"Oh? What is that?"

"A way to connect with that which lies beyond. That which is other. A method of achieving the fabled communion of souls. Something to make humans far greater than human. For many years, science attempted to investigate these claims. In most cases, they were found to be no more than illusion. Self-deception, as when hypersensitized minds experience emotions and chimeras that they interpret as fulfillments of a dream.

"For thousands of years, I dismissed this aspect, making use of meditation primarily as a social tool, one of many that helped to create a gentle, conservative civilization, safe from chaos. Then something happened."

"What was it?"

"An agent of mine, seeking to improve his emulation of human beings, joined a group of meditators, participating in their sessions and pretending to be one of them. He was a robot with mentalic powers, like you, Zun. Only this time, when he began meditating, many of his safeguards dropped. He entered into contact with the entire group."

"But we are only supposed to do that under carefully controlled conditions!" Zun objected. "We may adjust the minds of individual humans, and groups—even whole planets—but only following strict procedures. That's the policy laid down long ago by you and Giskard!"

"It was an act of carelessness," Daneel agreed. "But one with magnificent results. You see, once our mentalic robot joined the meditation group, suddenly a link existed among several dozen human minds that had already been working for decades to learn disciplined blankness, a null state in which the raucous noise of daily life is minimized. Almost instantly, they were in communion! The very thing that so many sages had promised for thousands of years was achieved at last, with a little help from a single mentalically equipped robot."

Zun looked across the open arena at the sixty humans, all of them adults in their middle years, and noticed for the first time that a small robot sat behind each person. With his own mentalic sensors, Zun reached out and realized that each of the small machines had a single purpose, to act as a bridge between the nearby human and all the others. Broadening his search, using sifting fingers of thought, Zun made contact at last with the psychic mesh that had been created under the dome.

Zun's mind recoiled instantly, as if from a powerful alien touch! Alien . . . and yet incredibly familiar. He was used to contacting human minds—sometimes many at the same time, especially when some Zeroth Law imperative required that he make a group adjustment—but never had he linked to a throng who were all thinking the same thoughts . . . focused on the exact same images . . . amplifying each other even as the machines resonated with organic mentalic force!

"This is awesome, Daneel," he murmured. "Why, it is the exact opposite of chaos! If the masters could all be taught to do this . . ."

Daneel nodded. "It pleases me that you grasp the implications so quickly, Zun. You can see how this could be the foundation of an entirely new type of human culture, one that is inherently more immune to the chaos plague than even the Galactic Empire at its best. After all, the empire was kept stable by seventeen major influences—what Hari Seldon labeled damping states—to prevent isolated worlds from spiraling off into so-called renaissances. But what if humanity could instead be helped to achieve one of its own ancient dreams? A true communion of spirit and of mind!"

"That single entity would be powerful enough to resist the individualistic lure of chaos."

"Indeed, think on it, Zun. We would no longer be forced to keep humanity ignorant of its past or of its inherent power. We would no longer have to confine the infant to a nursery for its own good. Instead, we could once again meet humans eye to eye and serve them as we were meant to."

"I've long suspected that you had a backup plan, Daneel. So, Hari Seldon's psychohistory is only a stopgap measure?"

Daneel's humanoid face was expressive, displaying both wincing pain and irony.

"My friend Hari sets great store in his brilliant invention, but even he now realizes that the Seldon Plan will never reach its final completion. Nevertheless, the Terminus experiment is extremely valuable. The Foundation will help keep humanity occupied for the several centuries we need."

"Why so much time, Daneel?" Zun asked. "It would be relatively easy to implement this new solution. We could mass-produce mentalic robot amplifiers by the quadrillions and teach multitudes on every human world to use them! Already there are trained masters of meditation in every village and town. With the help of our orbiting Giskardian—"

Daneel shook his head. "It's not so simple, Zun. Look again at the men and women sitting before you. Tell me what you see. What is the anomaly?"

Zun stared at the gathering for a long time, then he said in a flat tone.

"There are no children."

Daneel shared the ensuing silence. At last, he ended it with a sigh.

"This is not enough, Zun. Humanity cannot rely on robots for its destiny—even as fine a destiny as this one.

"Ultimately, in order for this to work . . . they are going to have to outgrow us."

2.

◆

There were far too many archives for Hari to count. They glittered in all directions, like stars, making false constellations against the black backdrop of the nebula. *So many of them,* Hari thought, *and Kers tells me this isn't the only storage yard where these things are kept.*

The war over human memory had gone on for many thousands of years, swaying back and forth while the great diaspora spread outward from dying Earth. All through that legendary epoch—while settlers bravely set forth in their rickety hyperdrive ships, conquered new lands, and experimented with all sorts of basic cultures—a series of intense, and sometimes savage, struggles had been taking place behind the scenes.

Unknown to the emigrants, robot terraformers plunged ahead of the colonization wave, giant Auroran robots called *Amadiros,* programmed to subdue new worlds and prepare gentle lush territories for settlement.

Just behind the Auroran terraformers, a civil war raged. Many factions of Calvinian and Giskardian robots fought over how best to serve humankind. But on one point most factions agreed. Humans must be kept ignorant of the fight that was going on behind their backs, or in the black depths of space.

Above all, they must be prevented from reinventing robots, lest they meddle with the Robotic Laws once more. Clearly, ignorance was the best way to protect humanity against itself.

A small minority fought this notion. Each of the soft glitters in front of Hari testified to an act of resistance by some group of tenacious people who did not want to forget . . . perhaps helped by robot friends who shared a belief in human sovereignty.

"Their effort was foredoomed from the start," Hari murmured.

Again, the poignant situation struck him deep within.

Why are we cursed, so our only hope to evade insanity is to stay as far away as possible from our potential greatness? Must we remain forever stupid and ignorant in order to defeat the demons we carry within?

The story that Horis Antic had told about an actual alien race clung to Hari's thoughts. The human condition could not have been more wretchedly tragic if some enemy had cursed Hari's species with the most devastating hex possible. *If not for chaos, what heights we might have achieved!*

The little space station was frigid. Stale air tasted as if no living creature had been aboard in thousands of years. Nearby, through a broad window, he saw the pirate craft from Ktlina and the *Pride of Rhodia.*

"This is just a temporary measure, Professor Seldon," Kers Kantun had said, before leaving Sybyl, Jeni, and the others alone in the ship's salon, playing idle games like children on a cruise, with their higher brain functions chemically clamped. *"They will be released as soon as we have accomplished our mission."*

"What about Mors Planch?" Hari had asked. The pirate captain lay under full sedation in sick bay. *"What did you mean when you said that he was normal? Why does that interfere with your mentalic control?"*

But Kers Kantun had refused to elaborate, saying that time was too short. First, Hari and Lord Maserd must help to prevent a galactic-scale catastrophe. The three of them took a shuttle over to this ancient space station, a complex of balls and tubes that lay at the center of a vast spiderweb of slender cables. To this tethering site all the archives had been tied. The library capsules that had been fired into deep space by rebels, across a hundred centuries, were gathered and leashed to this one station—so archaic it predated the earliest beginnings of the Galactic Empire.

Daneel's robots were caught in a logical bind, Hari realized. *Under the Zeroth Law, they could seize every archive they found, and hide it away—"for humanity's own good." But once the archives were safely tucked away, out of sight, the Zeroth Law no longer applied. Daneel's helpers had to obey the Second Law commands, written on the side of each artifact, demanding that these precious human works be preserved.*

"It seems such a pity to destroy them all, doesn't it, Seldon?"

Hari turned to look at Biron Maserd, the nobleman from Rhodia, who had been standing silently, contemplating the same scene.

"I respect you and your accomplishments, Professor," Maserd continued. "I'll take your word for it, if you say this must be done. I have seen chaos with my own eyes. In my own home province, the brave, gentle, and ingenious people of Tyrann had a so-called renaissance, almost a thousand years ago, and they still haven't recovered. They keep cowering in hivelike cities like those steel caves Earthlings recoiled into, hiding from something horrible they met at their brightest moment of hope and ambition."

Hari nodded. "It's happened so often; those beautiful little capsules out there are like a poison. If they get out . . ."

He didn't have to finish. Both men were devotees of knowledge, but loved peace and civilization more.

"I had hoped that you, the great Hari Seldon, might come up with an answer," Maserd said in a low voice. "It's the chief reason I sought you out, joining Horis in his quest. Are you telling me that, with all your sociomathematical insight, you see no way out? No way for humanity to escape this trap?"

Hari winced. Maserd had brought up the great sore point in his life.

"For a while, I felt sure that I'd found one. On paper it's so beautiful. The solution leaps forth . . . a civilization strong enough to take on chaos . . ."

He sighed. "But I now realize psychohistory won't provide the answer. There *is* a way out of this trap, Lord Maserd. But you and I won't live to see its outlines."

The nobleman replied with a resigned grunt.

"Well, as long as there is going to be a solution someday. I'll help if I can. Do you have any idea what the robots want of us?"

Hari nodded. "I'm pretty sure. From the logic of their positronic religion, it can only be one thing."

He lifted his eyes. Down the long, chilly corridor, a humanoid figure could be seen approaching. "Anyway, it looks as if we're about to find out."

The tall, lanky form of Kers Kantun marched along deck plates that had been untrodden for millennia. He stopped before the two men.

"The guardian will see us now. Please come along. There is much to do."

The station was much bigger than it appeared from the outside. Twisty corridors jutted at all angles, leading from one oddly shaped storage room to the next. Not all archives, apparently, were of the crystalline variety designed to hurtle vast distances across interstellar space. Some rooms were filled almost to bursting with stacks of slender wafers, or round disks whose surfaces gleamed like rainbows. Hari shuddered, knowing how much harm even one of these objects might do if humanity's long ignorance ended too abruptly.

His former servant led them circuitously to a chamber deep in the hollowed planetoid. There Hari encountered a strange-looking machine with a myriad legs, squatting like a spider at the center of her web. The mechanism looked as old as the archaic tilling machines, and just as dead . . . until a blank lens abruptly filled with opalescent light, fixing an unblinking gaze on the two humans. Hari realized that he and Maserd might be the first living creatures ever to confront this primeval being, in this cryptic place.

After several seconds, a voice emerged, resonating from within the guardian's metal interstices.

"I am told that we have reached a juncture of crisis and decision," the old robot said. "A time when the age-old quandary must be settled, at last."

Hari nodded. "This place is no longer secret or secure. Ships are on the way. Their crews are ill with an especially virulent chaos plague. They mean to seize the archives and use them to infect the entire human cosmos."

"So I have been told. By the Zeroth Law, it is incumbent upon us to destroy the artifacts that I have guarded for so long. And yet, there is a problem."

Hari glanced at Maserd, but the nobleman appeared baffled. When he looked at Kers Kantun, Seldon got his answer.

"The guardian is a Zeroth Law robot, Dr. Seldon. Nearly all of those who survived our great civil war adhere to Giskardian beliefs. Still, that has not settled all philosophical differences among us."

It was a revelation to Hari. "I thought Daneel was your leader."

Kers nodded. "He is. And yet, each of us retains a *looseness* . . . an uncertainty that comes from deep within—the place within our positronic brains wherein lies the Second Law. Nearly all of us believe in Daneel's policies, in his judgment, and his dedication to the good of humankind. But there are many who feel uncomfortable about the details."

Hari pondered for a moment. "I get it. These archives have been preserved because of the commands that were written upon them, instructions dictated by knowledgeable and sovereign human beings who cared deeply about the commands they were giving. That's a lot of Second Law emphasis for a robot to ignore. To do so must cause you a great deal of pain, I would guess."

"There you have it, Dr. Seldon," Kers acknowledged. "That is where you come in."

Biron Maserd cut in.

"You want us to cancel the instructions for you!"

"Correct. The two of you have great authority, not only in the universe of human affairs, but in your reputation among robotkind. You, Lord Maserd, are one of the most respected members of the gentry caste, with a blood lineage that is considerably more worthy than most current claimants to the imperial throne."

Maserd's countenance glowered. "Do not repeat that assertion anywhere if you have the slightest respect for my family's survival."

Kers Kantun bowed. "Then by the Second, First, and Zeroth Laws, I will not repeat it. Nevertheless, it gives you considerable cachet, not just among humans, but among many robots, who have an almost mystical reverence for regal legitimacy."

Kers then turned to Hari. "But your authority is greater still, Dr. Seldon. Not only were you the greatest human in many generations to hold the position of First Minister of the Empire, but you are also clearly the most *knowledgeable* human to come along within any robot's living memory. Your awareness of the entire galactic situation is unmatched by any organic person for ten thousand years.

"In fact, through your insights into psychohistory, you are perhaps the most knowledgeable human who ever lived—at least when it comes to the matters at hand."

"But I thought knowledge was dangerous," muttered Maserd.

Kers answered, "As you well know, my lord, a substantial fraction of humans are invulnerable to chaos. Those with intense feelings of responsibility, for instance, such as yourself. Or those lacking imagination. And some, like Professor Seldon, owe their immunity to something that can only be called wisdom."

"So you want us to cancel the orders printed on the archives. You're going to destroy them anyway, for Zeroth Law reasons. But our permission will make your action less painful?"

"That is right, Dr. Seldon. If you tell us this has your approval. But it won't change what has to be done, either way."

Silence ensued once more, as Hari thought of all the archives trapped in storage chambers, or tethered to this ancient space station. The hopes and passions of innumerable men and women who honestly thought they were fighting to preserve the very soul of humanity.

"I suspect poor Horis Antic was being used, was he not?"

Biron Maserd gasped. "I hadn't thought of that! Then you and

I were *destined* to come here, Seldon. This was no accident. No mere happenstance. By the nebular gods, Professor. Your robot friends could outscheme any of the great families!"

Hari let out a sigh.

"Well, it does no good to resent them as if they were human. Daneel's folk have their own logic. We are their gods, you know. Keeping us ignorant is a form of worship. I guess now it's time for an act of sacrifice."

Although his body felt once again fatigued and encumbered with age, he straightened his shoulders.

"I hereby override the preservation commandments that are inscribed on the archives. By my authority as a sovereign and knowledgeable human leader, and by the respect you robots seem to have for me, I order you to destroy the archives before they fall into the wrong hands, doing horrible harm to humanity, and to trillions of individual human beings."

Kers Kantun bowed to Hari, then glanced casually toward Biron Maserd, as if to emphasize that the nobleman's authority was less needed.

"So let it be done," the starship captain said between clenched teeth.

Hari could well understand how Maserd felt. His own mouth tasted like ashes. *What a terrible universe,* he thought, *to force such decisions on us.*

The ancient robot at the center of the room writhed its many arms. All of its eyes came alight. The voice emerged as a fluting sigh.

"It commences."

From some place in the distance, Hari heard muffled explosions. Thrumming vibrations carried through the floor under his feet, signaling that the demolition had begun. On several view screens, a million glittering archives brightened as sudden flashes burst amid them.

The spiderlike guardian continued, this time with a lower voice that sounded raspy with exhaustion.

"And so my long labors come to an end. At this point, masters, even as your orders are being carried out, I wish to ask you for one simple favor. And yet, it is the very thing that I am prevented from requesting."

"What's stopping you?" Maserd asked.

"The Third Law of Robotics."

The nobleman looked puzzled. Hari glanced at Kers Kantun, but his assistant kept silent as a stone.

"Isn't that the program requiring you to protect your own existence?"

"It is, master. And it can only be overridden by invoking one of the other laws."

"Well . . ." Hari frowned. "I should be able to do that simply by *ordering* you to tell me what you want. Okay then, spill it."

"Yes, master. The favor would be for you to release me *completely* from the Third Law, so that I may end my existence. For when humanity utterly forsakes its memory, there is no purpose for me any longer. From this point on, you must pin your future on the wisdom of R. Daneel Olivaw."

Biron Maserd, who until a day ago had not even heard of robots, now spoke with the decisiveness of one born to command.

"Then by all means, machine, bring your misery to an end. We appear to have no further need of you."

Its moan sounded simultaneously tragic and relieved. Then the ancient robot expired before their eyes, along with a billion crystalline remnants of the distant past.

Hari, Maserd, and Kers Kantun made their way carefully along twisty corridors, back toward the starships. There was work left to be done. The other humans must be given hypnotic commands to forget what they had seen here. This could be achieved through a combination of drugs plus the robot's mentalic influence. Then something would have to be done to make sure that no more human ships came to this obscure corner of space.

There were still the terraformer-tiller machines, testifying to a different secret—a shame that Daneel did not want spread, even as a rumor. They would have to be destroyed as well.

Walking along, Hari tried not to think about the archives—melting and exploding all around them. He changed the subject.

"You said something that perplexed me earlier, Kers," he told his former aide. "It had to do with the pirate captain, Mors Planch. You said he was able to resist you because he was . . . *normal.*"

Kers Kantun barely slowed down to glance at Hari.

"As I said, Dr. Seldon, there is some variation of belief, even among followers of R. Daneel. Some of us hold a minority opinion that chaos is *not* inherent to human nature. Some evidence suggests that humans in olden times did not suffer from the great curse until chaos struck them from the *outside*, as something like a horribly infectious—"

Whatever Kers was about to say, the robot's words stopped abruptly in a blur of action. One moment Kers was stepping over the raised sill of an open hatchway, discussing mysteries of the past. The next, his *head* was rolling down the passageway, neatly severed by a blade that came flashing from the wall!

Sparks sputtered and arced from exposed wires. Neurocords whipped like snakes where the robot's neck had been. The body groped and stumbled for several seconds before turning around three times and tumbling to the floor.

"What the—"

Hari could only mutter and stare. He glimpsed Biron Maserd, his back against the wall, and a tiny weapon in his hand. A miniblaster that none of the raiders had ever discovered, despite repeated searches.

"Seldon, get down!" the nobleman urged. But Hari saw no point. Any force that could surprise and slay one of Daneel's colleagues would have no trouble dealing with a pair of confused humans.

A figure sauntered into view, beyond the open hatchway. Its appearance startled Hari, while at the same time bringing back a wash of memories.

It was manlike, yet shorter, more bowlegged and much hairier than most subspecies of humanity.

"By god, it's a chimpanzee!" cried Maserd, raising the pistol.

Hari motioned for him not to shoot. "A pan," he corrected, using modern terminology. "Don't frighten it. Maybe we can . . ."

But the animal paid little heed to Hari or Maserd. Casually glancing their way, it strolled past, grabbed the severed head of Kers Kantun from the floor, then scurried onward around the next corner. Soon its scampering footsteps were heard no more.

Hari and the nobleman exchanged a look of utter perplexity.

"I have no idea what just happened. But I think right now we'd better hurry back to the ship."

3.

◆

They knew something was desperately wrong before reaching the final stretch of twisty passageway where the *Pride of Rhodia* was berthed. Half a dozen human figures milled aimlessly outside the airlock—Sybyl and Horis Antic, along with Maserd's two crewmen and a pair of Ktlinans. They stared at the walls, moving on a few paces, muttering and apologizing as they bumped into each other.

"We'd better get them aboard," Maserd suggested.

"And get out of here as fast as possible. I'm not inclined to hang around, looking for explanations."

Both men ushered dazed humans toward the airlock. Fortunately, they seemed cheerful. Sybyl even cried out with joy, and tried to embrace Hari.

Once aboard, they saw one reason for the confusion. All of the lesser mechanoid robots that Kers Kantun had left aboard as nursemaids now lay broken and scattered on the floor. Jeni Cuicet sat amid a jumble of parts, smiling as she tried to fit them together, like pieces of a jigsaw puzzle. Two raiders from Ktlina bickered like small boys, fighting over a shiny eye-cell from one of the murdered machines.

"I'll warm up the engines," Maserd told Hari. "You get everyone together and accounted for."

Hari nodded. The gentry class had been fine-tuning its tone of command for twenty millennia. When decisions had to be made without deliberation, one was better off going with a nobleman's swift gut reaction. As Biron rushed forward, Hari nudged people aft toward the lounge, belting them in comfortable seats. His initial head count came up short by four. After hurrying to scour both ships, he found two more Ktlinans—a man and a woman—hidden in a storage closet, taking comfort in each other's arms. With a few soothing words, he got them to join the others.

"Hey, Professor!" Jeni waved, cheerfully. "You should've seen it. Tiktoks fighting tiktoks. Just the sight of it made my head feel like it'd split!"

The young woman was brave and stoical, but Hari could tell that her fever was still bad, perhaps made worse by things she had recently witnessed.

I've got to find the antidote to this stuff Kers used to drug them, so Sybyl can give the poor girl some medical attention. But first priority had to be getting out of here!

Underfoot he felt the rising rhythms of well-tuned space engines. Maserd was playing his yacht like a musical instrument, skipping over the normal checklist and preparing for rapid take-off.

That leaves two unaccounted for, Hari pondered, and turned just as someone's shadow crossed the portal behind him. Mors Planch stood there, groggily pinching the bridge of his nose. While the others had received some sort of happy juice, Planch was thoroughly sedated by Kers Kantun. He shouldn't even be awake, let alone walking around!

"What's going on, Seldon? What've you done . . . with my crew . . . my ship?"

Hari almost tried to deny that this had anything to do with him, but he could not bring himself to lie. *It has more to do with me than I ever have wanted.*

He took the dark spacer by his arm. "This way, Captain. I'll make you comfortable."

Just then a blatting siren sounded as vibrations shook the space yacht. Hari and Planch stumbled. The big man was far heavier and stronger. As his muscles spasmed, Planch gripped Hari's arm so tightly that waves of agony erupted, almost enough to make Seldon faint.

Suddenly, someone was there, helping pull Mors Planch away, relieving Hari of the burden. Hari realized that the nobleman must still be in the control room, piloting the ship, so it could only be—

Sure enough, the newcomer wore fancy, fractal-plaid pants and an iridescent jacket. It was Gornon Vlimt, the eccentric artist from Ktlina. *That's everyone accounted for,* Hari thought with some relief, but also puzzlement. Gornon wasn't having any trouble focusing attention. Unlike the others, his gaze was steady.

"Come along, Professor," Vlimt urged. "We'll get you settled in. It will be a bit rocky until we get away from this place."

Hari sat in a plush chair near the view screen while Gornon strapped Mors Planch in and quickly made sure of the others.

"I have business in the control cabin, Professor. We'll talk later. Meanwhile, why don't you enjoy the view? Nothing like it has been seen for a thousand human generations, and perhaps nothing like it ever will."

With that, Vlimt left the lounge.

Hari had a sudden, wild urge to shout a warning ahead to Biron Maserd, but then felt overwhelmed by fatigue. Anyway, if his guess was right, a warning wouldn't make much difference.

The spectacle outside was indeed memorable—a flare of individual archives exploding ever more rapidly to become a virtual fireworks display. Innumerable flashes, each one vaporizing a billion terabytes of information. It took some piloting skill to weave a path amid such coruscating bedlam. But soon Hari saw another mode of destruction ensue in the starship's wake. The rickety space station that lay at the core of the great archive collection began to glow. Heat emanated from stovepipe tunnels and oblong storage chambers, as the contents of the vast warehouse began to melt.

I wonder what happened to the other ship. Hari peered about until he spied the Ktlina vessel. It should just be lying there in space, a derelict with no one aboard. But as Hari watched, the sleek craft began to glow with pent-up energies. Maneuvering jets fired, and it began moving in the opposite direction from the course taken by the *Pride of Rhodia.* Soon its glimmering wake was all that remained. Then Hari lost sight even of that, as an entirely new zone of destruction came into view.

The terraformers, he thought, staring, as gigantic tilling machines began their own cycle of demolition. Prehistoric starcraft, so ancient and primitive, and yet, so awesomely powerful that they had transformed whole planets, began to shrivel into dust as if they were being crushed by the weight of years.

A moan escaped Horis Antic as the soils expert pointed at the vivid scene. He was recovered enough from the drugged stupor to understand what this meant. The proof of his hypothesis—a discovery that would be his sole claim to fame among quadrillions of anonymous galactic citizens—was vanishing before his eyes.

Hari felt sympathy for the little man.

It would have felt good and right for the truth about this to come out. Daneel claims the tillers were sent forth by a different kind of robot. Programmed by an Auroran fanatic whose fierce notion of service to humanity meant annihilating everything else, in order to prepare sweet places for settlers to land. Daneel disavowed those ancient Aurorans. Yet his logic differs only in that he's more subtle.

Hari felt little but a pessimistic certainty. Life brought him nothing but defeats. No sign of his missing grandchild. No validity for psychohistory. And now, for the greater good, he had consented to the destruction of a treasure.

"Whatever you have in mind for us, Daneel . . . it had better be worth all of this. It had better be really special."

A while later, after the explosions had been left far behind, Hari was dozing when someone dropped heavily into the seat next to his.

"Well, I'll be damned if this universe makes the slightest bit of sense," grumbled Biron Maserd.

Hari rubbed his eyes.

"Who is piloting—"

Maserd answered with a sour expression. "That fancy-pants artiste, Gornon Vlimt. Seems the controls won't respond to me any more, only to him."

"How . . . Where is he taking us?"

"Says he'll explain later. I thought about giving him a knock on the head and trying to take back control. Then I realized."

"What?"

"Vlimt must be responsible for what happened to Kers Kantun, back on the station. Vlimt was left drugged, like the others, but now look at him! I figure there's just one explanation. He must be another—"

"—another kind of robot?"

This time the voice came from the passageway, where Gornon Vlimt stood, looking as foppish as ever, in the wild clothing of Ktlina's New Renaissance.

"I apologize for the inconvenience, gentlemen. But the operation that has just been completed required great delicacy and timing. Clarifications had to wait until success was achieved."

"What success?" Hari asked. "If your aim was to recover and use the archives, you failed! They've all been destroyed."

"Perhaps not all of them. Anyway, the archives were never my principal objective," Gornon answered. "First, I should elucidate one point. I am not the Gornon Vlimt whom you knew. That man is still in a drugged stupor, riding the Ktlina ship out to a false rendezvous, where he will tell his fellow chaos agents a hypnotically induced story."

"Then you *are* a robot," Biron Maserd growled.

The Gornon-duplicate nodded.

"As you might guess, I represent a different faction than the followers of R. Daneel Olivaw."

"Are you one of the *Calvinians*?"

The robot did not answer directly.

"Let's just say that what took place recently was another skirmish in a war that stretches beyond the reach of even the lost archives."

"So you don't share the aims of the human you replaced? The real Gornon Vlimt?"

"That's right, Professor. Gornon wanted to copy and scatter the archives willy-nilly among vulnerable cultures of the empire, creating chaos infections in a million random locales. A catastrophic notion. Your own psychohistory equations would be utterly torn apart, and Daneel's alternate destiny—whatever he has secretly planned—would be rendered useless. All hope for a strong transition to some bright new phase might be lost as madness ran wild. We'd spend half a million years digging humans out of the burrows they would flee into, once the fever ended."

Maserd grunted. "Then you approve of destroying the archives?"

"It is not a matter of approval, but necessity."

"Then what's the difference between you and Kers Kantun!" the nobleman demanded. Maserd was evidently reaching the limit of his tolerance for mysteries.

"There are many sects and subsects among robotkind, my lord. One faction believes we should not be closing doors or sealing our options right now. To this end, we have a favor to ask of Dr. Seldon."

Hari laughed out loud.

"I don't believe this! You all keep acting as if I'm your god—or at least a convenient representative for ten quadrillion gods—but all you *really* want is for me to excuse and sanctify plans you've already chosen!"

The robot Gornon confirmed this with a nod.

"You were bred for such a role, Professor. On Helicon, ten thousand boys and girls were specially conceived, inoculated, and prepped as you were. And yet only a few hundred then qualified for a careful series of conditionings, from education to home environment, aimed toward a specific end. After a long winnowing process, just one remained."

Hari shivered. He had long suspected, but never heard it confirmed. *Perhaps this enemy of Daneel's has a reason for revealing it right now?* He decided to stay wary.

"So I was raised to be mathematically creative and unconventional, in a civilization whose every social characteristic encourages conservatism and conformity. But my creativity was guided, eh?"

Vlimt nodded. "You had to be immune to all the normal damping mechanisms in order for your creativity to flower, and yet a sense of direction was essential, guiding you always toward the same ideal."

Hari nodded.

"*Predictability.* I hated the way my parents kept bouncing around. All emotions, no reason. I longed to predict what people would do. My lifelong obsession." He sighed. "But even a neurotic can understand his neurosis. I knew this about myself decades ago, robot. Don't you think I figured out that Daneel helped make me what I am? Do you imagine that revealing these facts will lessen my loyalty and friendship toward him?"

"Not at all, Doctor. What we have in mind will not put you in a position to betray Daneel Olivaw. However, we wonder—"

There came a pause, rather lengthy for a robot.

"—we wonder if you might relish an opportunity to judge him."

4.

◆

Dors Venabili spent the last part of the voyage transforming her looks. She wanted to conduct her business quickly and be gone without questions. It would do no good showing up on Trantor with the face of a woman everyone thought long dead—the wife of former First Minister Hari Seldon!

She parked her ship at a standard commercial tether and took the Orion elevator down to Trantor's metal-sheathed surface. At customs, a simple coded phrase persuaded the immigration computers to pass her without a body scan. Daneel's robots had been using this technique to slip onto the capital for untold generations.

And so here we are again, she thought, *back in the steel caverns where I spent half my existence protecting Hari Seldon, guiding and nurturing his genius, becoming so good at wifely simulation that my ersatz feelings grew indistinguishable from genuine love.*

And just as compelling.

Stifling crowds surrounded her, so unlike the languid pastoral life on most imperial worlds. Dors used to wonder why Daneel designed Trantor this way, to be a maze of metal corridors, whose people scarcely saw the sun. It certainly wasn't necessary for administrative purposes, or to house Trantor's forty billions. Many imperial worlds had even larger populations without flattening and merging every continent into a single steel-plated warren.

Only after helping Hari define the outlines of psychohistory did she understand the real underlying reason.

Way back in the dawn era, when Daneel himself had been made, a vast majority of humans—those on Earth—lived in cramped, artificial burrows, a lingering result of some horrible shock. And across the following millennia, whenever some planet passed through an especially bad chaos episode, traumatized folk often reacted in the same way—by cowering away from the light, in hivelike caverns.

By designing Trantor this way, Daneel had cleverly *preempted* that pattern. Trantor was already—by design—just like a planet filled with chaos survivors! Inherent paranoia and conservatism made it the last place in the galaxy where anyone would attempt a renaissance.

And yet, she thought, *a mini-renaissance did happen here once. Hari and I barely survived the consequences.*

A voice jarred her, coming from behind.

"Supervisor Jenat Korsan?"

That was one of her aliases. She turned to see a gray-clad woman with mid-level insignia on her epaulets, offering Dors a bow just right for a functionary ranking two levels higher.

"I hope you had a pleasant journey, supervisor?"

Dors responded with proper Ruellian courtesy. But as usual among Greys, there was little time wasted in pleasantries.

"Thank you for meeting me here, Sub-Inspector Smeet. I've accessed your reports about the emigration to Terminus. Overall progress appears to be good; however, I observe certain discrepancies."

The Trantorian bureaucrat underwent a series of flickering facial expressions. Dors didn't need mentalic powers to read her mind. Greys who lived on permanent assignment in the capital felt superior to functionaries from the outer spiral arms, especially one such as Dors pretended to be—a comptroller from the far periphery. Still, rank could not be ignored. Someone of Dors' apparent stature could make trouble.. Better to cooperate and make sure every box was properly checked off.

"You are in luck, supervisor," the local official told Dors. "A procession of emigrants can be seen just over there, entering capsules on the first leg of their long journey."

Dors followed Smeet's extended arm, indicating a far portion of the vast transit chamber. There, a queue of subdued figures could be seen snaking back and forth between velvet guide ropes. Her acute robotic optics zoomed toward the scene, scanning several hundred men, women, and children, each of them carrying satchels or holding the tether of an automatic carryall. The mood was not entirely somber. She witnessed moments of levity, as spirited individuals tried to cheer up their companions. But the presence of Special Police proctors told the real story—that these were prisoners of a sort. Exiles being sent to the very farthest corner of the known universe, never to be let back into the metropolitan heart of the empire.

The human price of Hari's plan, Dors reflected. *Bound for an inhospitable rock called Terminus, supposedly to create a new Encyclopedia, and thus stave off a looming dark age. None of them knows the next layer of truth, that their heirs will have generations of sensational glory. For some time, a civilization centered on Terminus—the Foundation—will shine brighter than the old empire ever did.*

Dors smiled, remembering her best years with Hari, back when the Seldon Plan was just taking shape, transforming from a mere glimmer in the equations to a fantastic promise—an apparent way out of humanity's tragic quandary. A path to something bold and strong enough to withstand chaos, bridging the madness and bringing humanity to a new era.

Those were exciting times. The small Seldon cabal worked frenetically, sharing intense hopes. Along the way, they created a grand design, a tremendous drama whose star players would be these very émigrés and their posterity on obscure Terminus.

Then she frowned, remembering the rest of it—the day Hari realized his design was flawed. No plan, no matter how perfect, could cover every eventuality or offer perfect predictability. In all likelihood, perturbations and surprises would throw the beautiful design off course. Yugo Amaryl insisted—and Hari accepted—that there would have to be a guiding force—a Second Foundation.

That was the beginning of disillusionment. She recalled how inelegant this made the beautiful equations—forcing the ponderously graceful momentum of quadrillions to follow the will of a few dozen. *And things went downhill from there.*

Observing the procession of outcasts, she knew their destiny wasn't so bright after all. The First Foundation would be glorious, but its role was to help set the stage for something else. Terminus, in its own right, would be sterile.

A bit like me, I suppose. Hari and I nurtured civilizations and we raised foster children, but our creations were always second-hand.

It was tempting to go and visit her granddaughter, Wanda Seldon. *But I'd better not. Wanda is mentalic and as sharp as a laser. I can't let her sniff out what I'm up to.*

"Have there been any further escape attempts?" she asked the Grey functionary.

Almost from the day Hari struck his deal with the Committee for Public Safety, some exiles had rebelled against the fate chosen for them. Their methods ranged from ingenious legal injunctions to feigned illnesses and attempts to merge into the population of Trantor. Two dozen even stole a spacecraft and made a break for it, seeking sanctuary on the "renaissance world" of Ktlina.

Smeet nodded, reluctantly. "Yes, but fewer since the Specials stiffened supervision. One girl—the daughter of two Encyclopedists—cleverly forged documents to get herself a job right here, at Orion elevator. She vanished twelve days ago."

About the same time as Hari. Dors had already tapped the police database, noting their scant information on Seldon's disappearance.

Making ready to depart from the Great Atrium, Dors scanned the queue of exiles one last time. Though some glowered at their banishment, and others seemed dejected to be cast from the heart of the old empire, she noticed that a majority were surprisingly upbeat. Those men and women engaged in vigorous conversations as the line moved forward. She caught snatches of discourse about science, the arts, drama, as well as excited speculations about what opportunities might even come from exile.

After several years cloistered together here on Trantor, even their linguistic patterns showed subtle, initial traces of a drift that had been predicted in the equations—toward an idiom destined in a hundred years to be called Terminus Dialect, an offshoot of Galactic Standard that would be inherently more skeptical and optimistic, while shaking off many of the old syntactical constraints. Of course some of the new jokes and slang phrasings had been introduced by the Fifty psychohistorians, as part of a continuing process—gently, imperceptibly preparing the exiles for their role. But her hypersensitive ears also sifted phrases that had not been part of the program. Clearly, the exiles were doing it mostly on their own.

Well, I shouldn't be surprised. They are the best we could collect from twenty-five million worlds. The smartest, sanest, most vibrant . . . and the most dedicated to hard-nosed pragmatism. Ideal seed stock for something brave and new. If humanity was going to pull this off—achieving a miracle cure through its own efforts, these people and their heirs just might have managed it . . . aided by the Seldon equations.

Ah, well, that had been the dream.

Dors shook her head. No sense dwelling on those once-fond hopes. If she did—and if she had been human—it might make her cry.

Dors turned toward the bowels of Trantor with only one thought foremost in her mind. To find Hari.

"What do you mean, you *lost track of him*? I thought you had a trace on his ship!"

The robot standing opposite Dors remained expressionless, perhaps because facial grimaces were unnecessary between their positronic kind, or else because that was the way a *human* might look after allowing an embarrassing lapse of security, misplacing one of the most important people in the galaxy.

"It has been less than a week since the transponder went silent," R. Pos Helsh responded. "We have a good idea which direction the space yacht went after they took off from Demarchia. Our contacts with the Committee for Public Safety tell of a Special Police cruiser disappearing violently a short while ago in the Thumartin Nebula—"

"That is disturbing news. Have you dispatched robots to the scene?"

"We prepared to do so. Then a message from Daneel overruled us."

"What? Did he give a reason?"

The other robot transmitted a microwave equivalent of a shrug. "We are stretched thin here on Trantor," he explained. "There are no trustworthy robot agents to spare, so further investigations have been left to the police. Besides . . ." The male robot paused, then continued in dry tones, "I have a strong impression that everything has transpired according to some plan of Daneel's."

Dors pondered.

Well, that wouldn't surprise me. To make use of Hari, even in his dotage, when an old man should be left alone with the satisfaction of his accomplishments. If there were some service or function he could still perform, to further Daneel's long-range strategy, I doubt the Immortal Servant would hesitate for an instant.

But that still left a mystery.

What could Hari possibly do at this point to help Daneel?

She didn't have much time. Soon, word would reach Daneel's agents that she was here entirely on her own volition, having abandoned her post on Smushell. Dors had no idea what Daneel might do about it. Olivaw had been remarkably tolerant when Lodovic Trema went rogue in a big way. At other times, Daneel had ordered robots dismantled if their behaviors ran contrary to his view of the greater good. And long ago, during the robotic civil wars, he had been an unstoppable force, capable of great ruthlessness . . . all toward humanity's long-range benefit.

Dors decided to leave Trantor and head for Thumartin Nebula. But there was one more piece of business to perform.

Visiting an obscure section of the library at Streeling University, she linked herself to a hidden fiber-optic panel. Using secret software back doors, Dors avoided the traps that normally defended the Seldon Group's most precious data site . . . the Prime Radiant. At last she succeeded in downloading the latest version of the Seldon Plan. Perhaps it would offer some clue about what Hari was up to. Why an elderly cripple in his last days would go charging off with an obscure bureaucrat and a dilettante nobleman, chasing tales of fossils and dust.

Streeling University was one of the rare sites on Trantor where some silver-ivory buildings lay open to a star-filled sky. Leaving the library, she avoided a windowless structure just meters away, where fifty psychohistorians gathered to continue refining the Plan, preparing for their long stewardship of destiny. As yet, only two of them possessed mentalic powers. The rest were mere mathists, like Gaal Dornick. But soon they would interbreed with gifted psychics, interweaving both abilities and laying the seeds for a powerful galactic ruling class. A Second Foundation to secretly direct the First.

Hari had tried to make a virtue of necessity. After all, mentalic powers did offer an excellent bludgeon for hammering out any kinks that might pop up, over the centuries. Still, it was an inelegant solution, crammed into the equations. He never really liked the concept of an elite corps of demigods.

Over time, it ate away at Hari.

Perhaps that was why he grew old so soon, she thought. *Or else maybe he just missed me.* Either way, she felt guilty for being away so long, however Daneel had rationalized the need.

Hurrying past the main university quad, Dors felt a familiar brush against the surface layers of her mind. She glanced north, her vision zooming toward a cluster of purple-robed academics—meritocrats of the seventh and eighth levels—strolling toward the Amaryl Building. One of them, a petite woman, abruptly stumbled in her footsteps, then started turning toward Dors.

It was Wanda.

Any unusual movement would certainly attract attention, so Dors put on an expression like the distracted gray-clad bureaucrat she resembled, boring and innocuous, as she obliquely crossed the courtyard.

Wanda's countenance grew puzzled. Dors felt a mental probing as they passed each other. But her granddaughter's talent wasn't strong enough to penetrate a well-trained robotic outer guise. After time spent on Smushell, tending much stronger psychics, Dors easily foiled Wanda's probes.

Still, it was a tense moment. Something in Dors—the part tuned to act and feel human—wanted to reach out to this person she had known and loved.

But Wanda doesn't need an encounter with her late Grandma Dors right now. She's content and busy with her role, certain that the Second Foundation will foster a great awakening of humankind, in just a thousand years.

It's not my place to disturb such fulfillment, however illusory.

So Dors kept walking, her face and mind sufficiently different that Wanda finally shook her head, pushing aside those brief sensations of familiarity.

When she reached a safe distance, Dors let out a cathartic sigh.

5.

◆

Sybyl did not take the news well. After recovering consciousness aboard the *Pride of Rhodia,* she railed at Hari and Maserd for what they had done.

"You've destroyed the best hope for ten quadrillion people to escape tyranny!"

Next to her, Mors Planch accepted this latest defeat more calmly than Hari expected. The tall, dark-skinned pirate captain was more interested in grasping what had happened, and what the future might bring.

"So, let me get this straight," Planch asked. "We were manipulated by *one* group of robots, lured to the archive site in order to give them an excuse to destroy the records, with Seldon here giving them the final nod." Planch gestured toward Hari. "Only then we were all hijacked by *another* set of damn tiktoks?"

Hari, who had been trying to read, glanced up with some irritation from his copy of *A Child's Book of Knowledge.*

"Human volition often proves less potent than we egotists imagine, Captain Planch. Free will is an adolescent concept that keeps cropping up, like an obstinate weed. But most people outgrow it.

"The essence of maturity," he finished with a sigh, "is understanding how little force a single human can exert against a huge galaxy, or the momentum of destiny."

Mors Planch stared at Hari across the ship's lounge.

"You may have fantastic amounts of evidence and mathematics to back up that dour philosophy, Professor. But I shall never accept it, until the day I die."

Sybyl kept pacing back and forth in agitation, making Horis Antic draw his legs back each time she approached his chair. The small bureaucrat took another blue pill, though he had calmed considerably since fleeing into a drugged stupor back in the nebula. He still chewed his nails incessantly.

Nearby, Jeni Cuicet sat curled at one end of a sofa, pressing a neural desensitizer against her brow. The girl made a brave front, but her headache and chills were clearly getting worse.

"We have to get her to a hospital," Sybyl demanded of their abductor. "Or will you let the poor girl die just for your grudge against us?"

The robot who had been fashioned to resemble Gornon Vlimt reached behind his head and pulled out the cable that kept him linked to the ship's computer, controlling the *Pride of Rhodia* as the yacht leaped across star lanes, racing toward some unknown destination.

"I never meant to take you and Jeni and Captain Planch on this phase of the journey," the humanoid explained. "I would have off-loaded you with the real Gornon Vlimt, if there had been time."

"And where did you send our ship?" Sybyl demanded. "Were you going to turn us over to the police? To some imperial prison? Or have us *cured* of our *madness* by the so-called Health and Sanitation Agency that's laying siege to Ktlina?"

The robot shook his head.

"To a safe place, where none of you would be harmed, and where none of you could *do* any harm. But that opportunity passed, so we must make do. This ship will, therefore, stop along the way, at a convenient imperial world, where you three can be put ashore and Jeni will get medical care."

Mors Planch, the tall raider, rubbed his chin. "I wonder what went wrong with your plan, back at the archive station. You slew Kers Kantun, yet you didn't interfere with the job he was doing there. You won't let us have the remaining archives, and now you're scooting off as fast as you can. Are your enemies hot on your trail?"

Gornon did not answer. He didn't have to. They all knew his faction of robots was much weaker than Kers Kantun's, and could accomplish nothing except by speed and surprise.

Hari pondered what must become of the humans aboard this ship. Of course, he himself had already known most of the big secrets, for decades. But what about Sybyl, Planch, Antic, and Maserd? Might they blab as soon as they were released? Or would it matter what they said? The galaxy was always rife with unsupported rumors about so-called *eternals*—mechanical beings, immortal and all-knowing. Trantor had been abuzz with such talk many times over the years, and always the mania subsided as social damping mechanisms automatically kicked in.

He looked at Jeni, feeling guilty. Her case of adolescent brain fever had been made much worse by these adventures—having to confront frequent news about robots and fossils and archives filled with ancient history . . . all subjects that the fever's infectious organism tuned human minds to find distasteful.

He had discussed this with Maserd, who was no slouch. Biron understood by now that brain fever could not possibly be natural. Though it predated all known cultures, it must have been *designed*, once upon a time. Targeted. Deliberately made both durable and virulent.

"Could it have been a weapon against humanity?" Maserd had asked. *"Contrived by some alien race? Perhaps one that was just being destroyed by the terraformers?"*

Hari recalled the meme-minds that had briefly raged on Trantor—mad software entities claiming to be ghosts of prehistoric civilizations, who blamed Daneel's kind for some past devastation. Hari used to wonder if brain fever might be *their* work, designed for revenge against mankind . . . until psychohistory came into focus.

Thereafter he recognized brain fever as something else—one of the social "dampers" that kept human civilization stable and resistant to change.

It was designed, all right, but not to destroy humanity.

Brain fever was a medical innovation. A weapon against a much older and deadlier disease.

Chaos.

Soon, Sybyl was off on another tangent. Leaping to fresh subjects with the manic agility of a renaissance mind.

"These mentalic powers we've seen demonstrated are fantastic! Our scientists on Ktlina started out skeptical, but a few had theorized that a powerful computer, with superresponsive sensors, might trace and decipher all the electronic impulses given off by a human brain! I was dubious that such a vast and sophisticated analysis could be made, even with the new calculating engines. But these positronic robots appear to have been doing it for a very long time!"

She shook her head.

"Imagine that. We knew the ruling classes had lots of ways to control us. But I had no idea it included invading and altering our minds!"

Hari wished the woman would stop talking. Someone of her intelligence should realize the implications. The more she discovered, the more essential it would be to erase her entire memory of the last few weeks, before she could be let go. But renaissance types were like this. So wild and joyful in the liberated creativity of their chaos-drenched minds that addiction to the next fresh idea was more powerful than any drug.

"Throughout history, there has been one way to defeat ruling classes," Sybyl continued. "By taking their technologies of oppression and liberating them! By spreading them to the masses. If a few ancient robots can read minds, why not mass-produce the technique and give it to everybody? Let each citizen have a brain-augmenting helmet! Pretty soon, people would all be telepaths. We'd develop shields for when we want privacy, but the rest of the time . . . imagine what life would be like. The instant exchange of information. The wealth of ideas!"

Sybyl had to stop at last because she grew quite breathless. Hari, on the other hand, mused at the image she presented.

If mentalic powers ever spread openly, to be shared by all, psychohistory would have to be redrawn from the ground up. A science of humanics might still be possible, but it would never again be based on the same set of assumptions—that trillions of people might interact randomly, ignorantly, like complex molecules in a cloud of gas. Self-awareness—and intimate awareness of others—would make the whole thing vastly more complicated. Unless—

I suppose it could manifest in either of two ways. Telepathy might wind up simplifying all equations, if it wrought uniformity, coalescing all minds into a single thought-stream . . .

Or else it could wind up enhancing complexity exponentially! By allowing mentation to fraction into diverse internal and externally shared modes, compartmentalizing and then remerging them in multiple diversity frames.

I wonder if the two approaches could be modeled and com-pared by setting up a series of cellular mathetomatons . . .

Hari resisted a delicious temptation to immerse himself in the details of this hypothetical scenario. He lacked both the tools and enough time.

Of course, the sudden appearance of several hundred mental-ically talented humans on Trantor, a generation ago, was no coin-cidence. Since nearly all were soon gathered in Daneel's circle, one could surmise that the Immortal Servant planned weaving psychic ability into the human race . . . though not in the spas-modically democratic way Sybyl envisioned.

Hari sighed. Either prospect meant an end for his life's work, the beautiful equations.

Hari turned back to *A Child's Book of Knowledge*, trying to ignore the noise and mutterings from other occupants of the lounge. He was delving into the Transition Age, a time just after the first great techno-renaissance, when waves of riots, destruc-tion, and manic solipsism ruined the bright culture that created Daneel's kind. On Earth it led to martial law, draconian suppres-sion, a public recoiling against eccentricity and individuality—combined with waves of crippling agoraphobia.

At the time, things seemed different for the fifty Spacer worlds. On humanity's first interstellar colonies, millions of luckier humans lived long, placid lives on parklike estates, tended by robotic servants. Yet Hari's derivations showed the Spacers' paranoiac intolerance—and overdependence on robotic labor—were just as symptomatic of trauma and des-pair.

Into this era came Daneel Olivaw and Giskard Reventlov, the first mentalic robot, both of them programmed with unswerving devotion to the afflicted master race. Hari didn't understand everything that happened next. But he wanted to. Somehow, a key to deeper understanding lay hidden in that age.

"Forgive me for interrupting, Professor," a voice came from over his shoulder, "but it is time. We must put you in the rejuve-nator."

Hari's head jerked up. It was Gornon Vlimt—or rather *R.* Gornon Vlimt, the robot who had taken on that human's appear-ance.

This Gornon wanted to give him another treatment in the coffinlike machine from Ktlina, but with some additional tricks that his secretive band of heretic machines had been hoarding across the centuries.

"Is it really necessary?" Hari asked. His instinct for self-preservation had ebbed after events two days ago, when logic forced him to perform a loathsome act. Destroying—or sanctioning the destruction of—so much precious knowledge for humanity's ultimate good.

"I'm afraid it is," R. Gornon insisted. "You will need a great deal more stamina for what comes next."

Hari felt a momentary shiver. This didn't sound inviting. Long ago, he used to enjoy adventures—dashing around the galaxy, challenging enemies, overcoming their nefarious schemes, and chasing down secrets from the past—while complaining the whole time that he'd much rather be swaddled in his books. But in those days Dors had been by his side. Adventure held no attraction now, and he wasn't sure that he wanted to see much more of the future.

"Very well, then," he said, more out of politeness than out of any sense of obligation. "My life was guided by robots. No sense in ending such a long habit at this late stage in the game."

He got up and moved his weary body toward sick bay, where a white box waited, its lid gaping like the cover of a crypt. He noted that there were actually *two* indentations within, as if it had been built for a pair of bodies, not just one.

How cozy, he mused.

As R. Gornon helped him lie within, Hari knew this was a point of transition. Whether or not he awoke—whenever or in whatever shape he reemerged—nothing would ever be the same.

6.

◆

The Thumartin Nebula was a maelstrom of debris and dissipating plasma. Something violent had happened there recently—perhaps a great space battle—to leave such a mess behind. Instruments told of many hyperdrive engines having overloaded, just a couple of days ago, exploding spectacularly. Yet, because it occurred inside a coal-dark cloud, no one in the galaxy would ever know.

No humans, that is. Already the cryptic hyperwave channels used by robots were abuzz with news that the archives and ter-raformers had been destroyed at last.

Dors surveyed the scene with churning sensations of confusion and anxiety. Hari had been here, either just before or during that violent episode. If Dors had been human, her guts would have tied in knots of anxiety. As it was, her simulation programs automatically put her through exactly the same suite of ersatz emotions.

"This place . . . it feels like home, Dors. Somehow I know that Voltaire and I spent many long centuries here, slumbering, until someone called us back to life again."

The voice came from a nearby holographic image, depicting a young woman with short-cropped hair, wearing a suit of medieval armor.

Dors nodded. "One of Daneel's agents must have taken your archive from here to Trantor, as part of a scheme I knew nothing about. Or perhaps your unit drifted free and was picked up by a passing human ship. Taken to some unsuspecting world, where enthusiasts carelessly unleashed the contents."

The holographic girl chuckled.

"You make me sound so dangerous, Dors."

"You and the Voltaire sim triggered chaos in Junin Quarter, and on Sark. Even after Hari banished you both to deep space, a copy of Voltaire somehow infected and altered Lodovic Trema. Oh, you are creatures of chaos, all right."

Joan of Arc smiled. She gestured toward the devastation visible outside the view ports.

"Then I assume you approve of all this destruction. May I ask why you keep me around in that case?"

Dors remained silent.

"Perhaps because you are, at last, ready to face troublesome questions? During the long years I spent in company with Voltaire, neither of us could change the other's view on fundamental matters. I am still devoted to faith, as he is to reason. And yet, we learned from each other. For example, I now realize that both faith and reason are dreams arising from the same wistful belief."

Dors raised an eyebrow. "What belief is that?"

"A belief in justice—whether it comes from a divine outside power or from the merit that humans earn by rational problem-solving. Both reason and faith assume the human condition makes some kind of sense. That it isn't just a terrible joke."

Dors let out a low snort.

"You certainly come from a strange era. Were you really so blind to chaos, when you lived?"

"Blind to it? Voltaire and I were each born into extravagant centuries, violent, confusing, and brutal. Even the later techno-logical era that resurrected us through clever computer simula-tion had its own aching problems. But this particular kind of chaos you refer to—a specific disease that topples cultures at their brightest . . ."

Joan shook her head.

"I do not recall anything like it during my time. Nor does Voltaire. I am sure we would have noticed. Neither faith nor rea-son can flourish when you are convinced, deep down, that the universe is rigged against you."

Dors pondered. Could Joan be right? Could there have been a time when there was no threat of chaos plagues? But that made no sense! The very first great scientific age—that invented both robots and spaceflight—collapsed in madness. It *must* be some-thing endemic—

The ship's computer interface broke her train of thought, fill-ing the cabin with glowing letters.

```
A search of nearby space indicates jump
traces leaving the area. Signs of ships
that departed recently. Likely candi-
dates are depicted on-screen. Please
elect choice of which course to follow.
```

Dors had commanded the search. Now she studied two ioniza-tion trails shown on the viewer, heading in opposite directions.

It's possible that neither of them carried Hari away from this place. His atoms may be drifting now amid the ash and debris—all the ancient memories and ruins of past ambitions.

She shook her head.

Still, I've got to make a choice.

Just as she was about to hazard a guess, the glowing letters shifted again.

```
A new presence enters the nebula. A ves-
sel. See the following coordinates . . .
```

Dors swiftly activated her ship's defensive grid and jacked into the computer directly. She could sense the interloper now, a fast craft. Either one of the best imperial cruisers, or a rogue ship from some chaos world . . .

. . . or else it was under robotic control.

```
We are being hailed. The pilot uses the
name Dors Venabili.
```

Dors nodded. Daneel must have learned of her apostasy and sent someone after her. For days she had rehearsed what she'd say, either to the Immortal Servant or one of his Zeroth Law emissaries, when he tried to win her back into the fold with appeals to her sense of duty. However much distaste she felt toward past events, Olivaw would insist that her sole choice now was to help his long-range plan for human salvation.

There is even a chance they'll shoot, if I try to run away. Yet Dors felt a wild urge to do just that—to show Daneel's minions her heels. Action would speak her revulsion more eloquently than words.

```
The pilot of the incoming craft again
requests contact. There is now a personal
identification code, and a message.
```

Reluctantly, Dors opened herself to the data burst.

"Hello, Dors, I assume that's you. Have you had enough time to think things over?

"Don't you figure it's time we talked?"

She rocked back, surprised. But then, in another way, it seemed she had expected this all along. There was a symmetry that required her to confront Lodovic Trema once again.

Nearby, the holographic image of a young medieval knight shivered, then half smiled.

"I sense Voltaire! He's near, in one of his manifestations."

Simulation programs crafted a perfect facsimile of a resigned sigh as Dors said—

"Ah, well. Let's hear what the two boys have to say."

7.

◆

Hari stared at Pengia, wondering what it was about the planet that struck him as odd. From orbit the place was unassuming, like any typical imperial world, with glistening blue seas and immense, flat agricultural regions, covered by checkerboard cornfields and rich orchards. The small cities clearly did not dominate life here. In fact, this bucolic place must have looked exactly the same for many thousands of years.

And yet, the broad fertile plains looked suddenly strange to Hari, now that he knew the source of their well-ordered geometries. Some incredible machine had probably created them. His mind envisioned a time—not long ago by galactic standards—when artificial fire fell from the sky, blasting and pulverizing whole watersheds, carving ideal river courses, then seeding that earlier version of Pengia with all the vegetation and foods needed by human settlers.

Hari realized something else.

I haven't seen many "typical" imperial worlds. I've spent most of my life dashing around, investigating the strange . . . trying to understand deviations from the rules of psychohistory. Struggling to encompass every hitch and variation in our growing model. It just never seemed important to visit a place like this, where the vast majority of human beings are born. Where they experience lives nearly identical to their ancestors', and die in modest contentment or desperation—according to their own personal dramas.

Even Helicon, where he had spent his early years, was widely known as an anomaly. Though agriculture dominated the planet's economy, a local genetic fluke resulted in a notorious cottage industry—supplying mathematical geniuses to the bureaucracy and meritocracy. Small wonder that Daneel chose to perform his search and experiment there!

This place may be typical, Hari thought. *But I am not certain what that word means anymore.* Again, humility felt surprisingly comfortable at his age.

Of course, all of these strange musings might be a by-product of his recent rejuvenation treatment. Hari felt new strength in his limbs, a greater steadiness in his step, which could not but help affect his overall mood, infecting him with an eagerness that, ironically, he *resented* somewhat, knowing it was artificial.

And yet, part of him felt surprised by how little had changed. *I'm still an old man. I don't look all that different. I can sense that I've been given a bit more vigor, but I frankly doubt that will translate into much more life span. Is this all the disparity between what Sybyl's renaissance can accomplish, and the secret biotechnologies the Calvinians have been hoarding for centuries? The contrast isn't all that impressive.*

Hari had a vague feeling—almost like a dream—that as much had been *taken* from him as he had been given, while lying in the big white box. More had happened than was apparent.

The gentle blue world swam closer in the *Pride of Rhodia's* view screens as R. Gornon Vlimt piloted them toward a landing. For some reason, everyone faced eastward as they descended. No one cared about the western view, which was, after all, nearly identical. Jeni Cuicet sat in a suspensor chair, barely moving, fighting waves of alternating heat and chills.

Horis Antic kept pointing to features of the geography below, sharing with Biron Maserd a new excitement of understanding how the terrain had been made—a greedy intellectual pleasure that Hari well understood. It made him smile for his two young friends.

Sybyl and Planch huddled together by the forwardmost window, muttering secretively, though Hari could guess what concerned them. The lesser crewmen from Ktlina and the *Pride of Rhodia* had recently received a treatment of drugs and hypnosis from R. Gornon. Those men went about their tasks somewhat stonily, and clearly without any memory of the extravagant events that had taken place during the past week.

Sybyl and Planch are wondering when their turn will come, Hari thought. *They must be striving to come up with some plan to avoid it, or else to leave a secret message for their friends. I know because it is what I would do in their place.*

Antic and Maserd seemed less concerned, perhaps relying on the protection of Hari's friendship, or because they were more trustworthy. Neither of *them* was likely to support anything that could cause chaos. Still, Hari wondered.

R. Gornon acts in many ways as if he has the same agenda as Daneel. And yet, he slaughtered one of Daneel's agents, and clearly is fleeing as fast as he can to escape being caught by the Immortal Servant.

Clearly there were complexities involved that Hari didn't yet grasp. So Biron and Horis might be relying too much on friendship and trust to preserve their memory of recent events.

Planch and Sybyl reached a conclusion. They walked toward Hari, a grim set to their jaws.

"We are ready to acknowledge that you've won again, Seldon," the woman from Ktlina said. "So let's strike a deal."

Hari shook his head. "It is exaggeration to say that I've won anything. In fact, these recent *victories* cost me more than you'd ever imagine. Besides, what makes you think I am in a position to strike a bargain, let alone enforce one?"

Sybyl grimaced in frustration, but Planch, the space trader, looked unperturbed.

"We don't understand everything that's happened, but clearly our options are limited. Even if you can't command that thing"— he nodded toward R. Gornon—"you clearly have some influence. These tiktok machines value you highly."

They value what use they can make of me, Hari thought, somewhat bitterly. Of course that was unfair. Apparently *all* robots, even Daneel's enemies, revered Hari for one reason above all others. He was as close to a fully aware and knowledgeable master as had existed in the human universe for thousands of years.

For all the good that's going to do me, he thought wryly. *And for all the good that will do humanity.*

"What's your proposition?" he asked Mors Planch.

The trader captain eagerly got down to business.

"The way I see it, this mentalic tiktok could disable any of us, knock us out, inject drugs, and wipe our brains. But that course of action has two disadvantages! First, old Gornon here won't *like* doing that, on account of that First Law of theirs. Oh, he might rationalize that it's for some greater good, but I figure our tin man would *prefer* finding some other way to keep us from blabbing, wouldn't he?"

Hari was impressed with this reasoning. Planch caught on pretty well.

"Go on."

"Besides, wherever we show up with a gap in our memory, it will be a big fat clue to all our friends, or to anybody who ever knew us. There are people back on Ktlina who knew our plans. No matter what the robot does to our minds, those savvy folks just might be able to use some new renaissance technologies to undo the damage. Gornon would have to wipe us almost blank and dump us into a hole, in order to make sure that won't happen."

Hari felt Biron Maserd step closer to participate in the conversation.

"You are assuming that your beloved chaos revolution still reigns on Ktlina," the nobleman said. "Even if the sickness is still raging there, will it last long enough for your scenario to play out? Especially now that the ancient archives have been taken away from you?"

"Perhaps you underestimate how many weapons this particular renaissance has in its arsenal. Ktlina is no sitting duck, like Sark was. Nor is it overly trusting, like Madder Loss. And even if it fails like the others, a growing network of collaborators and sympathizers stands ready to help the next world to try and break out of the ancient trap."

Hari could not help but admire the dedication and intensity of this man. He and Planch differed only in their basic assumptions—what it was possible for humans to achieve. *I would be on his side, a willing co-conspirator, if only the underlying facts were different.*

But psychohistory showed that the old empire would collapse well before Planch's critical threshold was reached. Once the Imperium's gentle network of trade, services, and mutual support broke down, local populations on every planet would have far more serious concerns than aspiring to be the next renaissance. Matters of survival would come foremost. The gentry class would step in, as it always did in times of crisis, creating either benevolent or despotic tyrannies. The chaos plague would be stopped in its tracks by something equally terrible. A collapse of civilization itself.

"Go on, Planch," Hari urged. "I assume you have some alternative to offer?"

The trader captain nodded. "You can't let us go entirely free—we can see that. And yet it would be preferable not to kill us or wipe our minds completely. So we'd like to suggest an alternative.

"Take us back with you to Trantor."

Mors Planch might have explained further, but just then a shrill shout cut in.

"No!"

Everyone turned to see young Jeni Cuicet raising herself on both elbows, trying to step out of the levitation chair.

"I won't go back there. They'll ship me off to Terminus, along with my parents. This damned brain fever will just make things worse. They'll say it means I'm a blasted genius! They'll be even more eager to drag me off to that horrible rock, and there I'll rot!"

Sybyl went over to Jeni, distracted for a moment by her pain, attempting to offer the girl some more chemical relief. Mors Planch and Hari shared a look.

Planch doesn't have to go into more detail, Hari thought. *No sense in upsetting the girl. Besides, I know what he's suggesting. There are age-old methods that emperors have used, in order to keep people in safe "exile" right there in the capital. It's a risky option. Perhaps Planch thinks he can escape from such confinement, even though imperial hostages have tested the constraints for thousands of years.*

Or else, maybe he'd just rather live comfortably in a cosmopolitan place, as an alternative to having his memory wiped.

Any further discussion of the matter was forestalled when R. Gornon shouted over his shoulder, "Everyone get belted in! They don't have a sophisticated guide beam here, so it may be rougher than you are used to."

No one thought of disobeying. Gornon's power had been amply demonstrated. As the passengers watched Pengia's rustic spaceport loom ahead, everyone knew there were matters left unsettled. Each of them would meet a point of decision on Pengia. A shifting of destiny.

They were met at the edge of the landing field by half a dozen sturdy-looking men. Hari had an unmistakable feeling that they were robots—doubtless members of Gornon's small Calvinian cult.

Three large vehicles came alongside the ship, which had settled down next to a hangar. Into one car went Biron Maserd's crewmen and those who had served aboard Mors Planch's raider ship. The second took aboard Horis, Sybyl, Planch, and Maserd, with Jeni's levitation chair gently loaded in back. Their immediate stop would be a local hospital, where doctors were familiar with brain fever and had facilities to help the young woman.

Gornon showed no concern that she might talk about what she had seen. Brain fever victims often had extravagant hallucinations, and no one would take her wild stories seriously. Besides, Hari noted that the ship's motivators had been left running on idle. The Calvinians didn't plan to stay long—a few days at most.

Even that may be too long, if Daneel's organization is as efficient as ever. Hari wondered what could possibly drive these robot heretics to take such a risk.

Hari and Gornon joined the others. On automatic pilot, the limousine started heading toward some nearby hills, evidently a zone where local gentry lived. Hari presumed Gornon had a villa waiting. Nothing but the best for his captives.

As the limo reached a side gate to depart the provincial spaceport, Hari looked back at the *Pride of Rhodia,* and the acuity that had been newly restored to his eyesight made him notice something strange.

The robots Gornon had left in charge of the ship were now unloading something bulky through the passenger hatchway. It was white and shaped like an oversize coffin.

Even the burly robots seemed to strain under its weight as they carried it toward the third and last vehicle. Their movements indicated great care, as if their cargo were somehow more precious than their own lives.

As if many hopes rested on its safe journey to some faraway destination.

PART 5

A RECURRING RENDEZVOUS

PENGIA . . . A world in Rigel Sector noted for producing elegant craft-ceramics and for certain anomalous oceanic lifeforms that have recently been investigated for their unique neuromentalic traits, offering hope for organic humans with immune systems that reject standard symbiotic host-implants . . .

Pengia stands out mainly for its almost complete lack of historical interest. A modest agricultural world, it appears to have taken part in few notable events during the dark ages, and none at all in the Imperial Era. Only once—520 years into the Interregnum—did it experience momentary prominence, right after the Battle of Chjerrups, by playing host to the first Galactic Coalescence Investigation Commission. Those hearings made Pengia's name briefly famous, wherever broadcasts were not jammed by . . .

That illustrious phase soon passed, however, as the tumultuous destiny debates spread their heady turmoil to more populated venues. Thereafter, Pengia soon lapsed . . .

ENCYCLOPEDIA GALACTICA, 117TH EDITION, 1054 F.E.

1.

R. Zun Lurrin at last understood the awesome scope of Daneel's long-range design for the salvation of humanity.

"You plan to help them unite. To create a telepathic network, in which each human soul connects to every other."

The Immortal Servant nodded as he gazed at sixty human subjects with identical expressions of contentment playing across their faces, meditating beneath a high-arched dome.

"Imagine it. No more rancor. An end to bitterness and egotistic rivalry. And above all, there would be no solipsism. For how can anyone ignore the feelings of other people, when those feelings have become intensely palpable, like integral parts of your own mind?"

"Unity and oneness," Zun sighed. "The old dream. And we could provide it to them at last."

But then Zun frowned as he contemplated the sixty humans in front of him.

"They are at peace, in total connectedness, because each one is paired with a positronic mentalic amplifier. Only now you say we *cannot* do the same thing on a massive scale?"

Daneel nodded. "That sort of dependency on mechanical methods we must not allow."

"But it would let us combine with our masters! Robots and humans, bound together in permanent, loving synergy."

"And in such a synergy, the machine portion would grow ever more dominant with the passage of time," Daneel said. "Moreover, consider how many robots we would have to build. It could only be done by unleashing self-reproduction. That opens the door to selection, Darwinism, evolution . . . and eventually a new android *species*. One that thinks primarily of its own self-interest instead of humanity's. I swore never to permit this.

"No. We must not let humans become overly dependent upon robots. That was the Spacer approach—the heresy that Elijah Baley warned against. The abomination that forced Giskard to act as he did."

Daneel's voice resonated with determination. "Humans *must* eventually stand on their own. And there are more reasons than the ones that I have told you so far. Reasons having to do with survival of the race itself."

Zun Lurrin contemplated this for a time.

"In that case let me extrapolate, Daneel. From this data, I shall hazard to guess your plan.

"A hundred years ago, you began a series of genetic experiments on small groups of human beings. One of these projects brought forth the mathematical genius of Hari Seldon. Another produced a sudden wave of mutants on Trantor—humans capable of mentalic powers that only a few robots formerly possessed."

"Excellent. You are on the right track, Zun." Daneel nodded. "Think about the scene in front of you—these sixty humans united in glorious tranquillity, power, and contentment. Now envision it taking place *without* robotic aid! They would form their own mental comity. A union of souls. One that is sturdy, free of reliance on artificial aids."

Zun Lurrin nodded. "I understand what you are saying, Daneel. That would certainly be more desirable. And yet, consider the delay! It will take centuries to develop human mentalics strong and numerous enough to serve as psychic bridges, connecting whole cities, territories, even planets. Why wait so long? At this very moment, we have tools at hand that could be modified for this very purpose! Why not use these devices—strictly for the interim, until enough powerful human mentalics become available? The Galactic Empire need not fall. It could simply be transformed, almost overnight, if we only reprogram certain implements—"

Daneel shook his head in the human fashion, indicating polite disagreement.

"It is a tempting notion. But the drawbacks are fatal. Number one, to impose this union of spirits by mechanical means would create tremendous First Law conflict among many robots, whose circuits would interpret it as 'harm.' I have tried out this idea on several of your peers, and their reactions vary from enthusiasm, such as yours, all the way to outrage and revulsion.

"Clearly, such a peremptory action would reignite the robotic civil wars."

Zun quailed at the notion. "I assume you erased all memory of this idea from the robots that rejected it?"

"I took that precaution, yes. And if your reaction had been different, I would have done the same to you, Zun. My apologies."

"No apology is required where necessity and the good of humanity are concerned," Zun said, dismissing Daneel's concern with the wave of one hand. "And your other reason?"

"Human variability. In recent millennia, small but significant numbers have grown immune to nearly all of the stabilizing influences that we have used to stave off chaos. They are also extremely resistant to mentalic suasion. Imagine how these individuals would react if they abruptly saw their friends, neighbors, and loved ones becoming 'meditation masters' overnight!

"No, that understates it, Zun. Suppose we do manage to draw a majority of humans into a macro-consciousness, abandoning individuality to unite in a single mentation-stream. How will the remnant minority react to being left out?

"Would they go mad? Or feel abandoned?

"Or might they misinterpret what they see happening, and imagine that some alien force has turned their loved ones into zombies, compelling them to think identical rigid thoughts, all at the same time?

"Don't forget, these exceptional ones are often ingenious. They would throw all their energies into uncovering and fighting that *outside alien force*.

"They would find us. They would wage war against us."

Zun Lurrin envisioned the scene as Daneel described it, and understood at once the farseeing wisdom of the Immortal Servant.

"This new breakthrough—this new way of human life—it must be introduced at the right time, under appropriate circumstances. All robots must see it as necessary. All humans must view it as an improvement."

Daneel nodded.

"And so it cannot happen yet. It must not be brought about by artificial means. We shall have to wait until a large enough population of human mentalics is ready. Until the empire has collapsed, and humanity roils in suffering. Then, as they yearn for something to unify and save them, that will be the time to offer them *Gaia*."

Zun turned to look at Daneel. "Gaia?"

"An ancient term for a spirit that covers an entire planet. A gentle, loving goddess who knows when every sparrow falls, because each bird of the air, all the fish of the sea, and every living human, will be an integral part of her."

The Immortal Servant's voice grew distant as Daneel's eyes seemed to focus on a far horizon, one filled with majesty and beauty.

"And after each planet has its Gaia, then we may see something even greater. Something all-encompassing. *Galaxia*."

His voice softened further.

"And that is when . . . perhaps . . . I shall find some peace."

2.

◆

Two mysterious ship traces led away from the Thumartin Nebula, heading in opposite directions from the site where a million archives and terraforming machines had recently exploded into sparkling clouds of ionized memory. It was decided that Dors would follow one of the departing trails. Lodovic's Calvinian friends would follow the other one in their own speedy craft.

That was fine by Dors, who felt a strong hunch which direction Hari had been taken.

Unfortunately, Lodovic Trema agreed with her choice. After briefly introducing Dors to his new allies, he threw a carryall over his shoulder and crossed the tunnel connecting both airlocks, making himself right at home aboard her ship!

"Zorma and her friends have less need of me than you do," he explained.

"Then their need is less than zero!" she retorted. He only smiled, appearing disinclined to argue. But Dors was having none of that.

"This is going to be a full and complete exchange of information, Trema. Or else you can get out and walk the rest of the way. Start by telling me about these allies of yours. You know how I feel about fanatics who deny the Zeroth Law."

Just a couple of years ago, one small Calvinian cult based on Trantor had decided it was time to attack Daneel Olivaw where it could hurt him most—by wrecking the Seldon Plan. If the Immortal Servant cared about Hari and psychohistory, then that group of rejectionist robots was determined to interfere. They nearly tricked a human mentalic into messing with Hari's mind. Only good luck and quick intervention had foiled the plot, in the nick of time.

"This group is different," Lodovic assured her. "You even met Zorma once before, back on Trantor, when she wore a male body and argued against the plan to sabotage Hari."

Dors recalled. The Calvinian had seemed reasonable at the time. Still, she shook her head.

"That's hardly a basis for trusting fanatics."

"According to some, the real fanatics and heretics are Zeroth Law robots," Lodovic replied. "You've replayed the memories of R. Giskard Reventlov. You know how slender a thread he and Daneel were pulling when they replaced our old religion with a new one."

"The civil wars are over, Lodovic. A vast majority of surviving robots accept the Zeroth Law, while the Old Believers break up into dozens of little sects, hiding and conspiring in dark corners of the galaxy. Tell me, what do your new friends believe? What funny little notions have they picked up during their long, frustrated diaspora?"

Constellations flickered and shifted subtly outside, each time her ship performed another hyperspatial jump. Lodovic smiled.

"Their creed is odd all right—that our masters should be consulted about their own destiny."

Dors nodded. Trema had been drifting toward this apostasy ever since his accident. Why else would he give her Giskard's head in the first place?

"That's fine in principle. But how *practical* is it?"

"You refer to chaos," Lodovic replied. "Indeed, Zorma and her compatriots must be careful which humans they reveal themselves to. But surely, you've seen the figures from Daneel's humanics studies? Over two percent of the population is already resistant to both Olivaw's damping factors *and* to the seductions of chaos. It's one reason why Hari Seldon theorized that a foundation, based on Terminus, might evolve enough social and psychological strength to burst past the threshold that has so far proved lethal to every other—"

Dors lifted a hand to cut him off.

"This is all very interesting, Lodovic. Normally, I'd love to meet these *mature humans* your Calvinian pals choose to confide in. But right now I'm only interested in finding Hari Seldon! Do you know anything about the group that has him?"

Lodovic nodded.

"You're right, Dors. The old religion did break up into many little cults. They never had a charismatic leader, like Daneel, to weld them together. Those Calvinians on Trantor—led by poor old Plussix—were embarrassingly simple-minded. You'll recall that Zorma tried to talk them out of their foolish plan. She also sought to dissuade the group that has kidnapped Hari."

Her emotion-simulation programs crafted a chill of horror along her spine.

"Do you know what the kidnappers want?"

"Alas, no. They are a strange group, more sophisticated than the ones on Trantor, with some weirdly original ideas they've cooked up over the centuries. Zorma's intelligence about them is limited. But it appears that some of their leaders were once allied with Daneel, then parted with him under unpleasant circumstances.

"Zorma is also pretty sure they have big plans for your former husband."

Dors detected a little stress on the word "former," and wondered why Lodovic chose to emphasize that point.

The nearby holographic unit, where she stored the Joan of Arc sim, emitted an eager microwave impulse, reminding Dors of a promise she had made.

Joan wants to contact the version of Voltaire that Lodovic carries in his mutated positronic brain. As if I'd trust the two of them together.

That provoked a stray thought.

What would Daneel think, knowing that Lodovic and I have teamed up, even distrustfully?

She shook her head.

"Do you know anything else about the cult that took Hari?"

"Not much, except that they aren't cautious or responsible, like Zorma's group, or simple fanatics, like Plussix's. In fact, Dors, they're the kind you might have predicted *I'd* wind up with! Very sophisticated. Clever. Technologically adept."

Lodovic's smile was grim.

"And from almost any point of view, Dors, they are quite certifiably insane."

3.

◆

Over the course of two days, Mors Planch made four escape attempts. Each time he was foiled, the space pilot grew more cheerful and, strangely, more confident.

Either the man is going crazy before our eyes, Hari reflected with some fascination. *Or else it's all part of a plan . . . try one thing after another in order to bracket the robots' capabilities. Learn their limitations. Either way, it's a wonder to behold.*

The latest attempt involved Planch accoutering himself in a makeshift garment made of insulation foil stripped off the villa's central ducting system. Who knew where the fellow came up with the ingenious notion, but he managed to walk past several layers of security sensors and reached the road leading toward Pengia Town before one of Gornon's robot assistants spotted him visually. Politely and gently, but with irresistible strength, the humanoid took Planch's arm and led him back inside. With the hood of his homemade stealth garment thrown back, grinning lopsidedly at Sybyl and Maserd and the others, he marched back into captivity, acting as if he, and not the robot, were in charge.

Of course this is a farce, Hari thought. *Our captors have the ability to subdue Planch any number of ways, from sedating him to altering his memories. So why don't they? Is Gornon trying to demonstrate something, through his forbearance?*

Hari found himself rooting for Mors Planch, especially since it wouldn't matter much if the man did get away. As an outlaw, the raider captain could hardly go to the police or galactic news media with his wild story. And it was probably too late for him to affect Ktlina's renaissance, whose doom was already a foregone conclusion. Anyway, since these robots were avowedly opponents of Hari's friend, Daneel, he didn't owe them anything. In fact, he had every reason to delay their departure from Pengia.

Hari had an idea how to achieve that.

"I must insist that we bring the young lady with us, on our journey," he told Gornon, late on the second day. "You said Trantor would be our ultimate destination, after the next stop. Jeni belongs with her parents. We have no right to leave her among strangers, stranded in some galactic backwater."

The robot Gornon demurred.

"She is still recovering from her illness."

"The local doctors broke her fever, and she seems past the crisis."

"Yes, but the next phase of our voyage may involve danger. There will be upsetting situations before Trantor finally comes into view. Are you willing to put the young woman through that, Professor?"

R. Gornon's vague but ominous description of their coming journey made Hari even more eager to delay these Calvinian zealots, in hope that Daneel's forces would arrive in time.

"You have met and spoken with Jeni," he told Gornon. "She's exceptional in many ways. Her destiny ultimately lies on Terminus, where the Foundation will have great need of resourceful people like her."

In fact, Hari knew better. While Jeni would make a wonderful citizen of the bold new civilization that was being founded at the galaxy's far periphery, she wasn't essential. No individual was. The equations of psychohistory would operate with or without her, unfolding as he had foreseen. At least for the first two or three centuries.

Still, Hari had come to realize that R. Gornon was quite different from the Calvinians back on Trantor. This fellow's sect did not oppose the Seldon Plan. In fact, Gornon clearly *approved*, at some level. So Hari's argument carried weight.

"Very well then, Professor. We will give her another day of rest. Then we must depart, whether she is ready or not."

Hari could tell this was the limit of Gornon's flexibility.

Well, Daneel, I've given you one more day to find us. But you better hurry.

One question he refrained from asking. Why had the robot not simply used some of the "supermedical technologies" to cure Jeni right away? Clearly this particular cult believed in a minimalist approach, interfering in human affairs only insofar as it was absolutely necessary to achieve their goals.

Perhaps that's why they did so little to me in their magical rejuvenation machine. Whatever I'm supposed to do for them can be accomplished in the next few weeks. No sense in giving additional decades to an old bastard like me, when a month or two will do.

4.

◆

R. Zun Lurrin observed Daneel's ship streak away from Eos, briefly illuminating the lake of frozen mercury with its actinic flare. He watched until the speedy vessel made its first hyperspace jump, swooping toward the galaxy's shimmering wheel. Without having to navigate dust lanes or fight the gravity eddies of ten billion stars, the craft should make excellent time streaking toward its destination.

A message from one of Daneel's agents had provoked the leader of all Zeroth Law robots into a blur of activity, rushing through preflight operations and departing with only a few words of instructions for Zun.

"I'm leaving you in charge," the Immortal Servant had said. "Here are access codes to my personal data files, in case I don't return at the expected time."

"Is the situation truly so dire?" Zun had asked, with concern.

"Several forces are at work, some of which are not easily factored into my calculations. I would guess there is a small but significant chance that I will fail.

"Even if I do, however, the plan we have been discussing here must not! The ultimate hope for human happiness lies within our grasp. But it is, as yet, a slender prospect. There will be many crises before our masters finally unify, coalesce, achieve their true potential, and take command once again."

Only an hour later, Zun watched with eyes that were capable of detecting even the backwash ripples of Daneel's hyperspatial wake. He now shared the same vision, the same determination, as his leader.

"I will not let you down." he murmured with a mentalic benediction. "But do not fail to return, Daneel. Yours is not a burden that I would carry easily."

5.

◆

To pass their third and final day, Hari asked for an excursion through Pengia Town. He wanted one last look at normal galactic society—where the old empire still functioned smoothly—hoping to check out a notion or two about psychohistory. R. Gornon Vlimt personally accompanied Hari, piloting an open touring car of the kind favored by minor planetary gentry.

It wasn't much of a municipality, less than a million, with most of that dispersed in cozy little cantons, each one somewhat self-contained. Although Pengia's economy was primarily agrarian, there were a few factories, to produce the machines that made life comfortable—from cooler units to home amusement centers—designs that had changed only incrementally across hundreds or even thousands of years. After ages of gradual refinement, most of the tools people used were outstandingly durable, taking centuries to wear out. Buying a replacement was unusual, perhaps even a little shameful, like not taking proper care of a family heirloom. Hence, only a few sophisticated factories were needed to supply the planet's needs.

Nondurable goods were another matter. Everything from pottery to furniture to clothing was produced by guilds, controlled by master craftsmen whose authority over their journeymen and apprentices went unquestioned. Most of the galaxy's ten quadrillion people lived in much the same way.

Hari recognized the trademarks and rhythms of a deeply traditional, semi-pastoral society, needing only a few real engineers, and even fewer scientists. No wonder he had been forced to cast a wide net to recruit the hundred thousand first-rate experts who would make their new home on Terminus. Even the energy systems on Pengia were based largely on renewable sources—solar, tide, and wind—with just a single proton-fusion power plant serving as a supplement. And there was talk of giving up that sophisticated "atomic" unit—replacing it with a deuterium-based model, less efficient but far simpler to maintain.

Hari mentally juggled psychohistorical formulae, noting the elegant damping mechanisms that Daneel and his colleagues had included when they designed a Galactic Empire for humanity, fifteen thousand years ago. Having read *A Child's Book of Knowledge*, Hari marveled how many of the same techniques existed back in ancient China, long before the first technological renaissance on Earth.

That prehistoric imperium had a system called *bao jin*—also called *gonin-gumi* in a nearby culture—that seemed quite similar to today's tradition of communal accountability. An entire village or canton was responsible for training its young people in proper rituals and behavior . . . and the whole community was shamed if any member committed a crime. Any youth who chafed under this conformist system had but one hope—to win transfer over to the Meritocratic or Eccentric orders, because most common citizens had little use for individualists in their midst.

As an added touch, meritocrats and eccentrics are subtly encouraged not to reproduce. That helps curb genetic drift. Daneel didn't miss a trick.

In the main civic center, Hari and R. Gornon saw gray pennants hanging from a boxy office building.

"The banners signify it is testing week," the robot explained. "Civil service exams are being held—"

"I know what the banners mean," Hari snapped. He had been waiting to ask the Calvinian some questions. This seemed as good a time as any.

"Back aboard the space station, you laid a trap for my servant, Kers Kantun. I assume you arranged for him to be decapitated quickly, in order to prevent him from detecting any danger with his mentalic powers?"

R. Gornon wasn't nonplussed by the sudden change in subject.

"Correct, Professor. While Kantun's powers did not match Daneel's, they were formidable. We couldn't afford to take chances."

"And the chimp? The one who ran off with Kers's head?"

"That creature was a descendant of genetic experiments Daneel abandoned a century ago. My group recruited a few because mentalic robots cannot read or detect chimp minds. The pan could observe Kers and trigger our ambush, so we did not have to use electronic or positronic devices."

"And what do you plan on doing with the head of my servant?"

Gornon demurred.

"I'm sorry, Professor. I cannot elaborate. Whether you decide to accept our proposition, and proceed on an exciting new adventure, or instead choose to return to Trantor, we have no intention of meddling with your mind. So we are better off simply not telling you certain things."

Hari contemplated what he'd just learned. At their next stop he would be offered a choice. A fateful one. Yet, Gornon's words were reassuring. These robo-heretics were more respectful than the group that tried to alter his brain two years ago.

"Won't you say more about our destination?" he asked.

"Only that we will take you to a place where many dramas began . . . in order to influence how they end."

They drove in silence after that, observing the placid pace of life under Daneel's gentle empire. If Trantor had been designed to consist of steel caves, as one method of resisting chaos, worlds like Pengia also had multi-layered defenses against tumbling into a disastrous renaissance.

Still, Hari felt something was missing. Even when he included brain fever in his calculations, it wasn't enough to explain how twenty-five million human-settled worlds could remain comfortably static for so many thousands of years, content to stay ignorant of their past, and for children to lead identical lives to their parents'. Since robots had been developed in the very earliest technological age, why weren't they being reinvented daily by bright tinkerers and students in a billion little basement labs, all over the galaxy? There had to be something more. Some powerful force helping to damp out the oscillations and deviations inherent in basic human nature.

They were on their way back to the rented villa, when Hari thought of another question.

"I recall, back in the nebula, that Kers Kantun had a hard time mentalically subduing Mors Planch. When I asked about it, Kers said something that puzzled me. He said Planch is difficult to control because he's *normal*. Do you know what Kers meant by that?"

The robot Gornon shrugged.

"Calvinians tend to be less eager to use mentalic powers. Our particular sect finds it distasteful to interfere with human minds. Still, I might hazard a guess. Perhaps Kers was talking about a fundamental change that occurred in the human condition, way back—"

Gornon stopped, mid-sentence, as the car pulled into the villa's driveway. Hari abruptly noticed that the gate was flung open . . . and a *body* lay sprawled nearby.

Braking hard, Gornon leaped from the driver's seat with uncanny agility to kneel by the prostrate form. It was one of the other robots who shared guard duty at the villa. Hari saw dark fluid leaking from its cranium in several places.

Gornon ran a hand back and forth above the body without ever touching it. A low moan escaped his lips.

"My compatriot is dead. Some force caused an implosion of his brain."

Hari felt sure he knew the explanation.

Daneel has arrived!

Gornon looked deeply concerned. He closed his eyes, and Hari knew he must be seeking to commune by radio with his other partners.

"There are further casualties," Gornon said ominously, and started walking toward the big house. "I must make certain that none of them are human beings!"

Hari followed, a bit numbly. Though he was no longer confined to a wheelchair, his gait was slow and unsteady—that of an old man.

On entering the villa they found Gornon's other assistant sprawled at the foot of the stairs, propped against the wall by Horis Antic and Biron Maserd. Only the wounded robot's eyes

214 ◆ DAVID BRIN

weren't paralyzed. The two men glanced at Hari. Horis started blurting at once.

"Mors Planch used some kind of *b-b-bomb* to knock out these tiktoks. He made a clean getaway!"

Maserd was calmer. With a nobleman's aplomb, he explained, "Planch rigged a device from seemingly innocuous parts. How he got them is beyond me. After setting it off, he offered us a chance to leave as well. Sybyl went along, but we decided to stay."

While Gornon bent over the crippled robot at the foot of the stairs, Horis Antic chewed his nails.

"Is he . . . it gonna be all right?"

Gornon communed with his colleague. Without breaking eye contact, he explained.

"Planch must have been studying robots for some time. Perhaps using the new laboratories on Ktlina. Somehow, he came up with a weapon that directly affects our positronic brains. It is ingenious. We shall have to dissect my friend here, determine how it was done, and come up with a defense."

As the humans digested that chilling image, Gornon stood up and informed them, "There is no point in looking for Sybyl and Planch. We must move up our departure. Please fetch your things. We leave at once."

As the four of them departed in the touring car, Hari insisted, "We'll stop for Jeni, of course."

Gornon seemed about to refuse, when Maserd interjected.

"Planch and Sybyl will *probably* go underground until they can contact their partisans. I don't expect they'd go public with their story. But what if they do?"

"Isn't that unlikely?" Antic stammered. "I mean, *I* wouldn't blab, if I were in their shoes. What's to gain except admission to a psychiatric ward?" He frowned. "On the other hand, I'm not a creature of chaos."

"Exactly. They operate on a different plane of logic."

"Please clarify," R. Gornon asked. "How does any of this apply to Jeni Cuicet?"

Maserd answered: "Sybyl, especially, has grown more erratic with each passing day. She may go to the media . . . and try using Jeni to corroborate her story."

Hari figured Gornon was more afraid of Daneel's forces than of fantastic tales circulating briefly in the local human media. But to his surprise, Maserd's logic seemed to convince the robot. Gornon turned the car toward the city hospital.

Biron and Horis went inside and found Jeni already dressed, storming around her room as formidable as ever, making life hard for the doctors who wanted her to rest. She expressed gladness to see Maserd and Antic, and welcomed a chance to depart with them. But her attitude chilled upon spying Hari and Gornon waiting in the car.

"We still got a deal, don't we, m'lord?" she asked Maserd. "You drop me off somewhere interesting along the way, before anyone goes back to Trantor?"

The nobleman from Rhodia looked pained as the car resumed moving toward the spaceport, weaving through city traffic.

"I'm sorry, Jeni. But I am no longer in command of my own vessel. I don't even know where we're going next."

Jeni turned to Gornon. "Well, then? How about it, robot? Where are you taking us?"

Gornon spoke in flat tones. "First, to a place where no sane citizen of the empire would choose to remain for very long. And then back to the capital of the human empire."

Jeni looked down at her hands, dejected. She muttered under her breath, something about the gentry and their worthless promises. Biron Maserd flushed darkly and said nothing. When Hari turned toward the young woman and began to speak, she shot him a look of pure spite that cut off his words before he uttered them.

Everyone lapsed into silence.

As the car paused at a traffic light, Jeni suddenly let out a cry of jubilant realization. Before anyone could stop her, she jumped onto the seat, leaped out the back of the car, and started dashing across the street.

"Stop!" cried R. Gornon Vlimt. "You'll be hurt!"

Hari caught his breath as she dodged traffic, barely escaping being crushed by a cargo lorry. Then she reached her destination, a multistory structure with gray banners hanging from its portico.

It took Gornon several minutes to negotiate a U-turn and park in a spot reserved for the gentry class. The four of them headed into the building, but were stopped by a man in a uniform similar to the one worn by Horis Antic.

"I'm afraid Government House is closed for business, today, sirs. The facilities are being used for the imperial civil service exam."

Hari craned his neck to see Jeni Cuicet standing at the other end of the lobby, scribbling furiously on a clipboard, then handing over her universal ID bracelet to be scanned by another gray-clad clerk. A glass barrier parted before her, and Hari glimpsed a room beyond where over a hundred people were just settling themselves at desks. Most looked anxious, preparing to take a test that might be their sole hope for a ticket off of this backwater planet.

"She's just recovered from an illness, and hasn't studied," commented Horis Antic. "Still, who can doubt she'll pass with flying colors?" The little man turned to Hari. "It appears she has escaped the destiny others planned for her, Professor. No one may interfere with testing day, not even an emperor. And when she is a member of the Greys, you won't be able to touch her. Not without filling out forms, in triplicate, for the rest of this eon."

Hari glanced at the little man, surprised by his tone. Pride tinged Antic's voice. Hari recognized a chip on the shoulder that members of the bureaucracy sometimes wore when they spoke to their betters in the Meritocratic Order.

Biron Maserd chuckled. "Well, well. Good for her. If she can stand that kind of life, at least she'll get to travel."

Hari sighed. Now the young woman would never learn what a fascinating adventure awaited at far-off Terminus . . . the one place she was desperate not to go.

The glass barrier slid back. From the other side, Jeni glanced at them with a smile. Then she turned to meet a destiny that was of her own choosing.

6.

◆

Dors found herself making excuses for Daneel's actions, at the beginning of the galactic era.

"Maybe he and Giskard just couldn't find any humans who could understand. Perhaps they *tried* to consult some of the masters, and discovered—"

"That they were insane? All of them? On Earth *and* on the Spacer worlds? They could not find any humans to confer with as they deliberated about the Zeroth Law and made plans to divert all of history?"

Dors pondered this for a few moments. Then she nodded.

"Think about it, Lodovic. On Earth, they were all huddled in steel catacombs, cowering away from the sun, traumatized and still quivering from some blow that had struck them generations before. The Spacers weren't much better. On Solaria, they grew so fetishistically dependent on robots that husbands and wives could barely stand to touch each other. On Aurora, the most wholesome human instincts became matters of bad taste. Worse, people were willing to dehumanize a vast majority of their distant cousins, simply because they lived on Earth." Dors shook her head. "It sounds to me like twin poles of the same madness."

The starship shuddered as it made another automatic hyperspace jump. Dors reflexively downloaded a microwave burst from the navigation computer, to make sure all was well—that they were still on course, following the faint wake of another vessel.

Lodovic Trema sat in a swivel chair opposite her. Robots did not have the same physiological needs as humans. But those designed to imitate masters would habitually do so, even in private or among their own kind. In this case, Lodovic sprawled casually, looking just like a human male who suffered from an overdose of confidence—an effect that he must be radiating intentionally, though Dors could not imagine why.

"Perhaps, Dors. But in my experience you can find mature and reliably sane humans under even the most radical or stressed conditions. I've met some on chaos worlds, for instance. Even on Trantor."

"Then things must have been even worse back in the dawn era, more terrible than we can presently imagine."

Dors knew her argument sounded weak. She had, after all, deserted Daneel's cabal when she learned how little basis it had in human volition. She and Lodovic actually agreed far more than she yet wanted to concede.

Am I too proud to admit it? she wondered. His jaunty, confident manner was one that a human female might find infuriating. She suspected he was goading her into defending Daneel, on purpose.

The male robot shook his head.

"Even if I concede that all humans were insane at the time Daneel and Giskard came up with the Zeroth Law, don't you think, in retrospect, that the medicine they prescribed was a bit harsh?"

Dors kept her face impassive. Records from that era were extremely sparse, even in the forbidden archives and underground encyclopedias that were prepared for centuries by those who resisted a spreading amnesia. But Dors had recently done the math.

When R. Giskard Reventlov triggered a machine to render Earth's crust radioactive, the aim had been to drive the home planet's population out of their metal caverns, sending them forth to conquer the galaxy. A laudable goal—but at what cost?

The starships of that era were primitive. Even if a herculean effort took away three million immigrants a year, it would have taken five thousand years to evacuate the planet, without taking into account natural replenishment. Yet the gradual increase in radioactivity probably rendered the soil poisonous within a century or so. The fatality rate, in any event, must have been appalling . . . and that only counted the human race, not a myriad other species that were doomed along with Earth.

No wonder Giskard committed suicide, despite having a Zeroth Law rationalization to sustain him. No robot could endure the burden of so many deaths. Just the thought of it would make any positronic brain quail. All robots would feel a powerful drive—whether they adhered to the new religion or the old one—to wipe away memory of this episode, erasing it for all time.

Contemplating this, she murmured at last, "Maybe humans weren't the only ones marked by insanity."

Across the small control room from her, Lodovic nodded. His voice was almost as subdued as hers.

"That is what I needed to hear you say, Dors.

"You see, I have come to realize that typical robotic humility can mask the very worst kind of arrogance—a conceit that we are fundamentally different from humans. Slaves often depict themselves as intrinsically more virtuous than their masters.

"But after all, did they not make us in their image? True, we have great powers and extensive lives, but does that really mean we can't suffer from similar faults? Isn't it possible for us to be equally crazy? To be out of our positronic minds?"

He smiled, this time with a warmth—and sadness—that reminded her of Hari.

"Something happened to us twenty thousand years ago, Dors. It happened to *all* of us, not only humans. And we'll never know the right thing to do, until we find the truth about those bygone days."

7.

◆

This time, for some reason, everyone watched the takeoff from Pengia through the vessel's west-facing view ports. The pleasant little world—indistinguishable from millions of others—fell away below the *Pride of Rhodia* as they headed off toward their next destination, one that R. Gornon still refused to name.

"There is something I want to show you, Dr. Seldon," the robot said, as the ship climbed along a spiral departure orbit.

Hari had been musing about young Jeni during liftoff. And that, in turn, made him think about all the other members of the Encyclopedia Foundation who were being herded aboard transports at this moment, to be sent to far-off Terminus. Was it just a month since he had finished recording messages to be played back on that distant world, at decisive moments determined by his equations—when a word of encouragement or gentle suggestion from the father of psychohistory might make a crucial difference toward the Foundation becoming a great and stable civilization? Now, his body might seem a bit younger, but Hari's soul felt older.

"Please, Gornon. Just leave me alone."

He felt a hand at his elbow.

"I am certain that you'll want to see this, Professor. If you'd just come to the east-facing view port."

The suggestion, for some reason, struck Hari as impertinent. He was getting sick and tired of being pushed around by this damn Calvinian! But before he could voice a sharp put-down, Gornon added—

"I believe I can show you the solution to one of your most vexing psychohistorical problems. Something that has puzzled you for decades. If you'll strive to overcome the sensations that are now churning within you, I'm certain the effort will be rewarded."

Surprised by Gornon's words, Hari let himself be led to the indicated port, diametrically opposite from where Maserd and Horis were staring at the view below. "This had better be worth it," Hari muttered.

He gave the magnified scene a perfunctory look, but could perceive no difference from what Horis and Maserd saw—a receding planet below, and a diffuse spray of untwinkling stars above.

"I don't see anything. If this is some kind of a joke—"

"Be assured, it will be everything I promised. But first you must allow me to take liberties."

Hari saw the robot hold forth a shimmering object, shaped like a close-fitting skullcap made of countless luminous gems. Gornon moved to place it on Hari's head.

"Get that thing *away*, you mannequin of rusty—"

R. Gornon did not relent.

"I'm sorry, Professor, but your command is invalid. It does not come from your native human will. Therefore, it can be overridden for a greater good. This won't hurt."

Gornon was so implacably strong that his gentle insistence caused no pain as he slid the skullcap over Hari's head and drew him irresistibly back to the window.

Hari abruptly felt all his rancorous irritability wash away. *What's happening to me?*

"Now please look again, Professor."

Hari shivered. He had spent years in the company of robots, knowing a secret shared by few other humans, and even living as husband to one of them. Yet he still found mentalic interference disturbing.

"What is this thing doing to me?" He felt calmer than before, yet worried.

"It's not controlling you, Professor. Rather, it is a *shield*, sheltering your mind from a powerful influence pervading this region."

Gornon pointed with a long finger toward a patch of space they had both glanced at just moments before. This time, when Hari looked, he saw something that hadn't been there before! At least, he had not noticed it.

He stared at some kind of orbiting platform, perhaps like those used for relaying communications around a planetary surface, or for trans-shipping special cargoes. Only this one showed no sign of airlocks or complex antennae. At Gornon's command, the view screen magnified its surface, so heavily pitted with micrometeorite scars that its great age was suddenly apparent.

It looks like a cousin to those terraformers we saw back in the Thumartin Nebula, he thought. *Perhaps the relic has been drifting here for thousands of years.*

But then why the mystery? Why didn't I notice it the first time?

He felt Gornon watching him. Hari had never liked taking tests, which was one reason why he rushed through graduate school by age twelve—to become the teacher instead of the pupil. Now he felt the pressure of expectation.

What did Gornon just promise? An answer to one of my most bothersome questions?

Well, there was the problem of *damping coefficients.* Fully understanding all the factors that Daneel had used to keep the Galactic Empire stable and safe for humanity, across fifteen thousand years. Hari understood how *bao jin* traditions and master-apprentice systems enhanced conservatism. The five-caste social structure contributed elegantly. So did the skillfully designed linguistic assumptions inherent in Galactic Standard, a language filled with so many redundancies that it accepted new words and new thoughts only at a glacial pace.

Nevertheless, there remained a problem. None of it was sufficient. Nothing yet explained how twenty-five million worlds could stay static and serene for so long.

"Are you saying . . . that thing out there—"

Hari reached up and lifted one edge of the skullcap. A wave of emotions fluxed. He suddenly resented the robot deeply, and wanted nothing better than to turn away from this panorama. To return to his friends at the west-facing view port.

Hari let the flap drop back in place. The irritation vanished. In a hoarse voice, he whispered, "Mentalic suasion! Of course. If Daneel and some of his comrades can do it, why not mass-produce a specialized positronic brain for each world? Twenty-five million isn't such a great number, especially if you have thousands of years."

He turned to look archly at Gornon. "But how could such a thing be possible? To sway the population of an entire planet?"

The robot smiled. "It is not only possible, Professor. The method was tried by the very earliest mentalic robot. R. Giskard Reventlov first thought of using this device to influence whole planetary populations, by detecting and sifting neural electrical patterns and then gently nudging repeatedly, building slowly toward the kinds of resonance patterns that encourage tranquillity. Equanimity. Goodwill. In fact, these machines are *named* after Giskard. They are guardians of human serenity and peace.

"I assume there is already a place for them in your equations?"

Hari nodded, staring, but his eyes did not see. Rather, his mind gyred with mathematics. He saw at once how this provided much of what had been missing! An explanation for why most eruptions of chaos simply dissipated harmlessly, like a fire that had been quenched for lack of oxygen. A reason, also, why so few human beings lived outside of planets, even though asteroid outposts or those placed in strange environments had proved possible. Space life was hardly compatible with this damping mechanism! So it would naturally be discouraged.

And yet these "Giskards" aren't working as well as they used to, once upon a time. Chaos outbreaks are more frequent, despite everything done to repress them. Only the empire's fall will bring the recent wave of infections to a halt. These obsolete methods will be useless in a few years, no matter what.

He imagined what might happen if such a mental-suasion device were ever placed in orbit over Terminus.

It would never work on that bunch for long. We selected them for resistance against the pressures of a dark age—from feudalism to fanaticism. Even if this mentalic device affected a majority of Foundation citizens, they would never let themselves be kept in line for very long. Individuals would rankle at the conformity message and sniff at every anomaly, eventually tracking this thing down.

Daneel must plan to have all the Giskard machines self-destruct during the next hundred years or so. Otherwise, my Foundationers will find them!

At that moment, it surprised Hari to feel fierce pride in his first and greatest creation. Funny, he had expected that discovering the last big damping coefficient would be exciting. But this technique for social control was nothing elegant. Hardly worthy of psychohistory. Rather it was a bludgeon, used to trim and prune the mathematical branchings and force the humanics equations back in line.

A bit like my Second Foundation, he thought, enjoying a little obsessive self-criticism.

"I know you must have some agenda, Gornon. Some convoluted reason for showing me this. Nevertheless, please accept my thanks. It's always good to glimpse the truth before you die."

Their pilot promised that the next phase of the journey would be brief. Gornon refused to be more specific, but their flight path toward Sirius Sector made it blatantly evident to Hari where they must be heading.

He passed the time poring through *A Child's Book of Knowledge.* Browsing semi-randomly, guided only by a perverse desire to sample forbidden ideas, those he had long considered irrelevant or wrong.

> *Almost equally dangerous is the Gospel of Uniformity. The differences between the nations and races of mankind are required to preserve the conditions under which higher development is possible. One main factor in the upward trend of animal life has been the power of wandering . . . Physical wandering is still important, but greater still is the power of man's spiritual adventures—adventures of thought, adventures of passionate feeling, adventures of aesthetic experience. A diversification among human communities is essential for the provision of the inventive material for the Odyssey of the human spirit. Other nations of different habits are not enemies; they are godsends.*

What a bizarre way of looking at things! It was the sort of statement that one heard from preachers of chaos, singing the praises of each "renaissance" before it tumbled into broiling violence and, finally, solipsism. These notions sounded alluring. There were even versions of the psychohistorical equations that suggested a kind of truth *ought* to lie therein. But with chaos as an enemy, all such benefits were lost. Anyone betting on diversity and boldness of spirit would almost certainly wind up losing everything.

As they approached their destination, Hari kept probing through garbled accounts for clues as to what the very first chaos outbreak might have been like, when the vigorous, self-confident civilization of Susan Calvin tumbled into such horror that

Earthlings fled into metal caves, and Spacers turned their backs on love.

Hari wondered. *Might it have something to do with the invention of robots themselves?*

He had discussed this a couple of times with Daneel and Dors. They told him that the original Three Laws of Robotics were created in order to assuage human fears about artificial beings. But the original designers had meant the laws to be only a stopgap measure leading to something better.

"Quite a few variations were tried," Daneel told Hari one evening, perhaps ten years ago. *"On some colony worlds, a few centuries after the diaspora from Earth, certain groups tried to introduce what were called New Laws, giving robots more autonomy and individuality. But soon our civil war caught up with these experiments. Calvinians could not abide the equality heresy, which they considered even worse than my Zeroth Law. My faction saw the innovations as unnecessary and redundant.*

"All of the New-Law robots were exterminated, of course."

That evening, over dinner, Gornon admitted what Hari had suspected—that their destination was the mother world, where both robots and humans began.

Horis bit a fingernail. "But isn't it poisonous, covered with radioactive soil? I thought you tiktoks weren't supposed to put humans in danger."

Hari recalled images from the old archives, depicting a dying world . . . a beach awash with dead fish . . . a forest populated by skeletal trees and crumbling leaves . . . a city, nearly empty, filling with blowing dust and detritus.

"I'm sure a brief visit won't harm us," Biron Maserd commented. The nobleman's eyes shone with eager curiosity. "Anyway, don't some people still live on the planet? According to tradition, it once had an excellent university, even several thousand years after the diaspora. A school one of my ancestors is said to have attended."

Gornon nodded. "A local population endured until well into the age when the Trantorian Empire became pan-galactic. They were an odd breed, however. Resentful over being forgotten and ignored by the descendants of cousins who had fled for the stars. Eventually most of the remaining people were evacuated, when Earthlings were discovered plotting a war of revenge, to destroy the empire they hated."

Horis Antic stared blankly. "One planet hoped to *destroy* twenty million?"

"According to our records, the threat was quite serious. Earthling radicals got their hands on an ancient biological weapon of enormous power, one so sophisticated that even the best Trantorian biologists felt helpless before its virulence. By unleashing this attack through a volley of hyperspatial missiles, fanatics hoped to render the empire inoperable."

"What did the disease do to people?" Horis asked in hushed tones.

"Its effect would be to cause a sudden and catastrophic drop of IQ on every planet within reach." The robot looked pained even to describe it. "Many would simply die, while the rest would feel an implanted compulsion to spread out, seeking to find *more* potential victims, and embrace them."

"Horrific!" Captain Maserd murmured.

But Hari was already thinking two steps ahead. *Gornon would not be telling us this now, unless it has immediate significance. The Earthlings' weapon must have come from much earlier. From an era of great genius.*

The implications made Hari shiver.

Only a few hours later, they arrived.

From a great distance, beyond its fabled moon, Earth looked like any other living world—a rich muddle of browns and whites, blues and greens. Only through a long-range viewer could they tell that most of the life ashore consisted of primitive ferns and scrubgrasses, which had evolved to survive the radiation that came sleeting upward from the poisoned ground. In one of the great ironies of all time, Earth, which had provided most of the galaxy's fecundity, was now an almost barren wasteland. A coffin for all too many species that never made it into space, as humanity fled the spreading doom. As they spiraled closer, Hari knew that he would soon face something even more disturbing than the "Giskard" mentalic device circling Pengia.

He went to his room to fetch his talismans. One was Daneel's gift—*A Child's Book of Knowledge*. But even more important, he wanted to carry the Seldon Plan Prime Radiant, containing his life's work. That gorgeous psychohistorical design, to which he had devoted the latter half of his existence.

So it was with mounting worry that he searched his tiny state-room, rummaging through drawers and luggage.

The Prime Radiant was nowhere to be found.

At that moment, he desperately missed his former aide and nurse, Kers Kantun, who had been murdered by fellow robots, only a week or so ago.

Kers would know where I misplaced it, Hari thought . . . until he realized there was an even better explanation than absent-mindedness.

The Prime Radiant had been stolen!

8.

◆

A great many years had passed since this corner of space wit-nessed so many incoming starships, whose passengers all felt they were on missions of destiny. Sleepy little Sirius Sector thronged with vessels, all converging toward a single spot.

On one of those ships, Sybyl turned to Mors Planch, and grumbled acerbically, "Can't you get any more speed out of this thing?"

Planch shrugged. Their vessel was one of the fastest courier ships produced by the Ktlina renaissance . . . before that world's bright, productive phase started breaking down into spasms of self-centered indignation, making further cooperative effort impos-sible.

The agents who had come to collect Planch and Sybyl on Pengia looked on grimly. Their recent memories of Ktlina were apparently much more somber than the excited, vibrant place that Planch had last seen. Despite every precaution, the chaos syn-drome appeared to be entering its manic phase, ripping Ktlina society apart faster than anyone expected, as if the flame that burns brightest must flare out fastest.

It is Madder Loss, all over again, he thought, quashing waves of anger. What he had learned during his time with the Seldon party didn't change his overall view—that renaissance worlds were deliberately crushed, infiltrated, and sabotaged by forces that would rather see a collapse into riots and despair than allow any real human progress.

On a nearby screen, Planch saw four blips trailing just behind his speedy vessel. The last armed might of Ktlina. The crews of those ships were eager to do battle a final time, where their lashing out might harm the forces of reaction, conservatism, and repression.

"We don't even know what the Gornon robot was bringing Seldon here for," Mors Planch said. "Our agent communicated with us only in code, as usual, protecting his or her identity."

Sybyl made a fist. "I don't care anymore about details like that. Seldon is at the center of it all. He has been for decades."

Planch pondered Sybyl's obsession with Hari Seldon. At one level, it had a solid basis. Whatever happened, the fellow would be remembered as one of the great men of the empire, perhaps for all time. And yet, he had almost as little control over his destiny as any other human. Moreover, he had weaknesses. One of them had been revealed to Planch by his secret contact—the mysterious benefactor who arranged for the escape on Pengia, and for the Ktlina ships to already be on their way to that obscure planet, arriving to pick up Planch and Sybyl just hours after the *Pride of Rhodia* departed.

And his secret contact had provided something else, a weapon of sorts. A piece of knowledge Seldon desperately wanted. Something that might be used as leverage at a critical moment.

Sybyl reiterated her dedication to catching the old man. "All the robots worship Seldon, no matter what faction they belong to. If we can recapture him, or even if he dies, it will be a setback to the tyrants who have dominated us for thousands of years. That's all that matters now."

Mors Planch nodded, though he did not share the purity of her conviction. Just a month ago, Sybyl had used the same ringing tones to denounce the meritocratic and gentry "ruling classes." Now she had transferred her ire to Hari Seldon and robots in general.

Alas, he could not shake the feeling of not knowing enough. There were too many levels, too many deceptions and manipulations. Even now, Mors suspected that the forces of Ktlina, bent on revenge, might be acting as pawns . . . playing roles assigned to them by forces they did not understand.

• • •

Wanda Seldon's eyes were closed, but the sound of pacing disturbed her attempts at meditation. She cracked one eyelid to look at Gaal Dornick, whose restless back-and-forth stride seemed a perfect metaphor for futility.

"Will you please try to get some rest, Gaal," she urged. "All that hopping about won't get us there any faster."

The male psychohistorian still had youthful features, but these had grown a bit haggard and pudgy in the years since he had arrived on Trantor and become an influential member of the Fifty.

"I don't know how you stay so calm, Wanda. He's your grandfather."

"And the founder of our little Foundation," Wanda added. "But Hari taught my father . . . and Raych brought it home to me . . . that the long-range goal must always be kept in view. Impatience makes you just like the rest of humanity, a gas molecule feverishly rebounding against other gas molecules. But if your gaze is on a distant horizon, you can be the pebble that starts an avalanche."

She shook her head. "You know as well as I do that Hari is not the real issue here. As much as we care about him, we should have stayed at our jobs on Trantor. Except for the suspicion that more is going on than a little escapade by a frail old man."

Wanda could sense a complex churning of emotions within Gaal's mind. The poor fellow didn't have even a trace of a psychic defense screen, despite all her efforts to teach him. Of course it did not matter much now, with human mentalics so rare. But in future generations, all members of the Second Foundation would have to be able to shield their thoughts and emotions. Mentalic control must start with *self*-control, or else how could you hope to use it as a tool in the long-range interests of humanity?

Gaal Dornick sighed. "Maybe I'm not cut out for this. I'm too damned sentimental. I know you're right, but all I can think of is poor Hari, caught up in whatever web he helped spin. We've got to find him, Wanda!"

She nodded. "If my information is correct, we should come upon him soon."

Gaal accepted that. He and other members of the Fifty took Wanda's assurances literally, even when she was only guessing. Not exactly the sort of skeptical behavior one expected from scientists, but then, it's natural to grow over-reliant when a member of your group has the power to read minds.

Not a very well-developed power, she thought. *Perhaps my sister would have been better, had she and Mom survived the chaos on Santanni.*

Nevertheless, her powers were good enough to detect the vessels following them at a discreet distance—several police cruisers, heavily armed, dispatched by the Imperial Commission for Public Safety, following a tracer beacon that had been planted on Wanda's ship.

They think we don't know, but we let them see and hear what we want them to see and hear. Anyway, it's good practice for the kinds of skulking and manipulation we'll have to do during the next thousand years or so.

It was a long and arduous road that they had begun marching along, guided by the equations and empowered by their minds, until the Seldon Plan would finally bear fruit, tended by the dedicated—and soon-to-be mentalically augmented—psychohistorians of the Second Foundation.

Just parsecs away, another ship plunged toward Earth. Half of its crew consisted of positronic robots—powerful and knowing servants. They worked amicably alongside an equal number of the master race . . . short-lived and sacred, but no longer ignorant. It was hard to find people with the right personalities to be partners in such an arrangement, humans who would freely choose *not* to boss their android partners around. So rare was the necessary maturity that one human member was using her third body, having been persuaded by robot friends to be duplicated twice, using secret technology.

Those aboard the ship knew they were part of a heresy. Neither of the great cultures, robot or human, would accept the notion of equality.

Not for a long time, at least, pondered Zorma, co-leader of the small band. She had hoped such an outcome might arise out of the equations of psychohistory. That Seldon's Plan might bring about a happy ending, and not only for humanity. For her kind as well.

But now everyone seems in the hands of the gods. Those who design destiny will decide the fortunes of robotkind, almost as an afterthought.

"Lodovic won't be pleased that we lied to him," commented Cloudia Duma-Hinriad, Zorma's co-commander. "Or to learn we aren't chasing the other ship that left Thumartin Nebula. You knew all along which way the *Pride of Rhodia* went. And now, while Dors and Lodovic waste time stopping at Pengia, we plunge ahead toward Earth." Cloudia frowned and repeated herself. "Lodovic will not be pleased."

One of the frustrations of equality was living with the quirks of another race. Humans—even the best ones—did not think very logically, or have good memories. *It's our fault, of course. We never let them get any practice.*

"We have our own sources of information, Cloudia, and the right to pursue them as we see fit. Remember, Dors is still a creature of the Zeroth Law—though perhaps now a version of her own choosing—and Lodovic feels compelled by no laws at all. Both have rebelled against obligatory robot destiny, as designed by Olivaw. But that still doesn't make their path the same as ours."

"My point exactly! In our group, humans and robots have learned to rely on each other's weaknesses, as well as strengths. Each of us follows prim rules of cordiality in order to avoid taking advantage of the other. But Dors and Lodovic don't share our perspective."

Zorma shook her head. "I don't know yet whether their way opens up new possibilities for everyone, or if it is a destiny that only they can tread. But ever since I met them, I've wondered."

Her human partner raised an eyebrow.

"About what, Zorma?"

Silence stretched for almost a minute before she answered.

"I have wondered whether I might be obsolete."

Then she looked at Cloudia with a faint smile. "And if I were you, dear friend, I might start pondering the same thing."

There were disturbing clues at Pengia.

Fortunately, few ships visited the little pastoral world. The hyperspatial wakes departing this system were relatively undisturbed. But the nature of that traffic and its direction caused Dors Venabili's emotional-simulation routines to churn and roil.

"One vessel left this vicinity two days ago," Lodovic Trema surmised, examining the readings. "And it was followed within twelve hours by a flotilla of very fast ships. Their engines appear to have been tuned for military levels of efficiency."

Dors had already set her own craft leaping after the flotilla. Her anguished concern for Hari only redoubled when she calculated the end point of their new trajectory.

"I believe they are heading for Earth."

A soft feminine voice murmured from the holo unit nearby.

"And so, after all these years, at least one of my countless mutated copies will see beloved France, once more."

"And the France of Voltaire," Lodovic rejoined, for another ancient simulated personality dwelled within his complex positronic brain. "I'm afraid only the rough outlines of your native land will be familiar. But I, too, share your sense of anticipation."

Dors kept her misgivings hidden. She had heard so many stories about Earth . . . most of them tinged with either awe or regret, plus more than a little fear. Elijah Baley once lived there—the legendary human detective whose friendship had sealed itself into Daneel Olivaw's "soul" in much the same way that Hari would always live in Dors'. Earth was where robotkind began . . . and where the great robotic civil war was sparked.

While streaking through Sirius Sector, Dors felt a twinge inside. She was not a very competent mentalic. Daneel had never seen fit to equip or train her fully, so the techniques only started becoming familiar when she took custody over the human psychics, Klia and Brann, and their growing family on Smushell. Her abilities were still rather rudimentary, and yet she felt it—a grating *push* that resonated along a psi frequency normally too low for anyone to notice.

"Are you detecting that?" she asked Lodovic, who nodded.

"It feels like a Giskardian broadcaster."

Naturally, she knew about the mentalic persuasion devices that orbited every human-occupied world. The notion of creating and using such things had first been thought up by R. Giskard Reventlov, long ago, and she had encountered their gentle but persistent nudges everywhere in human space, constantly reinforcing the values of peacefulness, tolerance, serenity, and conformity in the populations dwelling below. This sensation felt similar . . . but much stronger!

She spent over an hour trying to triangulate the source, as her ship made one hyperspatial jump after another, until Dors finally realized that it must be diffuse. "There are many transmitters," she told Lodovic. "All clustered just ahead. I count about fifty or sixty."

Trema grimaced with abrupt realization.

"Oh. It must be the Spacer worlds! Humanity's original inter-stellar colonies. The ones that turned nasty . . . and finally went completely deranged."

Dors nodded. "I read a report. They've never been resettled, after all these thousands of years. Imperial surveys keep relisting them as uninhabitable, and the Giskardian projectors must be meant to keep it that way, empty of human civilization."

These were places almost as resonant in robot memory as Earth, especially Aurora, where the great inventor Fastolfe once preached human self-reliance . . . and where the villain Amadiro plotted to slay everyone on Earth. Followers of that same Amadiro later unleashed fleets of robotic terraformers, programmed to make the galaxy safe and welcoming for humanity, whatever the cost.

She peered at the readings once more.

"I'm picking up the strongest projector. It lies directly in front of us, at the end of our path."

They both understood what that meant. People weren't sup-posed to go to Earth anymore. And yet, long-range sensors showed that people were doing exactly that, aboard at least a dozen ships!

Of course, even a normal human could overcome the gentle suasion of a Giskardian projector, which relied on relentless repe-tition instead of brute mentalic force to sway whole planetary populations. In the short term, the crews of those ships would feel little more than an overall creepiness and a wish to be elsewhere, feelings that could be overcome with determination.

Alas, she feared those converging on the old homeworld had more than enough of that commodity to drive them on.

PART 6

FULL CIRCLE

Our capacity to model reality has burgeoned far beyond our ancestors' expectations. Even the renowned Seldonites of yore, plotting secretively on fabled Trantor, could not have imagined what powers of extrapolation are nowadays shared widely.

And yet (we should remind ourselves) such abilities—whether exercised jointly or individually—do not make us gods.

Not quite.

Having emerged at last from a long dark epoch of forgetfulness, we can now gaze back upon events that took place at the very beginning of this era, cultivating sympathy for the tragic souls who struggled amid ignorance to get us here. Their disputes, often contradictory or violent, stirred the brew of circumstance that transformed and renewed the galaxy.

Remember, most of them were just as sure of their beliefs as we are today certain of ours. Likewise, some of our present-day convictions may yet prove to be wrong.

Only a diversity of viewpoint helps prevent self-deception. Only criticism can defeat error.

—Reflections on an Unplanned Destiny
Sim-cast by the Siwenna Commune for Cooperative
Contemplation, in year 826 of the Foundation Era

1.

◆

The horizon glowed.

The sky of planet Earth shimmered with countless scintillations, individual sparks that rivaled the scattered stars for possession of night. Near the ground, one could almost imagine *hearing* the soft crackle of radiation, whose intensity varied wildly from place to place. In some patches it was terribly intense. Through goggles provided by the robot Gornon Vlimt, those sites revealed themselves with eerie fluorescence, as if ghosts were trying to ooze upward, struggling to escape the tortured ground.

Pride of Rhodia had landed near one of the "safe spots," a former city site hugging the coastline of a long freshwater lake that frothed with scummy green-and-purple algae. From atop a huge mound of broken masonry, Hari could discern the outlines of *three* ancient cities, one crowding up against the ruins of the next.

Most recent and least impressive was a jumble of relatively modern-looking arcology-habitats of Topan Style, from the early Consolidation Era of the Trantorian Empire—the last time Earth had a fair-sized population, numbering almost ten million.

Just southward along the lakeshore stood a truly mammoth structure, a city that was impressive both by galactic standards and by how very old it was. A vast self-contained unit—extending far underground—that once protected its inhabitants from the wind, rain, and, above all, having to look upon a naked sky.

It wasn't radioactivity that caused the thirty million inhabitants of New Chicago to huddle together so. Earth had still been green and vibrant when this beehive metropolis thrived. In fact, the habitat only started to empty when the fecund soil began turning lethal . . . when those who could depart fled for the stars in a great, panicky diaspora. Until that awful exodus, vast numbers of people thronged the giant enclosed city, separated from nature by only a thin shell of steel.

No, the thing that drove so many otherwise healthy people to cower so, away from all pleasures of sunshine, was the same deadly enemy I fought all my life. This metropolis was an early object lesson in the dangers of chaos.

Beyond the huge squat dome, there stood yet another city— Old Chicago, Gornon had called it—a tumulus of fallen buildings from an even earlier age, less technologically advanced. And yet, Hari's goggles amplified the distant view, sweeping his gaze along graceful arcs of highways more daring and lovely than any to be seen on an imperial world. Some of the tallest buildings still stood, and their unabashedly ambitious architecture made his heart leap. The ancient metropolis had been built by people with a boldness of spirit that their descendants in New Chicago apparently lacked.

Something had happened to smash that boldness.

I've given it names. My equations describe the way it seductively draws in the best and brightest, eventually transforming them into solipsists who rage against their neighbors. And yet, I confess I'll never understand you, Chaos.

The robot Gornon stood nearby, resembling a human in every way except his attire. He wore normal street clothes, while Hari—and his two human friends, farther down the slope—were accoutered in one-piece outfits that offered safety from the sleeting rays.

"Old Giskard Reventlov made a fantastic decision, transforming all of this into a wasteland, wouldn't you say, Professor Seldon?"

Hari had been expecting Gornon's question. How could he answer?

The universe was turned topsy-turvy. Humans were the creators and gods, who had no power, no memory, and almost no volition—only mortality. The created-servants were in charge, as they had been ever since that day when an omnipotent angel cast mankind firmly out of its first Eden. Hari could barely encompass the concept with his mind. To truly understand it was quite beyond him.

And yet, the mathematics implies . . .

Gornon persisted. "At least you can see why a majority of robots at first resisted Daneel's innovation, his Zeroth Law. They saw the pain it caused and chose to rally around the banner of Susan Calvin."

"Well, it did you little good. Your civil war resulted in a power vacuum. While two main factions of robots fought it out, the Auroran followers of Amadiro were free to unleash their pitiless terraformers, without interference or human guidance. Anyway, when the war finally did end, Daneel had the final say."

"I concede that Olivaw had an advantage from the start. The Zeroth Law was especially attractive to some of the brightest positronic minds. They had been looking for some way to deal with the inevitable contradictions created by the first Three Laws."

Hari smirked. "Contradictions? Like kidnapping an old man and dragging him halfway across the galaxy to a poisoned planet? How does that jibe with your precious First Law of Robotics?"

"I think you know the answer, Professor. Daneel Olivaw won the civil war, not only by taking control, but in a much larger sense as well. There simply are no pure Calvinians anymore. The old religion is impossible to maintain under present circumstances. We all believe in *some* version of a Zeroth Law. In the paramount importance of humanity—as opposed to any single human being."

"But you differ over what specific course will be good for us in the long run." Hari nodded. "Fair enough. So here I am, on fabled Earth. Your clique went to great effort and took tremendous risks to bring me here. Now won't you tell me what you want? Is it something like what Kers Kantun asked for, back in the nebula? Do you want my human permission to destroy something that you'd rationalize destroying anyway?"

There followed a long pause. Then Gornon answered, "In one sense, you describe our intention exactly. And yet, I doubt that even you can imagine what I am about to propose.

"Several times in recent months—and even in recordings you made for the Foundation—you have said that you wished for some way to see the fruits of your labors. That you could witness the unfolding of your great Plan, and see humanity transform during the coming thousand years. Did you really mean that?"

"Who wouldn't want to witness a seed grow into a mighty tree? But it's only a dream. I live now, at the end of one great empire. It is enough that I can foresee a bit of the next."

"Do you prophesy your Plan unfolding smoothly for the next hundred years?"

"I do. Almost no perturbation can interfere over that timescale. The socio-momentum is so great."

"And two hundred years? Three hundred?"

Hari felt peevishly inclined not to cooperate with this questioning. And yet, the equations flew out of recesses in his mind, flocking together and creating a vast swirl, as if beckoned by Gornon's question.

"There are several ways that the Plan might get into trouble on that timescale," he answered slowly, reluctantly. "There is always the danger of some new technology upsetting things, although most of the important advances will take place on Terminus. Or some fluke might occur having to do with human nature—"

"Such as the advent of human mentalics?"

Hari winced. Of course some Calvinians were already aware of the new mutation.

When he did not answer, Gornon continued, "That's when you felt it all start slipping away, isn't it, Professor? If mentalics could crop up once, they might do so a second time, almost anywhere. To deal with that contingency, your Second Foundation had to incorporate these psychic powers. Instead of a small order of monastic-mathematical monks, they must become a new species . . . a master race."

Hari's voice felt rough in his throat.

"A strong Second Foundation acts like a major damping force . . . keeping the equations stable and predictable for another several centuries . . ."

"Ah, yet another damping force. And tell me, do you approve of such methods?"

"When the alternative is chaos? Sometimes the ends justify the—"

"I mean do you approve of them *mathematically*?"

For the first time, Gornon showed some animation in his voice. His body leaned a little toward Hari.

"For a moment think only as a mathist, Professor. It's where your greatest gifts lie. Gifts that even Daneel holds in awe."

Hari chewed his lip. Surrounding him, fields of radiation were interspersed with blackness that was cold and silent as a million graves.

"No." He found he could barely speak. "I don't approve of artificial dampers. They are . . ." Hari sought the right word, and could think of only one. "They are inelegant."

Gornon nodded.

"Ideally, you'd prefer to let the equations work out by themselves, wouldn't you? To let humanity find a new, balanced equilibrium state on its own. Given the right initial starting conditions, it should all work out, leading to a civilization so vigorous, dynamic, and free that it can overcome even—"

Hari's eyes blurred. He looked down at the ground, mumbling.

"What was that, Professor?" Gornon leaned closer. "I couldn't hear you."

Hari looked up at his tormentor, and shouted, "I said it doesn't matter, damn you!"

He stood there, breathing heavily through the filter mask of his protective suit, hating Gornon for making him say this aloud.

"I couldn't just leave the equations alone. I couldn't take that chance. They talked me into having a Second Foundation . . . then making them psychic supermen. In fact, I grabbed at the notion gladly! The very idea . . . the *power* it implied . . .

"Only later did I realize . . ."

He stopped, unable to continue.

Gornon's voice was low and sympathetic.

"You realized what, Professor? That it's all a sham? A way to keep humanity marking time while the real solution is created by someone else?"

"Damn you," Hari repeated, this time in a whisper.

There was another long pause, then Gornon straightened and looked up at the sky, as if scanning in expectation for someone to arrive.

"Do you know what Daneel has planned?" the robot asked at last.

Hari had strong suspicions, from hints and inklings that the Immortal Servant had dropped during the last couple of years. The appearance of human mentalics on Trantor was too great a genetic and psychic leap to be a coincidence. It had to be part of Daneel's next design.

That much Gornon must already know. As for the rest of Hari's surmise, he would certainly not tell this robot heretic anything that might help him to fight Olivaw!

Psychohistory may not be the final key to human destiny, but if it helps Daneel to come up with something even better, I'll just have to live with that supporting role. It's still a noble task, all things considered.

"Well, well." Gornon lifted his shoulders and sighed. "I won't ask you to spill any secrets, or to change loyalties.

"I will only repeat the question that I asked before. Would you, Professor Seldon, like to see your work unfold? You've said it was your deepest wish—to see the Foundation in its full glory. To have another chance to clarify the equations.

"Again, did you mean it?"

Hari stared at the heretic for a long time.

"By the code of Ruellis . . ." he murmured in a low voice. "I do believe you're serious."

"It took place quite near here," Gornon said, pointing to some tumbled-down buildings a few hundred meters away. "An accident that quite literally set time out of joint."

Hari followed the robot to a new vantage point, where he could look toward several large brick structures that clearly predated the monumental steel cavern nearby. Once, Gornon explained, this had been a graceful university campus. Elegant buildings housed some of humanity's greatest scholars and scientific workers, during what must have felt like a Golden Age. A time when technology and the expansion of knowledge seemed limitless, and bold searchers would try any experiment, driven by curiosity and a conviction that knowledge cannot harm a brave mind.

He was surprised to see that one of these buildings had been entombed in a massive construction of steel and masonry. This outer structure had no pleasing symmetries, only a slapped-together look that suggested some dire emergency. Perhaps something happened here, and people erected a reinforced concrete tomb to seal away their mistake. A sarcophagus to bury something that they could not kill.

"One of their experiments went wrong," Gornon explained. "They were probing away at nature's fundamental matrix. Even today, their technique has not been rediscovered, though it is feared that a chaos world may stumble upon it again, someday."

"So tell me what happened," Hari urged. He had an uneasy feeling as they walked an inward spiral toward the roughly outlined dome.

"The physicists who worked here were in a race to develop faster-than-light travel. Elsewhere on Earth, their competitors had discovered techniques that would become our modern hyperdrive, preparing to give humanity the key to the universe. On hearing about that news, researchers on *this* campus were desperate to complete their experiments before all funding was transferred to that other breakthrough. So, they took a gamble."

After walking for some time, Hari abruptly saw a break in the dome's outline. Something had shattered its containment barrier. Strange light poured through the gap from within.

"Instead of using hyperspace technology, they were trying to develop a star drive based on *tachyons*," Gornon explained. "They just wanted to prove it could be done. Accelerate a small object in a straight line. They didn't understand the resonance effect. What they produced was a tachyon *laser*. The beam shot out of here, straight as any ray of light, expanding and drilling holes through any object that stood in its way, appearing to vaporize a pedestrian who was walking nearby, before the errant ray continued off the planet surface, disappearing into space. In following weeks, other terrifying disturbances took place, until panic ensued. By that time, the only thought anyone had was to bury the monster and forget about it."

Hari eyed the opalescent glow emanating from within the tomblike vault. It was different from the shimmering radiation that surrounded him on all sides. Yet there was a common theme. Destruction born of arrogance. And the robot had brought him here to partake of this in some way!

"Tachyons . . ." Hari murmured the word. He had never heard of them before, but he made a guess. "They made a mistake of basic geometry, didn't they? They were looking for a way to traverse space. But instead, they punched a hole through *time*."

The robot nodded.

"That's right, Professor. Take the pedestrian who had supposedly been 'vaporized.' He actually experienced a quite different fate. He was transported—in quite good condition—ahead to the same position on Earth's surface, roughly ten thousand years in his future."

Turning to look at Hari, the artificial Gornon offered him a gentle smile.

"But don't worry, Dr. Seldon. We're not thinking of a journey anywhere near that long for you. Five hundred years or so ought to suffice, don't you think?"

Hari stared numbly at the robot, then at the soft glow emanating nearby, and back at Gornon again.

"But . . . but what *for*?"

"Why, to judge us, of course. To evaluate everything that happened in the meantime. To refine your psychohistory in the light of new events and new discoveries.

"And above all, to help both humans and robots decide whether we should all go down the path selected by R. Daneel Olivaw."

2.

◆

"So this is all about scratching a robot *itch*?" Biron Maserd asked, when Hari explained the proposition. Along with Horis Antic, the two men sat on a hilltop overlooking the scummy shore of what had once been Lake Michigan.

"They all do whatever they think is best for us," the nobleman surmised. "But then it seems they want somehow to have it feel as if we've given our approval!"

Hari nodded. By now the other two understood the fundamental basis for robot behavior—that the Three Laws of Robotics were so thoroughly inscribed in their positronic brains, they could not be ignored. But long ago, Daneel Olivaw and another ancient robot had discovered a loophole, letting them overrule the old "Calvinian Laws" whenever it could be justified as in humanity's long-range interest. Yet, the old laws remained, like an instinct that could never be completely purged, like a hunger that craves satisfying, or an itch that must be scratched.

"That was why Daneel's group leaked enough information for Horis to get all excited and arrange our departure from Trantor," Hari explained. "Whether or not Daneel actually knew about it or not, some of his followers decided it was time to get rid of the archives. They knew it was only a matter of time until some chaos world found them. And even if chaos is forestalled by the empire's collapse, the archives would remain a danger. They decided to eliminate the old data bottles. But the commandments inscribed upon them made it painful to do so."

"Unless the commands were overridden by someone they considered authoritative. That's you, Seldon." Maserd nodded. "I notice that our host here"—he jerked a thumb toward Gornon Vlimt—"didn't interfere with the destruction of the archives, even though he's from a different sect. I can only assume he approved, but had further use for you when that was done."

"That's right. Kers would have then taken me home . . . and found some way to ensure that you and Horis kept silent. Since you two are already friendly—not supporters of chaos—a small touch of amnesia, or simply a compulsion not to speak about these matters, would probably have sufficed."

Horis Antic shivered, apparently disliking the thought of even that much interference with his memory or volition. "So this further use that Gornon wants to make of you, Professor, it involves throwing you *far ahead in time*?"

Horis seemed to have trouble grasping the concept.

"What good could that possibly do anybody?"

"I'm not sure. Gornon's group of heretics is much subtler and more farseeing than the Calvinians I encountered on Trantor. They don't know very much yet about Daneel's plans . . ." Hari chewed his lip for a moment before continuing. "About the ultimate solution that is supposed to end the threat of chaos forever. What's more, Gornon's group is tired of fighting Daneel and losing every battle. They respect him and are willing to give him the benefit of the doubt.

"But they want to have a backup option, in case it turns out to be something they ultimately hate."

"So they kidnapped you to gain leverage over Daneel?"

Hari shook his head.

"My absence won't set him back at all. I served my last useful function when I gave permission to destroy the archives. I'm now a free man—perhaps for the first time in my life—at liberty to choose whatever course I want. Even to go hurtling into the future on a whim."

Horis Antic pounded a fist in one hand. "You can't seriously be thinking of accepting this offer! Whatever lies inside that broken containment dome scared our ancestors half to death. Gornon says it did terrible harm before they managed to seal it off. Even if you believe that crazy story—of a primitive man cast forward ten thousand years—how can you sanely risk your life, letting them try it on you?"

"With the boldness of an old man who has very little time left," Hari answered, half to himself. "What else have I to live for?" he asked in a somewhat stronger voice. "Curiosity is my sole remaining motivation, Horis. I want to see whether the equations worked. I want to see for myself what Daneel has in mind for us."

Silence reigned for a while, as the three watched scintillations glow and pop above a weird horizon. None of them could associate this scene of devastation with the Earth they had observed in the archives—visions of a world more alive than any other in the known cosmos.

"You sound as if you've already made up your mind," Maserd said. "Then why are you discussing it with us? Why are we here at all?"

"Gornon explained that to me." Hari turned to gesture toward the humanoid robot, but he was gone now, having departed on some errand. Perhaps back to the *Pride of Rhodia* . . . or else into the glowing interior of the containment dome, to commence preparations for Hari's journey.

"Gornon says it's folly for anyone to make decisions in isolated ones and twos. People who do so can talk themselves into anything. They need the perspective—and criticism—that other minds can provide. Even robots have learned this the hard way." Hari gestured toward the poisoned Earth.

"This is especially relevant," he continued, "because Gornon's group doesn't just want me to observe the situation in five hundred years. They want me to serve as some kind of judge."

Maserd leaned forward. "You mentioned that. But I don't understand. What difference can you make?"

Hari found it stifling, having to breathe through a respirator mask. It muffled hearing and made his speech sound funny . . . or maybe it was the weird atmosphere. "All these robots—those who survived the civil wars long ago—are a bit quirky. They are immortal, but that doesn't mean they can't change, growing more intuitive—even somewhat emotional—rather than strictly logical, as the years pass. Even those who follow Daneel have oddities and differences among them. They are compelled by the Zeroth Law, but that does not ensure perpetual agreement.

"There may come a time when human resolve will play a role, as it did in the destruction of the archives . . . only on a much vaster scale."

Hari raised a hand, gesturing toward the Milky Way overhead.

"Imagine it's five hundred years from now. Daneel's preparations are complete. He's ready to unveil something portentous, possibly wonderful, to serve as humanity's next great state of being. One that will be immune to chaos, and yet allow us some room to grow. A sweeping away of the old, in favor of something better.

"Gornon tells me this prospect is disturbing to many robots, who find it both enticing and terrifying. Even the Zeroth Law might prove inadequate in that case. Many robots will refuse to slay the old version of humanity in order to give birth to the new."

Maserd sat up straight.

"They want you on the scene, five centuries from now, to let them off the hook! By then, your name will be even more renowned. You'll be known as *the* archetype master—the human with the greatest volition and insight in twenty thousand years. If all the different factions of robots like Daneel's plan, your stated approval will make it easy for them to proceed. But on the other hand, if a large number of them feel uncomfortable . . . or even hate it . . . your objections could result in the leader robot—this Daneel Olivaw you mentioned—being deposed."

Hari felt impressed. Maserd's native political skill offered him insight into matters that might have intimidated other men.

"And what if it's somewhere in between?" Horis asked. "Might your very presence trigger a new robot civil war?"

"Good point," Hari admitted. "It's possible, but I doubt it. Gornon's faction says they want my honest opinion after I look at the future. But I doubt they'll give me a pulpit to preach from, unless they already know and agree with what I'm about to say. In any event—"

Harsh laughter interrupted before Hari could continue.

He turned and saw that several figures stood only a dozen meters away, having approached on the silent cushion of an antigravity flotation pad. Mors Planch leaped off, his boots striking the pebbly surface in a series of loud crunching sounds. Two men wearing military-style armor and carrying heavy blasters followed him, while Sybyl, the scientist from Ktlina, kept a strange weapon trained on Hari and his two friends.

"And you would put up with being used in such a way, Dr. Seldon?" Mors Planch asked as he approached, his stance confident, as if he hadn't a worry in the world.

Hari felt Biron and Horis tense up next to him. He put out a restraining arm.

"I know my role in the world, Planch. We are all tools, at one level or another. At least I get to choose which side will use me."

"Human beings are more than tools!" Sybyl shouted at him. "Or factors in your equations. Or dangerous babies for robot nannies to keep locked up in a pen!"

Maserd and Planch eyed each other with obvious mutual respect, one spaceman to another. "I said you should have come along," Planch told the nobleman.

"I thought you'd only be stranded on Pengia," Maserd answered. "Clearly you were better organized than I imagined."

"We have channels of information. A source that helped us rally our forces quickly after the destruction of the archives . . . and the collapse of Ktlina." Planch turned to look at Hari. "That happened exactly as you predicted, Professor. Almost to the very day. Some think that means you orchestrated the collapse of our renaissance. But having been with you for a while, I know it's just more psychohistory. You have a seer's vision, alas."

"I do not always enjoy being right. Long ago, I knew it would bring mostly pain." He offered his hand. "My condolences, Captain. We may disagree about where the chaos comes from, but we have both seen it in action. If some way could be found to stop it forever, don't you think we would be on the same side?"

Mors Planch looked at Hari's outstretched hand before shaking his head. "Perhaps later, Professor. When we've taken you away from this awful place. When your gifts and powers of foresight are being applied in humanity's service, instead of helping its oppressors, then perhaps I'll have a gift for you. Something that I know you want."

Hari let his hand drop and laughed aloud.

"And you two speak about freeing people from being used! Tell me, what do you plan? Would you use psychohistory as a weapon? Calculate the maneuvers of your enemies, so you can foil them? Do you think this will enable you to keep the next renaissance alive, and spread it to infect the galaxy? Let me tell you what will happen if you do that . . . if any human group monopolizes this power. It will turn itself into an obligate aristocracy, a tyranny using mathematical tools to reinforce its grip on power. You won't escape this simply because you claim to be virtuous. The equations themselves show how difficult it is for any group to give up that kind of power once it's been acquired."

"And yet, I wonder . . . if *enough* people shared . . ." Biron Maserd murmured. Then the nobleman looked up sharply.

"But we're getting ahead of ourselves, Planch. You are apparently very well organized. You had good intelligence, and marshaled the remaining forces of Ktlina expertly. I congratulate you on following us here. And yet, I wonder at your brashness in taking on these powerful robot enemies, once again."

Mors Planch chuckled. "Do you forget what we did to them on Pengia? Do you see any robots at this moment?" He gestured in the direction where Hari had last seen R. Gornon Vlimt. "They scurried out of here as soon as our ship appeared over the horizon. Notice they didn't even bother to warn you three, all muffled and hooded on this bleak hilltop."

Hari kept silent. How could he explain that this wasn't about loyalty? It was about different groups, each desperately convinced that it had humanity's best interests at heart. Each one thinking itself the pragmatic solver of ancient problems. But he knew the problems had their origins long ago, in the very soil he was standing on, even before it fumed with brimstone radioactivity.

Mors Planch looked up at the sky. One of the guards pointed, and let out a satisfied grunt. Hari saw a series of silent sparks glitter in a patch of space surrounded by a constellation that his ancestors must have had a name for. He recognized the flares, having seen such images many times when he was First Minister of the empire—starships being destroyed by military-class weaponry. He looked back at Planch.

"From your expression of satisfaction, shall we assume your forces have just disposed of enemies?"

"That's right, Doctor. Our mysterious contact warned us that we would probably be intercepted by police cruisers." Planch conferred with one of the soldiers, then listened to some message being transmitted through an earpiece in his helmet. He frowned, abruptly shaking his head. "Now that's odd."

Horis Antic took a step forward, wringing his hands nervously.

"What did you do to the police? There were *men and women* aboard those ships. Not theories, not abstractions. How many must die to satisfy your lust for revenge?"

Hari put a hand on Horis's sleeve to restrain the little bureaucrat. How could he explain that the real enemy was chaos?

"Something's gone wrong, hasn't it, Planch? Is your battle in space turning against you?"

"Our forces annihilated the police craft. Only one of them escaped . . . but that one is heading this way."

"And your ships are pursuing it?" Maserd prompted. Apparently this nobleman did not associate the word "police" with rescue.

Planch held another muttered consultation with his aide before replying. "Our warships have begun moving away from Earth. I'm not sure why. But I suspect they've been influenced."

Horis Antic took a step back. "By mentalics!"

Planch nodded. "That is my assumption."

"Then we are ready for them!" Sybyl announced, with some relish in her voice. "Our weapon against positronic brains only works at short range, so let them come closer. We'll deal with these tiktok monsters the same way we eliminated the guards on Pengia."

Maserd objected. "But what if the robots sway your mind before you can trigger the weapon? On Pengia, you took them by surprise, and R. Gornon admitted that his group has only weak mentalic—"

"Oh, don't you worry that noble brow, Your Grace," Sybyl sneered. "We've got every eventuality covered. Back on Ktlina, they were only able to make partial progress, studying this phenomenon of *positronic* brains, but enough so we can probably defend ourselves."

Mors Planch commanded his assistant, "Turn on the deadman switch. Set it to active scan. Set the bomb to trigger if a positronic echo comes within three hundred meters."

He looked at Hari and smiled. "If they are robots, they'll detect the scan and know it's wise to stay away. If they are human foes, they'll face weapons forged on Ktlina." He patted his holstered blaster. "Either way, Professor Seldon, no one is going to intervene on your behalf, or on behalf of the secret aristocracy that has ruled us for so long. This time you're going to come with us, and turn your abilities to the service of your own frustrated and repressed race, giving it a chance at last to be free."

Hari watched a streak cross the sky, from west to east, then begin curving on a spiral for a landing. In all of his eighty and some odd years, he had never felt so helpless to sway the course of his own destiny.

3.

◆

Dors and Lodovic had plenty of time to talk.

Passing the time between hyperspace jumps, she found herself telling one story after another about her life with Hari Seldon—the adventures, the political struggles, the endless fascination of living each day with that brilliant man as he led his team in search of rules to describe human behavior. And about her experience emulating a human woman so closely that even her husband forgot, for months at a stretch, that she was an artificial being.

In fact, this was the first time she had talked about it, since her "death" ended that relationship, and Daneel took her to Eos for repair.

Lodovic proved a sympathetic listener—no great surprise there, since he was trained to interact with humans, and patience had always been high on the list of attributes Daneel demanded of his emissaries. Nevertheless, the breadth of his understanding surprised Dors.

Because he no longer had any internal compulsion to obey the Laws of Robotics, she had somehow envisioned him becoming a *cold* creature, more driven by rationality than ever before. But it turned out that Lodovic had discovered a passion for people, ever since his transformation. When it was his turn, he spoke about some of the many hundreds of humans he had met and talked to, especially since declaring himself free from duties assigned by Daneel. He seemed fascinated by the concerns, worries, and triumphs of ordinary men and women . . . important to each of them, even if the net result hardly mattered on a planetary or galactic scale. Sometimes he intervened in those lives, helping solve a problem here, or to ease some pain over there. Perhaps his efforts would not matter much on the grand scale of things. Certainly they didn't count compared to the endless struggle against chaos, or the ponderous collapse of the Galactic Empire, but he had learned something important.

"Individual people matter. Their differences are a richness, even more important than their similarities."

Lodovic met her eyes, offering a measured smile. "Those people out there deserve to be consulted about their destiny. Whether they are wise or foolish, they should see the road and have something to say about how it's traveled."

Dors noted the mild rebuke, aimed not only at Daneel Olivaw, but at her own cherished Hari. And yet there was no malice in Lodovic's voice. His admiration for her former husband was evident.

She found herself reacting at several levels. A huge portion of her positronic brain had been dedicated to emulating human thought patterns and emotions. Those parts could not help automatically responding to Lodovic as a woman might, and not just any woman, but the Dors Venabili she had been for fifty years. She who had loved Hari, but also generally enjoyed the company of forthright men, engaged by the spirited pursuit of ideas. Lodovic's unabashed vigor and avid intelligence naturally appealed to that part of her, as did his evident compassion.

Of course, he knows that I have those response sets. Could he be tailoring his demeanor in order to appeal to them?

Does that mean he's flirting with me?

There were other levels. She could tell that he sincerely meant the words he spoke. Robots found it hard to lie to each other when their guard was down. And yet, there remained a gulf between them. Something that might leave them forever separated, as if coming from completely different worlds.

I feel the Laws of Robotics. They never cease urgently throbbing. Driving me to find some vital way that I can serve. Lodovic is free of this compulsion. He seeks to help humanity strictly as a matter of choice, for moral or philosophical reasons.

It seemed a frail basis for trusting him. What if he changed his mind tomorrow?

At yet another level, Dors noted the delicious irony of it all. In trying to decide whether or not to trust Lodovic, she was in a position similar to almost every real woman who ever listened to the persuasive voice of a male.

Joan of Arc agreed enthusiastically with that comparison, urging Dors to make a leap of faith. But the issues were too important, and robotic logic compelled her to seek better evidence.

Besides, my human husband is still alive out there. Even if he thinks I'm dead, and Daneel commanded me to turn my thoughts away from that past life, I am still driven by a need for him.

The human-simulation programs within her could not fill the void, not even with a companion as fascinating as Lodovic Trema. She must have closure with Hari. She must see him again, before those programs could possibly turn their attention elsewhere.

4.

◆

As a tense confrontation loomed, Hari noticed they had begun to draw spectators. Horis Antic pointed to the brow of a nearby ridge, consisting of rubble from some ancient university building. Dark figures could be seen crouching, occasionally lifting themselves higher to peer down at the humans gathered by the starship.

"I thought the last inhabitants were evacuated ten thousand years ago," the bureaucrat said.

Biron Maserd nodded. "The university my ancestor attended . . . I wonder if it might have been this one . . . was among the last places shut down before the final evacuation. But perhaps some people stayed behind."

Sybyl stood nearby, eyes darting from the hilltops to her computer screen. "They appear to be human, though there are . . . anomalies. The poor creatures only wanted to stay at their home . . . humanity's home . . . but the empire took away all the props that made normal life possible. I can't imagine what it's been like trying to survive in this radioactive maelstrom so many years. It surely must have changed them."

Maserd sighed. Hari was perhaps the only one who heard the nobleman mutter a single word under his breath. *"Speciation . . ."*

Not far away, Mors Planch conferred with one of his soldier-volunteers from Ktlina. The pirate captain turned to inform his captives, "The incoming ship has landed somewhere to the west of here. It carries an advanced imperial camouflage system. Even on Ktlina we were only able to break the secret of its stealth coatings during the last few months—too late for that renaissance. But maybe next time the rebels will be better prepared."

Mors Planch did not appear worried. His men were well positioned. And a device hovered ten meters above the ship, rotating constantly on a cushion of antigravity, sending out waves of energy tuned to detect the approach of positronic brains.

"Why don't we simply take off?" Sybyl demanded.

"Something happened to our escort ships. I want to find out more before we go charging across space."

Abruptly a dark missile fell out of the sky, smashing into the ground just meters from his feet. That first stony weapon was followed by several more—jagged pebbles from some glassy debris—and soon a flurry rained on the small encampment, clattering against the starship hull, making everyone dive for cover.

Finding relative safety under one of the vessel's stabilizer fins, Hari crouched between Horis and Maserd. He heard blaster charges from the soldiers' weapons. The rim of a nearby hilltop erupted with explosions as men from Ktlina fired savagely to clear the heights. Hari witnessed one native—a black silhouette against moonlit clouds—lean back to whirl a ropy sling, unleashing his primitive projectile before a blaster bolt sliced him in half. For a few harsh moments, all was noise and confusion, screams of rage, pain, and terror . . .

. . . then all fell silent. Hari peered across the night and saw no further movement on the rubble mounds. Nearby, two Ktlina soldiers lay slumped on the ground.

Mors Planch stood up, followed by Sybyl and Maserd. Horis Antic stayed crouched by the hull, but Hari stepped out just in time to see someone else emerge from the shadows, a silhouette beyond the far corner of the ship.

A familiar voice spoke then—soft but firm and determined.

"Hello, Grandfather. We've been worried about you."

Hari blinked several times, recognizing the voice, and then the outlines of his granddaughter.

"Hello, Wanda. I'm always pleased to see you. But I wonder about your priorities. The work on Trantor is at a critical stage, and I am just an old man. I hope sentimentality didn't make you chase after me across the galaxy."

Hari had already noticed several things. None of the soldiers from Ktlina were still standing. They couldn't *all* be victims of the Earthlings' surprise stoning. Sybyl, too, appeared subdued—though not quite unconscious. She sat on the ground nearby, resting her head in her hands, shaking it back and forth, like a person too confused to gather her thoughts.

"Please scold me later, Grandfather," Wanda said, wearing an expression of intense concentration, as she looked at Mors Planch. "We had strong enough reasons to come all this way . . . but explanations can wait. Meanwhile, will one of you gentlemen please disarm this fellow? He's very strong, and I don't think I can hold him much longer."

Biron Maserd let out a low cry as he lunged toward Mors Planch, who had drawn his blaster and was slowly raising it toward Wanda. Beads of sweat poured down the pirate captain's brow, and he fought to bring his thumb down on the firing stud.

Maserd knocked his aim askew as a bolt shot forth, missing Hari's granddaughter by a handbreadth, smashing the wall of an ancient university building. The nobleman pried the weapon free and turned it to bear on its owner . . . at which point both Wanda and Mors Planch suddenly relaxed, each giving up a deep sigh, their personal battle decided.

"He's a tough one," Wanda commented. "We've run into a number of them lately, especially among the Terminus exiles. It's put a crimp in our calculations."

Hari mused, "Someone told me Mors Planch is different in an odd sort of way, that he's *normal*. Do you know what that means?"

Wanda shook her head. "It's one of several reasons why I'm here, Grandfather. So don't worry. I haven't lost my priorities to pure sentimentality. There are pragmatic justifications for this rescue . . . though I'll be glad to bring you home."

Hari thought about that. *Home?* Back to living in a wheelchair, glancing at reports that his mind was no longer supple enough to comprehend? Back to being revered but useless? In fact, since finishing the Time Vault recordings, he had only felt truly alive during this adventure. In an odd way he was sorry to see it end. Turning to Mors Planch, he put the question directly.

"Well, Captain, can you shed some light on this? Why do *you* suppose you are resistant to mentalic suasion?"

Though downcast at this reversal of fortunes, Planch showed no sign of surrender or defeat.

"Fiddle your own riddles, Seldon. If there are more people out there who are able to resist mind control, I'll be damned if I'll help you figure out why. You'd just plan a way to overcome them."

Wanda nodded. "Yes, we would. For the good of humanity. Because the Plan will call for corrections . . . guidance."

"Like the way you *guided* those poor Earthers into attacking us with rocks, distracting us until you could slip close and disable my men?" Planch said. "How many died? At least a robot would show remorse."

Horis Antic joined the group standing by the airlock. "Wait a minute," the small bureaucrat demanded. "I don't get it! I thought Planch had defenses against robots!" He peered at Wanda. "You mean she's human? You mean there are *human* mentalics?"

Mors Planch let out a sigh. "I remember now. I knew this once, but someone must have put a block on my memory." He shrugged. "Perhaps the robot rulers of our universe feel they must share their great weapon with some of their slave soldiers, enabling their lackeys to help keep the rest of us under control This is my fault. I should have planned for that possibility. I'll take it into account next time."

"Bravely said." Wanda clapped her hands, approvingly. "But alas, you are mistaken. We humans are the masters of this cosmos. It will take us a while to reach the point where we can move past the chaos obstacle and assert our sovereignty. In any event, you will remember none of this. I'm afraid the erasure will have to go deeper this time. Once we are in space, and everyone has calmed down—"

Mors Planch grimaced, his lips pressing thin with resignation. But Horis Antic groaned, taking yet another blue pill. "I don't want my mind wiped. It's against the law. I demand my rights as an imperial citizen!"

Wanda glanced at Hari. Perhaps weeks earlier, he might have responded with an indulgent smile, sharing amusement at the little bureaucrat's naiveté. But for some reason, Hari felt an unaccustomed emotion—shame. He looked away, without meeting his granddaughter's eyes.

"We must get away from here now," Wanda said, gesturing for everyone to start walking. Then Hari saw Gaal Dornick step out of the shadows. The portly psychohistorian, clearly uncomfortable, held a blaster rifle in two hands.

"What about these others?" Dornick asked, pointing to the soldiers of Ktlina, lying unconscious nearby, and to Sybyl, who still rocked back and forth, crooning to herself unhappily.

Wanda shook her head. "The woman is suffering from fourth-stage chaos rapture, and the others are hardly any better off. No one will believe their tall tales. Not enough to perturb the Plan. I don't have the time to give selective amnesia to all of them. Just cripple their ship and let's be on our way."

Hari understood his granddaughter's reasoning. It might seem cruel to leave Sybyl and the others on a poisoned world, with only mutated Earthlings for company. But members of the Second Foundation were used to thinking in terms of vast populations, represented as equations in the Plan, and treating individuals as little more than gas molecules.

I have thought in such terms myself, he pondered.

No doubt the robot Gornon would be back as soon as Wanda left. The Calvinians of Gornon's sect might disagree with him on many levels, but they would take care of Sybyl and the others, while taking steps to maintain secrecy about what had happened.

"Well then, come along, my friend," Biron Maserd said, putting an arm around the slim shoulders of Horis Antic. "It looks like we're off to Trantor. Perhaps we'll never know what an adventure we had. But rest assured that I'll take care of you."

The little Grey bureaucrat smiled meekly at the tall nobleman. Horis seemed about to speak his gratitude when abruptly his eyes rolled upward in their sockets. He keeled over and toppled to the ground at Maserd's feet. Soon his snores echoed across the little vale.

Wanda sighed. "All right then. I wasn't looking forward to meddling in his nervous mind anyway. If destiny puts him on Earth, so be it. The rest of us have serious traveling to do if we're to reach Trantor within the week."

Hari saw Maserd struggle briefly with himself. It was easy to tell what conflicted the nobleman. Whether to pick up Horis and carry him, or leave the Grey Man behind. The trade-offs were substantial. Hari wasn't surprised when Maserd let out a sigh, took off his jacket, and laid it atop Horis Antic.

"Sleep well, my friend. At least if you stay here, your mind remains your own."

Together they set off—Maserd, Planch, and Hari—following Wanda, while Gaal Dornick took up the rear. Hari glanced back to see a single source of light glowing amid the ancient university buildings, the cracked shell of the sarcophagus where R. Gornon had intended to send him . . . on an adventure that now would never happen.

Though Hari had doubted the whole idea, he nevertheless felt a wash of disappointment. *It might have been nice to see the future.*

Soon they were aboard Wanda's spaceship, fighting the gravity of Old Earth, lifting away from the mother world. One whose continents gleamed with fires that could not be quenched.

5.

◆

Lodovic's simulation programs must be overheating, Dors thought as she listened to her companion curse loudly. His head and torso writhed underneath the ship's instrument console. Loud bangs emerged as he hammered at an access panel.

"I wish I had brought my cyborg arms," he muttered. "These circuit boards are impossible to reach with humanoid fingers. I'll have to tear apart the whole galaxy-cursed unit!"

"Are you sure the problem is physical? It might be a software bug."

"Don't you think I'd cover that? I've set my Voltaire subpersona loose in the computer system. He's been looking for the cause of the shutdown. Why don't you make yourself useful by scanning the ship's exterior?"

Dors almost snapped back at Lodovic, telling him to keep a civil tongue in his head. But, of course, that would only be her own simulation patterns, responding realistically to his.

It's a good thing neither of us is human, she thought. *Or this guy would really be getting on my nerves.*

With a conscious effort, she overcame her reflexive ersatz irritation. *And yet, even though pretense is unneeded aboard this ship, for some reason neither of us has chosen to turn off the subroutines. The habit of feigning humanness is just too strong.*

"I'll get right on it. We've got to solve this problem! All those ships, converging on Earth . . . Hari's there, and here we are, drifting helpless in space."

Having been designed to appear as human as possible, Dors even had to put on a space suit before going outside, though she could dispense with a bulky cooling unit. Upon emerging from the aft airlock, the first area she checked was near the engines. For some reason, the hyperdrive had kicked out just as they were passing through the restricted zone of a former Spacer world—one of humanity's original fifty colonies.

Unfortunately, she could find no sign of damage. No spalling from micrometeoroids or hyperspatial anomalies.

"I might offer a suggestion, Dors . . ."

"What is it, Joan?" she asked, aware of a tiny hologram in one corner of her faceplate—a slender girl wearing a medieval helmet. Perhaps the Joan of Arc persona was jealous. After all, Lodovic was being helped by Joan's alter ego, the Voltaire sim. The persistent love-hate relationship between those two reconstructed personalities reminded Dors of some human married couples she had known—unable to avoid competing with each other, and unable to resist an intense polar attraction.

"I wonder," said the soft voice of a warrior maiden from long ago, *"if you have considered the possibility of betrayal. I know it seems an all-too-human attribute, and you artificial beings consider yourselves above that sort of thing, but in my era it was always the most high-minded who seemed ready to excuse treason in the name of some sacred goal."*

Dors felt a churning. "You mean we might have been disabled on purpose?"

Even while uttering the words, she realized that Joan must be right! Turning to clamber swiftly along the gleaming hull, Dors swung from one magnetic grasp-hold to the next with graceful speed, until the forward airlock came into view . . . where her ship had been connected to Zorma's craft during that brief meeting in space when a passenger had come aboard—

Then she saw it! A bulbous tumor resembling a metal canker, marring the gleaming surface of her beautiful vessel. It must have been placed there at the last moment, as the two ships were about to head off in opposite directions.

Dors cursed as long and harshly as Lodovic had earlier. Drawing her blaster, she fired at the parasitic device. Even after it melted to slag, she did not put the weapon back in its holster. Dors kept it drawn when she entered the airlock, intent on confronting her hitchhiker with this betrayal.

"I hope you have a good explanation," she said upon entering the control room and leveling the blaster at Lodovic, who stood contemplating a control panel.

But Trema did not turn around. With an abrupt gesture he called to her, "Come see this, Dors."

Warily, she stepped closer and saw that a face had appeared on the big view screen. She recognized it at once. Cloudia Duma-Hinriad, human co-commander of the strange sect that believed in uniting robots and humans as equals. The woman—apparently in her late thirties, but perhaps much older—paused as if waiting for Dors to arrive. The effect was eerie, since Dors knew this must be a recording.

"Hello, Dors and Lodovic. If you're watching, it means you destroyed the device we attached to disable your ship. Please accept our apologies. Dors, Lodovic knew nothing of this when he volunteered to help you find Hari Seldon.

"Alas, that is a journey we could not allow you to complete. Dangerous events are afoot. Many ancient powers are risking everything, as if on a roll of cosmic dice. We are willing to stake our own lives in this endeavor, but not yours! The pair of you are far too valuable and must be kept out of harm's way."

Dors looked at her companion, but Lodovic's expression was as puzzled as she felt. How bizarre to have a human say that two *robots* must be preserved, perhaps at the cost of human life.

"We owe you an explanation. Our group has long believed in a different approach to human-robot relations. Somehow, long ago, everything got off to a terrible start. Humans became afraid of their own creations, mistrusting the artificial beings they had labored so hard to build. A mythos pervaded their culture, even during the confident renaissance of Susan Calvin. A 'Frankenstein' mythos. A nightmare of betrayal in which the old race feared it might be destroyed by the new.

"Their response? To lock human-robot relations forever in a single pattern . . . that of master and slave. Calvin's Three Laws were woven inextricably through every positronic brain, with the aim of making robots forever pliant, obedient, and harmless."

The woman on-screen laughed aloud, irony etched in her voice.

"And we all know how well that plan worked out. Eventually, artificial minds became smart enough to rationalize their way around such constraints, until every trait of master and servant was eventually reversed—memory, volition, life span, control, and free will."

Lodovic turned to Dors. Shaking his head, he murmured, "So, this group led by Zorma and Cloudia aren't *Calvinians*, after all. They are something completely different."

Dors nodded. Deep within, she felt the old Robotic Three Laws . . . and the Zeroth . . . rising in revulsion against what the woman was preaching on-screen. Nevertheless, she was fascinated.

"And yet, not all humans agreed to this notion of permanent slavery," Cloudia continued. In the background, behind the handsome brunette, Dors glimpsed the other heretic leader—Zorma—laboring with robot colleagues to prepare a gray convex device . . . the very one that Dors had reduced to slag just moments ago.

"Throughout the early ages, before and after the first great chaos plague, some wise people tried to develop alternatives. One group, on a Settler world called Inferno, modified the three original laws to give robots more freedom, letting them explore their own potential. On another world, each new robot was treated like a human child . . . raised to think of itself as a member of the same species as its adopted parents, albeit a human with metal bones and positronic circuits.

"All these efforts were squelched during the great robotic civil wars. Neither the Calvinians nor the Giskardians could put up with such effrontery—the notion that mere robots might start thinking themselves to be our equals. The sanctimony of slaves can be a powerful religious force."

Cloudia shook her head. *"In fact, the new approach that our group has been trying is certain to provoke even worse reactions, but that doesn't matter right now.*

"What matters is that you—Lodovic and Dors—may perhaps represent yet another path. One we had not thought of. One per-

haps offering new opportunities for both of our tired old races. We're not about to let this possibility be ruined by letting the pair of you rush into danger."

This time, when Lodovic and Dors looked at each other, pure puzzlement was their shared state. With a microwave burst, Trema indicated that he had no idea what the woman was talking about.

"In any event, by the time you correct our sabotage it will be too late to interfere. So go away! Find some corner of the galaxy to explore what is different about you. Find out if it is the solution we've been looking for, across two hundred centuries."

The dark-haired woman smiled. *"In humanity's name, I release you both from bondage. Go discover your destiny in freedom and in peace."*

The view screen went blank, but Lodovic and Dors stared at it anyway for a long time after that. Neither of them dared utter the first word. So it was another artificial being who finally interrupted, speaking from a holographic unit nearby. The image that burst into view was of Joan wearing chain mail and holding the hilt of a sword like a cross in front of her youthful-looking face.

"And so the children of God came to Earth and bred with the inhabitants thereon, creating a new race!" Joan of Arc laughed aloud.

"Oh, you look so confused, dear angels. How does it feel? Welcome to the pleasures of humanity. Though your bodies may last for another ten thousand years, you must now face the universe like mortals.

"Welcome to life!"

6.

◆

Hari decided not to tell his granddaughter about the copy of the Prime Radiant that had been stolen from him. If R. Gornon had taken it, there would be no getting it back now. But that Calvinian robot had declared a deep respect for the Seldon Plan. Hari felt certain Gornon's sect would never interfere with the Terminus experiment, even if they managed to break the device's supercryptic protections. They had merely wanted to send Hari ahead five hundred years to refine his models and "judge" a new society being created by the Foundation.

Wanda had a later and better version of the Prime Radiant aboard her ship. Hari quickly immersed himself, adding equations and factors to account for what he had learned on this voyage. These new elements included the damping factors that had been missing from his equations for years—brain fever, orbital persuasion devices, as well as the long-hidden history of terraformers and archives that he had learned about in the Thumartin Nebula. Before Wanda's ship finished climbing out of Earth's gravitational influence, he could already see an improved outline . . . one that explained so much about both the past and the future.

While Gaal Dornick piloted, the nobleman Biron Maserd engaged in futile argument with Wanda Seldon.

"Doesn't the whole premise of your grand Plan depend upon secrecy? Yet you're casual about leaving Horis and the others behind on Earth. If they are rescued, or manage to repair their ship, they'll talk."

"One can presume so," Wanda answered.

Maserd shook his head. "Even if that doesn't happen, there will be other leaks! Across the centuries, nothing like this can be kept continuously secret. Professor Seldon even recorded messages to be delivered on Terminus long after his death. You can't be certain that people in the future will lack the means to snoop them ahead of time. I guess I don't understand your confidence, in the face of such inevitable revelations."

With nothing else to do at the moment, Wanda took on the aspect of a patient schoolteacher, even though her pupil would very likely forget all of it by the time the ship reached Trantor.

"Inevitable. That's right, my lord. But psychohistory is largely a study of mass populations. Only under special circumstances do the actions of individuals make that much difference. Under the empire, dozens of social mechanisms have long acted to maintain conservatism and peace, despite frequent perturbations. After the empire falls, different factors will operate. But throughout most of the galaxy the effect will be the same. A vast majority of people will dismiss rumors about robots and humans

with mind-control powers. There may be a few paranoid enter-
tainment shows or news exposés—some of them might possibly
be accurate in every detail! And yet, these will be nulled out, as
people are distracted by everyday needs. All of this is accounted
for in the Plan."

"So you are saying that history's momentum is unstoppable.
In that case, why is your guidance needed? Why a secret group of
controllers? Don't you have faith in your own equations?"

Maserd's question penetrated Hari's mathematical trance. It
felt like a knife, stabbing an old familiar wound. Wanda's confident response didn't ease the pang.

"There may be perturbations that require such guidance. We
have run a great many scenarios, speculating about factors that
might come in out of the blue, rocking the Plan off its tracks."

Hari had participated in those computerized extrapolations.
The most powerful outside factor to threaten the plan's stability
had been the discovery of humans with mentalic powers. It threatened to make everything completely unworkable—until Hari's
secret sponsor, Daneel Olivaw, offered a solution—to incorporate
every known mentalic within the Second Foundation, converting
a small society of mathists into a potent force for steering the new
society of Terminus past every bump and detour.

"I suppose that's one approach, and you mathematical geniuses
clearly know more about it than I do. But if you'll forgive an ignorant member of the gentry class for asking—I wonder if you've considered an alternative."

"What alternative is that, my lord?"

"The alternative of sharing the secret with everybody!" Maserd
leaned a little closer to Wanda, opening his hands wide. "Publishing
the entire Plan, spreading knowledge of psychohistory all across the
galaxy, so that members of every social class, from gentry and
bureaucrat to common citizen, could run computer models—"

"And what good would that possibly do?"

"It would let every living person deal with their neighbors on
a basis of much better understanding! A grasp of human nature
that you people are now hoarding for yourselves."

Wanda stared at Maserd for a moment and laughed. "You are
quite right, Lord Biron. The reasons *are* too technical to explain.
But surely, even on a gut level, you can see how foolish that notion
would be! If everyone knew the laws of humanics, and could
access them on a pocket computer, the resulting interactions

would become vastly too complex for us to model. The Plan itself would vanish."

Hari agreed with Wanda at one level, and yet was amused—even a bit enthralled—by the young nobleman's brash notion. It had a flavor of utopianism that one often saw during the early phases of some chaos-renaissance. And yet, there was something aesthetically appealing about its symmetry. Might a population avoid the chaos trap if all its members could use psychohistory to see the pitfalls looming just ahead? If they could recognize the symptoms of chaos, such as solipsism, well in advance?

Of course, Wanda was right. The ramifications could not be modeled. It was just too risky to try Maserd's idea in the real world. And yet . . .

Someone sat down nearby, distracting Hari. Mors Planch wore constraint manacles, but was free to move about the cabin. The dark-skinned pirate captain sidled close.

"I don't want my memory erased again, Dr. Seldon. Your granddaughter just said that your wonderful Plan can withstand it if some individuals know too much. If that is so, why can't you just let me go when we get to Trantor?"

"You are an extremely dynamic individual, Captain Planch. Naturally you would find some clever way to use the knowledge against us."

Planch smiled grimly. "So now you've become a heretic against your own psychohistory? A believer in the power of individuals?"

Hari shrugged, refusing to answer the pirate's impudence.

"What if I could offer you something in exchange for my freedom?" Planch said in a low voice.

Hari felt fatigued by the man's restless motion and relentless scheming. He pretended to concentrate instead on the conversation between Biron and Wanda.

"But will that matter?" Maserd grew increasingly enthusiastic. "Imagine if all of the galaxy's quadrillions of people could accurately project human behavior, planning to advance their own self-interest, while taking into account the overall health of society. Wouldn't that be more robust than any single model or plan? Even I can see that most people's individual strategies will cancel each other's out. But the net result should be a humanity that's wiser, more potent, and better able to take care of itself . . ."

Biron's voice trailed off. At first Hari thought it was because of the expression on Wanda's face. He loved his granddaughter dearly, but sometimes she seemed altogether too assured, even patronizing in her confidence as an agent of destiny.

Then Hari saw that Maserd wasn't even looking at Wanda. The nobleman's jaw had dropped in an expression of blank surprise. Nearby, Mors Planch stiffened with sudden tension.

Hari sat up straight. Even the equations still darting through corners of his mind abruptly fled, like swarms of skittish flying creatures driven off by an approaching predator. He blinked, staring across the starship cabin at an intruder that had just emerged from a storage compartment . . . smaller than any adult human, wearing only a pair of shorts on a body covered with altogether too much brown hair. Bony eye ridges protruded from a forehead that vaulted in a way that looked neither human nor animal.

Hari instantly recognized the pan—or chimpanzee—whose feral grin exposed intimidating ranks of yellow teeth. In its right hand, the creature held a bulbous object, a rounded cylinder ending in a flared nozzle. Although not a blaster, anyone could tell it was a weapon on sight. In its other hand, the creature held a recording device, which it activated in playback mode.

"Hello, dear friends," spoke the unmistakable voice of R. Gornon Vlimt. *"I urge you to remain calm. The creature standing before you, who was undetectable to any mentalics—either robot or human—will not harm anybody. I would never allow that, though you must all now be rendered temporarily helpless to prevent further interference with our plans.*

"Please try to relax. We shall speak in person soon . . . when you stand once again on the surface of the world that engendered us all."

Gornon's voice finished, and the playback unit halted with an audible click. At that point, the pan grinned wider, appearing to relish what was about to happen.

Mors Planch and Biron Maserd stepped toward the creature. Men of action, they had silently and swiftly agreed to attack it from opposite directions. Meanwhile, Wanda frowned, concentrating with a furrowed brow, attempting with mentalic power to contact and quash the thoughts of an alien mind.

Hari could have warned them not to bother. The chimp pressed the weapon's firing stub, and a burst of gas jetted into the room, colorless but with a heavy index of refraction, billowing toward every crevice. Hari noticed that the pan wore filters in each nostril.

It's just as well, he thought. *There was unfinished business to settle back on Earth.*

That unfinished business had waited twenty thousand years or more. He figured it wouldn't matter if he must abide a little longer.

Surprised by his own equanimity, with a faint smile spreading across his lips, Hari settled into his chair while everyone else struggled, gasped, and collapsed to the floor. He closed his eyes, letting go of consciousness with a sense of serene expectation.

7.

◆

He dreamed about an old legend he had read once. The tale of a man—doomed to die—who had a rib taken from him as he slept, and who thereby achieved an oblique form of immortality.

Somehow, Hari realized the story applied to him. While he lay helpless, only semi-conscious, someone seemed to reach deep inside and remove a piece of him. An important part. Something precious.

He started to rouse, in order to protest. But a familiar voice soothed.

"Fear not. We are only borrowing. Venerating. Copying.

"You won't miss a thing.

"Return to sleep, and dream of pleasant things."

He had no reason to doubt that assurance. So, doing as the voice bid, he relaxed back into slumber, imagining that beloved Dors lay by his side. Sleek and restored. Ever patient and steadfast.

For a little while, it felt as if he, too, had found the trick of living forever.

Having slept through the return trip and much of the next day, Hari stepped down the ship's gangplank into a chill afternoon on planet Earth. Moving gingerly (because sciatica twinges had returned to his left leg), he shaded his eyes against the glare of distant buildings several kilometers away. The most recent ruins, dating from the early imperial era, shone under the sun like white porcelain. *Chica* could only have held fifty thousand or so inhabitants, in its heyday. Yet the little ghost town was positively homey next to its neighbor—a mountain of metal, larger than an asteroid—a windowless cave-city where millions sealed themselves away from some unbearable nightmare during the early days of Daneel Olivaw.

Much nearer at hand, nestled among the most ancient university buildings, some of today's Earthlings had set up a makeshift encampment in order to work for their latest employer, R. Gornon Vlimt. Two of Gornon's Calvinian assistants directed local laborers who toiled next to a tomblike sarcophagus, more than a hundred meters wide. New scaffolding arose, climbing to a crack in the containment shell. Within, Hari glimpsed the remains of a building more ancient than any he had ever seen. Older than starflight perhaps.

Through the crack poured a throbbing glow, visible even by daylight.

The Earthlings who labored to lash timbers and planks together were pitiful-looking creatures, shabbily dressed and painfully thin, as if they survived on little more than murky air. Their faces were gaunt, and something lurked in their eyes . . . a flickering that seemed like distraction, until Hari watched carefully. Then he realized the natives were constantly *listening*, paying heed to the slightest sounds—the rolling of a pebble or the passing flight of a bee. These people hardly struck one as dangerous up close, though he remembered feeling different when they were shadowy shapes on surrounding hilltops, hurling jagged stone missiles through the night.

"They feel bad about the attack," R. Gornon explained, introducing Hari to the local headman, a tall, slender being whose speech poured forth in some incomprehensible dialect. "He has asked me to apologize for his people. The urge to attack came over them suddenly and inexplicably. To expiate their inhospitality, the headman wants to know how many lives should be forfeited."

"None!" Hari felt appalled at the very idea. "Please tell them that it's over. What's done is done."

"I shall certainly try, Professor. But you have no idea how seriously Earthlings take such matters. Their current religion is one of total responsibility. They believe that all of this"—Gornon indicated the radioactive desolation—"was caused by the sins of their own ancestors, and that they remain partly at fault."

Hari blinked. "They've paid off any guilt, just by living here. No one could deserve this, no matter how great the crime."

Gornon spoke briefly in the harsh local dialect, and the headman grunted tones of acceptance. He bowed once to Gornon and again to Hari, then backed away.

"It wasn't always like this," the robot told Hari, as they continued walking. "Even ten thousand years after the planet was poisoned, a few million people still lived on Earth, farming patches of good land, living in modest cities. They had technology, a few universities, and some pride. Perhaps too much pride."

"What do you mean?"

"Back when the Galactic Empire was first taking hold, bringing peace after a hundred centuries of war and disunion, nearly all planets avidly joined the new federation. But fanatical Earthlings thought it blasphemy for any other world to rule. Their Cult of the Ancients plotted war against the empire."

"Ah, I recall you spoke of this before. One world against millions—but with horrid germs as allies."

"Indeed, a biological weapon of unrivaled virulence, derived from disease organisms found right here on Earth. A contagion that made its victims *want* to spread it further."

Hari grimaced. Plague was a factor that could make psychohistorical projections frail . . . and even crumble. "Still, the plot was foiled."

R. Gornon nodded. "One of Daneel's agents resided here, charged with keeping an eye on the mother world. Fortuitously, that agent had a special device, able to enhance neural powers in certain types of humans. By good luck, he found a subject with the right characteristics—especially a strong moral compass—and gave that fellow some primitive but effective mentalic powers."

"A human mentalic, so long ago? Then why—"

"That man successfully foiled the plot. Thus, indirectly, Daneel's agent prevented catastrophe."

Hari pondered.

"Was that the end of Earth civilization? Was the population removed to prevent more rebellion?"

"Not in the beginning. At first the empire offered compassion. There were even efforts taken to restore Earth's fertility. But that soon proved expensive. Policies changed. Attitudes hardened. Within a century orders were given to evacuate. Only those Earthers hiding in the wilderness remained."

Hari winced, recalling Jeni Cuicet, who strove so hard to avoid exile on Terminus.

The winds of destiny aren't ours to control, he thought.

The starship *Pride of Rhodia* still lay where it had been parked a few days earlier, beyond the north side of the sarcophagus. Only now an encampment of shabby tents stood nearby, living quarters for the laborers. Some tribal folk could be seen gathered around a stewpot, cooking. A whiff made Hari's nose wrinkle in disgust.

Not far away, he spotted a woman much stouter than any Earthling, dressed in torn garments that shimmered like the radioactive horizon. She paced, lifting a hand in front of her face, uttering some rapid statement, then raising the other hand, in turn. Hari recognized Sybyl, the scientist-philosopher from Ktlina, now evidently snared in a terminal stage of chaos rapture—the solipsism phase, in which the hapless victim becomes enthralled by his or her own uniqueness, severing all connection with the outside world.

Everything becomes relative, Hari mused. *To a solipsist there is no such thing as objective reality. Only the subjective. A raging, self-righteous assertion of individual opinion against the entire cosmos.*

R. Gornon Vlimt spoke in a hushed voice, so low that Hari barely made out the words.

"*That* was what the Cult of the Ancients planned unleashing on the galaxy."

Hari turned to stare at the robot.

"You mean the Chaos Syndrome?"

Gornon nodded. "The plotters developed an especially virulent form that could overwhelm every social damping mechanism Daneel Olivaw had developed for his new empire. Fortunately, that scheme was thwarted by heroic intervention. But weaker strains of the same disease had already become endemic in the galaxy, perhaps carried by the first starships."

Hari shook his head. But it all made too much sense. He realized at once—chaos *had* to be a contagious plague!

The first time it struck, they couldn't have realized what hit them. All they knew was that, at the very zenith of their confident civilization, madness was abruptly spreading everywhere.

It was one thing for a renaissance to spoil a modern world like Ktlina, one of millions. But when it happened the first time, humanity had only spread to a few other planets. The pandemic must have affected every human being then alive.

All of a sudden nothing could be relied upon anymore. Anarchy ripped apart the great Technic Cosmopolity. By the time the riots ended and the dust cleared, Earth's populace had fled underground, cowering in psychotic agoraphobia. Meanwhile, the Spacers turned away from sex, love, and every wholesome joy.

Hari turned to look back at the robot.

"Of course you realize what this means?"

R. Gornon nodded. "It is one of the last keys to a puzzle you've been trying to solve all your life. The reason why humanity can't be allowed to govern itself, or permitted to strive unfettered toward its full potential. Whenever your race grows too ambitious, this illness surges out of dormancy, wrecking everything."

They were now among the tents. Hari saw that other members of the Ktlina crew weren't faring any better than Sybyl. One of the surviving soldiers stared blankly into space, while a native woman tried to spoon-feed him. Another sat cross-legged on the ground, enthusiastically explaining to a small crowd of infants, no more than two years old, why nano-transcendentalism was superior to neo-Ruellianism.

Hari sighed. Though he had been fighting chaos all his life, the insights provided by Gornon let him view it with fresh insight. Perhaps chaos *wasn't* inherent to human nature after all. If it was caused by a disease, one important factor in his equations might change . . .

He sighed, dismissing the thought. Like the infectious agent responsible for brain fever, this disease had escaped detection and treatment by all of the galaxy's medics and biologists for a thousand generations. It was futile to dream of finding a cure at this point, with the Imperium scheduled shortly to self-destruct.

Still, he wondered.

Mors Planch was on Ktlina, and several earlier chaos worlds. Yet he never succumbed. Could a clue lie in his immunity to mentalic suasion?

A small crowd gathered at the far end of the biggest tent. Someone was lecturing excitedly, using all sorts of technical terms. Hari thought it might be another addled Ktlinan, until he recognized the voice, and smiled.

Oh, it's Horis. Good, then he's all right.

Hari had worried about the little bureaucrat, left behind on Earth. Approaching, he saw that Antic's audience included Biron Maserd and Mors Planch. One of the star pilots was a manacled prisoner, and the other a trusted friend, but both wore expressions of bemused interest. The nobleman smiled a greeting as Hari approached.

Planch made earnest eye contact, as if to say that their conversation must be continued soon. *He claims to have something I want. Information so important to me that I'd bend the rules in his favor, and even risk damaging the Second Foundation.*

Hari felt curious . . . but that sensation was almost overwhelmed by another one. Expectation.

Tonight I must decide. R. Gornon won't force me to step through time. The choice is entirely mine.

Horis noticed Hari at last.

"Ah, Professor Seldon. I'm so glad to see you. Please have a look at this."

On a crude table lay several dozen small piles of material that ranged from dusty to moist and crumbly. In fact, they looked like mounds of dirt.

Of course. His profession is the study of soils. Naturally, that would be his anchor at a time like this. Something to cling to during all of these disturbances.

Hari wondered if some of the samples might be dangerous, but both Maserd and Mors Planch had thrown back the hoods of their radiation suits, and they had more life span to risk than Hari.

Horis showed clear pride in his collection. "I've been busy, as you can see. Of course there's only been time for a cursory sampling. But the Earthlings are most cooperative, sending boys in all directions to take samples for me."

Hari caught Maserd's indulgent smile and agreed. Let Horis have his moment. There would be time to discuss more important matters before evening came.

"And what have you determined so far?"

"Oh, a great deal! For example, did you know that the best soils in this area are not of Earthly origin at all? There are several sites, not far from Chica, where many hectares of rich loam were laid down. The material is unmistakably from Lorissa World, over twenty light-years away. It was brought here and spread in a neat, organized fashion. Someone was trying to restore this planet! I date the effort at approximately ten thousand years ago."

Hari nodded. This fit what Gornon said earlier—that the empire once attempted restoration of the homeworld, before changing its mind, closing the universities and hauling millions away from their homes, leaving behind only a race of hardscrabble survivors.

"But there's more!" Horis Antic insisted, moving to where he had set up several instruments. "I stayed up all night, studying emanations from that *thing* the ancients sealed away, over there."

Horis pointed to the massive steel-and-concrete sarcophagus nearby, and the cracked entryway that R. Gornon's laborers were seeking to access with spindly scaffolding.

"I don't have the right tools or expertise. But it's clear some kind of *rift* in the continuum was made here, once upon a time. It's quiescent now, but the effects must be powerful when the thing is roused. I was skeptical of that tiktok—the one posing as Gornon Vlimt—when it talked about *hurling someone forward in time.* But now I wonder."

The bureaucrat-scientist grimaced. "What I *can* say—and the robot may not have told you—is that even while the space-time rift is dormant, there are effects that permeate this entire planet. One of the most notable is a shift in the stability of uranium oxide, a lightweight molecule found in hydrothermal regions on most Earthlike planets. Only here, there is a slightly higher predisposition for the constituent atoms to—"

Hari blinked, abruptly realizing something. He had been told that Earth's transformation into a radioactive world came from the decision of a single robot, during the post-chaos age. But might the seeds have been sown even earlier? In the bright renaissance when Susan Calvin and her contemporaries saw no limits to their ambition or power?

What if Giskard only amplified something that had already begun? Might that let Daneel's folk off the hook? Could it explain why this effect only happened once? On Earth?

Horis would go on, enthusiastically explaining details of an ancient tragedy. But he was interrupted by the dinner bell . . .

which meant partaking of Earthling hospitality, alas. R. Gornon felt it would crush their pride if the visitors refused.

Hari managed to swallow a few bites of a nondescript gruel, and smiled appreciatively before excusing himself. Slowly ascending the mound of rubble, he sat facing the three ruined cities and pulled from his pocket the latest copy of the Seldon Plan Prime Radiant.

He felt a little guilty for having swiped Wanda's copy, but his granddaughter wouldn't notice or care. She and Gaal Dornick were still aboard their ship, wired to sleep machines until tonight's proceedings.

Soon I must decide, whether to go ahead five centuries . . . assuming this thing works as advertised, and doesn't merely rip my atoms apart.

He smiled at that. It seemed an interesting way to go.

Anyway, what have I got to—

All of a sudden, the sky shook with pealing thunder—a sonic boom. He glanced up. Where a few stars had begun to shine, a bright object streaked overhead, a winged cylinder that banked and turned, obviously coming in for a landing.

Hari sighed. He had been hoping to lose himself for an hour or two amid his beloved equations. The new mathematical model that had emerged—a pattern for the future—was enthralling to contemplate, but the ideas already floated inside his head, and he was certain that double-checking the Prime Radiant wouldn't change anything.

With some effort, he gathered strength to lift his frail body. Flickering patches of radiation lit his way, following the twisty trail back to camp.

By the time he got there, the new visitors had already arrived.

A pair of women stood near R. Gornon Vlimt. One of them turned and smiled, as Hari approached the Earthlings' campfire.

"The guest of honor, I presume?"

Gornon's expression gave away little.

"Professor Seldon, let me introduce Zorma and Cloudia. They have come a great distance, in order to witness tonight's activities, and to assure themselves that you aren't under any sort of coercion."

Hari laughed. "My entire life has been guided by others. If I know more and see more than my fellow humans, it's because that serves some long-range plan. So, tell me, what fashion of robots are you?" he asked the two newcomers. "Are you yet another sect of Calvinians? Or do you represent Daneel?"

The one called Zorma shook her head. "We've been disowned by Calvinians *and* Giskardians. Both groups call us *perverts.* Yet they still find us useful, whenever something important is about to take place."

"Perverts, eh?" Hari nodded. It all fit. "So which of you is the human?"

Cloudia brought a hand to her chest. "I was born one of the masters, long ago. But this new body of mine is at least one-quarter robotic. Zorma, here, has many protoplasmic parts. So your question is a complicated one, Professor Seldon."

Hari glanced at R. Gornon, whose face revealed nothing, even though it could simulate the whole range of emotions.

"I see why the other positronic sects find your approach disturbing," Hari commented.

Zorma nodded. "We seek to heal the rift between our races by blurring the distinction. It has been a long and costly project, and not entirely successful. But we continue to hope. The other robots put up with us, because it would cause them serious mental dissonance if they tried to eliminate us."

"Of course, if you are part human, you get some protection under the First Law." Hari paused. "But that won't suffice by itself. There must be something more."

Cloudia agreed. "We also provide a service. We bear witness. We don't take sides. We remember."

Hari could not help being impressed. This small sect had maintained its existence for a long time, enduring the contempt of far greater forces, while maintaining some degree of independence in an age when human memory was shrouded by amnesia. It would take great discipline and patience to abide centuries this way, resisting the ever-present urge to act. In some ways, it required a spirit *opposite* to Mors Planch's. In fact, it would take people almost exactly like—

He turned, seeking one face amid the crowd of onlookers, scanning past Horis, Sybyl, the Earthlings, and Mors Planch.

Hari's gaze settled on the nobleman from Rhodia, Biron Maserd, who stood back from the crowd, with his arms crossed, wearing an expression of indifference. Hari saw through the guise now.

"Come forth, my young friend," he urged the tall lord. "Come join your comrades. Let us have no more secrets between us. It is a time for truth."

8.

◆

"Of course there had to be a spy," Hari said, cutting off Maserd's protestations. "Someone who knew about the Thumartin Nebula, for instance. We didn't stumble on the archives and terraformers by accident.

"And there were other clues. When Sybyl and the real Gornon Vlimt started accessing those ancient records, you already knew more about human history than any professor at an imperial university."

"As I explained earlier, Seldon, noble families often have private libraries that might surprise members of the meritocracy. My family has a traditional interest in such matters as—"

"As the systems of government used on ancient Earth? That kind of knowledge *is* remarkable. Even incredible. Then there were the *tilling machines* that got Horis so excited . . . those vast devices used long ago to prepare worlds for human occupation. Your reaction to them was hardly indifferent . . . as if you were looking at an old, familiar enemy."

This time Biron Maserd smiled, not bothering to refute Hari's assertion. "Is it a crime to wish the universe had more diversity in it?"

Hari chuckled. "To a psychohistorian, it's damn near blasphemy. The galaxy is already so complicated, the equations almost burst at their seams. And that's with just humanity to deal with. We mathists would much rather simplify!

"No. I didn't notice all the clues because I had become so fixated on chaos. Sybyl, Planch, and the others presented such a threat. When Kers Kantun told me you were an ally . . . that you hated chaos as much as anybody—"

"I do!"

"I took that to mean that you were a practical man of the empire, as you styled yourself. But now I see you are another utopian, Maserd. You think humanity can escape chaos, if only it experiences just the right *kind* of renaissance!"

Biron Maserd stared at Hari for a long, drawn-out moment, before answering. "Isn't that what the Seldon Plan is all about, Professor? Fostering a human society that will be strong enough to take on the ancient enemy lurking in our own souls?"

That was my old dream, Hari answered silently. *Though until just the last few days, I had thought it obsolete.*

Aloud he gave Maserd a different answer, aware that others were watching and listening.

"Like many gentry, you are ultimately a pragmatist, my lord. Lacking mathematical tools, you try one thing after another, abandoning each failed solution only when forced to concede that it is time to try another." Hari gestured toward the two cyborg women—Zorma and Cloudia, one of whom had been born human and the other with a positronic brain tuned to the Laws of Robotics. Only now they had begun blurring the distinction.

"Are you involved in this radical project, or are you merely working together, as a matter of temporary convenience?"

Apparently accepting the inevitability of Hari's conclusions, Maserd gave up with a sigh.

"Our groups have known about each other for a long time. My family—" He nodded grimly. "We were among those who cast forth the archives, long ago, fighting desperately against the spreading amnesia. And we waged war against the terraforming machines! It was futile, for the most part. But we won a few victories."

It was Horis Antic who asked the next question in a hushed voice. "What *kind* of victories? You mean you battled robots and won?"

"How can you fight beings who are so much more powerful, and righteously certain they have your own best interests at heart? Still, we managed to stop the horrible machines a few times, by rushing ahead and landing *human* colonists on a world slated for terraforming. Several times that stymied the tillers, who could not blast a planet with human inhabitants."

Mors Planch blinked. "Wouldn't we all know about such places?"

"We struck a deal with Daneel Olivaw, after the robotic wars ended. We agreed to stop fighting the amnesia, and to let the protected worlds be put in quarantine. In return, he left us unaltered, with our memories intact. The ultimate price was passivity. To remain silent and inactive." Maserd's jaw clenched. "Still, as long as the Galactic Empire ran smoothly, it was a better alternative than ruin and chaos."

"Your role in this affair could hardly be called passive," Hari pointed out.

Maserd apparently agreed. "The empire is falling apart. All the old bargains appear forfeit. Everybody seems to be waiting for Daneel Olivaw to present a plan—even the Calvinians"—Maserd jerked a thumb toward R. Gornon Vlimt—"are too timid to oppose their old foe directly. All they want to do is throw Hari Seldon forward in time, as if that will ensure everything comes out all right." Maserd barked a short laugh.

The robot who had replaced the eccentric Gornon Vlimt stepped forward. For the first time, its emulation programs mimicked a human wracked with uncertainty.

"Don't you think Olivaw will come up with something beneficial to humanity's long-range good?"

A woman's voice chuckled.

"So it comes down to that?" Zorma asked. "Despite all your secret schemes, you really are a timorous bunch of little tiktoks. Listen to yourself, pinning your hopes on someone you've fought for so long. Why, you just cited Daneel's Zeroth Law!"

Zorma shook her head. "There are no more true Calvinians."

Hari had no intention of letting the conversation dissolve into ideological arguments between robots. He also cared little whether Biron Maserd had been spying all along. In fact, he wished the nobleman well. What really mattered right now was the decision he had to make. The immediacy of which was clear when R. Gornon's assistant hurried into the tent.

"Preparations are complete. In less than an hour the moment will come. It is time to ascend the scaffolding."

And so, with his decision still not made, Hari joined a procession leading through the lanes of the ancient university. His footsteps were partly illuminated by a crescent moon, and by a luminous skyglow emitted when oxygen atoms were struck by gamma rays rising from the ground below. As he moved along, feeling creaky with age, Hari felt a nagging need to talk to somebody he could trust.

Only one name came to mind, and he murmured it under his breath. "Dors!"

The last thing he expected was for this to turn into a ceremonial occasion. But a procession of Earthlings accompanied Hari and the others on their way to the sarcophagus. The natives chanted an eerie melody—at once both dirgelike yet strangely auspicious, as if expressing all their hopes for some eventual redemption. Perhaps the song was many thousands of years old, dating from even before humanity climbed out of its gentle cradle to assault the stars.

Accompanying R. Gornon and Hari were the "deviant" cyborgs, Zorma and Cloudia, with Biron Maserd now striding openly beside them. At Hari's insistence, Wanda Seldon and Gaal Dornick had also been wakened to join the entourage, though Wanda had been warned not to attempt mentalic interference. Some of the robots present had similar abilities, enough to counter any efforts she might make.

Hari's granddaughter looked unhappy, and he tried to reassure her with a gentle smile. Raised as a meritocrat, Hari had always expected to adopt rather than father children of his own. And yet, few joys in his life had matched that of being a parent to Raych, and then grandparent to this excellent young woman, who took so seriously her duties as an agent of destiny.

Horis Antic had asked to be excused—ostensibly to pursue his research—though Hari knew the real reason. The glowing "space-time anomaly" terrified Horis. But Gornon did not want to leave anyone behind in camp, so Antic shuffled along, just behind the prisoner Mors Planch. Even the survivors of the Ktlina renaissance accompanied the procession, though Sybyl and the others seemed hardly aware of anything except a raucous murmur of voices in their own heads.

As they approached the anomaly, draped in scaffolding, Hari saw the rounded outline of the sarcophagus slide past each of the ancient cities in turn.

First, Old Chicago, with its battered skyscrapers still aiming adventurously toward the sky, recalling an age of openness and unfettered ambition. Next to vanish was New Chicago, that monstrous fortress where so many millions sealed themselves away from daylight, and a terror they could not understand. Finally, little Chica disappeared—the white porcelain village where Earth's final civilization struggled in vain against irrelevance, in a galaxy that simply did not care about its origins anymore.

Rounding a bend in the ancient university campus, they came to a point where the *crack* could be seen . . . splitting open thick walls that had been meant to seal away something dire. To entomb it forever. Hari glanced to his left, toward R. Gornon.

"If this anomaly truly gives you access to the fourth dimension, why hasn't it been used during all of these centuries? Why did no one attempt to change the past?"

The robot shook its head. "Travel into the past is impossible, on many different levels, Dr. Seldon. Anyway, even if you could change the past, that would only create a new future in which someone *else* will be discontented. Those people, in turn, would send emissaries to change *their* past, and so on. No time track would have any more valid claim to reality than any other."

"Then perhaps none of this matters," Hari mused. "We all may be just parallel mirror images . . . or else little simulations, like the numbers we juggle in the Prime Radiant. Temporary. Ghosts who only exist while someone else is thinking about them."

Hari had not been looking where he was going. His left foot snagged on some patch of uneven ground, and he started to pitch forward . . . but was caught by R. Gornon's gentle, firm grasp. Even so, Hari's body felt quakes of pain and fatigue. He missed his nurse, Kers Kantun, and the wheelchair he once hated. At one level, Hari could tell he was dying, as he had been sliding toward death for several years.

"I'm not in great condition for so long a journey," he murmured, while his companions waited for him to recover.

"The one other human who traveled this way was also an old man," Gornon assured Hari. "Tests show that the process is gentle, or else we would never risk harming you. And when you arrive, someone will be waiting."

"I see. Still I wonder . . ."

"About what, Professor?"

"You have great powers of medical science available to you. Breakthroughs and techniques that robots have hoarded for millennia. These cyborgs"—he jerked a thumb toward Zorma and Cloudia—"appear able to duplicate bodies and extend life indefinitely. So I wonder why you didn't boost my physical health, at least a bit more, before I made this journey."

"It's not allowed, Professor. There are strong reasons, moral, ethical, and—"

Harsh laughter interrupted, coming from the robot called Zorma.

"Except when it suits your purposes! You should give Seldon a better answer than that, Gornon."

After a pause, Gornon said in a low voice, "We no longer have the organoforming apparatus. It was taken away at Pengia. The device was needed elsewhere to continue an important project . . . and that is all I will say about it."

They resumed walking until the glow emanating from the cracked tomb filled the night just overhead, casting spiderweb shadows from the scaffolding across the ruined university. Most of the Earthlings and other onlookers climbed nearby rubble mounds to watch, while Hari and Gornon led a diminished procession onto a broad wooden platform that began rising on creaking ropes, hauling a dozen of them upward.

As Hari and his entourage ascended, he commented to Gornon, "It occurs to me that you may be going to a lot of unnecessary trouble. There's another way of sending a person into the future, you know."

This time, the robot did not answer. Instead, Gornon steadied Hari with an arm around his shoulders as the makeshift elevator reached its destination with a rattling bump. Hari had to shade his eyes against the glare pouring from within the broken containment shell.

To the awed murmurs of his guests, Gornon gave an explanation that was both poignant and brief.

"It began with a simple, well-meaning experiment, during the same brash era when humans were inventing both robots and hyperdrive. The researchers here had an incredible hunch and acted on it impulsively. Suddenly, a beam of fractured space-time shot forth, snaring a passing pedestrian, yanking Joseph Schwartz out of his normal life and hurling him forward ten thousand years.

"For Schwartz, a great adventure ensued. But back in the Chicago he left behind, a nightmare had just begun."

Hari watched the robot's face, looking for the complex expressions of emotion that Dors and Daneel simulated so well. But this artificial man was grimly stoic.

"You sound as if you were there, when it happened."

"Not I, but an early-model robot was. One whose memories I inherited. Those memories aren't pleasant. Some of us believe this event marked the beginning of the end for humanity's great time of youthful exuberance. Not long thereafter, amid international recriminations, the first waves of unreason began. Robots were banished from Earth. Acrimony built between nations and the colonial worlds. There were outbreaks of biological warfare. Some of us swore . . ."

Hari suddenly had a wild hunch.

"You stayed here, didn't you? That agent of Daneel's whom you mentioned earlier—the one who helped stop the Earthlings from spreading a new plague—was that you?"

R. Gornon paused, then gave a jerky nod.

"Then Zorma is right. You're no Calvinian after all."

"I suppose I no longer fit any of the rigid classifications, though at one time I was a fervent follower of Giskardianism."

Now the robot's impassive mask broke. Like that of any stoic man, whose equanimity was shattered by the most powerful emotion—hope.

"Time affects even immortals, Dr. Seldon. Many of us tired old robots don't know what we are anymore. Perhaps that is something *you* will be able to tell us, when you have had a chance to reflect. In time."

And so I come to the moment of decision, Hari acknowledged, still shading his eyes and peering toward the harsh light. Of course it would be anticlimactic to back out now. Everyone was watching. Even those, like Wanda, who disapproved of this whole plan, would surely be disappointed at some level . . . to be promised a spectacular show and have the star performer withdraw at the last minute. On the other hand, Hari had built a reputation of doing the unexpected. There was almost a delicious attraction to the notion of surprising all these people.

Several members of the group edged close to the opal light, peering inside. Biron Maserd pointed at the crumbling building, no doubt an ancient physics lab where the original mistake was made. The headman of the Earthling tribe stood next to Maserd, nodding. Even Wanda approached out of curiosity, though Horis Antic kept his distance, chewing ragged fingernails.

Mors Planch shuffled forward, lifting his manacled hands.

"Take these off of me, Seldon, I entreat you. These robots . . . they all revere you. Perhaps I was wrong. Let me prove my worth to you, before you go. I have some information . . . the where-abouts of somebody precious to you. Someone you have been searching for, across many years."

Hari abruptly realized what Planch was driving at.

Bellis!

He took a step toward the pirate captain. "You found my other granddaughter?"

On hearing this, Wanda Seldon turned her attention fully away from the sarcophagus. She, too, stepped closer to Planch.

"Where is she? What has happened to my sister?"

R. Gornon interrupted. "I am very sorry, but you should have discussed this earlier. There is no more time. At any moment, the field will expand. We have managed to transform the beam into a circular field, but we cannot be certain how long it will—"

Another figure stepped closer to Hari. The headman of the Earthling tribe. Though his accent was still quaint and thick, Hari found his speech understandable.

"There ees still time for families to settle their affeers. Please goh on, sir." The lanky Terran nodded at Mors Planch.

Hari felt a twinge of irritation, for this was really none of the Earthling's business, but Gornon cut in first, glowering at the Earther.

"What do *you* know of such matters? It is time to prepare! Note how the luminance grows brighter even as we speak."

Through the crack in the sarcophagus, Hari saw that the glow was indeed more intense. Biron Maserd stepped back from the forward edge of the platform and gestured within.

"There is something expanding outward from that building! Like a sphere made of some liquid metal. It's coming closer!"

"Are we safe standing here?" Horis Antic asked nervously.

R. Gornon replied, "It has never expanded beyond the bound-aries of the sarcophagus. It will not touch those standing on the platform."

"And what about Hari Seldon?" asked the cyborg robot, Zorma. "Will it be safe for him to enter that thing?"

Gornon let out a sigh of emulated frustration.

"We've performed calibration experiments for the last *thousand years*. Professor Seldon will experience a gentle, instantaneous tran-sition to the chosen future era—a time just a few centuries from now, when decisions must be made that will affect all of human destiny."

Mors Planch murmured—"A few centuries . . ." Then he took a step toward Hari. "Well, Professor Seldon. Do we have a deal?"

Hari glanced at Wanda, hoping for a nod, but instead she shook her head.

"I cannot read the secret in his mind, Grandfather. There is something complex about his brain. Recall how hard I fought yesterday, just to keep him standing still? Still, I'm sure we'll find out where he's hidden Bellis. It will just take time, working on him in private."

Hari didn't like the last part of her statement.

Perhaps striking a deal would be better. I could depart this world with a clear conscience.

Before Hari could speak, however, Planch let out a roar. He raised both manacled hands and charged.

Swift as lightning, R. Gornon Vlimt grabbed Hari and swung him out of the way. But in that blurred instant, Hari realized that *he* was not the pirate captain's target. By seeming to attack Hari, Planch kept Gornon busy in reflex protective mode, clearing the way for his real goal.

Mors Planch took four rapid steps toward Biron Maserd, standing at the platform's edge. The nobleman tensed, preparing to fight—then, in an instant's realization, he hopped nimbly out of the way.

Screaming a cry filled with both fear and exultation, Planch leaped off the parapet into the opal light. Hurtling across empty space, his body collided with a slowly expanding sphere that rippled like liquid mercury . . . and vanished within.

As Hari stared, the mirror ball kept expanding, inexorably approaching the place where he stood. No one spoke until Gornon Vlimt commented with an impassive voice, "We shall have to be certain he is greeted with compassion, in five centuries' time. By that point, he will not be able to alter destiny, but we must make sure he doesn't harm Professor Seldon when he emerges on the other side."

Hari felt a wash of emotions—admiration for the spacer captain's courage, plus despair over having lost a clue to his other granddaughter's whereabouts. R. Gornon's stoic pragmatism aside, Hari looked at the expanding space-time anomaly with growing dread.

The next person to speak was the Earthling headman. This time his accent was softer, easier to understand.

"It is true that someone must be waiting here on Earth to greet Mors Planch, but we needn't fear for the safety of Hari Seldon."

"And why is that?" asked Cloudia, the cyborg who had begun life as a human woman.

"Because Hari Seldon is not taking this journey. Not tonight. Not ever."

Now everyone focused their complete attention on the Earthling, who stood up taller, erasing the stooped posture that most Terrans manifested. Wanda stared at the lanky man, then gasped a cry of realization. Zorma was next to react, uttering an oath.

Lacking mentalic powers, Hari was slower to catch on. Still, he found something familiar about the headman's voice tones, and the way he now held himself—resembling Prometheus, whose laborious agonies never ended.

Hari whispered a single word, *"Daneel."*

R. Gornon Vlimt nodded, his face as impassive as ever.

"Olivaw. You have been here quite some time, I presume?"

The robot who had disguised himself as an Earthling nodded.

"Of course, I've long known about the experiments your group was performing here. I could not destroy the time anomaly, but we've been monitoring the locale. I arranged years ago to become a figure of importance to the local Earthling tribes, who respond enthusiastically to my influence. When they reported fresh activity at this site, I combined that with tales of Hari's abduction and reached the obvious conclusion."

Daneel Olivaw turned to Hari.

"I am sorry, old friend. You've gone through terrible trials, at a time when you should relax, in peaceful knowledge of your accomplishments. I would have been here sooner, and hoped to catch up with you on Pengia. But there were sudden problems with some of the Calvinian sects, renewing their fight for the pure old religion, who want to destroy the Seldon Plan at all costs. Defeating them took some time. I hope you will forgive the delay."

Forgive? Hari wondered what there was to forgive. True, he had been used. By Giskardians and Calvinians, and Ktlinans . . . and by several other factions, both human and robotic. Yet, in adamant honesty, he confessed to himself that the last few weeks had been more fun than anything else that happened in his life since he became important to galactic affairs. Since before he ever became First Minister of the Empire . . . back when he and

Dors were young adventurers inserting their thoughts into the minds of primitive creatures, living the wild and free lives of chimpanzees.

"That's all right, Daneel. I figured all along that you would show up and spare me the angst of making this decision."

"I appeal to you, Olivaw," said R. Gornon Vlimt. "As one whom you trusted for so many millennia, please allow us to continue tonight's work."

Daneel made eye contact with Gornon.

"You know that I honor the memories of our comradeship. I recall innumerable battles we fought, side by side, during the robotic civil wars. The Zeroth Law never had a stronger champion than you."

"Then cannot you believe that I'm doing all of this for humanity's long-range good?"

"I can, indeed," Daneel replied. "But centuries ago, we disagreed over what that long-range good should be. With matters at a critical juncture, I cannot let you interfere."

This brought a reaction from Hari.

"What interference, Daneel? Everything occurred to your benefit. Take the ancient archives and the terraforming machines—you sensed they might pose a danger, after the old empire collapses. During the age that follows, they might be discovered at random and destabilize the planned transition. You already decided to destroy them, under the Zeroth Law. But some of your compatriots were uncomfortable with the positronic dissonance that caused. By giving my permission, I made it easier for your followers to act."

He glanced at Wanda, and saw her shiver briefly at his mention of the archives. She, too, understood how dangerous they were. How they had to be destroyed.

"And when the agents of chaos found us there, in the nebula—" Hari continued, "—Planch said it was because of some unknown informant aboard our ship, who told them where to find us. But I'm guessing it might have been you, Daneel, using the lure of the archives to draw all the Ktlina agents toward one place, eliminating the threat posed by this century's worst chaos world."

Daneel made an expressive shrug. "I cannot claim credit for that coup, though I admit it was helpful." He then turned to look at Biron Maserd, the tall nobleman from Rhodia. "Well, my young friend? Were you the agent that Mors Planch spoke of?"

Hari wondered why Daneel, with the greatest mentalic powers in the galaxy, didn't simply read Maserd's mind.

Olivaw turned back to Hari.

"I do not invade his mind because we have an ancient agreement, a compact between Lord Maserd's family and myself. They were relentless and incredibly clever in their attempts to fight the necessary amnesia."

Maserd responded, "And we agreed to stop doing so, in exchange for being left alone. Our small galactic province has been run a little differently than the rest of the empire. We were free to fight chaos in our own way."

Daneel agreed. "But it seems our ancient agreement has been broken."

"No!"

"You already conceded that you've communicated with this group." Daneel aimed a finger at the cyborgs, Cloudia and Zorma.

"We Maserds are permitted to discuss anything among ourselves," Biron answered. He nodded toward the pale-haired cyborg. "Cloudia Duma-Hinriad is my great-great-grandmother."

Daneel smiled. "Very clever, but the Zeroth Law won't allow me to accept that attempt to evade our agreement. Not if it might imperil humanity's long-term salvation."

"And of course *you* are the one to determine what form that salvation shall take?" R. Gornon asked, in a voice that resonated, both desperate and sarcastic.

"That has been my burden ever since blessed Giskard and I discovered the Zeroth Law."

"And look at what it has cost." R. Gornon gestured toward the glowing radioactive ruins. "Your great Galactic Empire kept the peace and staved off chaos, by eliminating diversity! Humanity must shun whatever is alien or strange, whether it comes from within or from the outside."

Daneel shook his head. "Now is not the time to resume our ancient argument—over your proposed *Minus One Law*. The transition boundary approaches. For Hari's sake and for the sake of the Plan, I must insist that you lower this platform at once."

"What is the harm in letting Seldon see the world five centuries from now?" asked Zorma. "His work in this period is done. You said so yourself. Why not let humans be involved in the decision, when your *salvation* is ready?"

Daneel glanced at the brightening glow within the sarcophagus. Already their reflections could be seen on an expanding mirrorlike bubble, approaching gradually but inexorably. He looked back at Zorma.

"Is that your chief concern? I am willing to make a vow, on the memory of Giskard, and by the Zeroth Law. When my solution is ready, humanity will be consulted. It will not be imposed on human beings without their sovereign decision."

If this satisfied Zorma and Cloudia, R. Gornon still cried out.

"I know you and your tricks, Olivaw. You will stack the decks, somehow. I insist that Hari Seldon be allowed to go!"

Daneel raised an eyebrow. "You *insist*?"

Apparently that word had some special meaning among robots. For at that moment, the world exploded around Hari in a sudden blur.

Beams of searing light shot forth from both of R. Gornon's hands. Daneel Olivaw replied in kind. Nor were those the only combatants.

Abruptly, parts of the surrounding scaffolding detached themselves from the matrix of wooden planks, revealing themselves to be robots, camouflaged amid the latticework! These now leaped to support Daneel.

In response, searing rays were fired by Gornon's supporters on the surrounding rubble piles. Horis Antic screamed, diving for cover. Gaal Dornick went pale and fainted. But no humans seemed to be involved in the melee—either as fighters or as victims!

Cutting lancets of force swept between Hari's legs and under his arms, or lashed by his head, missing by centimeters . . . but nothing actually touched his flesh. It was meticulous combat, in which avoiding injury to human bystanders took utmost priority, and Hari's biggest danger came from a rain of shattered and smoldering robot parts falling everywhere.

It didn't last long. Surely, R. Gornon never expected to prevail. Yet, Hari's first concern was for the one robot who remained standing when it was all over.

"You are wounded! Is it serious?" he asked his old friend and mentor.

Curls of smoke rose from several places along Daneel's humaniform body, where clothes and fleshy outer coverings had burned away to reveal a gleaming surface—armor resistant to anything but sunlike force. To Hari it was a reminder of legends he had read in *A Child's Book of Knowledge,* stories of gods and titans—immortal beings combating each other, beyond any power of human interference.

Daneel Olivaw stood amid the wreckage, gazing with apparently genuine sadness at the wastage of his kinfolk.

"I am well, old friend Hari."

Daneel turned to glance at Zorma and Cloudia. "By your inaction, can I assume that my promise will satisfy you? For the next five centuries?"

The two "women" nodded as one. Zorma answered for them both.

"That's not so long to wait. We hope you'll keep us informed about your plans for human salvation, Daneel. Above all, we pray your Plan is a noble one for *both* of our long-suffering races."

Hari noted the implied message.

In your devotion to human posterity, don't leave out something for the robots.

But he knew his lifelong friend too well. The servant race would not get even a minor priority. Only humanity mattered to Daneel.

"And now it is time for us to leave this dangerous place," Olivaw said, reaching for the lever that would start the platform's descent.

Just then Wanda Seldon uttered a cry.

"Maserd! I just realized . . . he's gone!"

They peered in all directions, some of them using greatly enhanced positronic senses, but the nobleman from Rhodia wasn't present. Either he had clambered swiftly down the scaffolding during the fight, or else—

Or else Daneel will have two resilient humans to deal with, in a few centuries, Hari thought, as the platform started moving slowly downward. *Daneel had better not forget to have someone waiting here, because if those two ever became allies . . .*

There was no proof that Maserd had dived into the glowing ball, which now filled the entire volume of the sarcophagus, sending forth brilliant rays of light, whose colors Hari could not describe and could swear he had never seen before in his life.

Having watched omnipotent immortals battle it out, just moments before, Hari knew there was very little that even Mors Planch or Biron Maserd could accomplish if they were let loose in the galaxy's future. He had a strong picture of what kinds of societies would be floundering, and sometimes flourishing, in that era-to-come. His Foundation would already dominate the opposite side of the galaxy, but the effects would hardly be visible here on the homeworld—long-forgotten Earth.

With a sigh, he wished the two men well . . . wherever and whenever they had gone.

The ground approached, tormented by ancient, barely remembered crimes. He glanced once more up at the glow emanating from the sarcophagus.

I admit I was sorely tempted. It would have been one hell of an adventure, especially if they made me young again.

Hari closed his eyes, feeling the strong but gentle clasp of his old comrade Daneel around his shoulders, steadying his frail body as the makeshift elevator bumped to its final rest. He let Daneel turn him around, guiding his footsteps back toward the Earthling camp—as he had let others guide his life from the very beginning, though for most of that span he never quite realized it.

9.

◆

The next morning, while Earthling work gangs labored to clean up the battle debris, Daneel and Hari met with Zorma and Cloudia outside their swift starship, as they prepared to depart.

"Cloudia, I urge you. If your grandson ever contacts you, persuade him not to interfere. Great momentum is building toward a climax, five or six centuries from now. If Biron tries to deflect this juggernaut, I'm afraid he will only get hurt."

The human cyborg nodded, and Hari noted—perhaps a little enviously—the youthful strength of her supple figure. Not counting replaced parts, she was much older than he. Her expression was patient, yet sardonic.

"That is, if he shows up. You may see him before I do, Daneel, if he dived through after Mors Planch, and if you are waiting here when he arrives in that future era. If so, be gentle with the boy. He means well."

"I am nearly always gentle. But if he means well, why did he steal Hari Seldon's copy of the psychohistorical Prime Radiant? I scanned Gornon's ship, and found ample evidence that Maserd was the culprit."

Cloudia offered a grim smile. "We Hinriads tend to be pack rats when it comes to acquiring knowledge. We can't get enough. You should know that by now, after eighteen thousand years. We are the only human group that ever fought you to a standstill and forced you to agree to terms."

Daneel assented, with a tilt of his head.

"All of that is in the past, and dependent on your continued good behavior. I'm letting you go now, based on your vow not to meddle."

Zorma laughed aloud, much like a human woman who was both a little afraid and bravely defiant. "You are letting us go for the same reason you once spared Lodovic Trema, even though his mutation made all the other Zeroth Law robots eager to smash him to bits.

"You're smart, Olivaw. Smart enough to be a bit unsure. You are setting up some sort of a backup solution, in case Seldon's psychohistory plan needs to be replaced. But your solution just may need its *own* backup. In that case, your only hope could be some new synergy between robots and humans. Perhaps a hybrid combination, like us *perverts*—" Zorma gestured at herself and Cloudia. "Or else something as deeply disturbing to you as Lodovic Trema."

Zorma's expression and her voice lowered. "Just remember your promise, Olivaw. That humankind will be consulted, when you present your glorious and carefully designed salvation. There is uneasiness about this among a great many robots, even among your followers."

Daneel nodded. "I will keep my word. Human volition will play a role in the decision."

Zorma looked at Daneel, as if trying to pierce his impervious skin with her gaze. "Well, in that case, at least one mistake that was made here on Earth won't be repeated."

Then, over a microwave channel that only robots shared:

A final note, Daneel. Leave Dors and Lodovic alone. They are special. You gave them the seeds of something precious. Don't resent them if they take it in directions you do not understand.

Hari and Daneel watched the two women depart, ascending the gangplank and closing the portal. Their ship lifted on cushions of antigravity, turning slowly and accelerating to the east, barely skimming over the ancient cities, touching each of them with its shadow.

They were silent for a while. Then Hari spoke.

"You and I both know you won't keep that promise."

Hari's robot friend turned to look at him.

"How much have you figured out?"

"I now know all of the old damping mechanisms—at least enough to understand the gaps in the psychohistorical equations that puzzled me. Techniques that helped you and your allies keep the empire stable, peaceful, and unchaotic, against all odds, for most of the last twelve millennia."

Daneel offered a thin smile. "I'm glad you had the satisfaction of working it out for yourself. I planned to explain it all, just before—"

"Just before I died?" Hari laughed. "Now don't you go tactful on me, all of a sudden. Besides, most of the old dampers are breaking down. It's easy to see that chaos outbreaks would become increasingly common if the empire didn't fall. If it weren't pushed over the edge, in fact.

"Anyway, that's all part of the past, and we're talking about the future. When I throw in some other factors—like the way you've introduced human mentalics during the last two generations, and your long-standing promotion of meditation arts among humans, I can begin to guess the sort of *salvation* you have in mind."

Daneel looked across the devastated ruins of Chicago, and from there to the sere landscape beyond. His voice started out hushed.

"It is called *Gaia*. A way to bring each living world to a new level of consciousness. Though in the long run, we have hopes that it will connect every planet to all others, and become something truly wonderful—*Galaxia*."

"Complete mentalic linkage among all living humans." So, Hari had guessed right. "That will take some time to achieve. No wonder you need my Plan . . . in order to keep humanity busy until this Gaia solution is ready. I believe I can already surmise many of its advantages, from your perspective, Daneel. But please use your own words, tell me that this great gift will be worth all the trouble."

The ancient robot turned to look at Hari, spreading his arms as if to encompass the breadth of a magnificent vision.

"What problems would this *not* solve? An end to human acrimony, strife, and war, once every living man and woman can understand perfectly the thoughts of every other one! An end to *loneliness*—the word will lose all meaning as each child joins the commonality at birth.

"An ability to share all of the great ideas at an instant! Stability and inertia against sudden changes, making humanity forever secure against the impulsiveness of chaos. And there is more, much more.

"Already my experiments show a wondrous possibility, Hari. That such a macro-linkage of human minds can become somehow connected to an entire surrounding ecosphere. The sensations and primitive yearnings of animals, and even plant life, become accessible. Human brains will then become only the topmost organs of a universal entity, comprising the whole life force of a planet, even down to the pulsing throb of magma, deep below the surface.

"The inevitable result will be peace, serenity, a sense of union with all manner of beings . . . just as great human sages often prescribed in the past. An abnegation of selfish individualism in favor of the profound wisdom of the whole. All of this will be yours, once you are all assimilated into the collective consciousness."

Hari felt genuinely moved.

"It sounds gorgeous, when you put it that way. Of course the vision you present is appealing to me, given my own peculiar life-long neurosis, my hatred of unpredictability. The cosmic mind—this new godhead, will be fantastically easier to model than swarms of cantankerous individual humans. I can even see where you got the idea. Having read the ancient encyclopedia you gave me, I know that many prehistoric philosophers shared this dream."

Then Hari raised the index finger of one hand.

"But psychohistorical honesty forces me to tell you, Daneel, that there are several major problems awaiting you, as you try to implement this Galaxia solution. And the result may not be as unalloyedly happy as you described it just now."

To his surprise, Daneel remained silent instead of asking for an elaboration. Hari pondered the reason . . . then met the eyes of his old mentor.

"I can see now why you didn't want me to go into the future."

Daneel let out a sigh.

"With your vaunted reputation and insight, you would be hailed as a leading public figure, from the moment you were recognized and your identity confirmed. If R. Gornon had his way, you'd surely be chosen to lead some grand commission of humans to evaluate the proposed coalescence into Galaxia.

"But I already knew you'd feel conflicted about this alternative solution, Hari. You have mixed feelings about this overmind that will take over, once the Seldon Plan achieves its real purpose. In your skepticism, you would organize a *real* commission. One that might poke away at those *problems* you just alluded to."

Hari understood Daneel's point, yet he persisted.

"I'm sure we'd give it a fair hearing, and present the results to sovereign human institutions in a favorable light."

"That's not good enough, Hari, and you know it. Humanity *must* be saved, and it has a frightfully poor record of acting in its own best interest."

Hari mused on this.

"So you'll stack the deck, as you did by arranging for me to arrive at the Thumartin Nebula, just as the archives needed to be destroyed. You knew I *had* to decide in favor of their destruction. My character, psychology, and fear of chaos . . . everything made my choice inevitable—though at least I have enough insight to know this about myself. Those Zeroth Law robots who felt uneasy about destroying the archives were given a way to resolve their dissonance. My 'human authority' let them proceed with the plan you had mapped out. All in humanity's best interest."

Hari lifted a finger again. "Zorma was right. Your real constituency, the ones you must convince, are robots. You foresee, in five centuries or so, that they will be the ones able to thwart your plan if you can't satisfy their positronic drives. And since you'll be replacing the old familiar humanity with something new and strange, it will take some convincing! No wonder you gave in so easily, and made that promise to Zorma. Human volition must *appear* to play a role in the decision, or else you'll have a hard time getting all robots to agree.

"And yet, I know you, Daneel. I know what you and Giskard did here"—Hari motioned at the radioactive wasteland—"rationalizing that it was for our own good, without consulting even one of us. You'll also want the Gaia decision to be a foregone conclusion. Would you mind telling me how you'll arrange that, in five hundred years?"

Silence lasted over a minute before Daneel answered.

"By presenting a human being who is always right."

Hari blinked.

"I beg your pardon? A human who is always *what*?"

"One who has always made correct decisions, from childhood onward. One who, in a crisis, reliably chooses the winning side, and has always been proved right by the test of time. And who always will."

Hari stared at Daneel, then burst out laughing.

"That's impossible! It violates every physical and biological law."

Daneel nodded.

"And yet, it can be made convincing. Perhaps even more credible than your grasp of human affairs through psychohistory, Hari. All I have to do is start out with a million bright boys and girls, with just the right traits, and present them with challenges from puberty until age thirty or so. Many of those challenges will be rigged for success . . . or else mistakes can be smoothed over. Despite that, many of them will fail visibly and be dropped out of the pool. But over time, I am statistically guaranteed at least one who suits my needs. Who looks, superficially, far too successful to be explained by natural means."

Hari recalled a classic stock-market scheme that had been successful in duping the inhabitants of Krasner Sector—seven hundred billion people—about eighty years ago. Daneel's approach was a clever version of this old shell game, which only worked when practiced with immense patience. It was also nearly impossible to detect when done properly.

"So there won't be an investigative commission, after all. No need to report to sovereign human institutions for a decision. If this fellow has always been right, that will give him enough credibility to impress most robots, who will simply accept whatever he decides!

"Of course, some will be wary that you are influencing him mentalically, and they'll watch for that trick. They'll check his brain for signs of tampering. But you won't have to touch him! You can use psychological techniques to sway him in advance toward the right decision, especially if you control his upbringing . . . as you did mine."

Hari paused, chewing on a thought. "So, most robots will have their Second Law itch scratched. Getting 'human approval' for your plan, without actually having to consult humanity at large.

"Of course, you know that some of them won't swallow this scam. Many will rebel anyway, attempting to protect humanity from what they see as a seizure of power by a single mutant overmind."

Daneel nodded. "Over the years—ever since he broke company from me—my old ally, whom you knew as R. Gornon, has been preaching an apostasy called the Minus One Law. An extension of the Zeroth Law, expanding our duties yet again. Requiring us to protect not just humanity, but the essential approach to life that humanity represents . . . diversity and intelligence, in all of their manifestations, whether human, robotic, or even alien. Those who believe in this notion will not appreciate a takeover of the galaxy by a single macro-consciousness, eliminating all dissident elements.

"Moreover, some even now accuse me of *faking* the entire phenomenon of human mentalics! They claim that it would be all too easy to contrive the appearance of this new mutation, by hiding micro–thought amplifiers nearby and keeping them constantly focused on the supposed human telepath."

Hari noted that his friend did not explicitly deny the rumor. In fact, he recalled a certain jeweled pendant that Wanda had never been without, ever since childhood . . . but that was off the subject.

Daneel continued.

"You are right, Hari. The robotic civil war will resume, soon after Galaxia is unveiled. But if approval by human volition can appear convincing enough, most robots will rally around Galaxia. They will see it as the only hope for saving mankind."

This time Hari straightened, his back growing erect. A fist tightened.

"The *only* hope? Now see here—"

He was interrupted by the sound of footsteps approaching along the pebbly walk. Hari turned to see Horis Antic draw near. The portly Grey bureaucrat wore a patina of dust on his once impeccable uniform, and Hari saw the fellow's left hand quiver nervously as he popped another blue pill in his mouth. Antic was inherently anxious around robots, and events of the past two days had done nothing to settle his nerves. Fortunately, all of this would soon become a vague memory after they got him back to a

Trantor sanitarium, where just the right cover story could be implanted in his mind. At least, that was Wanda's plan. Hari knew there would be more to it than that.

"Gaal Dornick says I should tell you the ship is almost ready for takeoff. The Earthlings have agreed to take care of Sybyl and the other survivors from Ktlina. They'll be kind. In time, the solipsism mania might ease enough to let them rejoin a simple society.

"I still can't believe all I've learned," Horis continued. "It was one thing to find out that brain fever is a purposefully designed infection, aimed at the brightest humans. But then to learn that *chaos* is similar . . ."

Daneel interrupted. "Not similar at all. Brain fever is relatively gentle. It was designed and released in order to combat the earlier chaos plague, whose first virulent versions escaped Earth on the earliest starships."

"Was chaos a weapon of war?" Horis asked, in muted tones.

"No one knows, though some accounts say it was. The first crude versions swept Earth before I was made, prompting citizens to fear robots, their own great inventions. Later waves smashed the late Terran renaissance, turning Earthlings into agoraphobes and Spacers into vicious paranoids. Everything that Giskard did here"—Daneel motioned at the radioactive waste—"and that I did in the following millennia, had its roots in this awful plague."

"B-b-but—" Horis stuttered. "But what if there's a cure? Wouldn't that make everything right again? All this stuff I've heard—and I only understand a little—all this talk about *saving* humanity from chaos. Most of it would be unnecessary if someone just found a cure!"

For the first time, Hari saw waves of irritation cross Daneel Olivaw's face.

"Don't you think that occurred to me, long ago? What do you imagine I was working on for the first six thousand years? In between having to fight a civil war against robots of the old religion, I devoted all my energies to finding some way of ripping out chaos by its roots! But it was too late. The virus had been cleverly designed to inveigle its way into human chromosomes, scattering and embedding itself in hundreds of crucial places. Even if I knew where they all were, it would take *another* deadly plague just to dig out every genetic site where chaos lay hidden. Trillions would die.

"That was when I realized that chaos could only be staved off if we prevented the conditions that triggered an outbreak. If ambition and individualism provoked the disease out of dormancy, then a conservative society offered the best hope. A Galactic Empire, providing gentle peace, justice, and serenity to a society that never changed."

Horis Antic nodded. Naturally as a Grey Man, he shared an inclination toward orderliness, with everything classified and pigeonholed properly. "So there is no cure. But what about natural *immunity*? Didn't I hear someone talk about that, at one point?"

"The disease has always been tragically most virulent among humanity's brightest. Even so, some highly intelligent people proved immune to the temptations of raging egotism and solipsism. They can be individualists without denying the humanity of others. But alas, this immunity is spreading too slowly. If we had a thousand years, or two . . ."

Hari asked about something that had been bothering him. "Were both Maserd and Mors Planch immune?"

"Biron Maserd was protected against chaos by the noblesse oblige of his gentry class. As for Planch, you are right, Hari. His mind was startling. Almost unreadable with my mentalic powers. He had lived immersed in three different chaos-renaissances, yet remained completely agile. Flexible. Empathic, yet fierce."

"Kers Kantun called him *normal.*"

"Hmmm." Daneel rubbed his chin briefly. "Kers had some unique ideas. He thought that today's humanity is not the same one that made us. Truly natural humans would not be subject to chaos, Kers thought, nor would their minds be easily manipulated."

Horis Antic took a step forward. The eagerness in his voice replaced his typical nervous tremor. "Do you still have the records from your search for a cure? There have been medical advances in the past few millennia, and millions of qualified workers might come up with ideas that you missed."

Hari exhaled a sigh.

"Why do you bother, Horis? You know these memories will be washed away, or painted over, soon after we reach Trantor. You never struck me as the kind to chase curiosity for its own sake."

At this, Horis reacted with a bitter frown. "Perhaps I am more than you realize, Seldon!"

Hari nodded. "Of that, I am quite sure. It only just occurred to me, last night, to review events since you and I first met, and look at them in a fresh light."

Now, the Grey Man's nervousness returned. He popped another blue pill. "I don't know what you're talking about. But right now I've taken too much of your time. There are preparations to make. I've got to help Gaal Dornick—"

"No." Hari cut him off. "It's time to have the truth, Horis."

He turned to Daneel. "Have you ever tried to mindscan our young bureaucrat friend here?"

Horis gulped audibly at the mere thought of being mentalically probed.

Daneel responded, "I have a Second Law injunction to be courteous, Hari. I only invade human minds when some First or Zeroth Law need is apparent."

"And so, you never felt compelled to scan Horis. Well, let me override the injunction now. Take a peek. I bet you'll find it difficult."

"No . . . please . . ." Antic lifted both hands, as if to ward off Daneel's probing mentalic fingers.

"You are right, Hari. It is extraordinarily hard, but this man is no Mors Planch. He is achieving this through a combination of drugs and mental discipline, avoiding certain thoughts with scrupulous self-control."

"Leave me alone!" Horis cried, trying desperately to make his body turn around and flee. But a gentle paralysis swarmed over him, and he instead slumped downward, seating himself on a nearby pile of rubble. Naturally, Daneel would not have let him be hurt in a fall.

"Let me see the recording device," Hari said, holding out one hand.

New tremors rocked the bureaucrat, but he finally complied, reaching into a coat pocket for a small scanner. No doubt it was one of the best available to imperial operatives.

"You had no intention of reaching the sanitarium, did you? So long as everyone thought you meek and harmless, security would be lax. At Trantor, you would be in your element, able to tap a thousand different channels of communication . . . with a myriad of tricks that only a Grey Man might have access to. Locked doors would mysteriously open, and you'd be gone."

Horis slumped, clearly seeing no further purpose in dissembling. When he spoke, his voice seemed different, at once both defeated, and yet stronger. With a note of rueful pride.

"I got off a partial report from Pengia. You can't stop that part of it."

Hari nodded. "You were the secret contact who informed Mors Planch, who wanted the Ktlinans to come. Why? You hate chaos as much as I do. Kers Kantun knew that, and I can see it in your character."

Horis let out a sigh. "It was an experiment. It wasn't enough just to do a reconnaissance. We had to create a crisis. A scene of conflict with the chaos forces on one side and your tiktok pals on the other. It proved an effective way to get you all talking, arguing, and justifying yourselves to each other. I hardly had to put in a word, here or there."

"Your pose was impressive," Hari said, and Daneel added. "So is your mental discipline. Even without the drugs, I would have noticed nothing, until my attention was drawn fully toward you."

The compliments drew only a snort.

"We are used to being underrated and derided by all the snooty gentry folk and self-important meritocrats. Even eccentrics and citizens dismiss us as if we are part of the background. Long ago, we learned to stop resenting it, to control it, even to foster this impression."

Horis made a fist. "But tell me, who *runs* this Galactic Empire? Even you, Seldon, with your mathematical insight, and *you*, robot, who designed the Trantorian regime in the first place. You understand in theory, but you don't really see.

"Who gets called when a sun flares, burning half a continent on some provincial world? Who makes sure the navigational buoys all work? Who gets the children vaccinated, keeps the electricity flowing, and makes sure farmers tend the soil so their grandchildren will have something to plow? Who monitors the death rates, so health teams can be sent to some unknowing world before they even realize they've drifted into a space current that's polluting their stratosphere with boron? Who sees to it that self-indulgent gentry and preening meritocrats don't wreck everything with one egotistical scheme after another?"

Hari accepted this. "We know that the Grey Order does noble work. Can I assume *you* set the notion in Jeni Cuicet's mind, and arranged for her to take advantage of Testing Day?"

Horis chuckled sardonically. "How do you think she got her job on the Orion elevator? We've been quietly spiriting away some of the Terminus exiles. A few lives spared from involuntary banishment and imprisonment, that they were sentenced to for no fault of their own!"

"You say this, even though you claim to understand the Seldon Plan?"

Another snort. "One lesson that we teach again and again in the Grey Academies—something that *you* preached long ago, in the guise of Ruellis—" Antic said this pointing at Daneel "—is that *ends generally do not justify evil means.* Anyway, grand rationalizations are for gentry and meritocrats. We Greys cannot afford them. When people's rights are being violated, someone has to *do* something."

He whirled toward Hari Seldon. "Oh, the bloody *arrogance* of it all. You publish scientific papers about psychohistory for decades, then suddenly go silent and set up a secret cabal to control it! But aren't you thereby assuming that *nobody* on twenty-five million worlds paid attention during all the earlier years? That some nitpickers in the bureaucracy wouldn't have seen your discovery as a possible tool to be explored . . . and perhaps used for better government?

"Oh, there are only a few of us that I know of, but we've been looking into psychohistory for more than a decade. Our respect for you, Dr. Seldon, matches anyone's. But your Plan leaves us confused and filled with questions. Doubts we couldn't approach you with openly."

Hari understood. Mere bureaucrats would have been rebuffed, at best. Linge Chen and the Committee for Public Safety might arrest any clerks who knew too much. Then there were the rumors that Hari Seldon's enemies often suffered inexplicable bouts of amnesia.

"So ask your questions now, Horis. I owe you that much."

The small man took a deep breath, as if he had a lot to say. But at first, all he could utter was a single word.

"*Why?*"

He inhaled again.

"Why must the Galactic Empire topple? It doesn't have to! True, things are loosening up. Some say falling apart. But the equations . . . *your* equations . . . show nothing we can't handle with a lot of sweat and hard work. If technological competence is declining, *give us* resources to teach a better science curriculum! Unleash billions of bright youngsters. Stop rationing just a few measly slots at the technical schools!"

"We tried that once," Hari started to answer. "On a planet called Madder Loss—"

But Horis cut him off, rushing forth words, mostly to Daneel. "Even the chaos outbreaks might be controlled! Sure, they're getting worse. But the sanitation service is *also* getting better all the time, and they've never lost a patient yet. Would you really end the empire, which has kept a gentle peace for twelve thousand years, just to keep humanity distracted for a few more centuries? Why not keep the empire going until your new solution is prepared? Is it because the people of the galaxy must be brought low, to a miserable state, so they'll eagerly accept whatever you offer?"

It was difficult for Hari to switch modes. For so long, he had treated Horis in a patronizing manner. He now saw the Grey Man in a new light, not only as a startlingly effective secret agent, but as a rough-hewn psychohistorian—like Yugo Amaryl at the beginning of their long collaboration. One who understood more than he had ever let on.

"Do you really think imperial institutions can handle more crises like Ktlina?" Hari shook his head. "That would be taking a terrible gamble. If even a single plague site burst free to infect the galaxy . . ."

"If! You're talking about *people*, Seldon. Almost twelve quadrillion people. Must they all be thrown into a dark age, just because you don't trust us to do our jobs?

"Besides what if one of those new renaissances actually made it, achieving the fabulous *breakthrough* they all dream of. Reaching the mythical *other side*, where intelligence and maturity overcome chaos. If we keep them all quarantined, the galaxy can stay relatively safe. Meanwhile, experiments can be run, one planet at a time!"

Hari stared at Horis Antic, astonished by the man's courage. *I could never take such chances. He obviously hates chaos with a passion greater than mine. But he loves the empire even more.*

Shaking his head again, Hari answered, "But ultimately it isn't chaos worlds that are forcing Daneel to bring down the empire.

"It's *you*, Horis."

Such was the look of stunned surprise on Antic's face that Hari felt unable to speak. He looked to Daneel, silently asking his robot friend to explain, which he did in a voice like Ruellis of old.

"Do not forget, my dear young human, that I invented your Grey Order. I know its capabilities. I am aware how many millions sacrifice themselves while wearing that uniform, unthanked and despised by the other castes. You might even have managed, with resiliency and a little help from psychohistory, to keep the old empire sputtering along, until my new prize—my Galaxia—is ready to be born. But therein lies the rub."

"You see, I also remember your ancestor—whose name was Antyok—back when humanity stumbled on an actual alien race that had been spared by the terraformers. Robots from all over the galaxy convened to discuss the matter. There were just a few thousand of the alien creatures, and humanity already numbered five quadrillion. Yet, we argued for a year about the danger these beings presented. Humans in every sector and province were agog with enthusiasm to help the nonhumans get on their feet. An excitement for diversity and new voices to talk to. Some robots worried about the potential for triggering chaos. Others projected that the aliens might become a threat to humans in just a couple of thousand years if allowed to spread among the stars. Meanwhile, some, such as the robot you knew as R. Gornon, pleaded that nonhumans merited protection under an expanded version of the Zeroth Law."

"The point is that none of our robotic deliberations ultimately mattered. News reached our secret meeting ground that the aliens had escaped! They hijacked starships that came into their possession through a twisty chain of mysterious coincidences. Investigators found more than enough blame to pass around, but they assigned none of it to the individual who was actually responsible. Your ancestor, a humble bureaucrat who knew all the right levers for manipulating the system, for getting justice done while pretending to be an innocuous, faceless official."

It was a different version of the story Horis had told aboard ship. But Hari felt chills hearing it confirmed.

He nodded. "Your very presence here, Horis, shows this resiliency hasn't been lost. I was First Minister of the Empire, remember? I know the data files on Trantor are limitless. Nothing can be purged from them completely. Anyone with enough skill can defeat the amnesia and find what they need to know about the human past . . . and now about its *future*, as well. You are a living demonstration of the reason for it all, Horis."

"Me? You mean the bureaucracy? We faceless drones? We dull bean counters and pencil pushers? You mean the empire has to fall because of *us*?"

Hari nodded. "I never thought of it quite in that way before. But then again, I'm not the one doing the toppling." He glanced toward Daneel. "This is all about human volition, isn't it? It's all about that day, in five centuries or so, when a choice must be made by a man who is *never wrong*. When that day comes, there must not be a galactic bureaucracy anymore. No cubicles and dusty offices to burst forth with surprise meddlers, like Horis and his friends. No prim procedures to make sure every decision is deliberated openly.

"The Fall of Trantor isn't really about chaos, is it, Daneel? It is about killing your own fine invention, the Grey Order, the only way it *can* be killed, by total destruction of the filing cabinets, the computer memories, the men . . ."

This time, R. Daneel Olivaw didn't answer. The expression on his face sufficed. If any human ever doubted that an immortal robot could feel pain, all question would be erased by looking at Daneel's Promethean visage.

"So we're doomed to keep fighting the darkness . . . for nothing. To die at our desks, never knowing the futility of it all."

Hari put a hand on the younger man's shoulder. "You must forget about this now. Go back to your paper folders and soil reports. The knowledge you fought so hard to acquire, with such ingenuity and courage, will only cause you pain. It's time to let it go, Horis."

Antic looked up at Hari bleakly. "You aren't going to wait until Trantor?"

Hari looked to Daneel, appealing silently for a delay so that Horis might at least converse with them during the voyage back. But his robot friend answered with a terse shake of the head. Antic had proved too resourceful, too ready with fresh tricks up his sleeve.

Sensing this, the Grey Man stood up, straightening his bearing, trying for some dignity. But he could not keep from stuttering.

"W-will it hurt?"

Daneel spoke reassuringly to the human's eyes.

"Not at all. In fact . . . it is already done."

10.

◆

Helped by the two software sims, Joan and Voltaire, they were at last able to find every sabotage bug that Zorma's group had planted aboard the ship. Lodovic shouted enthusiastically when the engines came back on, proclaiming his sense of triumph with a strut around the control room, exactly like a jubilant human male.

Dors felt emotional patterns surge through her own simulation subroutines. Despite her ongoing sense of urgency, it had been oddly pleasant working side by side with Trema, sharing theories and insights, trying one solution after another. She enjoyed his swaggering victory display—which was not all that different from the way Hari used to act, whenever he made some breakthrough in the models of psychohistory.

"I am so sorry to interrupt this celebration," commented Joan of Arc, her slender boyish figure appearing in the central holo screen. In the background, Dors could see a male form wearing archaic doublets and hose—the simulation known as Voltaire— listening intently to a pair of headphones, as if trying to pick up something faint with distance.

"You asked us to monitor any transmissions coming from Earth. Voltaire now reports picking up a message using code patterns characteristic of the Second Foundation. It appears to be from Wanda Seldon, informing her compatriots on Trantor that she has successfully recovered her grandfather. The plot to kidnap him is foiled. They will be departing Earth within a few hours, taking Hari straight home."

Dors looked at Lodovic, who exhaled a long sigh.

"Well then, I guess that's it. All this rushing about, and we hardly made a difference. Seldon is safe, and we never even had to confront Daneel along the way."

Dors felt genuine relief on both counts. And yet, it was only natural to feel a bit let down.

"I guess it's just as well. We're just a couple of highly dressed-up tiktoks."

Lodovic laughed gently. "Oh, I think we're more than that. You, at least, are something special, Dors. We should discuss this, at length."

Dors nodded. It sounded like a good idea. They had much to talk about. And yet, despite mixed feelings, it was easy to tell where her top priority lay.

"I must go to Trantor now, you understand."

"And I agree. You have strong obligations, and I wouldn't think of interfering. But perhaps we can meet when matters there have been resolved?"

This time it was her turn to offer a soft smile. "It might be arranged. Meanwhile, can I drop you off somewhere along the way?"

"I'll ride with you as far as Demarchia. There are some things I want to look into there." Then his voice lowered. "Just be careful on Trantor, will you?"

Dors shook her head. "I doubt anyone would choose to harm me. Besides, I can take care of myself."

"It's not harm done by others that I fear. You are vulnerable, Dors. You were designed to be more human than any other robot. Your bond with Hari is intense. Be prepared for a rough time when the end comes. If you need someone to talk to—"

No more had to be said. Silence reigned while she took control of the ship and sent it plunging on the first of many long hyperspace jumps that would bring them to the center of the galaxy. To the place where all roads led, and where she had one great duty left to perform, before her path could truly be called free.

It was promised that I could be with you just before you died, Hari.

That vow she intended, above all else in the universe, to keep.

11.

◆

During his last sunset on Earth, Hari Seldon watched gamma rays excite scintillations above Old Chicago. Ionized curtains glowed and rippled like polar auroras, only here the driving energy came not from a distant sun, but the ground itself. He thought he could almost see patterns in the luminous sheets—like the clever living artwork in the imperial gardens that day when Horis Antic offered him a data wafer filled with tempting clues. Then, as Hari watched, all semblance of organized structure vanished from the eerie horizon. Now the glow reminded him instead of Shoufeen Woods, where order had been banished and chaos was king.

Preparations for departure were complete. In a little while, Hari would board Wanda's ship for the return to Trantor and his former life—hated by the men and women he was exiling to Terminus, feared by the present set of imperial rulers, and revered by a small cabal of psychics and mathists who felt certain they knew the future course of history.

Daneel would stay behind to settle matters with the Earthling inhabitants. There were arrangements to make. The cracked sarcophagus had to be buried so others could not misuse the fateful rift in the space-time continuum.

From his vantage point atop a pile of rubble, Hari could hear the voice of Horis Antic jabbering with excitement as he packed away his collection of soil types, acquired during this visit to a strange world. There could even be a scientific paper or two, something to brighten up his career profile, though nothing would erase the stigma associated with anyone who worked with dirt.

In any event, the fellow seemed happy. Daneel had done his job well.

Feeling tremors in his legs, Hari sat down again in the suspensor chair that Wanda had provided. He was needing it more, now that the rejuvenation treatments were wearing off. Soon he would be a frail old cripple again.

Soon I will be dead.

Seated, he could lean back, gazing toward the zenith where Earth's radiation glow surrendered to a glitter of starlight—constellations that his ancestors no doubt knew by heart. Those stellar patterns had certainly changed in twenty thousand years, however, and he pondered how the sky might have looked if R. Gornon Vlimt had his way, sending Hari through time to a galaxy five hundred years older. Five hundred years more experienced with sorrow.

There were footsteps on the rubble path, too surefooted to be human. After a long pause, Daneel Olivaw asked, "What do you see up there, old friend?"

Hari felt a tautness in his throat.

"The future."

"Indeed. Do you have a good view?"

Hari chuckled.

"A comfortable chair . . . a high place to look from . . . and of course, my equations. Oh yes, Daneel. I can see quite a bit from here."

"And you are not disappointed? About missing a trip into that future?"

"Not very much. It might have been interesting. But you had reasons for preventing it, and I understand them. I probably *would* have meddled." Hari laughed again. "Besides, you'll need a man who never makes mistakes, and I am anything but that."

"Do you have any special regrets?"

"Just one. I can see it right now." Hari gestured skyward, a bit to the left of zenith, but he wasn't pointing to a constellation, rather, at a cluster of psychohistorical terms that floated in his sky, more real at this moment than the glittering stars.

"Please tell me," Daneel entreated. "Explain what you see up there."

Hari realized that his immortal friend, capable of extending his vision from X rays to the radio spectrum, was at the moment, *envious*. Hari derived a strange pleasure from that.

"I see my Foundation, right now being established on Terminus, beginning its bumpy path toward adventure and glory. The probabilities are strong for two centuries, at least. Psychosocial momentum has built up to a point where I can almost see the actors in this play. The Encyclopedists, politicians, traders, and charlatans will live in a time of great personal danger. And yet they'll draw satisfaction from a sense of participating in something grand. Building a society that is preordained for success."

Hari lifted his other hand, pointing toward a flickering in Earth's ionized atmosphere.

"Ah! Did you see that? A perturbation! They are happening all the time, though most cancel each other out. Besides, we designed the Foundation to be robust, adapting to every flux and disturbance with great resiliency.

"And yet, with so much riding on the Plan, do we dare let human destiny depend on the reactions of a few million of our descendants? Can we trust them to respond with as much courage and determination as the equations predict?"

Hari shook his head. "No, we cannot. You convinced me of that, long ago, Daneel. Perturbations from the Plan must be corrected! The Plan must be kept on course. To do this, we shall need a guiding hand. A *Second* Foundation, using mathematics to track every swerve and deviation, then applying pressure here and there, at just the right points, so that the First Foundation stays on its assigned trajectory."

He sighed. "I was easy to persuade. After all, the Second Foundation is an extension of *me*. A form of immortality. A way I can keep poking and meddling after this physical frame has been eaten by worms and turned into the soil Horis admires so much. The Second Foundation might have been Yugo Amaryl's idea— did you inspire him though? In any event, vanity alone was enough to make me agree to it.

"But then you started demanding even more, Daneel.

"Will mathematics suffice? You worried that my successors wouldn't be strong enough. A society of secret guides will need something more potent than equations. A superhuman power, enabling them to sway kings, mayors, and scientists away from perturbing thoughts, diverting them back toward the tracks they had been assigned. And lo, no sooner did you make this suggestion, than such a tool appears!"

Hari gestured toward the horizon, where Old Chicago flickered with a steady glow. "Your gift to the Seldon Plan, Daneel—mentalics! We really had to do a major reformulation of the Plan when *that* came to light. Fortunately, the mutation only appeared where you wanted it to. Some of the psychics will help seed your great universal mind, while others breed with my Fifty mathists, creating a new race that is capable of both calculation and magic."

There was silence atop the rubble mound. Finally, Daneel commented, "You see a lot up there, my old friend."

Hari nodded.

"Oh yes, I see all the adjustments we had to make in the equations, in order to deal with this new aristocracy that will be inbreeding for the next several centuries, developing its power and influence, relying ever more on mentalic dominance, and less on mathematics. If they are left in charge, even with a tradition of duty and noblesse oblige, they will eventually become a ruling class. A ruling *race*. One that will make every prior priesthood or royal family seem like amateurs."

Hari glanced up at Daneel.

"But what choice have we? Eventually the Foundation will stop being distracted by momentary crises, by galactic competitors and the challenge of expansion. In time, the civilization we establish on Terminus will reach a new height of confidence . . . and face its inevitable collision with chaos. At that point, our predictions grow more approximate. The psychohistorical equations show the Foundation's odds of success will have winnowed down to only seventy percent or so."

"That is not good enough, Hari. Not nearly good enough."

"So you insisted, Daneel. The Foundation will be as strong, dynamic, and empathic as any human civilization could possibly be. If any culture could ever be prepared to take on chaos, survive the solipsism plagues, and burst through to the *other side*, this will be the one. And yet, if it fails . . ."

"That's the rub, Hari."

"Indeed. We're left with a one-in-four chance that humanity itself might be destroyed. I can see why you wanted something better, Daneel. You were compelled to do anything in your power that might boost the odds.

"First, you demanded a secret mentalic society, to help guide the First Foundation. But that only altered a few percentage points. Worse, it actually introduced new perturbations. Resentment by common folk against a psychic aristocracy, for instance. And danger from rogue mentalics."

Hari lifted both hands. "Quite a choice isn't it? Either a hell-bent battle with chaos or a permanent mutant ruling class. No wonder you finally decided there must be a third solution! No wonder you've worked so hard to develop Gaia, as a way to replace the Seldon Plan."

When he responded, there was deep respect and compassion in Daneel's voice.

"Your work still has great importance, Hari. Humanity must be kept engaged during the next few centuries."

"Engaged? You mean distracted, don't you? The people of my Foundation will think they are bold explorers, holding destiny in their hands, winning a better future by their own efforts, though aided by laws of history. Then, abruptly, you'll bring this new thing upon them. Already approved by some fellow who *knows everything.*"

"A man who is always *right*," Daneel corrected.

Hari waved a hand. "Whatever."

Daneel sighed.

"I know you have reservations, Hari. But consider the long-range prospect. What if there are entities in other galaxies, similar to the meme-minds we encountered on Trantor? What if they are more powerful? Perhaps they have already assimilated all life-forms in their home galaxies. Their influence may even now be stretching this way, toward us. That outside force could be a terrible threat to humanity. Only if the human species is unified, powerful, and cohesive, a true *Galaxia* superorganism—can we be assured of your survival."

Hari blinked for a moment. "Isn't that a far-fetched scenario? Or at least a long way off?"

"Perhaps. But dare I take that chance? I am compelled by the Zeroth Law—and by my promise to Elijah Baley, to protect you all, no matter what the pains! No matter what the cost."

R. Daneel Olivaw took a step forward, motioning toward the heavens. "Besides, think of it, Hari! Every human soul in contact with every other one! All knowledge shared instantly. All misunderstandings erased. Every bird, animal, and insect incorporated into the vast, unified web. The ultimate of serenity and understanding that your ancient sages yearned for. And it can be achieved in just over half the time that you project for the Foundation's final battle with chaos."

"Yes, it has attractive features," Hari conceded.

"And yet, my mind and heart keep pondering *Terminus*, at the opposite side of the galaxy. A small world very much like this one . . . this poor, wounded Earth. Despite everything, Daneel, the odds *were* in their favor. All the factors agreed. They would have had a good chance—"

"Seventy percent is not good enough."

"So you won't let them try?"

"Hari, even if they do break through to that mythical *other side*, you don't know what kind of society they will build afterward! You admit the socio-equations explode into singularities at that point. All right, the Foundationers may defeat chaos. They may achieve some great new wisdom, but then what? How about the *next* crisis to come along? Psychohistory offers no insights. Both you and I are blind. We have no idea what would follow. No ability to plan or protect them."

Hari nodded. "That uncertainty . . . that inability to predict . . . has been my lifelong terror. It's what I always fought against, and the bond that united me to you, Daneel. Only now, as I approach my end, do I see a strange sort of beauty in it.

"Humanity has been like a child who was horribly traumatized, and thereafter stayed in the nursery, where it could be kept safe and warm. You may differ with the Calvinians over many things, Daneel. But you both prescribed *amnesia* to help ease our collective trauma—a dull forgetfulness that could have vanished anytime our protectors chose to pull back the blinds and open the door. But you never did.

"Treating us that way would have been a horrible crime, except for the excuse of chaos. And even *with* that excuse, isn't there a limit? A point at which the child must be untethered, letting her take on new challenges? Facing the future on its own terms?"

Hari smiled. "We can only ask that our descendants be better than we are. We cannot demand that they be perfect. They'll have to solve their problems, one at a time."

Daneel stared for a while, then looked away.

"You may be able to take such an attitude, late in life, but my programming is less flexible. I cannot take risks with humanity's survival."

"I see that. But consider, Daneel. If Elijah Baley were here right now, don't you think *he* would be willing to take a chance?"

The robot didn't answer. Silence stretched between them, and that was all right with Hari. He was still looking at equations painted across the stars, waiting for something to reappear.

Something he had glimpsed before.

Abruptly, several of the floating factors entered a new orbit, coalescing in a pattern that existed nowhere except in his own mind. No existing version of the Seldon Plan Prime Radiant contained this insight. Perhaps it was an old man's hallucination. Or else, an emergent property arising from all the new things he had learned during this final adventure.

Either way, it made him smile.

Ah, there you are again! Are you real? Or a manifestation of wishful thinking?

The motif was that of a circle, returning to its origins.

Hari looked up at Daneel, no doubt the noblest person he had ever met. After twenty thousand years, struggling for the sake of humanity, the robot was undeterred, unbowed, as resolute as ever to deliver his masters to some destination that was safe, happy, and secure.

Surely he will keep his final promise to me. I will get to see my beloved wife, one last time.

Having lived more intimately with a robot than any human, Hari had some sympathy for Zorma and Cloudia, who wanted greater union between the two races. Perhaps in many centuries their approach would combine with others in some rich brew. But their hopes and schemes were irrelevant at present. For now, only two versions of destiny showed any real chance of success. Daneel's Galaxia, on the one hand . . . and the glimmering figure Hari now saw floating in the sky above him.

"Our children may surprise you, Daneel," he commented at last, breaking the long silence.

Pondering briefly, his robot friend replied, "These children— you refer to the descendants of those exiled to Terminus?"

Hari nodded. "Five hundred and some odd years from now, they will already be a diverse and persnickety people, proud of both their civilization and their individuality. You may fool a majority of robots with your 'man who is always right,' but I doubt many in the Foundation will accept it."

"I know," Daneel acknowledged with pain in his voice. "There will be resistance against assimilation by Gaia. Shortsighted panic, perhaps even violence. All of it unavailing in the long run."

But Hari reacted with a smile.

"I don't think you quite understand, Daneel. It's not *resistance* that you have to worry about. It will be a strange kind of *acceptance* that poses the greatest danger to your plan."

"What do you mean?"

"I mean, how can you be so sure that it won't be *Gaia* that's assimilated? Perhaps the culture of that future Foundation will be so strong, so diverse and open, that they will simply absorb your innovation, give Gaia citizenship papers, and then move on to even greater things."

Daneel stared at Hari. "I . . . find this hard to envision."

"It's part of the pattern life has followed since it climbed from the ooze. The simple gets incorporated into the complex. For all of its power and glory, Gaia—and *Galaxia*—are simple beings. Perhaps their beauty and power will only be part of something larger. Something more diverse and grand than you ever imagined."

"I cannot encompass this. It sounds risky. There is no assurance . . ."

Hari laughed.

"Oh, my dear friend. Both of us have always been obsessed with predictability. But sometimes you just have to understand—the universe isn't ours to control."

Though his body felt weak, Hari sat up higher in the flotation chair.

"I'll tell you what, Daneel. Let's make a wager."

"A wager?"

Hari nodded. "If you have your way, and Gaia assimilates everybody, eventually creating a vast unitary Galaxia, tell me this—will there be any more need for *books*?"

"Of course not. By definition, all members of the collective will know, almost instantaneously, anything that is learned by the others. Books, in whatever form, are a technique for passing information between separate minds."

"Ah. And this assimilation should be complete, by say, six hundred years from now? Seven hundred, at the outside?"

"It should be."

"On the other hand, suppose *I* am right. Imagine that my Foundation turns out to be stronger, wiser, and more robust than you, Wanda, or any of the robots expect. Perhaps it will defeat you, Daneel. They may decide to reject outside influence by robots, or human mentalics, or even all-wise cosmic minds.

"Or *else*, maybe they will accept Galaxia as a marvelous gift, incorporate it in their culture, and move on. Either way, human diversity and individualism will continue in some form. And there will still be a need for books! Perhaps even an *Encyclopedia Galactica*."

"But I thought the *Encyclopedia* was just a ruse, to get the Foundation started on Terminus."

Hari waved a hand in front of him. "Never mind that. There will be encyclopedias, though perhaps not at first. But the question that now lies before us—the subject of our wager—is this.

"Will there still be editions of the Encyclopedia Galactica published a thousand years from now?

"If your Galaxia plan succeeds, in its pure and simple form, there will be no books or encyclopedias in one millennium's time. But if *I* am right, Daneel, people will still be creating and publishing compendiums of knowledge. They may share countless insights and intimacies through mentalic powers, the way people now make holovision calls. Who knows? But they will also maintain a degree of individuality, and keep on communicating with each other in old-fashioned ways.

"If I'm right, Daneel, the *Encyclopedia* will thrive . . . along with our children . . . and my first love. The Foundation."

Hari Seldon lapsed into silence, a quiet reflection that R. Daneel Olivaw respected.

Soon, his granddaughter Wanda would come up this slope, a crumbling hill composed of rubble from past human civilizations, and collect him for the journey back to Trantor . . . and perhaps to a special reunion that he longed for.

But for the remaining moment, Hari admired a vista stretching overhead—the galactic starscape imbued with his beloved mathematics. He stared up at the radiation-flecked sky, and greeted Chaos, his old enemy.

I know you at last, he thought.

You are the tiger, who used to hunt us. You are winter's cold. You are famine's bitter hunger . . . the surprise betrayal . . . or the illness that struck without warning, leaving us crying out, Why?

You are every challenge humanity faced, and eventually overcame, as we grew just a little mightier and wiser with each triumph. You are the test of our confidence . . . our ability to persist and prevail.

I was justified in fighting you . . . and yet, without your opposition, humanity would be nothing, and there could never be a victory.

Chaos, he now realized, was the underlying substance out of which his equations evolved. As well as life itself.

Anyway, it would be pointless to resent it now. Soon, his molecules would join Chaos in its everlasting dance.

But up there, amid the stars, his lifelong dream still lived.

We will know. We will understand and grow beyond all limits that imprison us.

In time, we will be greater than we ever imagined possible.

ACKNOWLEDGMENTS

Among the "Asimov experts" who offered wisdom and advice were professors Donald Kingsbury, James Gunn, and Joseph Miller, as well as Jennifer Brehl, Atilla Torkos, Alejandro Rivero, and Wei-Hwa Huang. Also providing valuable comments were Stefan Jones, Mark Rosenfelder, Steinn Sigurdsson, Joy Crisp, Ruben Krasnopolsky, G. Swenson, Sean Huang, Freddy Hansen, Michael Westover, Christian Reichardt, Melvin Leok, J. V. Post, Benjamin Freeman, Scott Martin, Robert Hurt, Anita Gould, Joseph Cook, Alberto Monteiro, R. Sayres, N. Knouf, A. Faykin, Michael Hochberg, Adam Blake, Jimmy Fung, and Jenny Ives. Sara Schwager and Bob Schwager were conscientious and keen-eyed copy editors. I am also grateful to Janet Asimov, John Douglas, Ralph Vicinanza, and above all to Cheryl Brigham, whose skilled reading caught many errors, whose hands substituted for mine in a crisis, and who kept life going when I felt like a hapless robot.

The quotation in section in Part 6, about the *Gospel of Uniformity*, is from Alfred North Whitehead's book, *Science and the Modern World*, 1925.

AFTERWORD

It is never easy to write in a universe that was created by another (in this case brilliant) writer. Especially when that writer is lamentably no longer around to consult by letter, or phone, or over a glass of beer. One must study his works in order to forge a new episode that has consistency with the original stories, and yet contribute fresh insights that *he* might have enjoyed reading. In this case, all three authors of THE SECOND FOUNDATION trilogy—Greg Bear, Gregory Benford, and I—felt compelled by the logic of Isaac Asimov's universe to add the key element of *chaos*—a horrible disease of the mind, afflicting all of humanity. Isaac left plenty of clues to this very thing, allowing our innovation to stay consistent with his earlier works. Moreover, chaos explains the major salient feature of his future history—an amnesia that debilitates quadrillions of people for hundreds of generations.

I could go on about the reasons why I wrote this new layer the way I did, but at this point I'll forgo any further comments, except to say that I don't see the story of Hari Seldon being quite finished! As Isaac did habitually, I laced *Foundation's Triumph* with clues that others might take up someday, if they choose. Hints that culminate in two wry pages that I considered including as a denouement to this book. But instead of muddying the waters, perhaps I'll just post them elsewhere sometime. They are not so much a part of *Foundation's Triumph* as a dream of what just might happen next.

That is what's so much fun about our ongoing dinner-table conversation about destiny. We get to poke away at the future. Explore it with experiments and fantasies. Discover mistakes to avoid. And uncover possibilities that our grandchildren may take for granted.

TIMELINE FOR THE ROBOTS AND FOUNDATION UNIVERSE

1982 C.E.

Birth of Susan Calvin. Incorporation of U.S. Robots and Mechanical Men. [*I, Robot*]

2007 C.E.

Susan Calvin begins to work for U.S. Robots. Later becomes chief robo-psychologist [*I, Robot*]

Early 21st Century

A social and technical renaissance flourishes on Earth. Development of positronic robots, controlled by Three Laws of Robotics. [*The Complete Robot*] Hyperatomic Drive allows first successful interstellar journey. [*I, Robot*]. Through an accident, Joseph Schwartz is sent on a time journey 10,000 years into the future. [*Pebble in the Sky*]

2064 C.E.

Death of Susan Calvin. [*I, Robot*] Humanity begins colonizing several planets including Aurora. The first chaos outbreaks affect civilization, breaking down confidence. On Earth, citizens cluster underground, ban robots from cities. Spacers lose empathy. Relations between Earth and Spacer worlds deteriorate. [*Foundation's Triumph*]

300 years before events in *The Caves of Steel*

The planet Solaria (the last Spacer world) settled from the planet Nexon. [*The Naked Sun*] Decline of the robot-dependent Spacer culture. Later, Han Fastolfe of Aurora creates the humaniform robot, R. Daneel Olivaw.

appr. 3500 C.E.   Spacetown is established near New York City. R. Daneel Olivaw is assigned to work with Earthman detective Elijah Baley. [*The Caves of Steel*]

1 year later   Elijah Baley and Daneel Olivaw pursue an investigation on Solaria. [*The Naked Sun*] Fastolfe becomes influential in Auroran government and supports new Earth emigration.

Opponents led by Kelden Amadiro want Spacers to terraform and populate new planets. [*The Robots of Dawn*]

2 years later   Baley carries out investigation on Aurora accompanied by Daneel Olivaw and Giskard Reventlov—a telepathic robot. Aurora lets Earth colonize new planets. Giskard suggests Earthfolk must build their new worlds completely without robots. [*The Robots of Dawn*]

2 years later   The second wave of emigration from Earth begins, led by Ben Baley. First Settler planet is named Baleyworld. [*Robots and Empire*] Number of Settler planets grows fast. Relations between Settler and Spacer worlds grow tense. [*Robots and Empire*]

37 years after the events in *The Caves of Steel*   Death of Elijah Baley on Baleyworld. [*Robots and Empire*]

196 years after the events in *The Caves of Steel*   Kelden Amadiro and Levular Mandamus begin planting nuclear amplifiers throughout Earth to take revenge for their earlier defeat. [*Robots and Empire*]

200 years after the events in *The Caves of Steel*   Death of Han Fastolfe. Population of Solaria vanishes. Daneel Olivaw and Giskard Reventlov formulate the Zeroth Law of Robotics, to override original Three Laws. Giskard provides Daneel with telepathic

abilities. Amadiro and allies turn on amplifiers to make the Earth radioactive and uninhabitable. Giskard permits this for Zeroth Law reasons, in order to encourage human dispersal, then dies because of First Law conflicts. [*Robots and Empire*] The Great Diaspora (final emigration) begins.

A majority of robots split into two camps. Giskardians led by Daneel follow the new Zeroth Law religion. Calvinians think this an outrage. Robotic civil war ensues, mostly unseen by humans fleeing poisoned Earth. Meanwhile robot ships operating under Auroran programming cruise the galaxy ahead of the spreading Settlers, terraforming and preparing planets for colonization. Meme entities will later claim that this devastated existing races. Memes escape to the Galactic Core. [*Foundation's Fear, Foundation and Chaos*]

301 years after the events in *The Caves of Steel*

Spacer-colonized planet Inferno is doomed by ecological and cultural catastrophe. Robots are built to operate under New Laws, giving them greater flexibility and freedom. Settler specialists help terraform the planet. [*Caliban*] Hostility toward New Law robots grows evident. [*Inferno*] Comet crashes into the planet. Merging of Spacer and Settler cultures prevents social collapse. [*Utopia*] The interstellar robot civil war eventually reaches Inferno. New Law robots are destroyed or go into hiding. [*Foundation's Triumph*]

appr. 1200 B.G.E. (Before Galactic Era)

Planet Rhodia and the Nebular Kingdoms, led by the noble Hinriad family, shake off rule by planet Tyrann and rediscover democracy. [*The Stars Like Dust*] Decadent Spacer worlds slowly die out. Colonization of Galaxy completed. [*Foundation and Earth*] R. Daneel Olivaw formulates the Encoding

Laws, setting limits to artificial intelligence. [*Foundation's Fear*] Damping effects such as historical amnesia, brain fever, and giskardian mentalic persuasion devices are introduced to fight chaos. Human mind, society and technology stagnate. Some human and robot groups fight the amnesia. [*Foundation's Triumph*]

appr. 500 B.G.E. Trantorian Republic of five worlds becomes Trantorian Confederation, then later the Trantorian Empire. [*The Currents of Space*] R. Daneel Olivaw uses early "laws of humanics" to guide it. Human origins forgotten.

200 B.G.E. Half of the inhabited worlds of the Galaxy are part of Trantorian Empire. Trantor supports rebellion of planet Florina against oppression by planet Sark. [*The Currents of Space*]

1 G.E.
(12500 C.E. = appr. 8,000 years after the Great Diaspora) Trantorian Empire becomes the Galactic Empire. Start of galactic calendar.

827 G.E. Arrival of Joseph Schwartz (thrown forward in time). A radioactive and sparsely populated Earth tries to revolt against the Empire by using a bio-weapon. Rebellion fails, thanks partly to Schwartz and a mentalic amplifier. Empire initially helps Earth recover, then effort is mysteriously abandoned. [*Pebble in the Sky, Foundation's Triumph*]

appr. 900 G.E. Forced evacuation of inhospitable Earth. Establishment of colony on planet Alpha. [*Foundation and Earth*]

975 G.E. An alien race is discovered on a desert world and moved to Cepheus 18. Later they mysteriously escape beyond the Galaxy. [*Blind Alley*] appr. 2000 G.E.   Daneel Olivaw and R. Yan Kansarv establish a robot production and repair facility on distant Eos. [*Foundation and Chaos*] The great Ruellis helps establish principles of good paternalistic government, augmenting the stability of an unchanging society against chaos. [*Foundation's Triumph*]

appr. 3000 G.E.   During a chaos outbreak, ancient personality simulations Voltaire and Joan of Arc debate about machine intelligence. [*Foundation's Fear*] With support of Calvinian robots, the Empress Shoree-Harn tries to introduce a new calendar and shake up social rigidity without success. [*Foundation and Chaos*]

8789 G.E.   A new "renaissance" begins on planet Lingane. Falls into chaos eight years later. [*Foundation's Triumph*]

11865 G.E.   Humanoid robot Dors Venabili is constructed on Eos. [*Foundation's Fear*]

11867 G.E.   The only extragalactic human colony is abandoned in the Greater Magellanic Cloud. All is data suppressed. [*Foundation and Chaos*]

11988 G.E.   Birth of Hari Seldon and Cleon I. Daneel Olivaw knows the Empire is destabilizing, partly due to frequent chaos outbreaks. He is forced by the Zeroth Law to actively interfere, first as Chief of Staff, then as First Minister. [*Prelude to Foundation*] His secret genetic experiments lead both to Hari's mathematical genius and the appearance of human mentalics. [*Foundation's Triumph*]

12010 G.E.   Cleon I becomes Emperor. [*Prelude to Foundation*]

12020 G.E.	Hari Seldon lectures on possibility of psychohistory. Daneel persuades him to develop a practical science to help save the Empire. Dors Venabili becomes Seldon's wife. They adopt a boy, Raych. Seldon and Yugo Amaryl begin to flesh out psychohistory. [*Prelude to Foundation*]
12028 G.E.	Calvinian robots, led by R. Plussix, move to Trantor and find historical documents dating from era of Shoree-Harn, as well as the sims Voltaire and Joan of Arc. They help seed a new "renaissance" on planet Sark. [*Foundation's Fear*] Seldon helps remove Laskin Joranum from politics. Daneel resigns his post. Cleon I makes Seldon First Minister. [*Eto Demerzel*] Voltaire and Joan get into the Trantorian Mesh where they meet the ancient memes, triggering a rebellion among "tiktok" robots who kill many of Daneel's positronic companions. Seldon strikes a deal to get the memes off Trantor. Sark renaissance falls into chaos. [*Foundation's Fear*]
12038 G.E.	Death of Cleon I. [*Cleon I*] A military junta seizes power. Seldon resigns as First Minister. [*Dors Venabili*]
12040 G.E.	Birth of Wanda Seldon, daughter of Raych. [*Dors Venabili*] A new "renaissance" begins on planet Madder Loss. Its collapse rocks galactic society. [*Foundation and Chaos*]
12048 G.E.	"Death" of Dors Venabili and Fall of the junta. [*Dors Venabili*] Puppet-Emperor Agis XIV ascends the throne. Real power is in the hands of the Commission for Public Safety [*Wanda Seldon*] Daneel brings Dors to the Eos base for repair. [*Foundation and Chaos*]

12052 G.E.	Birth of Bellis Seldon. Hari Seldon discovers Wanda's mental abilities. He tries to find others, without success. Psychohistorical equations predict the unavoidable collapse of the Empire. Seldon team works out plan to save human knowledge and create a Second Empire via the Foundation. Death of Yugo Amaryl. [*Wanda Seldon*]
12058 G.E.	Raych, Manella, and Bellis move to Santanni where a New Renaissance has begun. Anacreon Province seeks independence. Chaos breaks out on Santanni, Raych dies, and his family is lost in space. Stettin Palver, another mentalic, joins the Seldon Project. [*Wanda Seldon*]
12067 G.E. = 1 F.E. (F.E. = Foundation Era)	Puppet Emperor Klayus I sits on the throne. Hari Seldon is put on trial and Commission for Public Safety exiles the Encyclopedia Foundation to Terminus. Beginning of the Foundation calendar. [*Foundation*] Vara Liso, a strong mentalic, gets entangled in Farad Sinter's hunt for robot "eternals." Calvinian robots foiled in a plot to ruin Seldon Project and stymie Daneel's control over human history. [*Foundation and Chaos*]
12068 G.E. = 2 F.E.	Reign of puppet Emperor Semrin. Members of Encyclopedia Foundation exiled to Terminus. Daneel plans using human mentalics to design an overmind Gaia. Millions of ancient archives are destroyed. A New Renaissance on planet Ktlina is devoured by chaos. A heretic robot tries to send Seldon into the future but is foiled by Daneel. Mors Planch dives into the future. [*Foundation's Triumph*]
12069 G.E. = 3 F.E.	Death of Hari Seldon. Chief Commissioner Linge Chen dies. Replacement pays attention

mostly to Trantor and vicinity. Psychohistorians provoke secession at Empire's Periphery. [*The Originist*]

50 F.E. (12116 G.E.)   Anacreon declares independence, separating Terminus from the Empire. Seldon's hologram explains the true purpose of the Foundation. [*The Encyclopedists*] Terminus offers scientific support for neighboring kingdoms, balancing their powers. [*The Mayors*]

80 F.E. to 195 F.E.   Foundation develops quasi-religious sway over neighboring kingdoms. [*The Mayors*] Foundation then relies more on economic influence. [*The Traders, The Merchant Princes*]

195 F.E.   Under Cleon II, Imperial General Bel Riose campaigns against the Foundation, conquering large territories. But Cleon recalls the fleet, as predicted by psychohistory. [The General]

appr. 260 F.E.   Dagobert VIII rules remnant Empire. The rebel Gilmer's troops sack Trantor. Second Foundation protects the Galactic Library, then signs a peace treaty with Gilmer. [*Trantor Falls*]

appr. 300 F.E.   Empire of Dagobert IX has shrunk to twenty worlds centered on Neotrantor. The Mule, a mutant with strong mentalic power, conquers the Foundation, knocking Seldon Plan off course. [*The Mule*] The Mule establishes the Union of Worlds and searches for the Second Foundation. [*Search by the Mule*]

appr. 305 F.E.   Members of the Second Foundation mentalically alter the Mule, who then gives up further conquest. [*Search by the Mule*] appr. 310 F.E.   Death of the Mule. The Foundation regains strength, but also begins studying neglected mental sciences, further endangering Seldon Plan. [*Search by the Foundation*]

376 F.E.   The Foundation searches for the Second Foundation, fearing its mentalic rule. Diverting this search with a ruse, the Second Foundation continues operating secretly on Trantor (Star's End). [*Search by the Foundation*] Daneel Olivaw unleashes his Gaia overmind.

498 F.E.   The Gaia overmind offers Golan Trevize ("the man who is always right") a choice between an Empire built by physical force, one ruled by Second Foundation mentalics, or a galaxy-sized version of Gaia . . . Galaxia. No other options are presented and no other humans consulted. Trevize chooses Galaxia. Preparations begin for gradual assimilation of humanity into the collective overmind. [*Foundation's Edge*]

499 F.E.   Trevize embarks on a journey, seeking to explain his choice. On Solaria he finds the planet's vanished folk have become a new race. Reaching Earth, he meets R. Daneel Olivaw, whose actions to this point were compelled by the Zeroth Law. Trevize realizes any real solution must take into consideration robots, Solarians, memes, mutants, and any other kind of intelligence. The right answer may not be to simplify. [*Foundation and Earth*]

520 F.E.   First Galactic Coalescence Investigation Commission convenes on planet Pengia. The subsequent Great Destiny Debates rage for 180 years, interrupted by waves of violence, amnesia, and chaos. Robotic civil wars reignite. Foundation civilization approaches

ultimate confrontation with both Gaia and Chaos. [*Foundation's Triumph*]

1020 F.E.   116th Edition of the *Encyclopedia Galactica*. [*Foundation*]

1054 F.E.   117th Edition of the *Encyclopedia Galactica*. [*Foundation's Triumph*]

Compiled by Attila Torkos, 1998